More praise for

"Sharp humor a... ...llmann's
Chicago-set debu... ...history
and suspense, thi... ...n engaging
amateur sleut... ...have to
wait too long for E... ...return." —*Publishers Weekly*

"You'll have to read *An Eye for Murder* . . . You won't be
sorry!" —*Midwest Book Review*

"A well-written and exciting account of how murder changes
an ordinary life, though Ellie Foreman hardly counts as ordinary. Readers will delight in her spunky approach to her career, single motherhood and ensuing romance, and are sure to
demand more books about Ellie." —*Mystery Times*

"A mystery in the great tradition, with sins of the past returning to haunt the present. I love the Ellie Foreman character
and I want more books about her." —Barbara D'Amato, author
of the Cat Marsala series

"A wonderful thriller . . . a clever mystery puzzle within a
beautifully wrought novel." —Jeremiah Healy, author of
the John Francis Cuddy mysteries

"Everything I want in a mystery: characters I care about,
credible motivations, a complex plot. Intelligent and gutsy,
the protagonist is someone I'd like to have for a friend. The
author knows Chicago and, more to the point, catches it on the
page. Wonderful." —Michael Allen Dymmoch, author of
the John Thinnes mysteries

continued . . .

To Kathy –
Be careful near
The water!

A PICTURE OF GUILT

LIBBY FISCHER HELLMANN

Libby
Hellmann

BERKLEY PRIME CRIME, NEW YORK

A PICTURE OF GUILT

A Berkley Prime Crime Book / published by arrangement with the author

PRINTING HISTORY
Berkley Prime Crime mass-market edition / July 2003

Copyright © 2003 by Libby Fischer Hellmann.
Cover art by Craig White.
Cover design by George Cornell.
Text design by Julie Rogers.

For information address: The Berkley Publishing Group,
a division of Penguin Group (USA) Inc.,
375 Hudson Street, New York, New York 10014.

ISBN: 0-425-19107-9

Berkley Prime Crime Books are published
by The Berkley Publishing Group,
a division of Penguin Group (USA) Inc.,
375 Hudson Street, New York, New York 10014.
The name BERKLEY PRIME CRIME
and the BERKLEY PRIME CRIME design
are trademarks belonging to Penguin Group (USA) Inc.

PRINTED IN THE UNITED STATES OF AMERICA

10 9 8 7 6 5 4 3 2 1

For Michael and Robin

ACKNOWLEDGMENTS

This book would not exist without the input of many people, all of whom I owe a tremendous debt of gratitude. Especially Don Whiteman whose knowledge, patience, and careful reading of the manuscript was a godsend. Also FBI Special Agent James Whitmer, Bob Egan, David Wechsler, Gerry Kessler, Leon Guaquil, Northbrook Deputy Commander Mike Green, Northfield Chief of Police Bill Lustig, Dave and Jean-Marie Case, and the Red Herrings.

To Jacky Sach and Samantha Mandor: your insights and support are remarkable . . . thanks for believing in Ellie. To Nora Cavin, I will always depend on your ear. And special thanks to Barbara Peters, TEE, who is really an angel in disguise.

Whoever destroys a single life is as guilty as though he had destroyed the entire world and whoever rescues a single life earns as much merit as though he had rescued the entire world.

—The Talmud, Mishna. Sanhedrin

ONE

THE RAFT PLUNGED straight down and slammed into a wall of water. It flew up at a ninety-degree angle, propelling me up and out into the river. The rapids spun me around and threw me from side to side, burying me under a blanket of waves. I tried to right myself so I could rise to the surface, but I couldn't tell which way was up. My lungs were on fire; my eyesight grew dim. Then a powerful force shoved me up, and I broke the surface, gasping for air.

Feet up, legs straight. That's what the guide said. I tried to stretch my legs out, but a fresh torrent wrenched me under. I tumbled over like a flimsy rag doll. Then, as if taunting me with the promise of release, the river raised me up again. Two giant boulders loomed ahead. I gulped down air and squeezed my eyes shut, certain my last sensation on earth would be the excruciating pain of bone splintering against rock.

When I opened my eyes, the boulders were behind me. A surge of foam and spray had pushed me through the narrow channel between them. Above the roar of the rapids, I heard screams. I twisted around. Rachel! Twenty yards away, my thirteen-year-old's yellow helmet bobbed in the churning waves.

My stomach clenched. I lunged and thrashed my arms, trying to swim to her, but the rapids carried me in the opposite direction. Just before I went under, I saw the guide throw her a lifeline. It landed short. When I came up, she was gone.

The river carried me another quarter mile. Then, as if underscoring its absolute control, it quieted. A hush descended. Tiny bubbles eddied across the surface. Gentle waves rippled peacefully. Hot sun struck my face.

I didn't care. Rachel was gone. I wanted to cry, but the tears wouldn't come. I wanted to scream, but the sound died in my throat. I stopped struggling. The water had won.

"**I SHOULD HAVE** known, when they said the river was kicking butt." I drained my third glass of wine.

"It was up two feet from the big storm the other day," Rachel added. She stirred her Coke with her swizzle stick.

"But you survived," Abdul, our dinner companion, said to Rachel.

Her blond curls framed her face like a soft, golden cloud. They bounced as she nodded. "Another raft picked me up."

Rachel inherited her coloring from her father, but we share the same gray eyes and feisty ways. I pushed a strand of thick, black hair behind my ears, thinking how close I'd come to never seeing those curls again.

"The guide said you weren't in any real danger, with the life preservers and helmets," David said.

I glared. "What did you expect him to say?"

We were finishing cocktails in the main dining room at the Greenbrier. Nestled in the backwoods of West Virginia, the resort is one of the plushest in the world. With its graceful columns, sculpted gardens, and antebellum buildings, it fairly drips Southern gentility.

Which is why it sounded like a perfect idea when David asked us to meet him there for the Labor Day weekend. It would be a grand finale to summer; an elegant start to fall. It was also a chance for the three of us to spend time together, since Rachel and I live in Chicago. To bond, in that trying-each-other-out-as-family kind of way. I'd even started to look forward to the trip, imagining myself sipping mint juleps on the veranda in a frothy summer frock. Of course, I don't have a frothy, mint-julep-sipping frock, but my friend Susan let me borrow hers. Susan has a dress for everything.

"Another glass of wine?" Abdul asked.

"I believe I will."

"Ellie," David cut in. "Haven't you had enough?"

"Not yet."

Abdul Al Hamarani had appeared at exactly the right time, like a fairy-tale genie magically released from his bottle. He was buying film inside the rafting company's small office as Rachel and I stumbled inside after our ordeal.

"We should never have left the Greenbrier," I'd muttered, collapsing on a chair.

He turned around. Wearing khakis with sharp creases, a pressed shirt, and a safari vest, he looked like he'd stepped out of a J. Peterman catalog. "You are staying at the Greenbrier?"

I nodded.

"I am staying there as well." He was round-faced, with dark hair slicked back from a widow's peak and had wide, lively eyes. Pocketing his roll of film, he introduced himself. After David joined us and settled up with the guide, he insisted we drive back together in his rented Mercedes. David started to decline, but after our experience, I wasn't eager for the bumpy ride in the van we'd come in. We accepted Abdul's offer.

During the trip we learned he was a Saudi petrochemical sheik and distant relative of the royal family. He'd come in a few days in advance of an annual energy conference, one of those international global-policy-making forums the Greenbrier is famous for hosting.

"I like to take pictures." Abdul explained and pointed to a canvas bag that had been slung on his shoulder. "Even your harshest summer is a relief from what I'm used to."

We continued getting acquainted over dinner.

"I beg your pardon, Ellie." He had a slight British accent. "But given your . . . your attitude, why did you embark on this rafting adventure to begin with?" He'd changed into a Savile Row suit for dinner. The softness around his belly said he'd dined at some of the best restaurants in the world.

"David suggested it." In truth, I'd been looking forward to a lazy day on the river, the hot sun beating down, the smell of blossoms perfuming the air. I'd been warned it was too late for the delicate pink and white laurel, but there might be some white rhododendron—a first cousin— in bloom. As the state flower of West Virginia, rhododendron grows in wild profusion at the side of the road, in ravines, and on mountains. Even the pat of butter on our plates was sculpted into the flower.

"Besides us, there were four teenagers. All of us first timers." The waiter set a fresh glass of wine down in front of me. "Everything was fine at the beginning. The first rapid was only a two. Nothing to worry about. But then we got to the Keeneys. They're the most powerful stretch of rapids on that part of the river."

I looked from Abdul to David, aware I was reworking and revising, turning the experience into a story. As if somehow that could blunt the terror I'd felt. But hey— I'm a filmmaker. I tell stories for a living.

"So we hit the Keeneys, which usually are a four, but because of the rains the other day, were closer to a five. Apparently, when we hit the first patch, the kids got spooked and forgot to stroke. Big mistake." I rolled my eyes and then clutched the arms of my chair. The room was starting to spin.

"Yeah." Rachel said. "Our guide kept telling us we had to keep stroking. All the way through the white water."

"If you stop, you lose control and balance, and you're at the mercy of the water." I took a sip of wine. "That's what happened."

Abdul patted his mustache and carefully trimmed goatee. A band of gold around his wrist glinted in the candlelight. "Yet you proceeded down the rest of the river without incident?"

David cleared his throat.

I looked away. "Actually, I told them they would either have to get a helicopter in to pick me up, or I would be hiking back. And since there weren't any helicopters handy—"

"And you're afraid to fly . . ." Rachel added.

I shot her a look. "You hiked back with me."

"I didn't want you to be alone." She swirled the Coke in her glass. The corners of her mouth twitched with silent laughter.

I settled back in my chair. The room was definitely starting to spin. I propped my elbows on the table. "One of the guides took us back. We climbed a fifty-foot cliff, then hiked five miles through the woods. That turned out to be the nicest part of the trip."

"Did you pass the abandoned railway and coal mines?" Abdul asked.

I raised an eyebrow. "How did you know?"

He thumbed his mustache. "I have been exploring the area myself."

"Of course. You said that." I looked at David and saw just the slightest shake of his head.

Abdul extracted a Gauloise from his pack and struck a match. Waving out the flame, he looked for an ashtray, but there was none. He casually dropped the spent match on the tablecloth. Our waiter, hovering nearby, promptly supplied an ashtray and whisked the match away, not even bothering to mention we were seated in the room's non-smoking section.

Abdul didn't seem to notice, either, and launched into a discussion with David about the Russian oil market. As the director of foreign currency trading for a Philadelphia bank, David keeps current on issues involving global finance. After their initial friction, they'd seemed to warm to each other.

I stared at the spot where Abdul dropped the match. A tiny smudge of gray marred the white damask tablecloth. I guess if you're related to the Saudi royal family, you can do things like that. After a moment I decided the smudge wasn't really jumping from one spot to another. I tried to focus on the men's conversation but heard only snatches of words, soft music, and the clink of silver on china.

I looked around. Ensconced in gilt-edged frames, a gentleman in a powdered wig and a lady in a low-cut gown gazed back at me. Did these stern representations of Southern society somehow sense my growing discomfort? After three days of rich food, soft accents, and scotch sprays, I was starting to feel overwhelmed. And that was before the river.

A curl of smoke rose from Abdul's cigarette, drifting into a haze above his head. I picked up a roll and buttered it, thinking how cruel it was to smash a tiny yellow flower with my butter knife. Who made those butterflowers anyway? Elves?

"So." I interrupted around a mouthful of bread. "You're here for an energy conference?"

Abdul looked over. "That's correct."

"Yeah? So what do you think? Have you decided what the government is gonna do for you next year?" I swallowed clumsily.

Irritation flashed in David's eyes. Rachel looked away.

"Don't look at me that way, David. Everybody knows the oil industry's in bed with the government. And—" I spread my hands. "What better place to be seduced? I mean, here we are in the lap of luxury in the poorest state in the country. And why is it so poor, you ask? Because all the coal that was so abundant here was stolen by certain interests while our government looked the other way."

"Ellie, that's enough."

"That's why those coal mines are abandoned, you know." I wagged a finger. "They were exploited by rich and powerful capitalishhts who didn't care what happened to the land after they raped it. And now they're shhtarting all over again with timber." I nodded in what I hoped was a sage manner. "Logging."

Abdul's mustache and goatee seemed to blur together.

"So you see, it's entirely fitting your meeting's at the Greenbrier." I went on. "Hey. I got an idea. Why don't we make a commercial? 'The Greenbrier—where the government goes to get grafted.' " I looked from Abdul to David. "Has a ring to it, don'cha think?"

Abdul inhaled deeply, the embers of his cigarette glowing orange. David avoided my eyes.

"You have passionate convictions, Ellie," Abdul said. "But you give me too much credit. I am just an observer, not a player in your politics." He picked up the menu. "Perhaps we should order our dinner."

AFTER DINNER RACHEL headed to the bowling alley, where the kids at the resort hung out. David and I went to our suite: two large bedrooms and a lavishly decorated living room with a wraparound porch outside.

David loosened his tie and disappeared into the bedroom. I sprawled on the living room couch. He came back out, minus his jacket, and sat on the other end. I made no move toward him, which, even through my alcoholic haze, surprised me. Usually, I can't wait to get him alone. He gazed at me expectantly, his deep blue eyes wide. Soft lamplight glinted off his thick, white hair. Muscles bulged through his short-sleeved shirt. Though he was well into his fifties, he could hold his own with any Generation Xer. The silence between us grew. Then,

"Why do you always do that?" he said.

"What?" I said, after a beat. "Get drunk?"

He shook his head. "Why do you always make sure everyone knows you're an outsider?"

"I am."

"No more than Abdul."

"Sure. And I just happen to have twenty oil wells in my pocket, too." I sniffed. "My God, David, look at this place. The garbage alone could feed an entire West Virginia hamlet. And Abdul flicks his burnt match on the table like we're in some greasy spoon. I know some people are used to being waited on. But that just isn't me." I slouched. "Of course, nearly drowning today didn't help much."

David took a breath. "Ellie, I wanted us to enjoy our time together. Frightening you or Rachel was the last thing I ever intended to do."

That was probably as close as he would come to admitting that we *had* brushed up against the void that afternoon. "But as far as belonging . . ." He sighed. "People spend their whole lives not knowing where they belong. Can't you just file this away as an experience?"

Maybe I was still too worked up. Or drunk. But his tone rankled. "Sorry. I forgot who I was dealing with. The guy who'll do anything to belong. Who needs acceptance from everyone."

He knelt in front of me. "Not from everyone," he said quietly. "Just you."

Something inside me came unhinged, and a weight in my chest I hadn't known was there began to melt.

"I'm sorry. That was way out of line."

"It's okay." He smiled and drew me into his arms.

TWO

"ELLIE?"

ABDUL HEADED over to my table carrying a plate loaded with French toast, sausage, and grits. Draper's Café was done up in so many bright pinks and greens I felt like a prisoner inside the petals of a giant laurel. I folded my newspaper. "Good morning."

"Where's David?"

"Showering. He was working out."

Abdul's mound of food almost obscured the pattern of laurels bordering his plate. He smiled ruefully as he set it down. "I should follow his example. But I am not as disciplined."

I smiled, too, remembering our very undisciplined activities the night before. As if reading my mind, Abdul's grin widened. Mine faded. I felt like I'd been hit by a bus, and I was nursing a headache the size of Montana. "Abdul, I want to apologize for my behavior last night."

He sat down. "Think nothing of it."

"I was ugly."

"You were refreshing."

"*You* are charming."

He pulled out a chair and sat down. Unfolding a pink linen napkin, he placed it on his lap, then reached for the syrup, drenching not only the French toast but the sausages and the grits in a sea of maple. My fruit cup looked Spartan in comparison.

He speared his sausage and swallowed it in two bites. If he was Muslim, he wasn't all that devout. "You are from Chicago, David tells me?"

"Born and bred." I braced myself, waiting for the inevitable comment about the Windy City or "my kind of town," or some other inanity non-Chicagoans feel compelled to express. As if we run around all day humming Sinatra, thrilled to live in a place with razzmatazz.

But all Abdul said was, "I am very impressed with your . . . your . . ."

"David."

"Yes. He has keen observations on the relationship between currencies and markets."

As much as I try, I can't summon up much enthusiasm for currency trading. Admittedly, I don't really understand it, and I keep wondering what I'm supposed to understand. As David explains it, it's a service that banks provide to their customers. The bank doesn't want to lose money, but they're not in it to make a killing. Except for the occasional scandal, which often turns out to be the result of poor judgment rather than deceit, currency trading just isn't very sexy. Which is fine by me. My ex-husband played the market. Badly. I have the debts to prove it.

But Abdul was clearly a man of wealth—and a member of the Saudi royal family. I should be polite. "I don't understand currency trading very well, but I imagine you need dollars because—well, why do you need dollars?"

A waitress in green and pink filled our coffee cups. He waited until she glided away. "You're a curious woman."

I shrugged.

He studied me closely, as if registering every detail of

my appearance. I found it unnerving. I'm usually the observer.

"It is not that complex." He lowered his fork. "The price of oil is quoted in U.S. dollars, and most of my business is transacted that way. I use the proceeds to purchase currencies for my other investments."

"And what would those be?"

He hesitated. "I am always looking for new ideas and technologies to bring back to my people. For example, I have invested in a genetic engineering company which is experimenting with drought-resistant seeds. Also an Internet search engine that teaches children how to retrieve information more easily."

"Really?"

"It may be your David Linden and I will have more to discuss." He laughed, scraping up a mouthful of grits. "But enough business. You seem more—how do I say it— anchored this morning."

"Nicely put." I smiled. "The rafting . . . well, it isn't anything I plan to do again."

He laughed again and went back to his food. When he'd finished, he pulled out a copy of the *Journal*. "You don't mind?" He motioned to the paper.

I held up the *Chicago Tribune* I'd bought earlier, and we settled back to read in companionable silence. I'd been surprised to find a Chicago paper in the mountains of West Virginia. But then, this was the Greenbrier. They probably had their own printing press in the back.

As I scanned the paper, a story on page nine caught my eye. A murder trial was about to get under way at criminal court downtown. The accused, a man named Johnnie Santoro, allegedly beat up and then shot his girlfriend at Calumet Park on the Southeast Side. He was pleading not guilty, but according to the article, there was a wealth of incriminating evidence. The last weeks of summer are usually the dog days in terms of hard news, so in the absence of anything more newsworthy, the case had been heavily covered by the media, the local stations promising all the legal maneuverings and high drama of the OJ trial. I'd paid scant attention until now, figuring that whatever local TV wants me to watch is exactly what I should avoid.

Today, though, there was a grainy newspaper picture of Santoro in the paper. He was twenty-six, the article said, but he looked older. His eyes were hooded, and his hair was cut close to his skull. He was looking off camera, but his eyebrows were so overgrown and bushy they met over his nose, which gave gave him a simian look.

I stared at the picture and felt my skin grow clammy. I reached for a glass of water.

"Something is wrong, Ellie?" Abdul asked.

I gulped down a swig, then held up the paper. "This man who's on trial? He . . . looks familiar. I think I know him."

His eyebrows shot up.

"Good morning, troops." Strong hands squeezed my shoulders. I glanced up. David leaned over and kissed my cheek.

"It's the face," I said to Abdul. "I've seen it before."

David pulled out a chair. "What did I miss?"

I passed him the paper. "Look at this."

"What am I looking at?"

"The man in the picture. Who's on trial for murder."

David studied the article.

"I think I know him," I said. "But I don't know how."

I felt Abdul's eyes on me.

"Guy beats up his girlfriend and shoots her to death." David handed me back the paper. "What a nice person for you to know."

THREE

RACHEL WAS RIGHT, I am terrified of flying. I always have been, even before September 11. Going home, I put up a brave front, but by the time we landed at O'Hare, having bounced around one thunderstorm and flown through another, I was a quivering, quaking mass of Jell-O. And that was an improvement over the flight out.

I tripped over Rachel's bag as I came through the front door. She was already on the phone, her newest CD blasting. I lugged our bags in the house, for once not minding the stains in the carpet, the nicks on the wall, and all the other imperfections and flaws. A modest three-bedroom on the North Shore of Chicago, I managed to hang onto it after the divorce, and it looks like I'll be there forever; I can't afford to move. Tonight I was grateful.

I dumped our dirty laundry in the basement and went upstairs to my office. It used to be the guest room, but I appropriated it when Barry moved out. My computer, scanner, and printer fill most of the space, but I'd invested in an ergonomic chair last year, and I happily swiveled from side to side as I downloaded my E-mail. There was something reassuring about the clicks, bells, and blue bars that accompanied the unspooling of my messages. All was right in my little corner of cyberspace. It hadn't always been.

After I trashed the usual spam, only a few messages remained, none of them urgent, so I decided to unpack. As I was digging through the canvas bag that doubles as my briefcase and overnighter, I came across yesterday's *Trib*. It was folded to the page with Johnnie Santoro's picture. I studied it again, feeling the same sense of familiarity.

I entered Santoro's name on a news database, and after a few seconds, more than a dozen articles popped up. I started scanning them. Santoro had been indicted for the murder of Mary Jo Bosanick, a young woman in her twenties. Mary Jo went to the Lakeside Inn, a tavern on the Southeast Side, to meet Santoro after a night-school class, but Santoro didn't show up until two hours later. A fierce argument erupted, and they both stormed out.

Mary Jo's body was found the next morning a few feet from Santoro's Chevy at the boat launch in Calumet Park. She'd been viciously beaten and shot twice in the head. Apparently, she tried to put up a fight; scrapings of Santoro's skin were found under her fingernails. The next day the cops arrested Santoro at the docks where he worked as a longshoreman.

I leaned back in my chair. There isn't much left of the dock life in Chicago—at least not on the same scale as Newark, Houston, or New Orleans. Back during the fifties and sixties, countless ships plied the Great Lakes, but traffic has since dried up. Competition from rail and trucks is one reason. The construction of larger, more efficient freighters is another. Weather also plays a part. Though they did dredge a terminal that operates year round, there's still only a nine-month season along the Saint Lawrence Seaway linking Chicago to the Atlantic.

What little shipping remains, mostly steel and steel products, is centered around Calumet Harbor, not far from

•

the park of the same name. On the rare day a ship does tie up, longshoremen queue up at waterfront warehouses for day jobs, like they've been doing for forty years. Most of the men are well past their prime, forced by meager pensions to take whatever work is available, but a few youngsters hang out there, too. That's where the cops found Santoro, stamping his feet in the morning chill, hoping for a few hours' work.

I looked through the window at the locust tree in my front yard. Its lattice of leaves, silvered by the moonlight, danced gently in the night breeze. Somewhere in the distance I heard the plaintive honk of a goose. Santoro might be a dock rat, but that didn't tell me how I knew him. I shut down the computer and went into my room.

Rachel had gone to bed, but I was still wired. I turned on the TV. The end of Ingmar Bergman's *Wild Strawberries* was running on cable. Ostensibly about a professor who confronts the void of his life, the film opens with one of the best dream sequences ever filmed: boarded-up windows, a clock with no hands, a hearse disgorging a coffin, the creepy, outstretched hand of a corpse.

Okay. Bergman is not what you'd call warm and fuzzy, but what can you expect from a Swede? His work even looks a little stagey now, but that's because every film-maker in the world has copied his style. The way he works with light and shadow. The nuances of his camera moves. The way he imbues his characters with personality through one simple but perfect gesture. In the journeyman work I do for a living, I might set up a pretty shot or a smooth pan, but there's no emotional investment. No fusion of form and function. Even Bergman's outtakes are works of art.

As good as the film was, my eyelids began to droop. I forced them open a few times, but it was hopeless. I snapped off the tube and burrowed under the covers—and then sat bolt upright in the dark. The water. Nighttime. Outtakes. I knew where I'd run into Johnnie Santoro.

FOUR

FOR A MONTH or so each fall, the mums take over Chicago. It's as if the Big Florist in the Sky has commanded, "Thou shalt have chrysanthemums and plant them everywhere." Huge planters of the red and yellow flowers, their spiky petals irrepressibly cheerful, flanked the door to Mac's studio as I headed inside.

When we started working together, MacArthur J. Kendall III had a tiny studio crammed with camera gear and editing equipment. Ten years later, his studio boasts two nonlinear editing suites, a soundstage, and one of the best editors in the galaxy.

Some people's bodies are made for the work they do. Michael Jordan. Martha Graham. Hank Chenowsky. With long, supple fingers, a lanky torso, and eyes that blink in sunlight like a mole's, Hank was destined to be either a concert pianist or a video editor. He chose editing, but to watch those fingers fly over the console is to watch a virtuoso perform.

He and I have spent more than a few late nights working, and he alone is responsible for the magic that makes our shows a cut above. I'm grateful to Mac, who appreciates what a talent he has and has managed to keep Hank happy. Though with Hank, happiness is more or less a permanent state of being. I've never seen him cranky.

I remember once asking him about his idea of heaven on earth.

"You first," he'd said.

"Okay." I squeezed my eyes shut. "A box of warm Krispy Kremes waiting for me . . . on a bed at the Four Seasons Hotel."

He cocked his head. "The Four Seasons?"

I opened one eye. "You ever been on one of their beds?"

"Uh, no."

"First of all, they're huge. Soft and firm at the same time. Perfect for sitting, and lying, and—well—they sell over two hundred beds a year, you know."

"And you know about beds at the Four Seasons because . . ."

"Um—uh—"

"Right." He cut in. "Okay. What flavor?"

"Pardon me?"

"The Krispy Kremes."

"Oh." I considered it. "Doesn't matter."

We exchanged nods.

"Your turn."

He bent over the keyboard to finish an edit. "Heaven on earth, huh?" He laced his fingers together and flexed them backward. "That's easy. Playing with Clapton."

"Where?"

"Shea Stadium."

"Instrument?"

"Bass, of course."

"Not piano?"

"That's my backup."

"What?"

"Playing with Count Basie at Carnegie Hall."

See what I mean about destiny?

But on this morning, garbled noise spewed out of the editing room door. It sounded like a flock of angry pigeons had taken up residence. I skirted the door and headed to Mac's office.

"Hey."

With his crew neck sweaters and khakis, Mac looks like an aging preppie, but it's dangerous to underestimate him. He's an excellent director and a shrewd judge of character. He looked up from a pile of paperwork. "What brings you here? A new client?"

I shook my head. "Things are slow." In my experience, industrial video production is an economic bellwether. When my work slows down, the economy isn't far behind. "I need the elements of the show we started for the water district."

"How come?"

"There's something I need to check."

He brightened. "They want to reedit?"

"You're slow, too."

He stood up. "It hasn't been this bad for years."

I followed him down the hall to a closed door, where he punched in a four-digit code on a wall panel. The door opened into a windowless room with gray walls and hundreds of gray cassettes on gray shelves.

"You'll be okay," I asked. "Won't you?"

"We'll survive." He started scanning the shelves. "You?"

"It's a little scary."

He tossed long brown hair back from his forehead. "I know that tune. Now . . . what were you looking for?"

"The Chicago water district."

"Our unfinished symphony."

"That's the one."

Last summer we'd started a video for the water district that showed how water travels from Lake Michigan to peoples' faucets. The journey begins at two intake cribs a few miles from shore. The cribs, anchored forty feet down on the lake bed, suck up enormous amounts of water, which is then piped through underwater tunnels to one of two treatment plants onshore. After the plants process and filter the water, it's piped through another series of underground channels to distribution centers at strategic points around the city as well as a hundred suburbs. These centers then pump it into homes. A simple concept; an engineering marvel.

Unfortunately, halfway through production, September 11 happened, and the water district canceled the video. Given the situation, a how-it-works video on Chicago's water supply didn't seem prudent. Happily, they paid us for the time we'd already put in. Which is probably more than Schubert got.

"Found 'em." Mac motioned to a group of cassettes on the top shelf. "Which ones do you want?"

"The B roll we shot during the reenactment."

Mac climbed up a stepladder. "That *was* one of your better ideas."

I smiled. We'd set out on the city tug from Navy Pier to scout one of the cribs. The Carter-Harrison crib is really two cylindrical structures joined together by a small suspension bridge. One cylinder has limestone and red-brick walls; the other has a white surface with pinkish stripes running down its sides. Except for a small tower rising through its center, it looks like a giant wedding cake. Although we wouldn't be shooting inside for security reasons, the Deaver crib, or candy striper, as boaters call it, is where the actual pumping takes place.

We'd disembarked at the limestone-and-brick cylinder, which houses living quarters for dozens of men. Before the pumps were automated, crews actually lived on the cribs to operate the machinery, and the facility, originally built around 1900, was equipped with bedrooms, a kitchen, and a dining area. Now, though, men bunk there only a few weeks each summer while they do maintenance and repair work. We'd planned to get some shots of them when the weather warmed up.

I remembered entering through a heavy iron door, half

expecting to see a drawbridge slam shut behind us. But once inside, I was surprised. The cribs had been rehabbed, and the interior was all white walls and bright lights. At one end was a large, high-ceilinged kitchen and eating area; at the other, a series of bedrooms. A suit from the water district's PR department explained that during re-modeling, some of the larger bedrooms had been divided up to accommodate more workmen.

As we passed one of the larger rooms, I saw a large wooden rolltop desk against a wall.

"What's that doing here?" I asked.

"Now, that's a great story." The PR guy glanced at the desk, then back at me. "But it's off the record."

I shrugged. I don't pretend to be a journalist; in no way does anything I do qualify as objective. In a pinch, you could call my shows infomercials, but—bottom line—if the client doesn't like it, it doesn't go in.

"It turns out that the cribs had quite a reputation. During Prohibition, this place was a speakeasy. And brothel."

I remember feeling my eyes widen. "No way!"

He laughed, clearly enjoying my astonishment. "You've heard of Big Bill Thompson?"

I nodded. Big Bill Thompson, aka William Hale Thompson, was one of Chicago's more avaricious may-ors. A friend of gangsters, a taker of bribes, he'd amassed two million dollars in assets during the twenties, almost twenty million by today's standards. However, he's re-membered most not for his shady dealings—he had plenty of company there, anyway—but by his famous advice to his citizenry: "Vote early and often."

"Right," the PR guy said. "Well, this was his party pad. You should hear the stories about the booze and wild women. Capone used to come out here, too—one of his favorite hangouts, they say." He motioned toward the desk. "They even brought their own furniture."

"Are you kidding?"

He raised two fingers. "Scout's honor."

I looked around. "I guess they weren't just *voting* early and often back then."

I'm still not sure how we did it, but we were so taken with the cribs' history that we persuaded the water district to let us stage a reenactment. We had to agree to shoot overnight so we wouldn't interfere with any work, but that was only a minor problem. We hired actors, dressed them in flapper costumes and sack suits, and through the genius of Mac's lighting, used smoky illumination and deep shadows to create a bordello atmosphere. The idea was to create a match dissolve, contrasting the bawdy revelries of the past to the techno-efficiency of today.

Now, Mac headed back to his office with the tapes and dropped one of them into his Beta player. I followed and settled into a chair. Color bars and tone appeared, followed by the drone of a motor. A dark blur filled the screen.

"That was a fun shoot," he said.

I stared at the screen. The night of the reenactment, Mac, the cameraman, and I set out from Diversey Harbor to shoot the trip out to the cribs. We were planning a sequence from the POV of the partygoers: shots of inky water, the gentle pitch of the boat, waves lapping the side. We'd gone as far south as Oak Street Beach when we started playing with the gain on the camera, trying to get the best exposure.

Shooting at night is tricky. Particularly on the lake and in the absence of artificial light. Not only do you lose detail, but if you're not careful, the image can turn grainy. You can use a night vision lens, but then your video might look green, like those shots of Scud missiles during the Gulf War. The solution is to try to include an existing light source, however dim, in the shot.

I watched as the shot on the screen panned from a red buoy back to shore where streetlights rimmed a small park. The sound was on, and for a moment, we could hear the slap of waves, the murmur of our voices, the drone of traffic on Lake Shore Drive. But then a low, steady hum buzzed the sound track, punctuated with a crackle of static. Seconds later, a series of white lines streaked across the image, and erratic bursts of snow obliterated the picture.

I looked at Mac. "What the . . . What's that?"

Mac leaned forward, a frown tightening his face. "That's weird."

The tape kept rolling. More dropout and static zipped across the screen. "Mac, what's going on?"

He got up and stopped the tape. He rewound it. Then he punched Play. The damage was still there. "There's noise on the tape."

"I see that. How come?"

"I don't know." He kept studying it. "It looks like some kind of RF interference."

We exchanged puzzled expressions. Twenty years ago RF, or radio frequency interference, was a problem. Video equipment could pick up radio signals, which penetrated down to the camera heads, ruining the sound track or picture. Shooting at Sears Tower was a particular nightmare. Most of the local radio and TV station antennas sat on its roof, and you were as likely to pick up Phil Donahue or a Top 40 song on your track as the audio from your scene. Today, though, cameras are better shielded, and the problem has, for the most part, disappeared.

"How can that be?" I asked.

"I don't know." Mac fingered the scar on the left side of his face, the result of a bad car accident as a teenager. "That's the first time I've seen it."

"There weren't any radio stations nearby, were there?"

He shook his head.

"A ship, maybe?"

"No way. Their frequencies are much lower. Anyway, it couldn't have been there when we first shot it."

"You know something? You're right. I would have seen it when I logged it in." I frowned. "In fact, I remember screening it before we set up for the match dissolve, and it was fine." I looked over. "So where have you been keeping this thing?"

"Ellie . . ." His scar started to turn red.

I raised my palm. "I'm sorry. Just kidding."

Mac always stores everything in his securely locked, temperature-controlled tape library. He fast-forwarded to the middle of the tape and punched Play.

"Look." I pointed to the monitor. "It's not so bad now."

Intermittent streaks still flashed the screen, but the snow was gone, and so was the low-pitched whine. We could plainly see a long shot of a park bench lit by a streetlamp. As the camera pushed in, what at first appeared to be a lump on the bench turned into a man curled up on it, his face toward the camera. As we zoomed in for a close-up, the man raised his head and looked into the camera. Thick, overgrown eyebrows cut across his forehead in an almost unbroken line, and there was a dazed expression in his eyes. He pushed himself up to a sitting position and tried to stand up, but as soon as he put weight on his legs, he collapsed back on the bench.

"Back up!" I said.

Mac rewound the tape. The man flew up, lay down awkwardly, and looked into the camera.

"Pause that!" I said.

Mac hit the remote.

"When does the log say we were there?"

He unfolded the piece of paper that had been inserted into the sleeve of the cassette. "Last July. The twenty-third."

"What time did we shoot?"

"Between midnight and one. Why? What's going on, Ellie?"

I opened my bag and pulled out the copy of the *Trib* from the other day.

Mac looked from the picture of Johnnie Santoro in the *Trib* to the image paused on the screen and back again. "It's the same guy," he said softly.

"Check out the time he supposedly murdered that woman."

"July twenty-third," he said "Sometime between midnight and three." The lines on his face deepened. "But he was in the park. On that bench. I don't get it."

Our eyes met. "Neither do I."

FIVE

HOISTING MY CANVAS bag over my shoulder, I locked the Volvo and walked to the elevators of the parking garage. The sharp, clean smell of gasoline tugged at my nostrils. I tried to smooth out my pants, but the two-hour trip downtown had welded permanent creases into the material.

Brashares and Associates had one of those LaSalle Street addresses that sounds much fancier than it is. Wedged between a real estate company and an accounting firm on the twenty-seventh floor, the office had an ordinary frosted glass door with black stenciling on it.

It was after five, but the lights were still on, and the door was unlocked. I pushed into a gloomy reception area with two chairs and a fern begging to be put out of its misery. A few feet away, a woman was bent over a keyboard. A copying machine in the corner spat out paper. Somewhere in the back, a phone was slammed down. The light on the woman's desk phone cut out.

"Gail, get in here," a churlish voice yelled.

The woman started, and then, as if embarrassed that I

had witnessed her loss of composure, winced.

I smiled. "Ellie Foreman to see Chuck Brashares. I have an appointment."

"Gail, where are you, dammit?"

The woman at the desk returned a strained smile, picked up her phone, and buzzed someone. "Ellie Foreman's here."

I heard a drawer close and a chair squeak. A moment later a tall, slim man emerged from the back. Bald on top, he sported a sparse blond mustache. Ice-blue eyes studied me from behind rimless glasses.

"Miss Foreman." He approached with feline, almost mincing steps, and we shook hands. "Thanks for coming down."

I figured him for a few years younger than me, but the tired expression on his face made him seem older. "Sorry to be late. The construction and the reverse commute are murder."

I cringed as soon as I said it, but he didn't seem to notice. He led me down a short hall.

His office had none of the upscale decor of my ex-husband's firm or the cheerful chaos of my father's old digs. A battered oak desk in the center of the room was piled high with folders. Two chairs sat in front, and a framed law degree from John Marshall Law School hung on the wall behind. Raised miniblinds gave onto a view of the building's air-conditioning shaft.

It seemed perfectly ordinary, if a tad shabby, until I stepped aside to let him close the door. Instead of the requisite family photos or framed landscapes, the wall behind it was covered with photographs of Brashares. There was a shot of him on skis wearing a red jacket and designer sunglasses. Another of him in a Sox uniform with a bat. Still another in running shorts with a number pinned to his shirt. There was even a shot of him with a helmet and an oar, white water swirling in the background. The shots were all eight by tens, and they were all precisely mounted in black matte frames, three to a row, three rows.

He watched me studying the wall. "I like to keep fit."

He seemed to expect some further response from me, maybe something along the lines of admiration.

"How'd you get the Sox uniform?" I asked.

"The Sox . . . I was high bidder for a day in the dugout at a charity auction," he said impatiently.

I smiled. Home run.

He gestured to the ski shot. "But that was Mount Snow. And that was the Boston Marathon. I run all over the world."

"Really."

He pointed to the shot of the rapids. "And that's the New River in West Virginia."

"I know that river."

His eyebrows shot up. "Do you raft?"

I stared him down. "Not anymore."

"Oh." He went back to his desk, pushed the files to one side, and sat down. "Well, let's go over what you said on the phone. You claim you have an alibi for my client?" He pulled out a yellow pad.

I sat down in the chair opposite him. "I'm a video producer, and I have tape of Johnnie Santoro in Olive Park at the same time he supposedly killed his girlfriend. I read you were representing him, and I figured you might want to see it."

"Olive Park? What—where is Olive Park?"

"It's a tiny enclosed area just north of Navy Pier. Near the water filtration plant. You can see it from Oak Street Beach."

"Santoro was at Olive Park?"

"Yes." I shifted. "But you already knew that."

His face was blank.

"You didn't?"

He pushed up the bridge of his glasses with his finger. "Why don't you tell me?"

"I was producing a video for the water district at the time. We were on our way out to the intake crib—"

"The intake crib?"

"The Carter-Harrison crib out on the lake."

He nodded.

"We wanted to get a few shots beforehand, so we took a boat out from Diversey Harbor. We were just south of Oak Street Beach when we started to try out different exposures. When you're shooting at night, well—" I shifted again. "Anyway, we took a few shots of the park, and Santoro was there. Passed out on a bench."

Brashares kept staring at me.

"There were two other people with me. I'm sure both of them would corroborate it." When he didn't answer, I crossed my legs. "You don't believe me."

"It's not that."

I waited.

He cleared his throat. "It—it's just that Johnnie Santoro wasn't—how do I say it—all there that night. His brain was fried. Booze, dope, I don't know. Neither does he. But there's no question he was loaded. He can't remember what he did." He picked up a pencil. "Makes it hard to come up with a defense."

I recalled his dazed expression on the tape. How he struggled to get off the bench. "What are you going to do?"

"What is there to do? Try to work around it. And be grateful he remembers his name."

The phone on the desk trilled. He grabbed the receiver. "Yeah?"

If Santoro was as strung out as Brashares said that night, was he even capable of taking someone's life?

"I'll get back to you." Brashares replaced the phone. "Look, this is the first I've heard of any alibi. Why did you wait so long to come forward?"

I uncrossed my legs, surprised by the question. "I just made the connection. I saw his picture in the paper, and he looked familiar. I didn't realize I had video of him until the other day."

"Why didn't you go to the police?"

I looked over. I'd considered it, of course, but I read

the papers. I know how Chicago cops can "lose" important evidence. Or "forget" to pass it through the system. But I'd just met Brashares. "The police are basically finished with their investigation." I answered carefully, "As I understand it, the ball's in your court."

"You know something about the legal system?"

"Both my father and my ex-husband are attorneys."

"Ah."

I got the feeling I'd climbed up a few points in his private opinion poll.

"Did you bring the tape with you?"

I dug into my canvas bag. "Do you have a VCR?"

"No. But you're prepared to leave it, I hope?"

I nodded and pulled out a copy of the tape, which Mac had made at the studio. "I also brought a copy of our video log. You'll see that it says we shot footage of the shoreline on the twenty-third around midnight."

Brashares took the tape and log and placed both at a precise angle to his pencil. For some reason, he didn't look as happy as a lawyer should who's just been handed a big break. But then, maybe he was just cautious. Or maybe he was already three steps ahead of me, formulating strategy to use in court. Or maybe he was just a lousy lawyer.

"There . . . there is a little damage on the tape." I explained about the RF. "You'll see some video dropout, and some snow from time to time. We just discovered it when we screened it the other day. But it wasn't there when we first shot it, and it didn't show up on any of the other tapes. I hope that won't be a problem."

He picked up the pencil. "I won't know until I take a look. But if it clearly shows Santoro in that park, we'll probably be okay."

"I hope so," I said. "I'd hate to think he was wrongly accused."

He frowned. "Up until now, I had no reason to believe he didn't do it."

"No?"

"They have a strong case. The car, the fingernail scrapings, his lack of an alibi. In fact, I'd almost persuaded him to cop a plea. He's taking a huge chance."

"Chance?"

"He's playing with a life sentence."

"Maybe he knows, in spite of his memory, that he really is innocent. They say even people with amnesia have gut feelings about these things."

"Sure. Him and all my other clients."

"You don't believe him?"

He shrugged. "He admits they fought. Says he might have taken a swing at her. But he claims she took his car and split. He never saw her again."

"So?"

"The other side has witnesses that saw two people driving into Calumet Park in his car."

"What does he say?"

"He can't remember."

"Which means the tape might be a real break."

"Maybe. But first I have to get it admitted."

"Why wouldn't it be? It's clearly Santoro. You'll see."

He leaned back. "Authenticity for one thing. Chain of custody for another. We have to prove both."

"Let's say you do. Then what?"

"Then, I'll do my best to see that he's acquitted."

"And then find whoever did kill the girl?"

He paused. "My job stops when I get him off. I'm not in the business of solving murders."

"But what if . . . what if someone framed him, and you get him off? What's to stop them from trying again?"

"You've just posed three hypotheticals, Miss Foreman. I can't deal with those. I deal with facts."

He got up and gazed at the wall of pictures, as if he was drawing inspiration from images of himself.

While he postured, I wondered how Santoro had become his client. Santoro didn't seem like the sporting type, and Brashares had probably never stepped foot on the docks. Then I recalled reading that Santoro's union card was up to date. Maybe the union had found him a lawyer.

He looked at me. "You're not planning to leave town in the near future, are you?"

"No. Why?"

"Because you'll probably have to testify."

SIX

I CALLED RACHEL on the way home to see if she wanted me to pick up a pizza.

"No, that's okay. Katie and I are going to the mall."

"You're going where?"

"Her mom's on her way over."

"Whoa, girl. I don't remember giving you permission to go to the mall. Especially on a school night."

"Mom," she said, stretching the word into three syllables. "School just started."

"I'm aware of that. What about homework?"

"It's done."

"All of it?"

"Yes."

"What are you going to do there?"

"Mother, why are you always on my case?"

"Uh—how about I care about my daughter, and I want to know what she's up to?"

"Jeez, Mom. It's just the mall."

"I get it."

"Mother, it's my life. Stop invading my privacy."

I gripped the cell phone, prepared to launch into a discussion about study habits, responsibilities, and boundaries. "Rachel, let's get—"

"They're here, Mom," Rachel cut in. "Gotta go. Pick us up outside the food court at nine."

I checked my watch. It was barely seven. "Rachel, I didn't say you could go." I heard a distinct click, followed by silence. "Rachel?"

I drove another block with the cell pressed to my ear, then tossed it across the front seat. The Martians had landed, and they'd taken her brain. With any luck they'd send it back when she was twenty-five.

Dusk settled, cloaking everything in a mantle of purple as I wound through Skokie. The occasional shout of a child, the tinkle of music, and canned TV laughter spilled through the window. I turned onto Golf Road, feeling a twinge of regret at the loss of innocence, though whether it was Rachel's or my own, I wasn't sure.

Dad was watching the news when I unlocked his door. He lives in an assisted-living retirement home, although to hear him tell it, the only thing they assist with is the steady depletion of his savings. He glanced up from his leather wing chair, the one with gold tacking that had moved from the house with him. A plate with a half-eaten hamburger sat on the hassock. The smell of grilled onions hung in the air.

"Hi," I said, closing the door. "How ya doin'?"

He turned back to the tube. "That's the problem when you get old."

"What?"

"People come, people go. All day long. And everyone's got a key. It's a real invasion of privacy, you know?"

The joys of the sandwich generation. I slid the key back in my bag. "Sorry. I should have knocked."

He turned up his cheek for a kiss. A lamp on a nearby table threw a soft glow across his head, which was as smooth and shiny as a marble. But at eighty-one, he's still

alert and engaged. In fact, Susan says he reminds her of
Ben Kingsley playing Ghandi.

I crossed to the window and opened it. "How's the new
prescription?"

He'd been having problems with heart palpitations, and
they'd changed his medication twice in two weeks. The
first prescription fatigued him so much I was ready to take
him to the ER until I tracked down his cardiologist, who
was at a conference in Hawaii. He phoned in a new prescription and told me not to worry; we were only on the
third of twelve possible drugs. If this one didn't work, he
said cheerfully, there were still nine to go.

Fortunately, Dad did have more color tonight. "Any
side effects?"

"Only if you call taking the boys to the cleaners today
a side effect."

"Stud or draw?"

"What do you think?" He grinned. "You shoulda seen
Marv's face after I bluffed the last hand. He thought he
was drawing dead. He still hasn't figured out when I'm
gonna do it."

It's hard to beat my father at five-card stud. I returned
the grin, then gestured to his plate. "You eating enough?"

"Ellie, would you stop? I'll let you know when I'm
about to die. Then you can worry."

"I'm not worried." I lied.

"I know." He chuckled. "So, what brings you here on
a weekday night?"

I snapped off the TV and dropped a CD in his player.
His face smoothed out as Sinatra started crooning. I felt
a stab of envy. I remember intense discussions about pop
music in my younger days. How it was an anesthetic,
foisted upon us by the establishment to numb us to our
suffering and political exploitation. Even now, I can't listen to a Motown riff without a twinge of guilt. But, as
Frank's voice slid through the air, Dad snapped his fingers
and closed his eyes, the tune clearly taking him back to
happier times.

I waited until the song ended to tell him about Johnnie Santoro.

He was massaging his temples before I finished. "Ellie," he said, a rise in his voice. "What are you doing? Stay out of it."

"I can't. They may want me to testify at his trial."

"But you don't know that he's innocent."

"He was passed out on a bench near Navy Pier the night of the murder. Calumet Park's at least seven miles away."

"That means nothing. How do you know he didn't hitch a ride down there—or back up afterwards? I mean if he's really as forgetful as this lawyer says—"

"Dad, the guy was wiped out. He couldn't even stand up."

Dad pushed himself up. "Ellie. You have no idea who this man is, or who he associates with. The man was a longshoreman."

"So that means I shouldn't get involved?"

He flipped up his hands.

"That's odd, because I seem to remember someone else—someone close to me—who did the same thing."

Dad blinked. He'd grown up in Hyde Park but spent time in Lawndale, currying favor and running errands for a gang of hustlers in that thriving Jewish community. It was only for a few months before the war, but he still talked about it sixty years later.

"This isn't the same thing. This man could be a career criminal. The Mob runs the docks. And their unions."

"But I don't think he did it."

"So, who made you his savior?"

"Well now, that is the issue, isn't it? Where do you draw the line? When do you get involved, and when do you just step over the homeless man and pretend you didn't see him?"

He aimed a finger at me. "Ellie, this man is a potential killer, not a vagrant."

I folded my arms, and we glared at each other. Then he settled back in his chair, shaking his head. "I should know by now. Your mother was the same way—bringing home strays every Thanksgiving and Pesach. I never knew where she found them."

"Dad, if he's convicted, and I could have done something to help but was too scared or busy or wrapped up in myself, I'd carry that guilt forever. That tape could make a big difference."

"Maybe. Maybe not." He stopped talking and tapped two fingers against his chin. "You know," he said more softly, "there comes a time that you don't have to keep apologizing for thinking about yourself. You're allowed to live your own life. You're even allowed to enjoy it."

"I—I'm not that busy. I have time."

"Maybe you should spend it with your daughter or your boyfriend. Not get distracted on some crusade for a stranger. Deal with your own issues as they say . . ."

I looked away.

"How is Rachel?"

"She's fine."

"You sure?"

"Dad . . ."

"She called me this afternoon after school. She wanted to ride her bike down to visit."

"Rachel?" I was astonished. "My daughter wanted to voluntarily expend energy on some form of exercise?"

"She said she was bored."

The thing they don't tell you about the sandwich generation is that the two pieces of bread can gang up on the stuff in the middle. "What did you say?"

"I told her it was too far to ride all the way down to Skokie, and why didn't she go to the pool?"

The municipal pool, where Rachel hung out from dawn to dusk—at least last summer—was only a short bike ride from our house.

"What did she say?"

" 'Opa,' she said—she sounded just like you do sometimes—'it's after Labor Day. The pool's closed. But even if it wasn't, swimming is for children.' " He got up, picked up his plate, and shuffled into the kitchen. I followed him in. "You know, it wouldn't hurt for her to have something to do after school." He dumped the remains of the burger in the trash and rinsed the plate in the sink. "Look. I'm not preaching. You've done a wonderful job. Considering. But she's thirteen. Sylvia said she still needs you, even if she doesn't think she does."

"Sylvia?"

I'm always surprised to find that an eighty-one-year-old man still blushes—all the way to the top of his head. "She just moved in."

"Uh-huh. And how old is Sylvia?"

"She's seventy-nine." He smiled. "But don't worry. She's pretty sure she can't get pregnant."

I giggled.

He smiled as he put the plate in the drainboard. "Sweetheart, I want you to stay out of this man's life. You have your own *tsuris*."

I noticed the determined set of his chin, and how much it resembled Rachel's. I felt like a piece of lunchmeat.

SEVEN

THE PHONE CHIRPED and the doorbell rang at the same time. I picked up the phone and opened the door.

"Fouad!" I smiled at the man standing outside. "What a nice surprise."

"This is Chuck Brashares."

"Sorry," I said into the phone. "Hold on, will you?"

I moved the phone away from my ear with one hand and shook Fouad's hand with the other. "It's so good to see you. How are you feeling?"

"And when I am sick, He restores me to health."

It's not unusual for Fouad Al Hamra, my friend and sometime gardener, to quote the Koran by way of greeting. He touched his fingers to his curly grizzled hair. He'd been shot a few months earlier but had recovered enough to resume work on a limited schedule.

I nodded and motioned to the phone. "I'll be out in a minute." I plugged the phone back in my ear. "Sorry, Mr. Brashares. You were saying?"

"I looked at the tape last night. Santoro is definitely on it."

I stifled an urge to say, "I told you so."

"I screened it several times, just to be sure. But I think we should proceed. I want you to testify. In fact, I've already spoken to the prosecution about it."

"So the quality of the tape isn't a problem?"

"Well, there is degradation, but it's not that bad when the camera's on him. You say you don't know how it was damaged?"

"No. It happened sometime after we shot it."

"Has the tape has been stored in one place ever since?"

"It's been in a locked room at the studio. Only a couple of people have access to it."

His silence said he was satisfied. Then, "Well, it might not prove anything, but it should cast some doubt. I gave notice that I'll be calling you as an alibi witness. Expect a call from the other side. They will want to depose you before opening arguments."

I coughed. A deposition—at least the divorce kind— was not the sort of activity I looked forward to.

"They'll want to know where you got it, the circumstances of the shoot, where it's been since then. Things like that."

"I don't know. I—I didn't expect—"

He ignored my reaction. "There is one thing I should caution you about. Anytime a new witness shows up this close to the start of a trial, there's apt to be some skepticism on the other side."

"What do you mean?" I said, remembering Barry's lawyers a few years ago. "Are they going to be hostile?"

"Probably—er—cautious," he replied. "But don't worry. You'll handle it. In the meantime, I'll show Santoro the tape. Maybe it will jog his memory."

"Would it help if I met with him? Explain how we found him? He might remember more."

Another short silence. "I don't think that's a good idea. It could taint your testimony."

"But if he *could* remember, wouldn't he make a better witness?"

"I'm not putting him on the stand."

"You're not?"

"He wouldn't make it past go. The prosecutor'll crucify him. Look. We're almost finished voir dire, and the judge will probably grant the other side a motion to get up to speed on the tape. If the trial starts next Monday, and I think it will, it should only last a couple of days. We could get to you as early as Wednesday. But you and I should go over the questions before that." He paused. "By the way, I'm going to need the original of that videotape for the trial."

"You can't use a copy?"

"The judge will never allow it, given the interference. Best evidence rule."

"In that case, you'll need to rent a different player. We shot Beta SP."

"What's that?"

"A different format than VHS. More professional. Kind of like the difference between sixteen and thirty-five millimeter film."

"More expensive?"

"Sure."

"Well, it has to be done."

"Okay, but could you return it when the trial's over? I would hate for it to get lost."

"No problem."

I said I'd make a new master for Mac's files and messenger Brashares the original. In the meantime, we set up a time to meet so he could walk me through my testimony.

"Do you think he's got a chance?"

"I don't know. But we've got more than we had before. Thanks for coming forward."

"Chalk it up to civic duty."

After I hung up, I tried to figure out what bugged me about this guy. I couldn't put my finger on it. He wasn't incompetent. He *was* doing the job, but I didn't have the sense he was committed to it. Then again, he was a de-

fense lawyer. He couldn't be emotionally involved with
every client. Still, I would have appreciated at least some
comment about justice being served, or the truth coming
out. I stood up. Maybe I was just reacting to his narcis-
sism.

I threw on some sweats and joined Fouad outside. It
was a brilliant, breezy day, the kind that triggers a yearn-
ing to be one with nature. Shading my eyes against the
sun, I watched Foaud unload the spreader from his pickup.
He'd lost weight, and the canvas pants he always wore
when he worked hung low on his hips. Though he'd never
had much excess flesh to begin with, his dark eyes seemed
enormous in his gaunt face.

My ex-husband considered lawn care a competitive
sport. During the four years we were married, Barry spent
thousands of dollars on landscapers, tools, and lawn care
products in an effort to make our lawn the greenest, thick-
est patch of grass on the North Shore. At the beginning
of April, even if snow still covered the ground, he'd demand that Fouad tell him precisely when fertilizer would
be applied, the bushes trimmed, the weeding done. He
suffered from an advanced case of "greenis" envy.

After we divorced, I didn't have enough money to keep
Fouad on. For a few years the grass languished, weeds
sprouted, and grubs feasted until the lawn looked like
something out of the dust bowl. Fouad came back on a
limited basis last spring, and we've made steady progress
reclaiming the land.

"This will be the last time I fertilize before winter." He
gazed ruefully at the grass, which bristled with weeds.
"I'm sorry I wasn't able to come more often."

I bent over to pluck a blade of crabgrass, but a ladybug
in speckled armor of black and orange was inching up its
stem. Ladybugs are good.

I left it alone and straightened up. "Mother Nature will
just have to understand."

Fouad smiled and poured a bag of what looked like
orange sand into the spreader. " 'Those who believe and

do good deeds shall have gardens in which rivers flow.' "

Fouad has built a flourishing landscape service and a garden supply store, but he remains, at heart, a modest, spiritual soul. He rolled the spreader in a neat, straight row. Tiny bits of orange coated the green lawn. I followed him as he worked.

"Your visit to West Virginia went well?"

"Upsetting." I explained about the white-water rafting.

He stopped with his hand on the spreader handle. "You and Rachel were not hurt?"

"We were fine. Can't say I'll ever do it again, though."

"I understand."

I thought back to the hike through the woods, Draper's Café, Abdul's plate. Then I remembered who'd warned me I wouldn't see much laurel. "You were right about one thing."

"What's that?"

"The only laurels I saw were in pats of butter."

EIGHT

THE FIFTH-FLOOR COURTROOM at Twenty-sixth and California has high ceilings, marble walls, and polished mahogany railings around the witness stand. Unlike the cramped rooms on the lower floors, where a thick glass wall separates observers from participants and the ambiance is like a driver's license facility, this courtroom looks like a place where justice is meted out.

The trial started on Monday. As a witness, I wasn't allowed to attend, but a producer friend of mine at Channel Eleven knew the sketch artist for one of the other TV stations and told her to fill me in. The first witness was the police detective, who, through questioning by Assistant State's Attorney Kirk Ryan, confirmed the bullets that killed the victim came from a .38 revolver, although they never recovered the gun. Next was the medical examiner, who explained the victim's cause and manner of death. He also recovered scrapings from the victim's fingernails, which DNA tests later proved to be consistent with Santoro's.

Ryan then led the victim's mother through a tearful testimony. Mary Jo was obedient, respectful, and ambitious, she said. Because her father was on long-term disability, the result of an accident at the steel mill, Mrs. Bosanick worked two minimum-wage jobs. Mary Jo aspired to something better and was taking night classes, hoping to become a bookkeeper in a Loop office.

"But now my baby is gone. And our lives are destroyed," her mother sobbed. "By him." She pointed dramatically at Santoro.

Brashares didn't tear her apart during his cross. Instead, he worked around the edges, gently eliciting the fact that she and her husband had met Santoro several times and had even invited him over for dinner.

Next the prosecution placed both Mary Jo and Santoro at the Lakeside Inn the night she was murdered. The Lakeside was a gritty but quiet neighborhood bar not far from Calumet Park, the kind of place a single woman could occasionally drop in for a beer and not get hassled. The bartender testified that Mary Jo came in around ten, looking for Santoro. He knew Santoro was one of the dockworkers who only came in when they had cash in their pockets. On the night in question Santoro showed up around midnight. He'd obviously had a few, the bartender said, and when Mary Jo lit into him for being late, he lit back. Their argument became so loud the bartender told them to take it outside. Her body was found at the boat launch in Calumet Park a few hours later, the prosecutor reminded the jury. Lying next to Santoro's car.

But the star witness for the prosecution was Mary Jo's best friend, Rhonda Disapio. They'd gone to the same school, the same Catholic church, and Mary Jo had been maid of honor at Rhonda's wedding. A plump woman with bottle-blond hair, too much jewelry, and scarlet lipstick, Rhonda testified that Mary Jo had been complaining about Santoro's lack of money and ambition. Not only was he abusive, she said, but Mary Jo thought he was a loser. She was sorry she ever got involved. In fact, she was planning to break up with him the night she was killed.

Brashares immediately objected to her testimony as hearsay. The judge sustained it, but Brashares made a big show of asking for a mistrial. It was denied, but the judge instructed the jury to disregard the witness's comments.

Which was like telling them not to think about pink elephants.

Ryan concluded his questioning, and Brashares approached the stand. Again he chose not to attack Rhonda on cross. He did shake loose some inconsistencies, racking up points when she admitted she didn't know how Santoro and Mary Jo first met, nor did she know what they were fighting about on the night in question. As she stepped down from the stand, the sketch artist reported, she dabbed her eyes with a tissue.

By the time the prosecution rested on Tuesday, momentum was on their side. It was a circumstantial case, which, Brashares said, was the kind of case a jury loved to get. Drunk boyfriend follows angry girlfriend; girlfriend shakes him off; boyfriend flies into a rage and shoots her. It was easy to connect the dots.

Wednesday morning the room was packed with reporters, court-watchers, and gawkers. I was glad I'd worn my gray power suit. Especially after I met Brashares outside the courtroom.

"Who's on besides me?" I asked.

He frowned at me through his glasses. "A vice-president from the water district who'll talk about the hours Olive Park was open."

It turned out Olive Park, adjacent to the filtration plant, was owned by the water district. It had been open to the public until Nine-Eleven.

I nodded. "Good. Who else?"

"That's it." He smiled thinly.

I stared. "I'm it?"

"I couldn't find anyone else who saw Santoro. Maybe if you'd come forward earlier . . ." His voice trailed off.

"You couldn't get a continuance so you could keep looking?"

"The judge denied it."

"What about the night crew at the water treatment plant? Maybe someone saw Santoro walking around."

Brashares shook his head.

"Well, what about Mac? Or my cameraman?"

"They'll say the same thing as you. You called the shots, anyway."

"But Ryan'll crucify me." Prosecutor Kirk Ryan's conduct on cross had earned him the nickname the Hammer.

"Don't worry," Brashares said optimistically. "We have the tape."

I know enough about the legal system to know that when a lawyer tells me not to worry, that's precisely when I should.

The judge asked Brashares if he was ready. He nodded and replied in a clear voice. "May it please the court, we call Eleanor Foreman."

I tried to ignore the stir in the courtroom as I walked down the aisle, but all eyes were on me, including Santoro's. I stole a glance at him. He wasn't a big man, but he had broad, powerful shoulders. His buzz cut had grown out into a thick mat of dark hair, and he sat at the defense table, wearing a cheap brown suit.

As I mounted the step to the jury box, our eyes met. At first his were vacant, with a curious lack of focus. But then, in the next instant, an expression of hope flashed in them.

I swallowed.

"Miss Foreman, thank you for coming today," Brashares said after I'd been sworn in. "Tell us what you do for a living."

"I'm an industrial video producer." I answered succinctly, not volunteering anything extra, just as Brashares had instructed.

"And what does an industrial video producer do?"

I wanted to say, "Whatever it takes to get the damn show made." Instead I explained that while a producer's role depends on the director, the budget, and other circumstances, I generally did all the research, handled pre-production logistics, wrote the script, and supervised the location photography and postproduction.

Brashares nodded. "Let's turn to July twenty-third of last year, the night Mary Jo Bosanick died. Were you engaged in your profession that evening?"

"I was."

"What were you doing?"

"My crew and I were preparing to shoot a scene on the Harrison-Carter intake crib for the water district."

"Intake crib?"

I told him what it was and where it was located.

"And what were you photographing?"

I summarized the reenactment and what we had planned. I heard a few snickers when I got to the part about Big Bill and Capone.

Brashares waited until it was quiet. "Now. On the night in question, you didn't begin filming at the intake crib, did you?"

"No." I told him how we experimented with the camera gain and took a few shots near Olive Park before going out to the crib.

"Tell me, Miss Foreman. Was anyone in or around Olive Park that you see in court today?"

I pointed my finger at Santoro, the way Brashares had coached me. A murmur went up from the crowd.

"Let the record reflect that the witness identified my client, Johnnie Santoro. Now, Miss Foreman, what was he doing?"

"He was lying on a bench under a streetlight. He looked like he might have been asleep."

"Was he?"

"Not at first. He did try to get up. But he couldn't make it, and he collapsed back on the bench. He didn't move after that."

"How do you remember that? I mean how do you recall exactly where he was and what he was doing?"

"Because I recorded video of him doing it."

More murmurs went up from the crowd. Smiling faintly, Brashares paused to milk the moment.

"And when did you come to realize that the individual on the video was my client?"

"When I saw pictures of him on the news. I knew he looked familiar, but it took me a few days to realize where I'd seen him. When I figured it out, I immediately called you."

"Now." Brashares took a measured step in my direction. "It was your understanding, was it not, that my client wasn't moving all that well because he'd had a few drinks?"

"Objection," Ryan cut in.

Brashares blinked.

Ryan stood up. "Leading the witness. Plus, the witness has no knowledge of what condition the accused might be in. Anything she says is speculation."

"Your Honor, we intend to recall a witness who will talk to the number of drinks he had at the Lakeside," Brashares countered. "And Miss Foreman saw how he moved. Or failed to move. She can testify to what she saw."

The judge pursed his lips. "I'll allow it, but rephrase the question, counselor."

Brashares smiled. Ryan sat down, shaking his head.

"Now, Miss Foreman, what did you see Mr. Santoro do?"

I explained again what I had seen.

"As far as you know, did Mr. Santoro get up and leave the park?"

"Not while I was filming him."

"And what time was that?"

"Approximately one in the morning."

Ryan looked like he wanted to object, but then, apparently decided not to.

"Now, Miss Foreman," Brashares continued. "You never completed the video for the water district, did you?"

"That's correct."

"Why not?"

I explained that it was canceled last September.

"However, even if it hadn't been canceled, you wouldn't have used any of the tape that my client appears on in your final product, isn't that right?"

"That's correct."

"Why not?"

"Those scenes were never meant to be part of the finished tape. They were outtakes. Shots we did to establish the right exposure."

"But since that time, you have since discovered something about those outtakes, haven't you?"

"That's right."

"Could you explain it to the court?"

"The tape with Mr. Santoro's image on it turns out to have been slightly damaged."

"Damaged how?"

"There appears to be some kind of interference on the tape."

"Radio interference?"

"Objection." Ryan shot up again. "She's not an expert on radio frequencies."

The judge looked at Brashares, then at me. "Sustained."

"Let me rephrase that," Brashares said smoothly. "Not being an electronics expert, perhaps you could explain the problem from a producer's perspective."

"Objection, Your Honor!" Ryan shouted again.

"Will both counsel please approach the bench?" The judge rose and stepped to the side of the bar.

While the lawyers and judge whispered, I looked around. Mary Jo's parents were sitting behind the prosecution's table. Next to them was Rhonda Disapio. Mary Jo's mother sat with her arms crossed, back straight. Her father stared at me with venom in his eyes. Only Disapio's face seemed to hold open the possibility I wasn't a lethal adversary.

I gazed at the row of people behind the defense table, wondering if any family members or friends of Santoro's had come to the trial, but from their detached expressions and body language, I surmised that wasn't likely.

Their side bar apparently now concluded, the two lawyers backed away from the bench.

"The objection is overruled," the judge said.

Brashares smiled at me. "Now, Miss Foreman, how did the problem manifest itself on the tape?"

I described what RF can do on a tape.

"And the RF was evident on the shots—excuse me, the outtakes—of my client."

"That's right." I was beginning to feel more comfortable. The questions were going the way Brashares said they would, and we were talking about subjects about which I had some knowledge.

Brashares moved to a separate table and picked up a videotape in a plastic sleeve. "Do you recognize this videotape?" He handed it to me.

"Yes. It's the original tape that I gave you."

"How do you know?"

I pointed to the label on the spine, which said Foreman Communications. "My label is on the edge of the cassette."

"Is this the tape that shows my client on the bench in Olive Park?"

"Yes."

"Does the tape fairly and accurately show how he appeared that day?"

"Yes."

"And to your knowledge, has that tape been tampered with or altered in any way, since it was recorded?"

"No."

Ryan scribbled furiously on his legal pad.

"Your Honor, I'd like to move this into evidence as defense exhibit number one," Brashares said. "With your permission, we will play it for the jury."

"Objection." Ryan again. "Chain of custody. Where was the tape from the day it was made until now?"

Brashares's eyes narrowed. "Counselor, I thought we

worked that all out." He turned toward the judge. "Approach the bench, Your Honor."

The lawyers had another side bar with the judge, after which Brashares asked me a series of questions that elicited the fact that the tape had been in Mac's tape library since we shot it, and that the tape library was locked and accessible to only two or three people. Ryan seemed satisfied and sat down.

Brashares wheeled a cart with a video player and monitor to the front of the room. The jurors leaned forward, and the room quieted. Brashares inserted the cassette and pushed Play. The tape was cued to the scene of Santoro on the bench. We heard the buzz on the track, saw the streaks on the picture. The entire scene lasted less than a minute, after which Brashares hit Pause. There wasn't a sound in the courtroom. Brashares stepped toward the jury.

"Again, Miss Foreman, who is the man on the videotape?"

"It's Johnnie Santoro."

"And when was this shot?"

"July Twenty-third of last year."

"Thank you, Miss Foreman." Brashares clicked his heels, turned around, and withdrew to the defense table. His face had a sheen, as if he'd just finished a five-mile run. He nodded to Ryan. "Your witness."

NINE

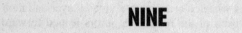

I TOOK A sip of water. The mood in the courtroom lightened. A low buzz came from the observers, and people seemed to relax, except for the Bosanick family, who sat tight-lipped and silent.

But when Kirk Ryan rose, the murmuring stopped. People shifted in their seats. A woman in the second row licked her lips. The door at the back of the courtroom opened, and my father walked in. How had he gotten downtown? He nodded at me and sat down in back.

Ryan, a squat man with the confidence of someone much bigger, pushed a hand through wavy blond hair. Pasting a smile on his face, he ambled toward me as if we had all the time in the world.

"Good morning, Miss Foreman. Nice to see you again." He was referring to the deposition I'd had last week with his staff. Brashares had been right. They hadn't been hostile; in fact, everyone had been quite polite. I returned a weak smile.

"You're a documentary filmmaker, correct?"

"Not exactly."

"You're not?"

"I produce industrials—corporate-sponsored videos."

"But you did produce *Celebrate Chicago* for the city's millennium celebration, which subsequently ran on cable television."

"Yes. The City of Chicago sponsored that."

"So." He cupped his hands around an imaginary sphere. "Some of your products eventually do end up on television?"

I didn't know where he was going, but I had a feeling I wasn't going to like it. "Yes."

"And prior to being on your own, you worked at a television station producing news documentaries, correct?"

"Many years ago, yes."

"Even so, would you say you have an understanding of the news process?"

"Objection!" Brashares jumped up. "I don't know where this is leading, or how it's relevant to the proceedings."

"I'm laying foundation, Your Honor," Ryan replied quickly.

The judge rubbed his nose. "I'll allow it."

"So." Ryan turned back to me. "Miss Foreman, would you say you have an understanding of the news gathering process?"

"I suppose so."

"You watch the news regularly?"

"Local or national?"

He dipped his head, as if to acknowledge I'd scored a point. "Let's start with local."

"Not that often."

"Pardon me, but didn't you say you recognized Johnny Santoro from his picture on the news?"

"I saw it in the newspaper."

He ran his thumbs underneath the lapels of his suit. "So you do keep up with local news. Through the newspaper."

I nodded.

"Please respond audibly."

"Yes."

"And when was it that you recognized Johnnie Santoro's picture in the newspaper?"

"About two weeks ago."

"But the crime with which Santoro is charged occurred over a year ago. Are we to believe that you, a former TV news professional, haven't watched the news or picked up a newspaper in all that time?"

"Objection!" Brashares again. "The prosecution is assuming facts not in evidence."

"I'm getting to them right now," Ryan said.

"See that you do, Mr. Ryan," the judge said.

"Well, Miss Foreman? Have you not watched the news or read a paper in that time?"

I squeezed my hands together. "Of course I have."

"Then you know the Santoro case has been one of the major news stories of the past year, correct?"

I nodded.

"Please respond audibly."

"Yes."

"For someone who was once in the news business, someone who knows the value of timely information, someone whose shows are still broadcast on the airwaves, why did you wait so long to come forward with your—" he made imaginary quotation marks in the air—"discovery?"

"I didn't realize that Mr. Santoro was the man on the intake crib video until last week."

"But you read the newspaper, and you watch television. Tell me, how many hours of coverage do you think have been accorded to the Santoro case since his arrest?"

"I don't know."

"Would it be fair to say it's been in the news frequently?"

"I don't know." My stomach was churning.

"Yes or no."

"Yes."

"Once a month, perhaps? And now, with the trial, even more?"

"I wouldn't know."

"And in all that time, you haven't seen one photo or image of Mr. Santoro until last week?"

"That's right."

"And that one image just happened to spark your memory?"

"Yes."

"Isn't that convenient?"

"Objection!"

"Sustained."

Ryan turned toward the jury, making sure they saw the smirk on his face.

Several jurors exchanged meaningful glances. I caught a glimpse of my father, a defiant glare in his eyes. My cheeks burned. Compared to this, maybe white-water rafting wasn't so bad.

Ryan strutted back and forth in front of the jury box. "Now, Miss Foreman, you saw the defendant on a park bench July the twenty-third, is that right?"

"Yes."

"How much time did you spend taking his picture?"

"About ten minutes."

"And while you were there, you photographed other things besides the defendant, correct?"

"We were trying to find the right exposure."

"Yes. Now, you arrived in the vicinity at about what time?"

"About twelve or twelve-thirty."

"And you left at what time?"

"About one."

"And when you left, you motored directly out to the intake crib, correct?"

"Yes."

"Where you spent the next five or six hours, correct?"

"We wrapped about seven in the morning."

"However, after you left the vicinity of Olive Park, you

really have no direct knowledge about what transpired, either at the park or onshore?"

"Objection!"

"Overruled. The witness may answer the question."

I looked at my shoes. "No."

Ryan faced the jury and smiled as if he had just revealed an important piece of information. "Now, Miss Foreman, let's talk a little bit about the damage to the tape for a moment. The alleged RF interference?"

I swallowed.

"What evidence do you have that the damage on the tape is indeed radio frequency interference?"

"I don't—I'm not sure I understand the question."

"Let me clarify. Have you taken the tape in for any kind of technical analysis?"

"No, but I didn't—"

"So you have no independent confirmation that RF interference really is the problem on the tape."

"My director agreed that's what it is. We've seen it before."

"But you didn't seek any kind of independent corroboration."

"We didn't need to. We knew what it was."

"Based on your experience."

"Yes. And that of my director."

"All right. Given that you knew what it was, you still never discovered where the problem originated, isn't that correct?"

"That's true."

"But it was serious enough that you wouldn't have been able to use this tape in the final product. If the project hadn't been canceled."

"That's correct."

"So, on this damaged tape, you know what the problem is, yet you can't adequately explain why it is there or where it's coming from. Is that right?"

"Yes."

"Very professional, Miss Foreman."

"Objection!" Brashares yelled.

"The jurors will disregard that last comment," the judge said.

"I apologize." Ryan smiled, baring his teeth. "Let's say we went back to Olive Park with a camera and tried to simulate the conditions that you found there. Would we be able to replicate the damage that we saw on your tape?"

The man was relentless. "I don't know."

"Why not?"

I hesitated. "RF interference can come from any number of different sources. And the tape didn't have any damage on it initially."

"How do you know that?"

"Because I screened it after we shot it, and it was fine."

Out of the corner of my eye, I could see Brashares stiffen, but Ryan's smile broadened, as if he knew he'd won big. "Let's see. The tape was fine after you screened it, but now, a year later, it shows significant damage. And you testified that it's been stored in a locked room at your director's studio for over a year, isn't that right?"

"Yes." I cringed. I knew what was coming.

"So, you don't know where the problem came from, and it's been a year since you looked at it. Yet you still maintain there's no possibility the tape has been tampered with." He didn't wait for my response but whipped around to face the jury. "Thank you, Miss Foreman. I have no further questions."

I sat on the stand for a moment, unsure who and where I was. Then I looked around the courtroom. A few faces looked back at me with sympathy, but most were curious, almost expectant, as if they were waiting for me to have a melt down then and there. After all, I'd just been bush-whacked. Discredited. Hammered.

My father leaped to his feet and made his way to the door. In the space he'd occupied, I caught a glimpse of a man sitting behind him. Young, dark, somewhere in his twenties, he had crisp features with high cheekbones.

Curly black chest hair poked through an open-necked shirt, and one arm was draped over the back of the bench. Even through my humiliation, I registered that he was sexy in a dark, Mediterranean kind of way.

I looked at him, hoping for a sympathetic nod or smile. He returned the look, but something on his face, a lilt of one brow perhaps, a narrowing of the other, gave me the feeling he could see through me and had decided there wasn't much there. A twinge of uneasiness passed over me. Averting my gaze, I stepped down from the box.

TEN

I TESTIFIED ON Wednesday, and the case went to the jury on Thursday. Ryan skewered me in closing arguments, implying I was the stupidest, most naive documentary filmmaker in the world. Why hadn't I come forward sooner? How did I know the tape hadn't been tampered with? Why couldn't I adequately explain the damage on the tape? Was I that technically incompetent? Either that, he said, or something else, something more sinister, was at work.

In either case, he declared scornfully, this was not an alibi. I might have seen Santoro at Olive Park, but what was to stop him from having traveled to Calumet Park either before or after? The tape was no more than a description of where Santoro ended up at a specific point in time. Indeed, when you added up the fingernail scrapings, the lovers' argument, and the fact that Mary Jo's body was found near his car, there was no way twelve intelligent jurors could possibly buy my story.

They didn't. On Friday they convicted Santoro.

The phone rang all afternoon—reporters, mostly, looking for a sound bite. Something that would sum up the conflict in ten seconds. Preferably at my expense. I decided I'd be damned if I'd give them one, and after a slew of calls during which my polite refusals to comment apparently weren't enough, I tried a new approach.

"Ellie Foreman?" A voice asked.

"Sí?"

"Is this Ellie Foreman?"

"Sí?" I stretched out the word.

"Uh—I'm looking for the video producer, Ellie Foreman. Is she there?"

"Meesus not home." I slammed down the phone before a fluent stream of Spanish could come back at me.

Small victories.

I was watching myself on TV when David unlocked the front door. I'd had no intention of turning on the tube, but, after polishing off half a bottle of wine, something drew me to the coverage—the same thing that draws gapers to an accident, perhaps. Or possibly a latent dose of masochism.

David took one look at me and went into the kitchen. The refrigerator door opened, a cabinet drawer closed. A minute later, he came into the family room carrying a plate of bagels, lox, cream cheese, and onions. He sat down on the couch.

"You haven't eaten today, have you?"

"I'm not hungry."

He spread some cheese on half a bagel, placed a thin slice of lox on it, and laid a strip of onion on top. The smell of the onion made my nose itch.

"You had a rough couple of days."

"It's a good life lesson. Never be a Good Samaritan."

He chewed slowly. "I suppose it won't help to say you did the right thing."

I gazed at the bagel and shook my head.

"What did your father say?"

"He said Brashares didn't do me any favors." I reached for the bagel. "Barry agreed with my father, by the way.

He was almost compassionate when he came to get Rachel." I bit into the sandwich. "Well, as compassionate as an ex-husband can be."

David went into the kitchen. "What's his take?" He called over his shoulder.

"He says Brashares left enough holes in the case to drive a truck through."

"Like what?"

"Not objecting when he should have, for one thing. Not calling any other witnesses, for another. He said Ryan ought to be thanking his lucky stars his adversary was so incompetent. In fact, he was surprised Brashares didn't get a continuance—based on the tape and what I brought to the case. Admittedly, Barry is usually looking for a way to needle me, but he said the guy ought to be sued for malpractice."

David came back out with another bagel. "He would know."

"He also said Ryan did a masterful job. You know, limiting me to yes and no questions. Not letting me give any opinions." I finished the bagel. "But you know what bothers me the most?"

"What?"

"I think he's right."

David frowned.

"I've been thinking about it. Brashares did his job. But there was no feeling in it. No soul. I got the sense he didn't really care about Santoro. Or me."

"Can you blame him? Think of the scumbags he represents every day. He needs professional detachment."

"This was beyond professional detachment. And how can you do a good job for your client if you're not invested emotionally—at least a little bit?"

"Not everyone has the same passion, the same commitment as you, Ellie. You see an injustice, and your heart cries out to fix it. Most people don't bother. It's part of what makes you special."

I balled up a napkin and threw it at him. "Why is it

you always know just the right thing to say?"

He tossed the napkin on the floor, moved over, and stroked the back of my neck. I settled back against the cushions, concentrating on the feel of his fingers. "That's good," I said thickly.

An hour later, I felt much better.

BEFORE I FELL asleep, I mentally played back the trial. I thought I was testifying for all the right reasons. Acting on principle. Serving justice. But now, lying in David's arms amid pillows, sheets, and blankets, I wasn't so sure. Was my concern the injustice that had been done or the fact that my ego had been bruised?

The comforting weight of David's leg fell over mine. Maybe I should give it all up. Ratchet down a few notches. He'd never admit it, but David probably found me high maintenance. Wearying. I sometimes thought he'd be happier with a woman whose worldview started and stopped with him. Someone who never questioned authority. Like the bimbo Robert Redford ended up with after he and Barbra Streisand broke up in *The Way We Were*.

I threw my arm above my head. David stirred, sleepily working the palm of his hand up my thigh. A shiver skimmed my nerves. Life with him would be easy. Pleasureable. I wouldn't have to work. I could dedicate myself to tennis. Join the garden club. And be bored—except in bed.

ELEVEN

THERE WAS A snap in the air as we came out of shul on Rosh Hashanah. My father rubbed his hands together. "I love fall days," he said cheerfully. "They always make me think of a fresh start. A new school term, new friends, a new suit for the High Holidays."

Rachel smoothed the skirt of her new outfit, a simple but elegant taupe knit from Nordstrom's. With her blond curls, blue eyes, and pale skin, she looked like a princess. And much too grown up.

Dad draped an arm around David's shoulder and headed to the car. Though David was half a foot taller than Dad, he made the movement seem natural.

"What's for lunch?" David asked.

"You'll see." I smiled.

I'd made most of the meal before services, though perhaps "assembled" was a better word. Blintzes, bagels, and salad. The omelets I'd make once we got home. And, of course, apples and honey. Cooking has never been one of my core strengths. Don't get me wrong; I love to eat. Especially when someone else feeds me. But today was special.

"Oh, boy." Dad grinned. "We're in for a treat. Your mother's cooking."

Rachel rolled her eyes. "You must be feeling brave."

"Rah-chel," Dad said, using the Hebrew pronunciation. "It's a new year. Let's start out treating your mother right."

Rachel threw me an icy look.

I shot her the old arched-eyebrow in reply.

Her eyes narrowed, and she skipped over to Dad. "I'll bet we don't go to services tomorrow."

"Want that extra day off of school, huh?" I cracked.

My father glared at us. "Stop it. Both of you."

David cut in. "I wouldn't mind going again."

The way he looked at me made me suddenly ashamed of myself. "You know something? That's a good idea." I turned to Rachel. "We'll all go, okay?"

She shrugged.

To be perfectly honest, though, Rachel does have a point. I'm not as observant as I once was. My father says it's because I'm the product of a mixed marriage. My mother was raised Reform, about as assimilated as you can get. Her mother used to host an open house every Christmas Eve during which she wore a tiny Christmas tree on top of her head. My father, on the other hand, grew up in Hyde Park among a tightly knit group of observant German Jews. In fact, Mother used to joke that she was about as far as he could go and still marry a Jewish girl. Still, I suspected she was grateful that my father was there to teach me who I was and where I came from.

After services the next day, Barry took Rachel for the rest of the day. I dropped David at the airport for his flight back to Philly, took Dad home, then changed and headed to the mall. All the talk about new suits was inspiring. Once I got there, though, I lost my nerve. I usually need Susan's approval for a major purchase. I've brought home too many mistakes.

I window-shopped for a while, then wandered into a

small, narrow gift shop with faux stucco on the walls. Merchandise was displayed on both sides of the aisle, and a blue-haired woman sat behind the register. She seemed to be the only employee in the store, but I was aware of one other shopper. I stopped in front of an end-aisle display of prettily packaged soaps, admiring the tiny butterflies, delicate flowers, and other designs painted on them. A sign declared that Soap Art was the latest thing. Guaranteed not to dissolve when wet. Maybe I'd get some for Rachel. A peace offering.

I kept browsing, admiring the wrapped baskets, ceramic pillboxes, and other *tsatskehs,* then headed back to the soaps. The other shopper stood with her back to me, juggling two soaps in one hand. I was about to say, "Excuse me," so I could take some when she slipped hers into her pocket.

I froze. After a moment she turned around—and froze, too, guilt and fear stamped on her face. I knew what I was supposed to do: demand she put the soap back, call the manager, shout for security. But I didn't. I was paralyzed, riveted to the floor.

We eyed each other warily, neither of us moving, until it must have dawned on her that I was either unable or unwilling to react. Then, something new edged into her eyes. Defiance, perhaps. Or triumph. She swept by me and exited the store.

I cowered in the aisle until the adrenaline drained out of my body. I picked out three soaps, took them to the counter, and paid. As the blue-haired woman handed me my bag, I felt an overarching guilt, as if I'd been the one to shoplift. It even crossed my mind to pay for the two the other woman took.

Instead, I left the store and trudged down the hall. I passed a colorful kiosk where a collection of nuts, sold by a woman who probably never shelled one in her life, gave off a pleasant, woodsy aroma. I moved on to the food court, bought a huge cookie with lots of chocolate chips, and wolfed it down. Heading toward the exit, I rationalized why I hadn't intervened. Since the trial, I was finished with trying to do the right thing. I'd been Hammered enough. Let someone else pick up the ethical gauntlet. I brushed cookie crumbs off my shirt.

I hadn't gone very far when I heard footsteps behind me.

I stepped up my pace. So did the footsteps.

I slowed. They did, too.

At first I thought the shoplifter was behind me, but I couldn't figure out why. Was she planning to thank me? Explain why she did it? She didn't need to. I understood. I used to shoplift.

Shoplifting involves cunning. And *chutzpah*. I'd had both, once upon a time. I knew the rush, the high, the shame. And knowing that, I knew there was no way she was behind me. She wasn't ready to return the soap. Or even express remorse. She'd have to hit bottom first. I did.

I kept walking.

So did the person behind me.

It was a beautiful fall day; the mall wasn't crowded. So who was following me? The cashier from the gift shop? I didn't steal the soaps, but I didn't do anything to stop it. Maybe she'd noticed my tacit complicity and wanted to confront me.

No. That was just guilt talking. I couldn't take the moral high ground, but cowardice wasn't illegal. Besides, what clerk would leave the store unattended? I stopped and turned around.

Aside from a woman pushing a baby stroller, the hallway was empty.

I made a three sixty. No one. Turning back, I caught my image in a shop window. I scanned the reflection for any quick, unexpected movements. I did see a silhouette half in and half out of a doorway a few stores back. It wasn't the blue-haired woman, and it didn't look like the shoplifter. I waited. The figure turned away from me.

I started forward again. Within a few yards, the footsteps were back. I tightened my hold on my purse. Last year, my wallet was ripped off at a restaurant downtown. One man jammed the revolving door as I went through, while another squeezed into the same compartment as me. As I banged on the glass, yelling for help, the nearer man grabbed my wallet out of my purse. He took off when his buddy let go of the door. I wasn't hurt, but within an hour they'd racked up three grand on my Visa.

I ducked into a perfume boutique.

"Can I help you?" A saleswoman suddenly appeared at my side, suspicion flooding her face.

"No thanks. I'm just looking."

She planted herself in front of me.

I took my time inspecting a display case filled with perfume, amused at the irony of the situation. Then I exited the store, pretending I had nothing more important to do than spend the afternoon window-shopping. The clerk's sniff followed me out.

I passed more stores, anxious, now, to get back to the car and go home. I had just reached a bend where a walkway angles off the main corridor when a hand clapped me on the shoulder.

TWELVE

I SPUN AROUND and wrenched free. I grabbed my purse, swung it backward, and launched it at a blond head. Thanks to the bars of soap inside, it connected with a resounding thunk. My pursuer staggered into the walkway and collapsed on the floor.

"Please. Stop. Don't hurt me."

I stepped back, hugging my purse until the machine-gunning in my chest slowed down. The blond woman cringed against the wall. We were a few yards down the narrow hall that jutted off the main promenade.

"It's all right. I won't hit you again," I said.

When she tentatively looked up, I felt a jolt of recognition. It was Rhonda Disapio, Mary Jo Bosanick's best friend.

"You?" I cried.

Her face said she was at least as scared as me.

I leaned over and extended my hand. She hesitated, then took it. As she stood up, the musky scent of Tabu drifted over me. I hadn't smelled it since high school when girls sashayed down the halls, a heavy cloud of it trailing after them.

"You want to tail someone," I groused, "you ought to brush up on your technique. It sucks."

I looked around. Fluorescent lights flickered overhead, and the floor was institutional tile, not marble. Opposite us was a supply closet. A sign at the far end pointed to an employee washroom.

"You want to tell me why you've been following me?"

She blew air into her cheeks, as if she was wrestling with how to begin. "I—I'm really scared." Her voice was squeakier, more timid than I remembered. "I don't even think I should be here. But I don't know what else to do. I need your help."

"How did you find me?"

"I followed you. You're listed in the phone book."

I rubbed my chin. At the trial Rhonda had seemed smooth and self-assured. I recalled thinking her friend's murder was the most exciting event in her life and that she was reveling in her fifteen minutes. Now, as I took in her sloppy clothes, smeared lipstick, and earrings that didn't match her outfit, I could see she was stressed. Maybe I should feel some compassion. No, I reminded myself. She did sneak up on me, and I don't do surprise well.

"So talk."

She hoisted the strap of her purse up on her shoulder. A blue and white polka-dot scarf was knotted around the base of the bag. "When I testified at the trial, there are—well, things happened that didn't come out. I should have left town afterwards. But I couldn't." She shrugged helplessly. "I have a kid."

"What kind of things?"

She picked at the knot on her scarf.

"Rhonda, you found out where I lived. You followed me all the way up here. You stalked me through the mall. If you have something to say, now's the time."

"Yeah, okay. But, please don't call the cops. At least, hear me out first."

"Call the cops?" I shifted uneasily. "Why would I do that?"

"Because of what I'm gonna say." She pressed her lips together. "The night Mary Jo got killed . . . I was with her."

"You were at Calumet Park?"

She nodded. "Mary Jo picked me up after she and Johnnie had that fight. She was driving his car."

"She took his car?" The fact that his car had been at Calumet Park was a key piece of evidence against Santoro.

"She had a set of keys. They were practically living together, you know."

"No I didn't." No one did.

"She'd tell her parents she was staying with me," she said. "Anyway, after he'd belted her, she got really pissed, jumped into the car, and took off for my place. We picked up a bottle and went to the park."

I frowned. "I thought you said you had a kid."

She waved a hand. "It was after midnight. You know how kids sleep. My sister lives downstairs, anyway."

I bit back a reply.

"We drove over to the boat launch, see? We done it before. It's nice there late at night. Peaceful and all. You can really feel the lake."

"So it was you and Mary Jo those witnesses saw driving into the park."

She nodded. "So we're sitting on the rocks, getting kind of loaded, and Mary Jo's telling me she really did want to break it off with Johnnie. He was a fuckup; he wasn't gonna amount to nothin'. So we're talking and drinking and laughing, and then we see this boat come in—"

"A boat? At midnight?"

"It was summer. People fish all night long. Anyway, it's dark, and we can't see much, but it looks like there's two guys in the boat, and they're heading over to the launch. So, we start kiddin' around, like maybe we should hook up with those dudes—we might have more luck.

Mary Jo even stands up, like she's gonna go over and start talking to 'em, you know? But I grabbed her and pulled her down. 'How do you know who these guys are, MJ?' I says. 'They could be creeps.' " Rhonda's voice wavered. " 'Criminals, sex maniacs, drug dealers, you know?' "

"Go on," I said softly.

Rhonda ran her tongue around her lips, succeeding in smearing her lipstick more than it already was. "So MJ turns around and says—she says, 'What makes you think I don't already know about shit like that?' "

"Shit like what?" I asked.

"I asked her the same thing, but she shakes her head and says, 'Nothing . . . forget it.' But then she says, 'If there's any shit on that boat, they're hiding it pretty well. Look at all that crap.' So I look and I see the boat is filled with junk."

"Junk? What kind of junk?"

"I don't know, sort of logs, you know, like fireplace logs, but they were metal."

"Metal?"

"You could see them in the moonlight, but I didn't really take a close look 'cause I had to pee." She paused. "I should never have done that." Her voice cracked. "But I couldn't hold it." She dabbed at her eyes with her scarf.

I waited while she pulled herself together.

"There are these trees at the other end of the parking lot, and I went behind them. I must have been longer than I thought, because all of a sudden I hear voices. First MJ, then a man, then her again. Then she's saying 'Hey—stop it!' Then I hear someone running across the parking lot. And then she screams, 'Run, Rhonda, run!' And there's more steps. And then I hear the shots . . . and, and . . ." She covered her face with her hands.

"My God, Rhonda."

She dipped her head, as if she were answering a question. "Then they started across the grass. Coming right toward me."

"What were they saying?"

"I couldn't tell. It sounded like they might have been cussing. But they were whispering. Like they knew they had to stay quiet."

"Then what?"

"Thank God there's this hole in the fence behind the trees. With this red building behind it. A garage or shed or something. I was able to find it, and I squeezed through. Then I ran as fast as I could. I thought I was safe. But now . . ."

I saw the fear in her eyes.

"I think they're following me. They figured out who I am."

"From the trial."

She started to cry. "I didn't want to testify, but they made me."

"Rhonda, why didn't you go to the cops? This would have blown the case wide open."

"By the time I got it together, they'd already arrested Johnnie. I was afraid that if I went to the cops, the guys that killed MJ would come after me. Or my kid." She touched her fingers to a gold cross at her neck. "But now, they're coming anyway."

"Even more reason go to the police. Or to Ryan."

A horrified look swept across her face. "I can't. He'd put me away for sure."

"At least you'd be safe," I said. "What do you think I'm going to be able to do?"

Her eyes flicked back to the head of the passageway, as if she feared whoever was following her might appear at any moment. "I saw you at the trial. I heard what Ryan said about you. You're one of those TV people."

"Not really."

"Yes you are. Like that blond on *Inside Edition*? You know."

"Deborah Norville?"

Her face brightened. "Yeah. Her."

"Rhonda, I—"

She cut me off. "You know people. I bet you can fix it so they won't put me in jail. You know, make me one of those secret sources or something."

"You want me to interview you, is that it? Put you on TV—without revealing your identity—to tell the real story of Mary Jo Bosanick's murder? Is that what you have in mind?"

"Well, yeah. Maybe."

A flash of heat shot through me. "How about we put you on with an exclusive report? We'll call it a special investigation, hype it with a sexy headline: 'Confidential Source Comes Clean . . . Tape at Ten.' "

Her cheeks colored. "I know you don't think much of me. But you've gotta believe me. At first, I thought maybe Johnnie *had* followed us down to the boat launch. But then I realized it couldn't have been him." Her eyes darted to the end of the corridor. "It was those guys. And now they're back."

"Why do you think they're following you?"

"Well, since the trial, I keep seeing the same car outside my place. One of them SUVs, you know? Dark. Like green or something. Then I saw it outside work—I work over at Hair Connection on Commercial. And then, yesterday, it parks outside my parents' house when we were there for dinner."

"Did you check the license plate?"

"I couldn't see it."

I was about to ask her if she knew the make when a series of noises suddenly exploded from the end of the corridor. Rhonda gasped. I spun around, clutching my purse like a club.

A group of teenage boys sprinted past the alcove, each of them trying to outdo the other with the loudest burps they could muster. When they saw us, one of them nudged his companion, and they erupted in wild, deep-throated laughs. I relaxed my grip, but when I looked back at Rhonda, her eyes were wild.

"Rhonda, you've got no choice. You have to go to the police."

"I told you. I can't."

I started to wonder why. Did she have a record of her own? Was she on probation? Or parole?

"Is there anything else you remember? Anything you saw or heard?"

She hesitated. "Like I said, they were whispering, mostly. But now that you mention it, I think I might have heard one of their names."

"Really?"

"I think one of them called the other Sammy. Yeah. Sammy."

"Sammy? Sammy what?"

"I don't know." She started in on the knot again.

"Anything else?"

"No."

She finally worked the knot on the scarf free, and it floated to the floor, a polka dot flag unfurled. As she bent down to retrieve it, there was a shuffling noise from the far end of the hallway, and a man in a beige uniform turned in, pushing a wheeled bucket ahead of him. He stopped, clearly surprised to see two shoppers in the alcove, but Rhonda was even more surprised. She let out a little scream. Then she lurched forward, snatched up her scarf, and sprinted past the man out into the mall.

THIRTEEN

BY THE TIME I got back to my car, the sun had surrendered to oily gray clouds, and a north wind was picking leaves off the trees.

As I drove down Skokie Boulevard, I tried to make sense of her story. Late-night drinking. Mysterious men on boats. Casual references to drugs. If any of this had come out at the trial, I'd lay odds the outcome would have been different. At least Ryan might not have come after me with such enthusiasm. Although maybe that was just wishful thinking. For all I knew, Ryan might have found a way to dismiss Rhonda's story. He was the Hammer. He wouldn't have cared.

But Brashares would.

I left a message on his machine when I got home.

I was surprised when he called me back a few minutes later. I'd imagined him taking time off, running in a triathlon in some exotic location. But he said he'd been working nonstop. I filled him in.

"Disapio says she was there?" I heard a slight edge in his voice.

"Yes. She was too scared to come forward. She thinks she's in danger."

More silence.

I scowled into the phone. "I would think that gives you powerful ammunition for the appeal. I mean, doesn't that open up a whole new set of possibilities about Mary Jo's murder? Or at least cast reasonable doubt on the prosecution's case?"

"It might, but unfortunately, you can't raise new facts on appeal."

"But this—this could change everything."

"It is interesting. I'll admit that."

Lightning strafed the sky, and a crack of thunder rippled overhead. A sudden autumn storm sweeping in from the west.

"Let me see what I can do. I'll call you tomorrow."

I disconnected and held the receiver to my chest. Brashares seemed awfully casual about the information I'd given him. We might have been talking about the point spread on the Bears game. It wasn't what I'd expect from a lawyer whose client was facing a life sentence. But then, maybe he thought I was trying to tell him how to run his case.

Rain pelted the roof, and wind gusts whipped the windows. I poured a glass of wine and thought about Rhonda Disapio. No question she'd boxed herself into a corner. She might well face serious consequences if she went to the authorities. But I didn't see any other solution.

I started to heat up a pot of water.

An hour later, the front door slammed, and footsteps pounded up the stairs. Rachel was home. I went upstairs and found her bent over her overnight bag, pulling out her clothes and flinging them on the floor. Rachel often comes home wired from the frenetic activity Barry puts her through; it takes a while to calm her down.

I kissed the top of her head. "Hi, sweetie. How was your visit?"

She whirled around. "Oh, hi, Mom." She went back to

her bag and turned it upside down. A pair of gym shoes fell out.

"What's going on?"

"Can I buy some Steve Maddens?"

"Steve Maddens?"

"They're shoes, Mother. Cool ones. Everybody's got them."

"I didn't think you needed new shoes."

She picked up her gym shoes and tossed them into the wastebasket. "I do now." She balled up a T-shirt and pitched it on top of the shoes. "A Michael Stars shirt, too."

"A who?"

"A Michael Stars shirt. It's—oh never mind. You'll never let me get one."

"I won't?"

"They cost a lot of money."

"How much?"

"About sixty dollars."

This was beyond wired. "That is a lot."

"See? I told them—" She clamped a hand over her mouth.

"You told who what?"

"Nothing."

"Rachel." I don't impose a lot of rules. But there is one: there shall be no gossip about the family—by the family—outside the family. You can attack, criticize, or scold in the bosom of the family, but never outside the home. It's probably a German thing I inherited from my father.

"Who did you see this weekend, besides your father?"

"No one."

Hmm. Daughter comes home, throws her clothes in the trash, and demands new ones. Yet claims she didn't meet anyone special over the weekend. Or tell them about her tightfisted mother. The rain drummed against the house like a bag of marbles.

I decided to try a different approach. I headed for the stairs. "You hungry? I'm making spaghetti and salad."

A puzzled look spread across my daughter's face. She shook her head.

"Well, I'll be downstairs." I started down.

Rachel was out of her room before I got to the bottom. I smiled.

"Daddy's girlfriend was there."

I stopped smiling. I'd heard about the new woman in my ex-husband's life. Washboard abs, buns of steel. Barry was now working out with her. Or on her. Whatever. "Marlene, the aerobics queen?"

Rachel shot me a look.

"Okay." I raised my palms. "So she lifts weights, too."

"Her daughter was there."

"I see."

"Her name is Carla."

"And how old is Carla?" I went into the kitchen.

Rachel followed me. "Sixteen."

I took out a knife and started chopping lettuce.

"She's got this really cool boyfriend. His name is Derek."

"And how old is Derek?"

"I don't know. But he drives."

I started chopping more briskly. I wasn't thrilled she was driving around with older teenagers. But Barry's a fairly responsible parent. They probably went out for ice cream. "Where'd you go?"

"Well, we heard there was this rave nearby, and—"

I spun around. "You went to a rave?"

Rachel immediately backpedaled. "We didn't go in. We just drove around the parking lot. And don't worry. I didn't do anything."

I clenched my fists so tight my nails bit into my palm. For a moment I thought I'd cut myself with the knife. "Rachel. You're only thirteen. You can't go to raves."

"I told you. We didn't go in. Everyone says I look older anyway."

I gazed at my daughter. Three inches taller than last year, she'd already lost that preteen, coltish look. Her body was starting to curve in all the right places. She could pass for sixteen. I forced myself to open my fists. *Stay calm, Ellie.*

"You're a beautiful girl, there's no question about that. But I don't care how old you look. You can't run around with sixteen-year-olds and go to raves."

"Why not?"

"Because you're thirteen. It's not appropriate. Or legal. Carla shouldn't be anywhere near them, either. I wonder if her mother knows? Maybe I should call—"

"Mom," she shrieked. "You can't!"

"If I hear anything more about raves, I will."

"I knew I shouldn't have told you." She fell into a sullen silence.

I turned back to the salad, but I'd lost my appetite.

BARRY WASN'T HOME when I called that night. Out with the aerobics queen, no doubt. I hoped they got drenched in the storm. An hour later, he still hadn't called back. I turned on the late news to make sure he hadn't been mugged, killed, or otherwise maimed and was using that as an excuse not to call.

The ten o'clock news is filled with let-it-bleed stories. Especially on weekends or slow news days, it's pretty much a litany of every accident, murder, and fire they can find within a fifty-mile radius.

I changed into a T-shirt and went into the bathroom to moisturize my face. Someone once told me I looked like Grace Slick, and I still consider it high praise, though both of us are now grayer, and, presumably, mellower. I was just finishing when the anchorman pulled on his serious face.

"A fatal accident on the Dan Ryan Expressway took the life of a twenty-four-year-old woman this evening. According to witnesses, the car veered out of control, skidded across the median, and hit an oncoming truck."

I jerked my head up and looked at the TV. Rain lashed

the camera lens, blurring everything except for a swirl of blue and red lights. The picture cleared, and I saw a cop standing on the shoulder of the highway. Behind him was a car, the front end crushed and mangled. The camera panned over to two paramedics loading a gurney into the back of an ambulance. The body was covered by a plastic sheet but a corner flapped in the wind, revealing a piece of blue and white polka dot material.

FOURTEEN

IT'S USUALLY AROUND three in the morning that rational thought disappears, leaving dark conspiracies to hatch in its wake. The storm fell off to a soft rain, the sound of each drop distinct and perceptible, almost like the crackle of burning paper. I tossed and turned, my mind doubling back on itself.

A young woman covers up important information about the night of a murder, and a man who is probably innocent is convicted. Soon afterward, the woman bares her soul to a video producer, telling her stories about boats and gunshots and fears that she's being followed. That night she dies in an automobile accident.

True, it happened at night, when drivers can be tired and less than careful. True, a storm made the roads slick. True, Rhonda Disapio might have been a rotten driver.

Still.

At six in the morning I ran across the grass for the paper. As if to apologize for last night, the sun was bright, and droplets of water sparkled like jewels on the grass. Mist rose from the ground, winding around the evergreens. The yard looked like an ancient fairyland. I took the newspaper in and brewed a pot of coffee, waiting for an elf or wood nymph to hop past the window.

I spread out the paper, dumped in a packet of sweetener, and sipped coffee from my When the Going Gets Tough, the Tough Go Shopping mug. Maybe it should say *shoplifting*. The steam from the coffee tickled my nose. Did cracking jokes about it mean I was cured?

The accident happened too late to make the morning edition, and TV didn't tell me anything I didn't already know. I thought about calling the state police, our version of the highway patrol. But they probably wouldn't disclose anything unless I had a compelling reason, and with my luck, I'd end up with a grumpy Broderick Crawford on the other end.

After dropping Rachel at school, I went upstairs sniffing my coffee. Why is it the smell is always better than the taste? Don't get me wrong—if it tasted any better, I might have to get a new husband, clean the house in a shirtwaist dress, and greet him after work like a good little Maxwell Housewife.

In my office, I dug out my client list. The only other slow work period I recall was during the early eighties, and I made an effort to hustle business. I culled through every corporate index at the library, wrote letters, sent demo reels. I even went on informational interviews—the kind where you know and they know there's no possibility of getting any work, but you go through the motions anyway.

I still think the only thing all that effort produced was the illusion that I was in charge. I had a plan. Kind of like the duck and cover drills the government made kids practice during the Cold War. About as effective, too. When the economy picked up, my work did, too, and it came in the way it always has: word of mouth.

I started making calls anyway. I didn't expect anyone to call me back; mornings are a hassle for most people. I left messages, figuring I'd start to get callbacks that afternoon. I was rinsing my coffee cup in the sink when a thump sounded at the window.

Susan waved at me through the glass. "How about a walk?"

I grabbed my shoes and threw on a sweater.

Susan Siler and I are yin and yang. A tall, willowy redhead, who always manages to look as if she's stepped out of *Vogue*, she's a gourmet cook, has impeccable taste, and seems to glide through life without the bruises, blows, and jagged edges that perforate mine.

The cool, rain-washed air was overlaid with the tang of pine and woodsmoke. We skirted a couple of puddles left behind by the storm.

"Did you hear about Phyllis Hartford?" Susan asked.

"What?"

"George moved out last week. After twenty-seven years."

I didn't know Phyllis well, except for her baked goods. No holiday, school function, or community event ever took place without a plate of her pastries on hand. It was her knee-jerk response to life cycle events.

"She has no idea what she's going to do."

"She can make lemon squares."

Susan shot me a fierce look. "Watch it. I have the recipe."

We made our way to the bike path that cuts a swath through the forest preserve. The leaves were just starting to turn, and the trees were shot through with glints of red and yellow. A carpet of newly fallen leaves, still holding their colors, muffled our steps. I found myself treading more respectfully, trying not to disturb the balance of nature.

"Speaking of baking, Rachel had a meltdown last night." I told her about the clothes on the floor, the shoes in the trash, the demands for new ones.

Susan giggled.

"You think it's funny? I just bought her some fall things. Including a really nice suit."

"Hormones, Ellie. Get used to it. It only lasts another forty years."

"Yeah? Well, get this." I told Susan about her budding friendship with Carla and Derek. "She just turned thirteen, started eighth grade, and she's already talking about driving in cars with boys.

"So find something for her to do."

"She already takes piano lessons and plays field hockey. But hockey ends in October."

"What about one of those after-school programs? Justin took a great photography class last year."

"Do you know what it's like to sustain the interest of a thirteen-year-old girl whose brain has been corrupted by MTV?"

She flashed me her Mona Lisa smile. "I'm sure you'll find something."

I dodged a couple of bumblebees hovering on some goldenrod. Happily, they'd be gone soon. I don't like flying objects with stingers. As we rounded a corner, I told her how Rhonda Disapio had accosted me in the mall.

"Do you believe her?" Susan pushed her sleeves up to her elbows. "I mean, if she committed perjury on the stand . . ."

"I don't think she would have tracked me down and come all this way just to make it up." I hesitated. "But there's something else that kind of makes me believe her."

"What?"

"She died in a car accident last night."

Susan's eyes widened and then narrowed.

I explained what happened.

"It was a pretty bad storm," she said carefully. "The power's still out in some places."

"She kept saying she thought she was being followed."

It had to be at least sixty degrees outside, but Susan shivered. "So what are you going to do?"

"I thought of calling the state police to see if they consider it an accident—"

"Why wouldn't they?"

"I—I'm not sure. But even if they didn't, they wouldn't tell me. I'm not a relative or a friend. I hardly know the woman. And since the trial, I doubt many people would believe much of what I said." I shrugged. "But I did talk to Brashares. You know, Santoro's lawyer."

"What did he say?"

"Not much. In fact, I don't think he's pursuing the appeal all that aggressively. For example—" I stopped short.

"What?"

I didn't answer.

"Ellie, what just happened?"

"I—I'm not sure. It's probably nothing."

"What is it?"

"I was just thinking that I told Brashares about my conversation with Rhonda as soon as I got home from the mall, and a few hours later, she was dead."

Susan slowed and arched her eyebrows. "Ellie . . ."

"You don't have to say it." I held up my palm. "I'm not jumping to any conclusions. In fact, I'm not even getting involved." I skipped a few steps ahead of her. "See? I'm fine. In fact, when I get home, I'm going to try to land some work."

We reached the end of the bike path and turned down Sunset Ridge. Ahead of us, a dark-colored SUV slowly turned the corner. I stopped and stared after it, shading my eyes with my hand.

"Now what?" Susan asked.

As it disappeared around the bend in the road, I felt my heart pumping. "Nothing." I couldn't say anything. Susan doesn't buy into conspiracies; she was just a baby when JFK died.

FIFTEEN

My MOTHER ALWAYS claimed I was a resilient child. I always bounced back like one of those inflatable dummies. Though I prefer to model myself after the Black Knight in Monty Python, who kept challenging the king to battle even when his arms and legs were chopped off, by afternoon I convinced myself to move on with life. Put Santoro, Mary Jo Bosanick, and Rhonda Disapio behind me. Under the circumstances, I didn't see what I could do. Maybe Rhonda's death was just an accident. Maybe Santoro really did kill Mary Jo.

I called around to park districts and schools. Most of the popular after-school classes—acting, soccer, photography, computers—had been filled since July, but I did find two with space: Let's Learn Latin and Science Club. Neither would be high on Rachel's top ten, but I jotted them down.

I checked my machine. No callbacks yet. I eyed my Rolodex, wondering whether I'd have to cast a wider net. I wasn't looking forward to it; the leap from friendly voices to cold calls is a big one. I picked up the clothes from Rachel's floor and did a few loads of laundry.

The phone finally chirped around four. It was Karen Bishop, my longtime client from Midwest Mutual.

"Karen, how are you?"

"Good. Sorry I didn't get back to you sooner, Ellie. What's up?"

"Just checking in to see if there's anything I can help you out with. We haven't spoken in—"

I heard an exhalation of breath. "I had a feeling that's why you called."

"Excuse me?"

Karen and I have worked together for five years. A working mother herself, she's a no-bullshit person who's managed to survive, even flourish, in a corporate environment. Still, I wasn't prepared for what came next.

She hesitated. "Ellie, I can't use you. In fact, I don't think anyone will touch you with a ten-foot pole."

"What are you talking about?"

"It was your testimony at that trial. You attracted a lot of attention. People are a little leery of you right now." She paused. "You know how it is."

I gripped the phone and stared at a crack in the wall I hadn't noticed before. "No. Karen. How is it?"

"You know the mentality around here. People don't like anything that disrupts the status quo. That actually requires them to form an independent opinion. And you were kind of out there. Visible. Everyone saw you on the news—"

"Hold on. Am I being punished because I testified?"

"No, of course not. Even though Ryan did poke holes in your story."

"Does that mean I'm no longer capable of producing videos?"

"I didn't say that."

"What are you saying, Karen?"

She cleared her throat. "Frankly, Ellie, it's the issue of consent. You released video that technically didn't belong to you. At least that's what I'm hearing from our attorneys."

"Karen, the water district released it. They knew all about it."

"But you were the one who initiated it. The lawyers say you overstepped your boundaries. It's a bad precedent."

"But there was nothing proprietary on it."

"That may be, but the problem was you made the decision for them. No corporation wants their hand forced— especially by a third party. It wasn't your tape to begin with. No one's going to do anything about it, but they are saying it's indicative."

"Indicative of what?"

"Of—well, let's just say they've lost confidence in your professionalism."

I stiffened. "I can't believe this. What do you say?"

"Ellie, come on. What do you think?"

Through my shock and anger, I could tell this was hard for her, too. "Jesus, Karen. The man was accused of a murder he probably didn't commit. What was I supposed to do? Look the other way? Pretend it didn't happen?"

"I know, I know. But you know as well as I do, whether you actually did anything wrong doesn't matter. Appearance is everything. You weren't a team player."

"But I didn't do anything wrong."

Karen sighed. "Look Ellie, I don't have to tell you that people in corporations have blinders on when it comes to their own interests. Or perceived interests. They'll do whatever it takes to protect themselves—and their jobs. The bad news is as long as I depend on them for my paycheck, I have to toe the line. But there is some good news."

"Yeah? What?"

"It won't last forever. Memories are short. A few months from now, this will all blow over. Call me in the spring, and we'll talk. In the meantime, why don't you take some time off? After what you went through, I bet you could use it."

"Thanks."

I disconnected. Now I understood why no one was calling me back. The Chicago video community is small, and word travels fast. Particularly when it passes through corporate communications. And, to be honest, the water district hadn't been all that happy about releasing the tape in the first place.

But this was my livelihood, and spring was six months away. What if it didn't "blow over"? I could be blacklisted indefinitely. They might never let me back on the "team." Given that Barry's child support was, at best, erratic, how was I supposed to make ends meet?

I started pacing, a white-hot anger skimming my nerves. Years ago, I would have been lauded as someone who, by virtue of suffering at the hands of the power structure, had become a person of value. But those days were gone, and I needed the corporate establishment—at least their largesse—to survive. Damn the suits. Damn Kirk Ryan. And damn Chuck Brashares.

It took six hours of self-pity, a hot bath, and two glasses of wine before I realized that Karen was right. No one had coerced me onto the stand. I'd come forward voluntarily. In a way, I had initiated the chain of events that destroyed my credibility. Karen was right about something else, too: *they* didn't care if I ever worked again. *They* had their interests to protect.

But I had mine.

I pulled back the sheets and climbed into bed. I'd gotten myself into this. I'd just have to get myself out.

SIXTEEN

YOU HEAR A lot about the North, South, and West Sides of Chicago, but no one talks much about the East Side, which was where I was going early Monday morning. Hugging Lake Michigan on its Southeast side, the area includes working-class neighborhoods like South Chicago, South Deering, and Hegewisch.

A gassy odor filtered through the car as I got off the highway at 130th. If Chicago is the city of big shoulders, this is the meaty part. Farther east are streets with tiny bungalows, a bar on one corner, a church on the other, but 130th and Torrence is the industrial hub. Factories, warehouses, and cranes crowd together, abandoned rail cars line the streets, and smokestacks belch grit and God knows what else into the air.

I'd made a strategic choice. If the objective was to restore my credibility, I had a couple of options. I could try to verify Rhonda Disapio's story. The problem was, I wasn't sure how to go about it, short of setting up surveillance at the boat launch. Plus, if the boat men really did kill Mary Jo, I wasn't anxious to put myself on their turf. The other option was to ferret out Santoro's background, in an effort to prove he didn't kill Mary Jo. I already knew his haunts: the bar and the docks.

It wasn't a tough decision.

The Calumet River flows southwest from Lake Michigan to Calumet Harbor and eventually to the Mississippi River. Through yet another miracle of Chicago engineering, the harbor was dredged and transformed into a deep-water port so it could accommodate freighters from the Saint Lawrence Seaway. Leading off the harbor are inlets that make the docks between them look like tines on a giant fork. It's at these docks that commodities are off-loaded. Years ago they were transferred to rail cars and shipped across the country. Now most of the cargo travels by truck.

I threaded my way around the Ford plant at Torrence and turned on 122nd. Turning again, I drove down a road that had been patched and repatched, and from the groan of my suspension, could stand yet another go-round. A mile down the road, a battered black and white sign said I had reached the Ceres Terminal. I swung into a lot studded with chunks of broken concrete and stopped behind a shabby brick building with a roof of corrugated metal. Two cars were parked at haphazard angles in front.

It was a cool October morning, and condensation coated the cars' windshields. Pulling on my Sox hat—I knew better than to wear a Cubs hat this far south—I wandered over to a group of longshoremen standing in front of a warehouse. Perched above them on a rusty steel scaffold was a fleshy, graying man with a clipboard. Most of the men looked old. Dressed in canvas coveralls and scuffed, steel-toed boots, several waved union cards in the air.

"Sorry, guys, that's all I need for today," the man with the clipboard said. "But I got a barge of steel coils coming in Friday. Be work for about a dozen of youse."

A collective grumble went up from the men, but it was surprisingly docile, as if they were used to disappointment. I shouldered my way through to the man with the clipboard, but he climbed down off the hiring stand and pretended not to see me. Pulling a tin out of his pocket, he opened it and pinched a wad of Red Man with his thumb and forefinger.

"Excuse me," I said as he packed it in his mouth. He squinted in my direction, one cheek plumped up like a chipmunk. "Do you know Johnnie Santoro?"

His eyebrows shot up, but he kept chewing.

"I know he used to work down here."

He spat out a clump of black goop, which landed a few inches from my left sneaker. "Haven't seen him in over a year. Don't expect to."

I stood my ground. "But you knew him, right?"

He looked me up and down. "You a cop?"

"No."

"Lawyer?"

"No."

"From the union?"

"No."

"Then I ain't got nuttin' to say."

He gave me his back and walked away. A few gulls swooped down in parallel arcs above his head, their bellies tinged with the morning sun. I considered groveling, beseeching him with the fact that my livelihood was at stake unless I could clear my name, but after glancing at the unemployed longshoremen still gathered by the warehouse, I reconsidered. I pulled the brim of my cap farther down and started back to the car. As I skirted a second warehouse with peeling paint on its sides, a flicker of movement caught my attention.

"Got a match?" A burly man with white hair, a bulbous red-veined nose, and skin the color of a dried apple drew a cigarette from behind his ear. The scent of booze clung to him, and there was a suspicious bulge in his pocket. I dug around in my purse and pulled out a frayed matchbook from the Italian Gardens, my favorite neighborhood restaurant.

He lit the cigarette with pudgy fingers and took in a deep drag. Then he blew it out so contentedly I was tempted to bum one, even though I haven't smoked in fifteen years. He grinned at me as if he knew what I was thinking, and slipped the matches into his pocket. "You're that dame I saw on TV." He studied me. "You stuck up for Johnnie. That took guts."

He could keep the matches. He knew Santoro. I tried to suppress my excitement. "It didn't seem to do much good."

"You never know." He brought the cigarette back up to his lips. "Why you come all the way down here? You ain't had enough?"

"I—I have some questions about him."

"Yeah." He spread his arms. "But how you know to come down here?"

"Oh." I'd misunderstood his question. "I called the union and asked where my best chance was to find some longshoremen. They said Ceres was the only place hiring today."

He nodded, then motioned for me to follow him to the edge of the dock. A barge was tied up a few yards away, its contents hidden under several tarps. Water lapped against the side of the barge. Across the inlet a freighter had tied up, and I heard shouts and saw men bustling to off-load materials. The smell of rotting fish was strong.

He flicked his ash into the water and took another drag, his belly ballooning in and out. "I'm Sweeney. What is it you wanna know?"

This was the best offer I'd had in weeks. "I'm not sure how to begin, but, well—tell me how you knew Santoro."

Sweeney inhaled. The tip of his cigarette glowed orange. "His daddy and me were buddies."

"Santoro's father is a longshoreman?"

"Was. He's passed on now. Died of cancer."

So did my mother. "Did he—Johnnie—come from a large family?"

He took another drag. "Not so big. Four kids, I think. Three girls and Johnnie."

"Do they live around here?"

"Not far." He flicked his cigarette off the dock. It landed in the water with a tiny hiss. "What is it you want, lady?"

I sucked in a breath. "Mr. Sweeney, I don't think Johnnie Santoro killed his girlfriend. But the jury didn't believe me, and unless I can prove it, I may not ever work again. I'm trying to find any information, any evidence, anything that would help prove he didn't do it. I figured I'd start by coming down here."

He stared at me, sizing me up for another long moment. Then, "In that case, I dunno if I'm gonna be much help."

"Why?"

"I—well, let's just say I didn't much like Johnnie."

A small boat chugged down the waterway. The barge rocked gently in its wake.

"Why not?"

"Johnnie was one of those guys who always wanted something for nothin'. You know what I mean? Thought just because his father worked down here, he was—entitled." He folded his arms.

"Did he work regularly as a longshoreman?"

Sweeney scoffed. "Not much. And when he did, he was always struttin' around like he owned the place. Mouthing off, too."

"About what?"

"His friends. His deals. How he was gonna score big. Bullshit like that."

"Deals? Was Santoro dealing?"

"Don't know." He looked off onto the water.

I waited.

He coughed hard, a smoker's hack, and took out another cigarette. "But seems to me, a couple months before he got busted, I can remember him sayin' he wouldn't have to be doing this much longer."

"Doing what?"

"You know. Scroungin' work down here."

"Why not?"

"Said he was working a big deal."

"But you never asked about the details."

He looked at me under hooded eyes. "Ain't none of my business, now, was it?"

"Did he ever mention a guy named Sammy?"

He dug out the Italian Garden matches, frowning. "Not so's I remember."

He lit another cigarette, waved out the match, and let it drop to the cracked concrete.

I cleared my throat, phrasing my next question carefully. "Did Johnnie have a union card?"

"Oh yeah, his daddy made sure of that. That was part of the problem. Charlie couldn't say no to Johnnie."

I paused. "Well, given the way things are down here, you think he might have been mixed up with the wrong people? People who didn't like the way he behaved, and—"

"You mean like the people what still control who gets hired and how much of our pension they're gonna rip off, even though there ain't no work? Those kind of people who you mean?"

I nodded.

He hesitated. "I couldn't say. All I can say is Charlie and I weren't never mixed up with that crowd. Those guys'll bleed you dry." He sniffed. "Of course, twenty years ago, it didn't matter. There was plenty of work. You could still make it. But now . . . it ain't never been this bad. A boat don't tie up but maybe once a week. No way you can live on that."

He stole a glance at me, then unexpectedly grinned, baring a set of yellow, stained teeth. "Now, I ain't gonna deny that Charlie and I mighta helped something fall off the back of the boat once or twice. Like the time a bunch of Corvette engines came in on a freighter. Some of 'em ended up in cars all up and down the South Shore. I heard the FBI took to casing the McDonald's over at Seventy-ninth and Phillips, making all them high school kids lift up their hoods so's they could check out what was inside their Chevys." His belly shook with quiet laughter. "But those days are gone. There ain't nothing left to steal. I mean, who'd want a load of steel coils?"

"So, it's not likely Johnnie was—"

"Like I told you. I keep my head down."

"I understand." I looked out over the waterway. The sun was sewing the surface of the water with tiny bursts of light. "Tell me something, Mr. Sweeney. Has anybody else come down here asking questions about Santoro?"

"Like who?"

"Cops, investigators, lawyers. Anyone."

"Not so's I'd notice. But this ain't the kind of place people come if they don't have to."

"Yeah. Well, thanks. You've been a big help."

He straightened up. "Like I said, Charlie was my friend."

I headed toward the car. Just before I rounded the corner, I turned around. Sweeney was gazing out over the water, as if the docks had stolen his soul, but it wasn't worth the effort to get it back.

SEVENTEEN

As I DROVE north on the Bishop Ford, a giant pair of red lips on a white billboard reminded me of Rhonda Disapio. How her mouth squeezed into a tight, crimson ball against her pale skin. How her lipstick was smeared the day we met. It occurred to me that she'd come north to see me on the same highway. Except she never finished the return trip.

I tightened my seat belt. The fact was, I probably hadn't done myself any good at the harbor. Johnnie Santoro sounded like a punk who was mixed up with the wrong people. Not someone I'd care to help. I wondered whether I'd have gotten involved with him in the first place if I'd known.

The Dan Ryan runs from ninety-fifth Street to the Loop. As I approached ninety-fifth, I slowed. Calumet Park, the lake, and the boat launch were only a few miles away. I could try to check out Rhonda's story. I'd never have incontrovertible proof—Mary Jo had died over a year ago—but at least I could see if Rhonda's version of events was feasible. I wouldn't even have to get out of the car. I could just drive around.

I made the turn.

East of the expressway the neighborhood is largely black until you hit the lake, where it turns Hispanic. The streets off ninety-fifth are narrow and lined with row houses and bungalows, but they're clean and neat, as if they're struggling to stay respectable.

They do parks well in Chicago, and Cal Park was no exception. The 200-acre stretch of land is a tranquil haven, with graceful curves, wide promenades, and lots of trees. I passed a few kids on bikes—they had to be playing hooky—and two women pushing strollers. I rolled down the window. Sun-warmed air swept through the car.

I swung into a parking lot at the northeast end of the park. Directly in front of me the lake curved around a wide bend. To my left were a few trees, but not enough to obstruct the view. I cut the engine and watched a few gulls march past the car, their tiny heads bobbing back and forth. The sun fired the trees with splashes of copper, red, and gold. A soft breeze skittered the leaves. I climbed out.

In front of me stretched four narrow wooden piers supported by pilings. Between them were lanes of water wide enough for a boat to navigate. Asphalt backed up to the water's edge, and two men were dragging their boat from the water to a trailer hitched to the back of their van. A metal breakwater angled around the north end of the boatyard, sheltering it from the worst of the lake's excesses.

To my right, an expanse of rocks hugged the shore, bordering a path wide enough for joggers and bicyclists. I walked over, trying to imagine the scene as Rhonda had described it. I hunkered down on the rocks, pretending it was late at night and I had a bottle. I gazed at the pilings, imagining a shadowy boat as it coasted into the launch, hearing the drone of its motor as it slowed. I tried to feel the spark of interest that must have run through Mary Jo and Rhonda when they realized two men were aboard. Though the launch was far enough away that you couldn't make out faces—I could barely see the men securing their boat to their van now—I could picture the two women giggling, daring each other to make the first move.

I retraced my steps to the parking lot. A grassy, leaf-strewn area, now stubbly and brown, lay in front of it. To my left, running the length of the lot, was a chain-link fence. Behind it was a one-story red building, a Park District facility of some sort, I thought.

Rhonda had said she'd escaped through a hole in the fence. I walked over and started down its length, jiggling and shaking it as I went. Halfway down, something went slack. I stopped and shook it again. The bottom of the fence had come loose. I leaned over and lifted a section of fencing. Was this where Rhonda slipped through and escaped?

I replaced the loose section and straightened up. Along the fence line was an accumulation of litter, pushed up against the links where grass had grown through. Discarded coffee cups, beer cans, fast-food wrappers, even a few swatches of material that might have been shirts at one time. A few yards farther down, up against the fence, something glittered. I explored it with my foot. A silver charm bracelet was tangled up in a comb. Bending over, I extricated it from the comb. It had a small silver heart. Probably belonged to some little girl who cried for days when she discovered it was lost.

I studied the bracelet, looked both ways, then dropped it in my bag. I still struggle to resist things that don't belong to me, but this time I was rescuing something from oblivion, not shoplifting. That was different, wasn't it?

As I headed to the boat launch, the two men with the van, having attached their boat to their trailer, were pulling away. More debris had collected where the breakwater met the shore. Soda bottles. A dented gas can. Shards of glass. I watched all of it disappear under a wave and reappear moments later. Did everyone expect someone else to clean up after them?

I was about to walk out onto one of the piers when I heard a noise behind me. I spun around. A couple of bikers were closing in on my Volvo. Though it's over ten years old, it's not a beater, and I planned on getting another couple of years out of it. I threw my bag over my shoulder and started over. As I did, one of the kids parked his bike and planted himself on the driver's side. Stretching out his arm, he strolled from the front to the back of the car, running his hand along the side. The other kid watched, laughing.

"Hey!" I sprinted toward them. "Stop messing with my car!"

The kid who'd been laughing turned around, his grin fading. The boy who'd been at the car ran to his bike and jumped on. They both pedaled furiously in the opposite direction.

"Hey you! Stop it right there!" I yelled.

But I was no match for young male bikers at warp speed. By the time I got to the car, they had turned the corner and were out of sight. Breathless and damp, I stopped at the spot where they'd been. A long, wavy scratch extended from the front end to the rear bumper.

EIGHTEEN

WHEN I GOT home I called Mark Lefferts, an old friend from high school who owns a body shop in Glenview. We dated for about a month during senior year, one of those relationships that burned hot and furious and then turned to ashes when he decided he liked Angie Sawyer more than me. Angie, a cute blond and a cheerleader, reportedly had a fondness for the backseats of cars. No wonder he made a career of automotives.

He could fix the scratch for about twelve hundred dollars, he said. Once I started breathing again, I said I'd learn to like it and hung up. So much for old boyfriends. Although he did have great weed, I recalled. Back in the days when grass cost thirty dollars an ounce, he had sinsemilla before anyone else.

I wandered into the kitchen. Thinking about grass reminded me of Mary Jo's statement to Rhonda at the boat launch. Something like "What makes you think I don't know about dealing?" At the time, I'd thought it was a strange comment. Out of context. But now, I wondered. Is that what this was all about?

I started wiping the counter with a sponge. Maybe the men in the boat were bringing in drugs from Canada through the Great Lakes. Hell, if the Calumet River was involved, they could have come up the Mississippi. Was it possible Mary Jo wasn't at the boat launch by chance? What if she was there to intercept the shipment for Santoro? Sweeney hadn't denied Santoro was into dealing; in fact, when I asked him point blank, he'd kept his mouth shut. And Mary Jo was Santoro's girlfriend.

But then, why would she have brought Rhonda Disapio with her? Unless Rhonda was involved, too. No, that didn't seem right. Maybe Santoro had ordered Mary Jo to intercept the stash, but she refused. Maybe that's what they were fighting about at the bar. Maybe she didn't want anything to do with dealing and was trying to make a break for it in his car.

I wiped the burners on the stove. Or was it the other way around? Maybe she was trying to get more heavily involved. Freeze Santoro out. Nobody ever said Mary Jo was an angel—except her mother. Maybe Mary Jo made off with Santoro's car, left him stranded, and proceeded to the boat launch herself. But then, after she got there, the deal fell apart. Maybe the men didn't know her. Or didn't buy her story. Or thought she was a cop. They panicked. She ran. They killed her.

Either way, Santoro would have been caught in the middle. He might not have been at Calumet Park, he might not be guilty of murder, but you wouldn't call him an innocent.

I rinsed the sponge in the sink. There was only one problem with my theory. There hadn't been any talk of drug dealing at the trial. Not a hint. And while I realize it's probably not a great idea to admit to one crime when you're on trial for another, I doubted if Brashares had even entertained the possibility. Which was too bad. If he could have established that Mary Jo was acting as Santoro's go-between, it might have buttressed the tape.

I squeezed water out of the sponge. I was spinning,

formulating theories without proof. Even so, Brashares should know. I called and got his machine.

"Hi. It's Ellie Foreman. Something's come up that I thought I should run by you. It's about Santoro's background and what those men might have been doing when Mary Jo was killed. It might give the tape more credibility. Then again, it could be nothing. But I thought I should at least mention it."

As I hung up, sun streamed through the window, and the reds, oranges, and yellows of the leaves put on a show. All this talk about scams and drugs and murders was making me feel dirty. I went up to take a shower.

THAT WEEKEND DAD and I barbecued on the tiny deck off my kitchen. Figuring it might be the last one for the season, I bought thick steaks and tried not to think how many arteries I was plugging.

Dad still fires up the coals better than any man I know. And he does it without any props except lighter fluid. Within minutes, he had flames licking the side of the grill. When the coals were edged with a thin border of white, I brought out the meat.

"You recovered from your experience in court?" He poked the steaks with the tongs.

I sank into a deck chair. "You know, I think you were right. In a way, I'm kind of sorry I ever got involved."

He slid the meat onto the grill. "Didn't the woman who testified just die in a car accident?"

"How did you know?"

"Ellie, I may be old and slow, but most of my cylinders are still firing. It was on TV."

"Rhonda Disapio was Mary Jo Bosanick's friend," I said. "What you don't know is that she came to see me on the day she died."

He looked up. "Why?"

"She had a pretty strange story." I told Dad about my encounter with Rhonda.

"What did she expect you to do?"

"Put her on TV so she could stay out of jail. She thought I worked for the news. Ryan did make a big point of that, remember."

"Why didn't she go to the police?"

"She said she was too scared."

"I'm not one to speak ill of the dead, but no one would ever accuse her of being the sharpest knife in the drawer."

"Could be. But I'm starting to wonder whether it all revolved around drugs."

"Drugs?"

I sketched out my suspicions but didn't tell him how I arrived at them. He wouldn't approve of my field trip.

"So," Dad said when I finished. "Santoro might not be the innocent you thought he was?"

"Maybe not."

He picked up his scotch. The ice cubes clinked against the glass. To his credit, he didn't come out with an I told you so.

"That might also explain why Brashares was so strange," I said.

"Santoro's lawyer?"

I nodded. "I kept thinking he was just going through the motions. Doing the minimum required but nothing more."

"You think he knew Santoro was dirty?"

"It's possible. Maybe Brashares didn't want to expend all that energy on a loser. Isn't that the way defense lawyers think?"

"If they do, they ought to stop being defense lawyers."

Through the kitchen window I caught glimpses of David and Rachel washing lettuce for the salad.

I turned back to my father. "I called Brashares to let him know. But he hasn't called me back."

Dad flipped over the meat, then eased himself into a chair. Sandburg had it wrong. It's age, not fog, that creeps in on "little cat feet."

"Ellie, why are you still calling this lawyer? The trial's over."

I shrugged.

"Ellie . . ."

"Okay." I sighed. "Since the trial, no one will hire me. I can't even get any callbacks. Karen Bishop, my client at Midwest Mutual, says it's because of the tape. Apparently, I forced its release, and people, especially corporate people, don't like that. I've lost a lot of credibility. I was trying to do some damage control."

"That's *meshuga*. Leave it alone," he said wearily.

"Dad, I have to work."

A peal of giggles came from inside. David and Rachel were playing catch with a cucumber, pretending it was a football.

"Where is it written that you have to support yourself forever?"

"Don't go there, Dad."

It was my dependency—or what Barry claimed was my dependency—that triggered our problems when we were married. I only worked when I felt like it, he complained, while he was expected to bring home the regular paycheck. But he was an attorney in a full-service firm, billing two thousand hours a year. He never really understood the nature of freelancing. It never comes in at a steady pace. You can write four proposals for every project you get. Go to appointments, lunches, and meetings that ultimately produce nothing. When I wasn't actually producing a video, he was quick to call me a princess. Or worse.

I didn't intend to revisit the pattern with David. But that was a conversation for another time. I picked up the tongs and checked the meat. "You know, there's another possibility. About Brashares."

"What's that?"

"He might be on somebody's payroll himself."

"Whose?"

"No one liked Santoro very much. Sweeney said—uh—I mean I heard he had a big mouth. Maybe some—someone with influence told Brashares not to try all that hard to get him off. Maybe they were happy to see Santoro take the fall."

"Now you think he was framed?" Dad's voice hardened.

I didn't answer.

"Now I know you're *meshuga*."

"Hold on. Suppose the business down at the boat launch did have something to do with drugs. We all know that where drugs are involved, organized crime isn't far away."

"You don't think you're stringing a few inferences together into a huge assumption?" Dad's eyes narrowed. "Ellie. You began this conversation saying I was right. That you were wrong to get involved. Sounds to me like you're getting in deeper."

"This isn't getting involved. It's just talking. I thought, given your experience, you might have some perspective."

"My experience?"

"Skull. Lawndale. Before the war."

My father snorted. "Sweetheart, that was sixty years ago. And Skull was no mobster."

"That's not what you implied."

"Skull was a . . . a street thug. With pretensions. Anyway, you're talking about a different world. A different time. Life wasn't as . . . as coarse. There were standards."

"A shark is a shark. No matter when they attack."

"You think so?" He got up to inspect the steaks. "Lemme tell you a story. When I went into practice for myself, a couple of guys came to me with one of those offers. You know. The ones you're not supposed to refuse." He faced me. "They wanted to help me build my practice. Said they could steer a lot of work my way.

"I knew what they were asking me. And I thought about it. It was tempting. You were a baby, and I was supporting your *oma* and your *opa*." He jabbed the steaks with the tongs. "But after a week or so, I called them back and said, 'Thanks. But no thanks. I'm going down a different path.' They understood. In fact, they said, 'You ever change your mind, come talk to us.' "

"That really happened?"

"What? You think I made it up? My point is there were boundaries back then. Limits. You could say no, and the Outfit would leave you alone. Not anymore." He waved the tongs. "Today they'd find a way to finagle it so I'd have to work for them. Threats. Extortion. Blackmail. There's no respect anymore. I mean, you're talking about the same scum who ripped off scrap metal from the World Trade Center."

"But Dad, in a way you're just confirming my suspicions. Maybe Santoro was mixed up with these goons. Maybe he pissed them off. Maybe—"

"Ellie, I love you dearly, but you're as headstrong as your mother. You can't live with ambiguity. So you latch onto some crazy idea and try to convince everyone it's true. Even if it isn't."

"At least I come by it honestly." I grumbled.

He waved a hand. "Let's say you're right, and he was involved with some scumbags. What are you gonna do about it? You got no idea who they are. They might not even be wise guys. Today you got your Russians, your Eastern Europeans, your Asians—"

"Tongs."

He looked towards the grill. "They're here."

"I meant—never mind."

"I'll tell you what the problem is." He brandished the tongs. "There's no respect for life anymore. The sanctity of life. Nobody gives a damn. Take these young suicide bombers. You know, the ones who kill themselves for the glory of Allah. How were these children raised? They're nothing more than cannon fodder. What kind of people are their parents? It's a *shonde*."

I watched him spear the steaks and take them off the grill. "You know why they're doing it. It's their jihad."

"Don't you believe it. They're doing it because some crazy Arab seduces these poor *shlubs* by convincing them they'll be heroes." He shook the tongs in the air. "You know, if I had a nickel for all the fools in the world, I'd be a millionaire. And something else . . ."

I realized that was all I was going to get out of Dad tonight. But, then, he was allowed; age confers a license to rant.

AFTER DINNER, DAVID, Dad, and I sat in the family room, trying to ignore the pounding bass that vibrated down from Rachel's room.

"I spoke to Abdul earlier," David said. "He said to send his regards. He hopes you're all right."

"Abdul?" I asked.

He smiled shyly. "He asked me to help him finance the purchase of a chemical plant in Indiana."

"Smooth. I guess the rafting trip turned out to be profitable. At least for you."

"You helped. He's very fond of you."

My father beamed. "You make a good team."

David went on. "I told him about the trial and what's been going on."

I shot him a warning look. I didn't want Dad to get curious again. I shouldn't have worried.

"Wait a minute. Did I hear you right? Abdul?" The lines on Dad's forehead deepened.

"We met at the Greenbrier," I said. "He's a relative of the Saudi royal family. He owns oil wells."

Dad looked over at David, then at me. "You couldn't find a Jewish sheik?"

David and I traded smiles. I got up to kiss my father, thinking how lucky I was to be surrounded by the people I love, when the phone trilled. I ran into the kitchen to get it.

"Ellie?" It was Susan.

"What's up?"

"You'd better turn on Channel Nine."

I ran into the family room and punched on the nine o'clock news.

"According to police," the anchorman was saying, "the body of attorney Chuck Brashares was found in his Loop office earlier tonight. Police say Brashares was shot in the head approximately three days ago."

NINETEEN

A POLITICAL SCANDAL in the governor's office pushed Brashares's murder off the front page, but the story on page three was chilling enough. His office had been broken into while he was working late. The cops found evidence of a struggle, there were bruises on his face, and it looked like his arm was broken. The office had been trashed, the safe cleaned out. Police speculated robbery was the motive.

His death cured me of any further involvement. I had no reason to think it was connected to Santoro's case, but three people were dead: Mary Jo, Rhonda, and now Brashares. That was enough. I forced myself back to the business of living: cleaning closets, washing the car—the key scratch gave the Volvo a tired dignity, I decided—and taking long bike rides.

David didn't come in the next weekend, and Barry didn't take Rachel. Friday night she came into the family room with a smile, a bowl of sudsy warm water, and a cigar box full of nail polish. After soaking my hands, she proceeded to file my nails, tighten my cuticles, and apply not one but three coats of polish. The result was a purple base, green tips, and a thin orange stripe separating the two. My nails were a vision.

Afterward, we made popcorn and watched a video. The film, a techno-thriller with big stars, great locations, but cardboard characters, was way too predictable, and I was dozing off when two beams of light suddenly poured through the window. Startled, I leapt up and ran to the window. A dark-colored SUV was pulling up to the curb.

A tiny ice crystal formed in the pit of my stomach. Hadn't Rhonda Disapio been followed by a dark SUV? And hadn't I seen one when Susan and I went for a walk? I wondered whether to double-lock the door.

But in that split second between thought and action, Rachel sprinted over and threw it open.

"Rachel—what are you—"

She ran out the doorway and down the driveway. A car window slid down, and she stuck her head in. I raced after her, my heart thudding, but there were no shots. No screams. No nothing. Rachel turned around, her eyes beaming.

"It's Carla and Derek. They want me to go out with them. Can I, Mom? Please?"

I sagged against the locust tree. "Whose car is that?"

Rachel looked at me, then back at the car. "Derek's parents."

I nodded, pressing my lips together. There were probably about five thousand dark-colored SUVs on the North Shore.

Rachel's face lit up. "Thanks, Mom. You're way cool. I'll be home in a couple of hours."

"Hold on." She'd misunderstood my nod. "You're not going anywhere."

"But you just—"

"That wasn't permission to go out." I started back to the house. "Rachel, it's after ten. You can't go out this late."

"But Mother—"

"We've been through this before. No driving around. No late dates. Anyway, you have that Science Club project to finish."

After a pitched battle a few weeks ago, during which I'd maintained it wasn't a yes or no option, she'd decided it was less humiliating to be a techno-geek than a linguist.

"But it's the weekend."

I glared at her.

She threw me a hateful look. "Daddy thinks you're neurotic, you know."

"You don't live with your father."

"Maybe I should."

"With behavior like this, I'm open to negotiation." I looked at the car. Two forms were in the front seat, their heads close together. "You just tell them you're not available tonight."

Rachel didn't move.

"If you won't, I will."

Her bottom lip curled, the way it does when she's about to scream or cry or shout. "You don't want me to have any friends."

"Rachel . . ."

"You don't want me to be popular. You want me to be a freak like you."

I pointed to the car. "Go."

She trudged back to the car and stuck her face in the window. A moment later, the car backed out of the driveway. As it sped off around the corner, she ran inside, tears streaming down her face, and raced up the stairs. The sound of the door slamming reverberated through the house.

TWENTY

MONDAY I GOT a call from Great Lakes Oil, which, until their merger with a British multinational, was one of the country's largest oil companies. An aide to Assistant Vice-President Dale Reedy asked if I was interested in bidding on a potential training video about the process used to extract oil from shale. Reedy would be out of town for a week or two but wanted to meet as soon after that as possible.

I tried not to accept too effusively. I've always felt somewhat proprietary toward Great Lakes; it was *our* gas station when I was a kid. My mother used to collect the glasses they gave out as premiums. I remember one sunny day riding my bike down to the corner to fill up my tires with air. How I told the manager we only needed one more glass to make up a set of eight. How he slipped me a free one, which I presented to my mother with a flourish.

The blue and white signs that used to dot the country have, for the most part disappeared, but the Great Lakes skyscraper still towers over the Loop, and every time I pass by it, I think of those glasses. Indeed, if it were possible for me to feel warm and fuzzy about any corporation, it would probably be Great Lakes.

I said I'd be delighted to meet Dale Reedy, and we set up a date. I hummed as I got off the phone. At least one corporation was willing to deal with me. And Great Lakes was a first-tier company. This could be major bucks. Things were looking up.

"**WHERE ARE WE** going?" I asked as David and I headed downtown Friday night.

"It's a surprise." He pulled into the left lane, weaving between cars.

"Pretty sure of yourself, for someone who didn't know how to find the lake six months ago."

"I had a good teacher. Plus . . ." he said, gunning the engine, "it isn't my car."

I fastened my seat belt, but I didn't need to. Chicago takes its cultural cues from the West Coast, and thanks to the snarl of traffic well past rush hour, we'd apparently absorbed their worst nightmares, too. There was no rational reason for the tie-up: no Cubs game, no accident, no construction. Nevertheless, we crawled down the highway for the better part of an hour. By the time we pulled up at the Four Seasons Hotel, I felt as wilted as yesterday's salad.

The doorman opened the door, his uniform festooned with more ribbons and buttons than a veteran on Decoration Day. David took my arm and guided me inside. He'd asked me to put on my black slacks, a white linen blouse, and the dangly silver earrings he bought me that make me feel dressed up. I laced my arm through his. He used to stay at The Ritz-Carlton, but after we met he switched—he was an equal opportunity hotel guest—and we'd spent our first nights together here. Long, languid nights, lost in the touch and taste of passion. Thoughts of the most perfect bed in the world danced in my brain. Could Krispy Kremes be far behind?

I grinned. "Is this the surprise?"

"Well, sort of."

"Sort of?"

He hesitated. "Abdul is in town, and he asked us to have dinner with him."

"Abdul?"

"I couldn't get out of it, and he really wanted us both to come."

My smile faded. Why would David think I'd want to share an evening with Abdul? I'd only met the man once. As a client of David's, especially a new client, he merited a modicum of courtesy, but he wouldn't be my first choice for a dinner companion. I was about to say so when David pulled a room card out of his pocket.

"This is the surprise." He said. "After dinner."

I eyed it longingly. A warm feeling started to radiate through me. "What about Rachel?"

He checked his watch. "Katie's mother ought to be picking her up right about . . . now."

"Okay." I kissed him. "I forgive you."

Our heels clicked across the marble floor of the lobby. We strolled past a polished mahogany table with a huge flower arrangement on top. Behind us was an oak hutch filled with elegant china, to one side a banister with ornate scrollwork. A silk carpet lay beneath our feet.

I stopped to smell the flowers, a mixture of giant sun-flowers, calla lilies, and smaller blossoms I couldn't iden-tify, though they looked like tiny orchids. Their sweet, delicate fragrance tickled my throat. David leaned over, picked one of the small blooms, and placed it behind my ear. Looking up, I caught our reflections in a gilt-edged mirror. Soft lighting bathed us in a warm, golden glow. The pale, cream-colored flower made a stark contrast to my black curls.

I touched my fingers to the flower. It was just a tiny flower; people take them all the time. But as I stroked its soft, velvety petals, it occurred to me that, innocent as it

was, David would never have done something like that
six months ago.

We crossed to the elevator. He clearly had loosened up
since we met. That was that a good thing, wasn't it? Then
why did I feel so uneasy? The walls of the elevator felt
like they were closing in.

"Are you okay?" David asked.

I looked over. I knew what was bothering me. It wasn't
the flower. I still can't accept it when good things happen
to me. If it seems too good to be true, it probably is. I
make sure of it. I ripped the flower out of my ear.

"What are you doing?"

I crushed it on the floor. "You've come a long way,
haven't you? I've even got you stealing now."

He gazed at me, then, without speaking, picked up the
flower and deposited it in the ashtray. The elevator slowed
and stopped on the forty-fifth floor. As the doors opened,
a young couple wrapped in each others' arms hurriedly
broke apart and edged past us into the car, giggly and
gay. We got out. The doors closed with a whoosh, but
not before the man reached for the woman.

David faced me. He had to be furious. He was probably
going to tell me how hypocritical I was. Attacking him
for one of my own failings. He'd be right.

Instead, he caught my chin in his hand and brushed his
fingers across my cheek. "Ellie, it was only a goddamn
flower. I'd give you a whole garden if I could."

I wasn't expecting that. Most men would have retali-
ated, at least become defensive. But David wasn't like
most men. He was utterly without guile. I sagged against
the wall. Maybe I was wrong. This was no big deal.
Maybe I'd been overreacting. Even a teensy bit maudlin.
This was supposed to be a pleasant evening. I straightened
up and pasted on a smile, determined to be a charming
dinner companion. David smiled back and knocked on
4520.

"Good evening, Ellie." Abdul opened the door and
planted a kiss on my cheeks. He was wearing a loose-

fitting dark blue silk shirt and white linen pants. He gave off a heavy whiff of cologne.

"Abdul. How lovely to see you again. When did you get in?"

"David and I took the same flight out." He smiled. "When he told me what a trying period you've been through, I insisted you join me for dinner."

I glanced over at David. "It was a wonderful idea."

He ushered us into his suite, which was furnished with settees, thick carpets, and Louis XVI chairs in rich patterns of red, gold, and blue. In the center of the room was a table set for three with crystal glasses and elegant china. Heavy drapes framed a picture window with a view of the Hancock and beyond that the lake. A breeze swept off the water, sharpening the edges of buildings and making the lights twinkle. The soft, dark blanket of water was pierced by an occasional flash from a boat or buoy. If the view from our room was half as beautiful, it would be heaven.

Abdul took a bottle of wine from a silver cooler and filled one of the glasses. "Try this."

I sipped. "Excellent."

He showed me the label. "It's Joseph Heitz. One of your Californias."

He put it back and picked up a crystal plate layered with triangular toast points. A small bowl in the middle held black caviar. I took one, scooping up a dab of caviar, scallions, and chopped egg. Abdul smeared his with a thick coating and bit into it.

The meal started with grilled shrimp marinated in a coriander lime sauce and progressed to rack of lamb with a caramelized shallot and thyme crust. Each course was served by two unassuming waiters, who whisked silver-domed covers off the plates. I reminded myself to tell Susan about it.

Abdul regaled us with stories about the small village in which he grew up, and despite his occasional lapse in manners that I attributed to the difference in cultures, I felt myself warming to him. The wine and the food did their job, too, and by the time the waiters served us sorbet topped with lavender blossoms, I almost believed my crisis over the flower was just a blip. An aberration. I'd been jumpy since Brashares's death. That's all it was.

"What brings you to Chicago?" I asked.

"I am looking at a small chemical company in Indiana. Great Lakes Oil has put it up for sale. David is helping me finance it."

I sat up straighter. "Great Lakes Oil?"

He nodded. "Since their merger, they're looking to spin off their smaller operations."

"What a coincidence."

Abdul angled his head. "Why is that?"

"I just got a call from them. Inviting me to bid on a video. An assistant vice-president wants to produce a video on shale oil. The industry flirted with it thirty years ago. But I guess with the price of oil what it is, they're resurrecting all their toys."

"Indeed." He smiled.

I felt myself color. I'd forgotten to whom I was talking.

He rose and went to a small table with a silver humidor on top. Bending over, he opened it and extracted two cigars. "What is the executive's name, out of curiosity?"

"Dale Reedy."

He hesitated, then pulled a clip out of his pocket and snipped off the end of one cigar. "I don't know the name." He lit it with a silver lighter, then handed David the other.

Surprise flickered through me; I'd never seen David smoke. "Why are you looking to buy an American chemical company? Why not build your own in—in Saudi Arabia?"

Abdul puffed on the cigar. "That is our ultimate plan," he said. "But Great Lakes produces an additive that extends the storage life of gasoline. It seems to work well in dry, hot climates." He blew out a stream of smoke. "We want to bring it to Saudi Arabia. As you may know, the money from petrodollars does not stretch as far as it once did. We have only one job for every two men. And if men don't work in our part of the world . . ." He waved his cigar, not needing to explain what could happen to a generation of young Saudi men with too much time and not enough money.

David cut in. "Did you get the correlations I faxed yesterday?"

Abdul turned to David. "You have anticipated me. As usual. However . . ." He handed his cigar clip over to David, who fiddled around with the tip. "It may be that our closing date is more fluid than I previously thought. Is there a way we can incorporate that into the hedging strategy?"

"Of course. Just remember, the more flexibility we incorporate, the more expensive the hedge."

Abdul touched the flame of his lighter to David's cigar.

"When you get a moment, E-mail me the parameters, and I'll work up some new strategies."

"I am fortunate to have you on my side."

David smiled.

I rose and moved to the window, queasy from the smoke. The side of the Hancock, its windows lit in random patterns, looked like a giant Tetris board. I grabbed the metal base of the window and pulled. To my surprise, the window opened, and a strong gust of air rushed in, peppered with the blasts from car horns, shouts, and squealing brakes. Startled, I sprang back.

David scrambled up. "Are you all right?"

"I'm sorry." I shook my head in embarrassment. "I—I didn't expect the window to open." I should have known. At the Four Seasons, everything works, including the windows.

"No." Abdul extinguished his cigar. "It's my fault. I did not ask if the smoke would be a problem."

Gusts of air whistled through the room, scattering a sheaf of papers on a small table nearby. I reached up and shut the window, then bent over to pick up the papers. "No. It's my fault. I should have said something."

"Here. Let me." Abdul crossed the room and bent down, too. Our heads bumped. He laughed nervously.

I patted my head. He retreated into the other room with the papers. A latch snapped open and shut. He came back out and motioned me back to the table.

"Now, tell me about this trial." He poured me a fresh glass of wine. "You must have been disappointed at the jury's decision."

I took the glass. "You could say that."

"After David told me about it, I read some of the stories online. I must admit I became curious about one thing."

"What's that?"

"The reports said something about RF interference. That it was raised during your cross-examination. What is this RF?"

"Ryan made mincemeat out of me on that." I sighed. "Radio interference. It affected our equipment and damaged the tape."

"And you never discovered the source?"

"We didn't even know it was there until just before the trial."

"Why did your lawyer not make that clear?"

"Well, first of all, he wasn't *my* lawyer. But to answer the question—" I hesitated. "As a matter of fact, that is a good question. I don't know."

"This is the same lawyer who lost his life."

"You *have* been keeping up." I paused. "The police say he was the victim of a botched robbery."

"What do you say?"

My gaze slipped from him to David. "I say . . . well, frankly, I'd rather not have to think about him, or Santoro, or Mary Jo Bosanick again."

Abdul scratched his goatee. "Then it is good that it is over."

OUR ROOM WASN'T as plush as Abdul's, but we weren't there for the decor. I padded over to the bed. My feet sank into deep pile carpeting. I perched on the edge of the mattress and bounced up and down. Perfect.

David smoothed a hand down my hair. I faced him, letting him trace the line of my jaw with his finger. Suddenly, we were full of each other. Hair, skin, smell. His arms wound around me, his mouth settled on mine. I fell back and pulled him on top. Our clothes came off, and our bodies took over.

Afterward, we lay beside each other in the dark. The light from the window threw spiky shadows across the room. David ran his hand down my leg.

"I'm sorry about tonight. But when Abdul called, he wouldn't take no for an answer."

I reached across and took his hand, ran it up my side, and covered it with my own. "It worked out just fine."

"He likes you a lot, you know."

I giggled. "Then I guess you better watch out."

"Why?"

"They're allowed to have more than one wife, aren't they?"

"He makes a move, he'll be one dead sheik."

"Proprietary, aren't we?"

He leaned over to kiss me, then buried his face in my neck. "I'm glad the trial is over," he murmured.

David's father died before he was born, and he'd lost his mother at seven. He'd gone into foster care after that, bouncing from one home to another. Some were good. Some weren't. He didn't talk about it much. But he didn't need to. I knew what he wanted. Stability. Security. Routine. For him it was more than a want. Or a need. It was a prerequisite—the defining quality of his existence.

Some time later, when his even, quiet breathing told me he was asleep, I crept out of bed. Our room faced west, and I stared out the window. Lights twinkled, marking the streets in a repetitive series of grids that stretched to the horizon. It was hard to get lost in this city. You always knew where you were. David liked it that way. I wasn't so sure.

TWENTY-ONE

"I THOUGHT WE'D go out for dinner," I said when I picked Rachel up from Science Club. "I have to go to the studio later."

There was no response.

"Want to go to that salad place?"

"With you?"

"Uh—yeah."

She rolled her eyes.

"I take it that's a no."

She leaned forward and snapped on the radio. A loud bass hammered the console, and an angry voice yelled about white sluts and guns. Mercifully, Rachel changed the station, but another rapster, sounding very much like the first, flooded through the speakers. Looking over, I was about to suggest she turn it off when it occurred to me that she'd reprogrammed the buttons in the Volvo. I keep classic rock and NPR at my fingertips; I don't do rap.

What's more, Rachel knew she wasn't supposed to play with the radio without special dispensation. I caught her watching me out of the corner of her eye.

That's when I got it. She'd changed them deliberately and was waiting for my reaction.

I had to make an instant choice, one of those small, perhaps insignificant parental decisions that, nonetheless, fills me with panic. Should I remind her of the rules and reinforce my role as a disciplinarian, which would escalate the conflict between us? Or should I let it slide, thus giving her a degree of power she hadn't yet earned? What was the right choice?

I mulled it over. It was a minor incident. Neither of us would remember it five years from now. But isn't that what parenting is? An aggregate of unimportant decisions that mold a child into adult? What if I made the wrong choice? Would she resent me for the rest of her life? Would she turn into an ax murderer? I waited for divine inspiration.

"Okay," I said when it didn't come. "How about Italian?" Better to have *shalom bayit*—peace in the house— at least for today.

She slouched lower in her seat. Her eyes slid to the radio, then narrowed into horizontal slits like they do when she's happy. "Cool."

I SANK ONTO the couch in Hank's editing suite, wrapping my jacket around me to ward off the chill. He'd agreed to stay overtime to help me edit a new demo reel for Great Lakes Oil. Styles in video production change, and I wanted to include some clips with an MTV look: quick cuts, strobed action, hot music.

While Hank set up the decks, I studied his collection of frogs, a cheerful jumble of amphibians given to him by clients, including a frog wearing a beret, a toad in a turban, and my contribution, a frog holding a menorah.

He swiveled around and saw what I was looking at. "Got a new one coming."

"What's that?"

"A frog with chopsticks. Guy's bringing it from Shanghai."

"It was probably made in Japan."

Shrugging, he turned back to the Avid and loaded a CD into the drive.

"Is that my old reel?"

"Yup. I backed it up."

"You're so smart. We'll be out of here in no time."

"It doesn't matter." He sighed. "Not much else is happening."

How could I resist with an opening like that? "And what does that mean, kimosabe?"

"Kimosabe?" He got up and headed down the hall. "You are a dinosaur."

I followed him to the tape library, where all Mac's shows are stored. "I'm donating my bones to the Field Museum."

He grunted as he punched in the code on the wall panel. "What shows do you want to add?"

"How about the most recent one we did for Midwest Mutual—you remember—the one for Claims? And the promo for the Jewish Broadcasting Network. And maybe the opening of Atlantic Wireless."

"No Marian Iverson?"

I shot him a look.

"Hey, we got paid."

"I thought we all agreed the price was too high."

Back in the editing room, he hunched over the keyboard. He set up the Avid for digitizing, then hit the Record button. As video played through the monitor, his shoulders sagged.

"Okay, Hank. What's wrong?"

For a moment, I thought he wasn't going to answer. Then, "There's this girl . . ."

The light from the monitor cast a pale glow across his face. For some reason, I'd never associated him with a woman before. Not that I thought he was gay. But with his slender build, ponytail, and magic fingers, he seemed almost androgynous. A sprite, too ethereal for the messy emotions the rest of us get mired in. But now, watching him fidget, it occurred to me how blinding the myopia of self-absorption can be.

"Tell me about her."

"She's a musician. Alto sax. I met her at the White Hen. She was buying cereal and milk." He smiled wistfully. "At two in the morning."

"What's her name?"

"Sandy. Sandy Tooley." It rolled off his tongue. "We got together a few times. She was really nice, you know?" His eyes were faraway and unfocused. I knew that look. It's the one that says, *I can still taste her skin, her lips, her body.* "I thought she really liked me. I mean, she acted as if—" He broke off.

"It's okay," I said softly.

He swallowed hard. "Everything was great for a couple of weeks. Better than great. Then I called her the other day—night—when I got off—to tell her I was on my way over. Except she said not to come. She said she had things to do. I wasn't—well—real happy about it. I really wanted to see her, you know?"

"So you went over there anyway."

He didn't answer.

I shaded my eyes. "And when you got there, she was with another man."

"How did you know?"

"I'm sorry."

"She said it was her old boyfriend, and that she would call me later." He took a shaky breath. "That was Monday, Ellie. I haven't heard from her."

Today was Wednesday.

"Maybe they were just talking."

"For three days?"

An hour later we'd finished digitizing the new pieces and cut in the excerpts. We were just winding up when the phone rang. Hank grabbed it. Though I only had a view of his back, I could tell it was Sandy. His spine straightened. His voice grew silky and eager. He ran a hand through his hair.

I ducked out of the room and wandered into Mac's office. It was a comfortable room with two floor-to-ceiling windows that spilled pools of yellow across the dark expanse of lawn. The studio was tucked away on an industrial block in Northbrook. At night, without the bustle from nearby businesses, it was quiet and isolated.

Hank's muffled voice drifted through the air. "He was? You're sure?" I heard a relieved exhalation. Then, in that eager, breathy voice, "Yes. About an hour." A pause. "Me, too." Then, "Don't get dressed." The receiver was replaced with a click.

I strolled back into the editing room. Hank was beaming, his smile so contagious I had to return it.

"She was out of town."

"Get out of here, Hank. We can finish tomorrow."

His smile broadened.

"Out." I pointed to the door.

"Tell you what. Lemme finish this edit, and I'll dub it in the morning."

"Better yet, if you set up the machines, I'll run the dubs myself."

"You don't have to."

"It's okay. I can lock up."

"Well . . ." Indecision and desire warred on his face. "Mac—"

"Don't worry. I'm sure he trusts me to lock a door."

Desire won. Hank finished the last edit and added black to the tail of the piece. Then he went into a side room to set up the dubs. After checking to see that the VHS machines were in sync, he started them rolling. "Thanks, Ellie. This means a lot."

"Go away before I change my mind."

He grabbed his backpack and bolted. I heard him race down the hall and out the door. Young love.

Seating myself in his chair, I swiveled in front of the bank of monitors. We'd added three new excerpts and deleted three others. As the signals changed from digital impulses to magnetic signals and then to images and sounds, I marveled at the magic of technology.

The reel was less than eight minutes. When it was over, I checked the dubs to make sure an image had indeed been recorded, then rewound and ejected them from the decks. The silence was sudden and deep. Hank had said not to shut down the Avid, so I gathered my bag and the shows we'd pulled.

As I walked back into the tape library, I mentally indexed my clients of the past few years: Midwest Mutual; Seagrave's Food Service; Van Allen, the paper company; Brisco Chemicals. I'd produced shows for them all. The corporate handmaiden.

It hadn't started out that way. I'd graduated college with dreams of becoming the American Lina Wertmuller who also produced substantive documentaries on the side. Seamlessly segueing from the arts to politics in a highly versatile and acclaimed career. Instead, I got married.

I was restacking the Midwest Mutual show on the shelf, thinking how time really does mellow us all, when the door to the library slammed shut. I stood where I was, uncomprehending. Then I realized it had to be Hank. He must have forgotten something.

"Hank?"

I thought I heard footsteps on the other side of the door. "What'd you forget, lover boy?"

No answer. I went to the door, intending to give him *shtick* about Sandy and how she'd be dressed to the nines if he didn't get over there soon.

I twisted the knob. It didn't move. I tried again. Nothing. "Hank, are you there? The door's locked."

Silence. I thought I heard a squeak. "Hank. Stop screwing around."

I listened again and thought I heard a quiet rustling on the other side. Like paper being shuffled. Then a sharp, pungent smell. Familiar. Almost tangy. I banged my fists against the door.

"Hank. Come on. Something's wrong. Open up."

No one responded. I kept banging until my fist was sore. I pressed my ear against the door. I felt a sensation of warmth. Strange. I hadn't expended that much energy. I leaned my palms against the door. More warmth. I looked down. At the bottom of the door, orange light flickered.

My brain connected. The smell. Like a parking garage! Gasoline!

I broke out in a sweat. Fire! And I was trapped. "Help!" I screamed. "Anyone. Fire! Open up!"

I beat on the door with my palms until they stung. When nothing happened, I threw myself against it, hoping to smash the lock. Pain radiated through my shoulder, but the door held.

The room seemed to have heated up ten degrees. "Help! Please!" I looked wildly around. Wasn't there supposed to be a fire extinguisher in every room? Not here. No windows. No pictures. Not even a nail in the wall. But when I scanned the ceiling, a wave of relief surged through me. A sprinkler. Of course. Water would gush down and extinguish the fire. All I had to do was wait.

I started pacing. I should call the fire department. I automatically looked for my bag, then realized I'd dropped it—and my cell—on the other side of the door. Damn! Meanwhile, crackles replaced the rustles on the other side of the door. The doorknob was too hot to touch. Wisps of black smoke seeped under the door. Didn't I read that most fire fatalities came from smoke inhalation, not flames? I covered my mouth with my hand. Why weren't the damned sprinklers working? Mac would never let fire prevention slip below code, would he? Should I stuff something under the crack in the door?

Another smell, like burning tires, wormed itself into my nose and throat. I tried to remember what I knew about fire. Never open a door if it was hot to the touch; a new source of oxygen would fan the flames. No problem. It was so hot I couldn't open it.

Now thick curls of smoke were rising on my side of the door. The heat pressed against my skin. I was starting to sweat. Where was the water? The only way out was through the door. I might have to break it down to open it. But if I did, I might create a back draft. What should I do? I couldn't wait much longer.

I started to case the library, trying not to feel desperate. But aside from the tapes, the shelves, and the stepladder, which was too heavy to lift, there was nothing in the room. No windows. No furniture. Not even a trash can. I sucked down hot air.

The shelves. They were the do-it-yourself kind that could be disassembled and put together in multiple configurations. Studying them, I got an idea. When they got going, the sprinklers would help douse the fire. If I could somehow use a shelf to break through the door when the water started, I might make it out.

But that required the sprinklers to kick in. I looked up at the ceiling. Sweat dripped down the back of my neck. What was taking them so damn long? The ones in the hall, at least, should have been on by now. My heart sank. Mac probably hadn't updated the system since he first moved in. And that was ten years ago. It was possible they weren't going to work.

Smoke billowed under the doorjamb and started to rise, saturating my clothes and hair. Heat blanketed the room like a shroud. I struggled to take a breath. If the sprinkler didn't start soon, it wouldn't matter. I dropped to the floor to find some breathable air. My stomach leapt to my chest. Flames licked the bottom of the door.

I got up and lunged at the closest shelf. As the tapes on it clattered to the floor, I banged on the underside to dislodge it. But the metal teeth gripped the slots in the frame. Nothing moved. The smoke thickened and moved lower. I coughed. Sweat poured off my forehead. I kept pounding the underside of the shelf.

Finally I was able to maneuver one of the teeth out of its slot. I kept banging; another one popped out. Grabbing the free end, I twisted and jerked. The shelf came free.

It was a bulky, awkward piece of metal, about a yard long, a foot wide, an inch thick. I looked up. Smoke was dimming my eyesight, but the sprinklers were still dry. I was running out of time. I stepped back, holding the shelf like a battering ram. I swung it back to gain momentum, then smashed it into the door. The door shook. Something cracked, but it held. I backed up, clutching the shelf, but a spasm of coughing stopped me. There was too much smoke. The shelf slipped from my hands.

I dropped to the floor and crawled to the other side of the room. But the air over there was just as smoky. I felt woozy. I forced myself to start naming the fifty states. I couldn't give up.

When the water finally streamed down, its force stung my skin and startled me awake. I was lying on the floor dazed and sleepy. The spray drenched me and seemed to dissolve the wall of smoke. I mouthed a prayer of thanks.

Slowly I got to my feet. I picked up the shelf one more time and rammed it into the door. This time the veneer splintered, and a jagged hole appeared. I tore at it with my hands, breaking off slivers of wood. Finally, the hole I'd made was large enough to thrust my arm through. I stripped off my jacket and wrapped a sleeve around my hand. Then I reached through to unlock the door from the other side. Grabbing the shelf, I flung myself into the hall.

Flames danced along the floor and walls, but no fireball engulfed me. The sprinklers were doing their job. Using the shelf as a shield, I staggered through rising steam toward Mac's office. I could make out the dim shape of the windows. I stumbled over to one, drew back the shelf, and rammed it as hard as I could. Glass shattered. An alarm sounded. Using the shelf, I broke off shards of glass that still clung to the frame and crawled through the window.

TWENTY-TWO

I WAS STILL gulping down air when the fire department arrived. My throat felt gritty, I was dizzy, and I was bleeding in two places on my legs. After checking my vitals, the paramedics insisted on taking me to the ER, but I refused. I did let them lead me to the ambulance, where they gave me a wet towel and a bottle of water, and bandaged my cuts. I wiped off some of the soot that covered me and slung my jacket over my shoulders. By the time Mac arrived, the fire had been reduced to a residue of sodden debris.

"A shelf?" After being briefed by the battalion chief, Mac came over and grabbed my shoulders. "You broke out of the library with a shelf?"

"Someone locked me in."

"Where was Hank?"

"He left."

"Are you okay?"

I thought about making a crack about being toasted on a stick like a marshmallow, but when I looked at Mac, I changed my mind. Usually a consummate prep, he was wearing wrinkled khakis and a stained T-shirt. That stiff-upper-lip Wasp thing he does had vanished, an expression of fear and relief in its place. I nodded.

"Christ, Ellie. You could have been killed."

I started to shrug, but the movement turned into a shudder, and the shudder into a sob. The tears started, and I sagged against Mac. He held me until it passed.

I WASHED MY hair three times, but it still smelled like smoke the next morning. Mac called to tell me the police had picked up Hank and held him for six hours at the station. They let him go around five.

"They can't think he had anything to do—"

"Not anymore." Mac's voice was grim. I got the feeling it hadn't been a fun time. "His girlfriend waited for him. They went back to her place."

Two points for Sandy.

"They *are* treating it as an arson, aren't they?"

"They won't confirm it, but I overheard the firemen talking about burn patterns and accelerant."

"Have you been back over?"

"The hall's totally gone. So is the Avid. Hank's editing room is in bad shape, too, and the tape library is ruined." He sighed. "And then there's my window."

"Oh, God. I'm so sorry, Mac."

"Yeah, well, I've been meaning to reorganize. But the camera gear is okay. And the other editing room is okay. Once we clean up the smoke damage, we'll be back in business."

Always the optimist. "No ideas who did it?"

"Not that they're telling me."

I cleared my throat. "Mac . . ." I stopped. Rachel was standing at the kitchen door. "I'll call you later."

I sat her down and told her an abbreviated version of what had happened. She blanched, then jumped up and threw her arms around me. "I want to stay home from school. With you."

"I love you, too, sweetie." I hugged her close. "But you can't get out of it that easily."

Somehow I forgot to call my father.

Village Detective Dan O'Malley showed up around nine. With shaggy red hair and freckled skin, he looks almost like a kid, except for his mustache and his height. He's at least six four, and he fills any room he enters. But I'd dealt with him before, and we'd achieved a grudging respect for each other—an accomplishment, considering my attitude toward law enforcement and his toward nosy women. I poured coffee, aware that he was looking me over. I imagined him opening with "A fine kettle of fish we're in now, Ollie."

He sipped his coffee. "How you feeling this morning?" His voice was surprisingly soft for a man of his bulk.

"Like a slab of ribs at an all-you-can-eat barbecue."

"You seem to have a talent for attracting trouble."

"I guess you could look at it that way."

"Why? How do *you* look at it?"

"The same way I did last night when your officers questioned me. I think it has something to do with Johnnie Santoro."

"The man whose trial you testified at."

I nodded. "His lawyer was killed a few days ago."

"So I hear."

I leaned against the counter. I was certain that the fire was linked to Santoro, Mary Jo, and Calumet Park. First Rhonda Disapio dies in an "accident." Then Brashares in a robbery gone bad. Now someone was trying to turn me into a crispy critter.

The problem was I couldn't prove it. I couldn't provide any evidence. And with nothing to back up my suspicions, the cops last night didn't take me seriously. But, then, why should they? I'd been put in my place at the trial. Hammered by a rising star in state law enforcement.

As if reading my mind, O'Malley looked over. "If there's something you want to tell me, now would be a good time."

I hesitated, then ran him through the events since the trial, including what I'd learned from Rhonda and Sweeney. "Bottom line: I think Santoro was working a deal, and Mary Jo was his mule or his courier or something."

"Drugs?"

I nodded. "It fell apart, they panicked, and Mary Jo was killed."

"They?"

"Before she died, Rhonda Disapio told me two guys showed up at the boat launch at Calumet Park. She said they killed Mary Jo."

"Why didn't she say that at trial?"

"She was scared. They tried to come after her, after they got Mary Jo, but she got away. She didn't want to take any chances."

"I don't know." O'Malley shook his head. "Sounds weak."

"Not if they were mixed up with the Mob."

"Who?"

"The guys at Calumet Park. Santoro, too. He might even have ended up taking the fall for them."

O'Malley brushed a finger across his mustache. "You have any proof?"

"It depends on your definition." I told him that Santoro was a longshoreman but wasn't well liked. And that he'd told Sweeney before the murder that he was onto something big.

"Like I said, do you have any proof?"

"Well, Rhonda Disapio did die in that 'accident.'"

"After she told you about the men at Calumet Park."

"And a few days later, Brashares was killed."

"And you think it's all connected."

"Brashares could have known the men who killed Mary Jo. Maybe they pressured him to make sure Santoro took the fall. But maybe he had second thoughts. Maybe he threatened to blow it wide open, and they had to shut him up."

"Got it all figured out, huh?"

"Just coming up with possibilities."

"And now you think the Mob's behind this alleged arson. That there's some kind of conspiracy—I don't know—to silence you."

"It is possible, isn't it?"

"But why? Why would they be coming after you?"

I bit my lip. "Because I figured it out?"

He shook his head. "Ellie, how would they know? It's not like you've been broadcasting it on the news."

He had a point.

"Tell me," he said. "What evidence can you provide that would help me find out?"

I didn't answer.

He tapped a finger on his cup. "Aside from this Santoro business, is there anyone else you can think of—besides the Mafia—who'd want to do you harm?"

I wouldn't meet his eyes. "Not at the moment."

"I see."

The most I could get out of him was a promise to call the detectives assigned to Brashares's murder.

A young investigator from the fire department showed up after O'Malley left. He ran through what I gathered was a required checklist. He asked where I'd been when the fire first appeared; what I saw, heard, and smelled. He asked about the color of the smoke and flames, and whether I heard an explosion. He pulled out a sketch of the studio's floor plan and asked me to retrace my steps from the time we finished the dubs until I crawled through the window. He left a few minutes later, a satisfied look on his face.

I'm glad someone was satisfied. I felt like I'd spent a hundred dollars at the grocery store and come home with nothing.

WHEN RACHEL ANDI got back from school that afternoon, Fouad was tramping across the lawn, waving a leaf blower. He turned it off when he saw us.

"I heard about the fire on the radio." He looked worried.

"News travels fast." I skirted the piles of leaves he'd collected.

"You are not hurt?"

I shook my head.

"That is good." His eyes fastened on something behind me.

I turned to see Rachel with a worried expression of her own. "Aren't you coming in, Mom?" She pulled on the straps of her backpack.

"I want to talk to Fouad for a minute. You could start practicing the piano."

"You'll just be a minute, right?"

"You bet." I brushed a curl off her forehead. "You can watch me through the window." She nodded and went inside.

"What is going on, Ellie?"

I turned around. "I think someone is trying to kill me."

Fouad moved here from Syria over thirty years ago, knowing his appearance, accent, and customs would always mark him as an outsider. That he would never be treated with the back-slapping heartiness white America reserves for itself. Yet this outsider had risked his life for me. There weren't many people I trusted more.

His eyes narrowed. "Who?"

"I don't know. I don't know anything—except that it began with Santoro."

I took him through the chronology. When I finished, he took the leaf blower off his shoulder. He doesn't dwell on it, but Fouad knows about the dark, evil underbelly of human nature.

"Why do you think it's the Mafia?"

"Because whoever is behind this doesn't want something exposed, and they're using a lot of resources to make sure it isn't. I don't know many other organizations with that kind of clout."

We walked back to his pickup where he put down the leaf blower. "But why are they after you?"

"I—I'm not entirely sure. I did meet with Rhonda Disapio before she died. She was the one who told me about the two men. She thought she was being followed. Maybe they saw us together."

He pulled out a rake from the truck. "But this has been the only incident directed against you? Since the trial?"

I thought about the SUV I'd seen when Susan and I took a walk. You couldn't really call that an "incident." I wasn't even sure it was significant. "There was nothing," I said, "until Brashares died."

"And he died—they broke into his office and attacked him."

"Tossed the place and cleaned out his safe."

Fouad was quiet as he raked the separate mounds of leaves together into one large pile. Then he looked up. "Perhaps there was something in his office that connected them to you."

"In his office?" I kicked a few leaves and watched them swirl in the air before settling. I hardly knew Brashares. I'd only been in his office once. In fact, since the trial, we'd only talked once or twice. Most of our communication was on answering machines. Playing phone tag.

The phone.

I looked up.

"What?" Fouad asked.

"I left a message on Brashares's machine."

Fouad's jaw tightened.

"I said something about Santoro and the men at Calumet Park." I hugged my chest. "Do you think that's it? I mean, if they were following Rhonda, they already suspected I knew something. And then, when they heard the message . . ."

"What are you saying?"

"I'm saying that the people who broke into Brashares's office might have listened to the messages on his answering machine. And heard the one where I mentioned the 'men at Calumet Park.' That could be the link." The temperature was in the fifties, but my palms were sweaty. "Oh God. Me and my big mouth."

Fouad tried to comfort me. "The Koran says, 'Allah does not impose upon any soul a duty but to the extent of its ability.' You were only doing what you thought you should."

"Even so, it backfired." I chewed on a finger. "Fouad, what do I do? The police don't believe any of this."

"Then you must convince them."

The plink of piano chords floated through the window. "How? I don't have any evidence."

He smiled. "You will find it, I am certain of that."

I wasn't quite sure how to take that, but coming from Fouad, it had to be a compliment. He bundled the leaves into a canvas tarp, tied the ends, and carried it to the back of his truck.

I followed him. "Oh. I almost forgot. I met someone from your part of the world the other day."

He looked over.

"A new client of David's. A Saudi oil sheik. He says he's related to the royal family."

"What's his name?"

"Abdul Al Hamarani. He's trying to buy a plant from Great Lakes Oil."

"There are thousands of royals in Saudi Arabia," he said. I must have looked crestfallen because he added, "I have a friend from Riyadh. I'll ask about him when I see him at prayers."

I went into the kitchen to think about dinner.

Rachel called from the living room, "Next week is the end of Science Club, you know."

"Already?" Where had the time gone?

"Well, the first session. They're having Parents' Day on Friday. Are you coming?"

I missed a lot when Rachel was young. Swimming lessons. Soccer games. Her violin recital. I remember thinking they couldn't possibly be as important as my work.

After the divorce, my priorities changed. Now I try not to miss anything.

I went into the living room. "Of course I'm coming. Why? What's up?"

"It's a surprise." She grinned. "But you'll like it."

I swatted her on her rear end. "Tease."

O'MALLEY GOT BACK to me that night. "I called down to Area Three and talked to the dicks handling Brashares's case."

"And?"

"They're sticking with the program."

"A botched robbery?"

"They say he was in the wrong place at the wrong time."

"Convenient, isn't it?"

"Ellie." O'Malley cleared his throat. "I know you had problems last summer. But lightning doesn't strike twice. Unless you can give me something, there's nothing I can do. Christ, I wouldn't know where to start anyway. Your story covers almost every friggin' police jurisdiction in Cook County."

"It's not a story."

"Well, it isn't a case." He paused. "Look, you know how it works. Give me something I can work with. Otherwise, all I got is a suspicious fire. Which could have been set by anyone."

I thought about the message I'd left on Brashares's machine. That wasn't evidence, either. At best, it was conjecture. But it was obvious O'Malley wasn't eager to take me on.

I kept my mouth shut.

TWENTY-THREE

I'D ALWAYS CONSIDERED our village a quiet place where nothing much happens until I discovered some history no one talks about much. Apparently, there used to be a bar behind the train station. It was a popular watering hole, especially on Fridays, when the owner took it upon himself to cash his customers' paychecks. Except for one Friday morning around three, when four masked men robbed the place at gunpoint and escaped with fifty thousand dollars. The community was shocked. Shocked. What sort of people would keep that much cash on the premises? It came out later that the owner was running a "finance and loan" business on the side.

The bar is now gone, but the owner's family isn't. Specifically, Joey DePalma, aka the Surgeon, and his brothers. They were part of the old Grand Avenue crew but moved to the suburbs in the sixties. His brothers didn't stay; their bodies were found in a Wisconsin field a couple of years later. DePalma made a precipitous retirement after that.

I once asked O'Malley why they called him the Surgeon. He said DePalma was known for his skill with a knife. But that was a long time ago, he added. DePalma led a quiet life now, enjoying his grandchildren and garden. And the careful scrutiny of village cops.

The next morning found me driving down a residential street a mile from my house. Some of the homes, products of remodeling, were upscale two-story structures, but most were modest splits and ranches. Midway down the block was a brown brick ranch with a cedar shake roof and a well-tended lawn. I was surprised how well the house blended in; I'd expected something showier.

I climbed out of the Volvo and made my way to the front porch. The screen door had one of those fancy *D*s in the middle. I was about to ring the bell when I stopped. What was I doing? You don't just drop in on a mobster for tea. I started back to the car.

"Can I help you?"

I spun around. Coming around the side of the house was a man pushing a wheelbarrow. He appeared to be in his seventies and had a big belly that spilled over baggy pants, but his shirt revealed brawny arms and shoulders. He wore thick black glasses, and his skin looked as if he'd a bad case of acne as a youth. Oddly enough, that made him seem more approachable.

I pasted on what I hoped was a sincere smile. "I was just—I was just admiring your garden."

He flicked his eyes toward his flower beds, which, since the frost last week, consisted of dead marigolds, withered salvia, and a few scraggly petunias.

"I mean, over the summer." I stammered. "It must have been gorgeous."

He looked me up and down, then picked up the wheelbarrow handles. "If you're selling something, we're not interested."

"I'm not selling anything," I said. "My name is Ellie Foreman. I live in the neighborhood."

He paused, then straightened up and motioned toward

the house. "My wife Lenora handles the charity dona-
tions."

I turned around. A soft, round woman was watching us
from the door. She wore beige stretch pants and a long,
flowery tunic, and her hair was tinted a brassy red. She
was wearing glasses, too. Oversized, with blue frames.

"I'm not here for money, sir." I took a breath. "The
truth is—I need your help."

He gave me another once-over. "You say you live
around here?"

"A few blocks away."

After a long moment, he beckoned me to follow him
and went inside the house. As he brushed by his wife, he
said, "Go into the kitchen, Lenora."

She disappeared without a word.

I followed him in. To the left was the narrow hallway
Lenora had just passed through, to my right a sunken living room. The carpeting was beige, the furniture, too. A
crucifix hung over the fireplace. End tables were crowded
with photographs of small children and young parents,
most with sunny smiles on their faces. But the hall we
were standing in was gloomy, and the open door hadn't
filtered out that musty smell that clings to old people's
homes.

"What's the problem, miss?"

"I think someone may be trying to kill me. But I'm not
sure who it is or why they're doing it." I felt the trepi-
dation in my voice. "I—I'm afraid, and I want it to stop.
I don't know who to turn to."

His eyebrows arranged themselves into an annoyed expression. "I'm a retired senior citizen, living on a pension.
Whaddaya think I can do?"

I swallowed. "I think it might have something to do
with my testimony at Johnnie Santoro's trial."

His expression didn't change.

"Somebody thinks I know something. But I don't know
who it is or what I'm supposed to know. I'm a single

mother. I have a daughter." I looked over at the photographs. "I'm all she has. Sir," I added.

DePalma looked me over for what seemed like a long time, though it probably was only a few seconds. Then, "You have a problem, get in touch with my lawyer. William Casey. At Brickman, Casey, and Scott. He'll help you."

"Mr. DePalma, with all due respect, your lawyer can't help me, and I think you know it."

"Young lady, like I said, I'm just a retiree on a pension. I can't help you." He took a step forward. "And now, you're gonna have to leave."

My stomach twisted. "Please, Mr. DePalma. I was almost killed in a fire the other day. It was arson. But the police don't know who's behind it. And it doesn't seem like they want to find out."

He paused. "Where was the fire?"

"In Northbrook. At a video studio."

He pulled out a clean, white handkerchief from his pocket. I took it as a hopeful sign.

"I thought perhaps you'd consider looking into it, and . . . well, maybe . . ." My voice trailed off.

He held the handkerchief to his face, blew his nose, and tucked it back in his pocket. Then he placed his hand on my arm. The back of his hand was covered with dark hair, and his fingers were thick and stubby. I could see that hand wielding a knife.

"Ms. Foreman, it's time for you to go."

The Surgeon guided me out. The door closed quietly behind me.

DAVID WAS EN route to London and wasn't reachable until evening. Because of the time difference, I woke him up. But when I told him about the fire, the drowsiness in his voice vanished.

"My God, Ellie. I'll fly back tomorrow."

"Don't. I'm fine."

"Are you sure?"

My throat was scratchy, and I still thought I smelled smoke everywhere, but he didn't have to know that. "I'm sure."

Silence. Then, "What about Rachel?"

"She's fine. Katie's sleeping over. It's Halloween."

When I was young, Halloween was my favorite holiday. Not anymore. Grisly costumes and nasty pranks have stripped the holiday of all its charm. I can't understand people who spend hundreds of dollars to celebrate the macabre.

Happily, Rachel was too old for trick-or-treating, but one of her friends was having a party the following night, and the girls were trying on every article of clothing in Rachel's closet in an effort to pull together some costumes.

". . . isn't good, Ellie."

I realized I hadn't been listening. "I'm sorry, David. What was that?"

"I said this isn't good."

"I know. But, at least no one was hurt, and—"

"No." David cut in. "Not that."

I stared at the broom closet. The door was half open. Maybe I should close it all the way. "What?"

He paused. "I'm concerned you might be in danger. I want to be with you."

"I don't need your protection." I bit my tongue. "I'm sorry. I didn't mean that."

"Maybe you did."

"David—"

"Look, I know you can take care of yourself. But when you care for someone, at least when I do, I want to make sure they're safe."

"Please don't take this the wrong way, but don't you think you might be projecting a wee bit?"

"What if I am?" His voice rose. "I'll admit I'm not a big risk taker." He paused. "The biggest risk I ever took was falling in love with you."

I swallowed.

"I didn't say that to make you feel guilty. I—I guess—I just wish none of this had happened."

"Do you think I should have kept my mouth shut? Even though I didn't—and still don't—believe Santoro killed Mary Jo?"

I heard his sigh over seven thousand miles. "No, of course not. But there isn't a day that passes that I'm not afraid for you."

I cleared my throat. This probably wasn't the time to tell him about DePalma.

"Ellie, I don't want this to sound like an ultimatum. But I'd like to suggest we both do some thinking."

I gripped the phone. "About what?"

"About us and how we can make this work. We're such different people."

"I thought that's why you were attracted to me. You know, action woman meets pensive man."

I heard a strangled sound on his end. I closed the door to the broom closet.

"Why don't we both do some thinking?" he said after a pause. "I'll call you next week."

"David?"

"What?" I heard the rise of his breath.

I bit back a reply. "Nothing. I—I'll talk to you later."

I hung up and started to load the dishwasher, but as I transferred a plate to the machine, it fell to the floor and shattered.

"Dammit." I kicked the cabinet under the sink. "Shit." My toes throbbed.

By the time I swept up the pieces, it was dark outside, a thick, heavy darkness in which objects lose definition. I put the broom away. What was I doing? Why was I picking fights with David? He was right about one thing. The bubble wrap of suburban life was no guarantee of safety. But his response was to avoid risk. Insulate himself with routine. Mine was to rush the front lines wielding a saber, refusing to cave in to fear.

It was a problem.

TWENTY-FOUR

MAC CALLED WITH good news on Monday. The insurance company would pay for most of the cleanup, plus the equipment replacement. In fact, Mac had decided to upgrade to a better Avid. Faster chips, better processor, and the ability to author to DVD.

"So everything in the tape room is gone?" I asked.

"I'm sorry, Ellie. I know a lot of your shows were in there."

"No. I'm the one who should apologize."

"Why?"

"I may have been the target."

"Yeah. The police asked me about that."

"What did you tell them?"

He didn't say anything, but I heard an entire conversation in his silence.

"Mac?"

"Look, Ellie," he said. "I have a lot of rebuilding to do. I have a family to support. If someone was sending us a message, I heard it loud and clear. I don't want to get involved."

"So you're—"

"I don't know who was responsible for the fire. Or why. And I don't want to. I just want it all to go away."

"So I'm out there on my own."

"You don't have to be."

I changed the subject. "How's Hank? I've tried calling, but we keep trading messages. Has he recovered?"

Mac laughed. "Let me put it this way. If this is how he reacts to stress, I'll have to pile more on."

Sandy must be something.

I hung up and looked outside. The sky was that heart-breaking shade of blue you only see in autumn. I called Susan to walk, but she works part-time in an art gallery and had already left the house. I threw on sneakers and sweats, feeling resentful toward everyone who had a place to go and a job to do.

I stretched and jogged over to Voltz Road. Twisting and turning through the forest preserve, Voltz has no sidewalks, just narrow shoulders of gravel. Huge trees shield the estates on either side. But the canopy of leaves now looked ragged, and leaves crunched under my feet.

Two years ago Rachel and I were driving down Voltz when we saw a fawn lying in the middle of the road. As we drew closer, it started to make small jerky motions, and I saw blood seeping out from under it. The creature's legs and back were broken, and it couldn't roll over, much less stand up.

We stopped and called the cops. Then I carefully picked it up and carried it to the side of road. As I carefully lowered it into a ditch, the fawn's large, obsidian eyes locked onto mine, and I was sure I saw an awareness in them that this was not the right order of things. That something very fundamental in its young universe had irrevocably shifted.

When the cop showed up, he inspected the fawn and said, "You know what I have to do."

"No." Rachel cried, clutching my arm.

I pulled her to me and spoke over her head. "Could you—would you wait until we leave?"

I led my sobbing daughter to the car and drove away. A shot rang out. Neither of us looked back.

Now, as I jogged past the ditch, caught up in the ache of the memory, I barely registered the black limo that eased past me. But limos weren't unusual in this neighborhood. Neither were SUVs, and I didn't make any connections when a dark green one passed behind the limo, followed, seconds later, by a gray sedan.

A moment later, I stopped. An animal, about fifteen inches long, was blocking my path. Clumps of straw-colored fur stuck out from scaly, pink skin. The creature had beady eyes, tiny floppy ears, and something that could have been a tail. I stared, not quite sure what I was looking at: a skinned rat, an albino raccoon, some mutant forest being. Then it trotted toward me on squat little legs.

A dog.

"Spike." A male voice cut through the air. "Get over here."

The animal hesitated, as if it were weighing whether to obey the command, but before it could decide, a man stepped out from the bushes. He was short, wearing a fancy sport shirt, slacks, and Italian loafers. Gray streaks ran through dark hair. He was holding a white leather leash studded with colored rhinestones that flashed in the sun. Dark glasses covered his eyes.

As we faced off, a fierce squeal came from the dog. I took a startled step back. The dog lifted his leg against a bush to mark his territory. When he was finished, his ears pricked up, and he barked again, though it wasn't clear at what. The man bent over and scooped up the creature with one hand. He flipped up his glasses with the other.

"Sorry." Cool eyes gazed at me. "Spike ain't having a good day."

"What's wrong with him?"

The man shrugged. "The vet don't know. Cushing's disease, he says. Maybe hypothyroid. Who knows? The little shit's on six different medicines. Costs me a fuckin' fortune."

"Oh." I started to resume my run. The man blocked my path.

"Hold on there, Miss Foreman."

I froze.

I briefly considered making a break for it. I might be able to put some distance between us—he was weighed down with the dog. But when a beefy man who looked like a linebacker suddenly materialized at the next corner, I changed my mind.

"The car's around the corner." Hitching his thumb, the man with the dog smiled. He had crooked but very white teeth. "How 'bout we go for a ride."

A cloud moved across the sun, not darkening as much as leaching the color out of things. I wiped damp hands on my sweats. The goon came forward and, clamping a firm hand on my arm, led me around the corner. He opened the door to the limo, unfolded the jump seat, and directed me in. Spike and the man climbed in the back.

We drove past the bridge at the west end of Voltz and headed north on Waukegan Road. Spike curled up on a blue blanket that lay on the backseat. At close range, I could see the dog's skin was flaking off. Large patches settled on the blanket, and his body gave off a sour smell.

"It started about ten months ago." The man ran his hand down Spike's back. "I thought it was cancer, but they keep tellin' me it ain't. Turns out Maltese get these weird diseases."

We passed the Park District pool Rachel lived at most of last summer.

"Just drive around for a while, Vinny."

"Sure thing." Vinny drove a few miles per hour under the limit.

"Who are you?" I asked.

He ignored the question. "You got a dog?"

Rachel had pestered me for one, but I didn't give in. I

saw *Old Yeller.* I know what happens when you let a dog into your life. I shook my head.

"Maybe you should. Keep you from bothering nice old men."

DePalma.

We passed a church with a billboard advertising their Friday night fish fry and bingo. The man picked up Spike, letting the dog lick his cheek. "You can't go up to people and ask them things like you done. These are quality people. They need peace and quiet."

"I didn't know what else to do."

"Someone torched a place you were in, huh?"

DePalma had briefed him. Or else he already knew.

Spike settled down in the man's lap, sinking his head on his paws. "Why don't you tell me about it."

I let out a nervous giggle. The fact that I was in the back of a limo, expected to spill my guts to a wise guy was pretty far out, even for me. "Do you know Johnnie Santoro?"

"The one who offed his girlfriend at Calumet Park."

My pulse sped up. He knew. "I was just wondering. Was he—"

"How 'bout you lemme ask the questions."

We crossed into Lake County where Waukegan Road slows. They say it's because of construction, but it's been that way for years. The cost overruns had to be lining a few pockets quite nicely by now. We inched forward, surrounded by cars, delivery trucks, and a yellow school bus filled with children.

"You had that videotape of Santoro. You testified at his trial."

"Yes."

"What makes you think I know him?"

I took a breath and launched into an explanation. I told him what I'd heard about Santoro's background, the men at the park, and Rhonda Disapio and Brashares's deaths. The fire. But as the words spilled out, the series of events I'd strung together sounded flimsier and more elusive in the retelling than they had in my mind. Not as conspiratorial. Possibly even coincidental. I felt foolish, and I could tell from my companion's expression, which changed from guarded to puzzled to exasperated, that he agreed.

"That ain't a lot to go on," he said.

I looked out the rear window. The dark-colored SUV was in back of us this time. I stiffened. "Are we being followed?"

"Of course." He waved a hand. "The most elite crime-fighting organization in the world checks in every day."

"The FBI?"

"You got it." He twisted around and saluted through the window. "They got these new mikes can pick up anything they point 'em at." The SUV dropped back and switched lanes. A few car lengths back was the gray sedan. It made for an odd procession. He twisted around. "Vinny, you can head back now."

"Yeah, boss."

We turned off Waukegan and started east. As if sensing the change in direction, Spike raised his head and sniffed the air.

"Listen." The man paused. "There ain't nothing there. This Santoro—he ain't connected. He ain't a friend. He ain't even a friend of a friend."

I shifted uncomfortably. "But I thought—"

"You thought wrong."

"I know I don't have what you'd call hard evidence. And I probably haven't done a very good job explaining it. But three people are dead, and I almost died in a fire. Someone's doing something."

His mouth tightened, as if he was losing patience with me. "Look, lady, I don't know who or what's causing your problems. I don't know who torched the place. And you know something? You're probably better off not knowing." He allowed his words to sink in. "I'll tell you what I think. I think You should get out of town for a while. Go on vacation. A nice, long one. It'll do wonders. You'll have a whole new attitude."

We turned south on Skokie Highway. Spike yawned and licked his hairless paws. The man picked him up and nuzzled his neck, oblivious to the flakes of skin that drifted down onto his pants. As we veered off on Sunset Ridge, I squinted against the glare of the sun. When we reached Voltz, we were a block closer to my house than where he'd picked me up.

"Vinny, let her out," he said. The car slowed. "By the way, this conversation never took place."

"How could it?" I said. "I don't know who you are."

He nodded. "Good way to keep it." He motioned for me to open the door. I slid over and climbed out. He leaned to the side to close it, but I kept my hand on the handle.

"I hope it works out for Spike."

He gave me a curt nod.

I TRUDGED BACK to the house. The sidewalk was flecked with chips that glinted like diamonds. DePalma's pal could be telling the truth; then again, he might not. But then, why come all this way to tell me the Mob wasn't involved with Santoro? I kicked a stone on the path. Dad was right. I was building a house of cards with my theories about drug scams and double-dealing. I'd made a fool of myself. That wasn't anything new, of course, but the fact remained that nothing made sense. If the Mob wasn't involved, if there was no drug deal, why was Mary Jo Bosanick dead? And Rhonda? And Brashares?

I picked up the stone and rolled it between my palms. I suppose I could visit Santoro in jail and ask him point blank, but I shuddered at the thought of going down to Cook County alone. What was I going to say to him? Are you or have you ever been involved in dealing? If he was as big a jerk as Sweeney said, my odds of getting a straight answer were low. And if they framed him as well

as I thought they did, he was just as much a victim as
me. Or Mary Jo. Or Rhonda. No. *Genug iz genug.* Enough
is enough.

I looked both ways, then hurled the stone as far as I
could. There's never an open declaration that a conspiracy
exists. They unfold gradually and subtly, through events
that, if they're connected at all, are often considered coincidental. Odd, perhaps, but not necessarily malevolent.
It's only in the revelation and retelling that one sees the
intent, the planning, the duplicity.

It's like a tree falling in the forest, I thought. *If no one
reveals it, is there still a conspiracy?* Maybe Rhonda did
die in a tragic accident, Brashares in a robbery. Maybe
the fire was some type of insurance-related arson.

And maybe pigs can fly.

I called David at his hotel that night. It was about four
A.M. London time, but he didn't pick up. I turned out the
light and stared at the wall in the dark.

TWENTY-FIVE

THE CHALK SQUEAKED as the handsome young man wrote on the blackboard, adding the words "baby monitor" to a list that included.

    garage door openers
    alarm systems
    cell phones
    walkie-talkies
    satellites
    GPS systems
    television

"Very good."

I crowded into the back row with the other parents, mothers mostly, all of us feeling the awkwardness of being in close quarters with strangers. The teacher turned around. Thick eyebrows and a pronounced chin made him look a little like George Clooney, and when he smiled, I realized why I hadn't heard any complaints about Science Club.

"You can see—just from this list—how many things depend on radio waves. Everyday items as well as the exotic." He picked up a chart and propped it against the blackboard. Across the top of the chart was a band of colors, identified by initials, such as VLF, LF, and EHF. Underneath were terms, such as AM Broadcast, FM Broadcast, and Radar bands. At the bottom were numbers: 10kHz, 1MHz, 100 MHz, and 10GHz.

"These are some of the frequencies of radio waves, and that's what your children have been studying. Radio waves are just one part of the electromagnetic spectrum, which also includes visible light, infrared, X rays, gamma rays, and other forms of electromagnetic energy."

I tried not to let my eyes glaze over. One of my biggest regrets is not having a better grounding in science. I thought I understood the concepts, but whenever I tried to apply them, I usually got it wrong. Apparently, speed isn't the same thing as velocity, and acceleration doesn't always mean speeding up. I had the poor grades to prove it.

It might have been my teachers. In high school, my science teacher was an Indian woman who wore beautiful saris but whose accent was so thick I could barely understand her. And in college, the TA taught us how to handicap racing forms but not much about physics.

Rachel, though, seemed to have lucked out.

"So. Bearing in mind that we were studying radio . . ." the teacher continued, ". . . we decided to build one."

"I didn't know that," one of the mothers whispered to another.

The second woman mouthed back, "Me neither."

"Don't worry," he added hastily. "I asked them to keep it a surprise. In case it didn't work."

The kids giggled, and the adults traded amused glances. "I'm Brian Matson, by the way. But this is really your kids' class. They're anxious to show you what they did."

Several kids rose from their desks. A young boy introduced us to transmitters, capacitors, and inductors. Another explained oscillating sine waves. Rachel got up to explain what a diode was and how it worked in a receiver. As I watched, I felt pride that this knowledgeable, confident young woman was my daughter.

The kids turned on a small receiver sitting on one of the desks and left the room. A few seconds later, we heard a click and some static from speakers on both sides of the blackboard.

"Afternoon folks, and welcome to WSCS. That's WSCS, the Science Club Sensation. I'm Paul in the P.M., and I'm here to play your favorite tunes."

We whistled, cheered, and clapped enthusiastically. The faces of the kids still in the classroom lit up. Two songs pulsed through the speakers: "Somebody to Love," which, knowing my hero worship of Grace Slick, had to be Rachel's doing, and something by U2. A girl handed out apple juice and cookies. When the songs were over, Paul signed off, and the kids returned to the classroom.

"That was an ultralow power AM radio station," Brian said. "Small. But real." We clapped again. "Thank you. It's been a great session. Your kids were terrific."

The kids broke out in cheers of their own. I heard snippets of "Way cool," "Best class I've ever had," "Awesome dude."

Brian waved an embarrassed hand. "Since we still have some time left, I thought you might want to take a look at other types of radio systems. I'm a ham radio operator, and I brought in some of my gear. I'd be happy to answer any questions."

I munched on a cookie as we milled around, thinking back to my first job in college, tearing copy at an all-news radio station. It wasn't glamorous, the pay was rotten, but I got hooked. Not just on the rush of breaking news, but also the thrill of shaping, in some tiny, insignificant way, the presentation of history.

The following semester, I signed up for a course on Edward R. Murrow, where I listened to his rooftop broadcasts from London during the blitz. By the time I saw his documentary on McCarthy, I knew what I wanted to do with my life, and I changed my major to film.

But that didn't mean I knew anything about the technology of broadcasting. Happily, Rachel now did. Maybe she would become a techno-geek. Maybe we would go into business together: she the technical expert, me the content provider. Foreman and Daughter. It had a ring.

"What's that?" I pointed to an object about the size of a cell phone that was plugged into a small black box with knobs on the front. A computer sat beside it.

Brian smiled. "That's called a handie-talkie."

"Is that like a walkie-talkie?"

"Well, it is both a transmitter and receiver. Like a walkie-talkie. But this is much more sophisticated. It's part of a packet radio setup."

"A what?"

"An amateur radio system. You know, ham radio. But this is digital. Packet combines radio and computers. The little box you're looking at can transmit and receive both voice and data."

"No way. That little thing?"

"Well, you need an antenna and a computer," he said. "And there needs to be an unobstructed view—a direct line of sight—between the transmitter and receiver. You also need this piece of equipment." He ran a hand over the black box with knobs on it. Now that I was closer, I could see a needle on a dial swinging back and forth.

"That looks like a VU meter," I said. "You know. It measures audio levels when you're working with video."

"This is a TNC. A terminal node controller."

"What does it do?"

"It's kind of the brains of the packet system. It's the interface between the computer and the handie-talkie. The chips inside have all the functions the equipment needs."

"Are you saying that if I have this, and a computer, and that handie-talkie, you can run a radio station?"

"Absolutely. Like I said, you also need an antenna, but you can put one of those almost anywhere these days."

"So, tell me something. If we already have the computer, how much would the rest of this cost?"

He laughed. "It's not as bad as you think. You could probably get a basic setup for a few hundred." He glanced over at Rachel. "Are we thinking Christmas?"

"Possibly Chanukah."

He was about to reply, when one of the other mothers buttonholed him and asked whether her son ought to apply to MIT.

BACK HOME, I turned on the news and boiled water for pasta. The trial of a suspected terrorist had begun on the East Coast, and, once again, they were replaying the video of the Twin Towers. I never thought I'd become inured to those images, but mindless repetition by the media had almost stripped away the horror. I snapped off the tube and turned on the radio. As Smoky warbled about the tracks of his tears, I tried to pretend I was fixing dinner for William Hurt and Kevin Kline.

Outside, the fading light turned everything into shades of granite, but a bunch of kids were still playing outdoors, determined to keep dusk at bay. One of them booted a ball past my house. Two boys scrambled after it, but it rolled under a gray car that was parked a few houses away. I was watching them retrieve it when I noticed two figures inside the car. A twinge went through me. How long had they been there?

As if hearing my thoughts, the men opened their doors and climbed out. The one who'd been in the driver's seat had steel-gray hair and a mustache. He wore a suit jacket, the material tight across the back. With his thick neck and barrel chest, he could have been an ex-boxer. The other man was lean and younger. He had on jeans, a blue T-shirt, and a billed cap.

The older man bent down under the car, got the ball, and tossed it back to one of the kids. The boy caught it and stared up at the man. The man smiled and gave the

kid a thumbs-up. The kid ducked his head and ran back
to his game.

The older man cut across the grass to my house while
the man in the billed cap strolled up the driveway. The
doorbell rang.

I opened it cautiously.

"Miss Foreman? Jerry Coates, FBI. We'd like a few
minutes of your time."

"Why?"

"We'd like to talk to you."

"Could I see some identification?"

The older man showed me a black leather billfold engraved with a gold shield on one side. When he flipped
it open, a grainy color photo identified him as Special
Agent Jerome Coates. The letters FBI were stamped
across the photo.

The second man held up his ID. "Special Agent Nick
LeJeune."

His hair was shorter in the picture, and he was wearing
a suit, but it was the same guy. I studied him, noticing
the crow's-feet around his eyes, the light stubble on his
chin. He tugged the brim of his cap, which was embla-
zoned with Different Drummer Fishing Charter in white
letters.

I led the way into the family room and sat primly on
the sofa. Coates sat on a chair. LeJeune settled on the
other end of the couch.

Coates began. "Your legal name is Goldman, isn't it?"

"That's my ex-husband's name. And my daughter's. I
changed mine back to Foreman when we divorced."

"And you've been living here for ten years?"

"That's right. Last August."

"And your daughter is thirteen?"

"Yes."

Coates took out a memo pad and made a note. LeJeune
ran his hands over the nubby beige material of the couch.

"So, you want to tell me why you were riding around
in Dominick Morelli's limo the other day?" Coates asked.

My jaw went slack. "That was Dom Morelli?"

Dominick Morelli was one of the leading figures in the Chicago Outfit, reputed to be involved in gambling, juice loans, labor racketeering, and most recently an aggressive—but thus far unsuccessful—effort to open a casino in the suburbs.

"He never told me his name."

Coates's expression said he didn't believe me.

I flashed back to the man who'd stroked Spike so lovingly. "He didn't identify himself, and I didn't think I should press it, you know?"

LeJeune covered his mouth with his hand. Was he stifling a smile?

Coates's frown deepened. "You always go for limo rides with strangers?"

"He wasn't a stranger. I mean, it was obvious he was someone. He knew my name. But I didn't think it was my place—"

"So you did know him."

If they were following him as closely as Morelli claimed and had that mike he was talking about, they already knew everything we said. I leaned back against the couch. "How come you're not in the SUV today?"

The two men exchanged glances.

"I mean, it's definitely more North Shore than a gray—a gray—"

"Plymouth," LeJeune cut in. I thought I heard a slight lilt in his voice. Southern. But soft.

"Right. Plymouth. Hey, how long have you been following me anyway?" Coates looked confused. "I wish you'd identified yourselves sooner. I was really scared. Rhonda Disapio was, too. In fact—"

"Mrs. Goldman—"

"Miss Foreman."

"Miss Foreman." He scowled. "What the hell are you talking about?"

I looked from one to the other. Then it clicked. "You were following *Morelli,* not me."

They exchanged another glance.

My stomach pitched. "In the Plymouth."

Coates nodded. LeJeune was eyeing me.

"Then who was in the SUV?"

"Why don't you let me ask the questions, Miss Foreman?" Coates said.

That was the second time in a week that a man had said that to me.

I studied the men more closely. They didn't seem like partners. Or even particularly close. There didn't seem to be much awareness of each other's rhythms, none of the shared patterns couples acquire when they've worked together over time.

LeJeune seemed more attuned to his environment, his gaze processing the posters on the walls, the crowded bookshelves, my mother's silver bowl. I hoped he didn't notice the tarnish. His eyes swept over a glossy news magazine on the coffee table where a woman was mirrored in endless reflections in a story on cloning. When he realized I was watching him, he looked up. The green in his eyes was flecked with black.

"How's about I do some summin' up?" His accent was definitely Southern. *S*'s that sounded like *z*'s, a bit garbled, as if he was talking around a marble in his mouth. "You were out jogging. Morelli picked you up. You went for a ride. Yes?"

I nodded.

"And you know who Mr. Morelli is."

"I do now."

Coates interrupted, a vein on his forehead starting to pulse. "What kind of business did you have with Dominick Morelli?"

"I didn't have any business with him."

He thrust a finger into his shirt collar. I frowned. Was it possible the Feds didn't know who was in the SUV? Maybe that's what they were trying to find out. If so, I should lighten up. The answer would benefit us all.

"I think he was doing a favor for Joey DePalma," I said.

"Joey DePalma?" Coates's voice spiked. "Now you're gonna tell me you know—excuse me—you *don't* know the Surgeon, too?"

LeJeune took off his cap and ran his hand through his hair. Sandy. Threaded with silver.

"I went to Joey DePalma's house a few days ago."

Coates folded his arms. "Why?"

"I needed some answers."

"And you needed answers because . . ."

"You know."

"Know what?"

His blank face sent another twinge through me. "You don't?"

"Look, Miss Foreman," Coates said, "it's been a long day. Let's not give each other a hard time."

They didn't know. "I thought someone was trying to kill me."

LeJeune laid his arm across the back of the couch. Coates leaned forward. "You want to run that by me again?"

I told them about the tape and the trial and what had happened since. Rhonda Disapio's version of the night in the park. The men on a boat. A man named Sammy. How she died. The fire. Brashares. I sounded more convincing than I had with Morelli, but whether that was because I was more composed or the danger seemed more real, I wasn't sure.

LeJeune spoke up when I finished. "You don't think Disapio's death was an accident?"

"The timing was suspicious. She died a few hours after we talked at the mall."

"Who else knew about your meeting with her?"

"Brashares."

"The lawyer who died."

I nodded.

He looked into space, his eyes clouding. "Why do you think his death has anything to do with you?"

"I'm not sure it does—anymore." I told them my theory

about Santoro being framed and how I thought I had stumbled into the middle of it. As a result of my conversation with Morelli, though, I'd seen the error of my ways. "I might have been overreacting," I admitted.

"Why is that?"

"I couldn't get any new clients for a while, and I was worried. But that seems to have worked itself out."

"Oh?"

"An executive at Great Lakes Oil wants to talk to me about a project."

"Great Lakes Oil?"

I nodded.

"But the genesis of all this—this worry—was that tape? The one you played at the trial?"

"Yes. Unfortunately, he was convicted anyway."

"Why do you think that happened?"

"I guess Ryan was a better lawyer. And there was that slight technical problem on the tape."

"Technical problem?"

"Some kind of RF interference." I shrugged. "Twenty years ago it was pretty common with video equipment."

LeJeune raised the brim of his hat. "You still have the tape?"

I nodded.

"I'd like to see it."

I got the tape from my office, dropped it into the VCR, and hit Play. When the breakup streaked across the screen, LeJeune scratched his chin. When it was over, he looked at me. "You mind if I take this?"

"Go ahead." I ejected the tape from the player. Coates took it, turned it over in his hand, then handed it to LeJeune.

LeJeune asked more questions about the shoot. What the weather was like. The lake traffic. Whether anyone radioed in to shore from the crib. I answered as best I could. Then he dipped his head and looked at Coates. As Coates nodded, a sound from the hall distracted me.

"Mom, when are we eating? I'm starved."

I turned around. Rachel stood at the entrance to the family room.

LeJeune moved to the door. "We won't take up any more of your time."

"I appreciate it." As I walked them out, I asked, "You'll let me know what you find on the tape?"

He dug in his pocket and pulled out a card. "If you don't hear from me in a week, give me a call."

I glanced at the card. "LeJeune—that's a French name, isn't it?"

"Acadian."

"You're from Louisiana?"

He grinned, his eyes crinkling up in the corners. "Yes, ma'am. Lafourche Parish."

"Where is that?"

"In the southeast part of the state. Between Thibodaux and Raceland." My silence apparently prompted him to add, "About fifty miles west of New Orleans. On the bayou."

"Cajun country?"

"Yes, ma'am. Most beautiful country you'll ever see."

Cajun. That was the accent. I opened the door.

Coates aimed a stern finger at me. "Be careful who you go joy riding with. You never know when you're gonna hit a speed trap."

I slid my eyes to LeJeune. He pulled on his hat and winked.

TWENTY-SIX

A BLANKET OF fog wrapped itself around the upper reaches of the Great Lakes Oil building, obscuring the view. In the heart of the Loop, the building is the second highest in Chicago, and on a clear day its gleaming white façade stretches eleven hundred feet into the heavens, an eighty-three-floor testament to fossil fuels and capitalism. Today, though, peering out at a curtain of gray from the sixty-eighth floor, I couldn't see the horizon or any landmarks. I felt an eerie sense of disorientation, like the passengers in that old *Twilight Zone* episode, when their plane disappears into a time warp.

I sat in the reception area and thumbed through last month's *Training and Development*. It was a boring read, but after encounters with wise guys and FBI agents, I was happy to be bored. I was back on familiar turf. The rules of engagement in the corporate world are predictable. I'd spent years learning them.

Two goals are paramount: profitability and accountability. Augment the first; avoid the second. The effort you apply to each depends on the state of the economy, last quarter's results, and your pecking order in the organization. Of course, appended to all this is one crucial corollary: everyone spins.

In fact, corporate politics, though often subtle, can be more insidious than the public kind. The media doesn't troll its inner sanctums; as a result, knives can be twisted more frequently. And if an "awkward" story does leak to the press, the company can always rationalize it in the name of shareholder value.

For me, the fascinating part is figuring out individual agendas. It isn't hard. People tend to confide in third parties, perceiving—correctly, in my case—that I don't have a stake in the outcome. As an outsider, though, I'm also the first to be blamed when something goes wrong, so, I end up measuring everything I say, too.

I was led down a corridor with impersonal art on the walls and thick beige carpeting. Assistant Vice-President Dale Reedy's office was big, but it wasn't a corner office. Still, he was clearly senior enough to have an aide call and set up an appointment. And usher me down to meet him.

I hate to admit it, but I was taken aback to see a woman rise and walk around the desk to greet me. She was about five two, with short, glossy blond hair, pale skin, and a pug nose. She wore a severe navy suit with no blouse. She looked somewhere in her thirties.

"Delighted to meet you, Ellie," she said in a clipped British accent. "I've heard good things about you." She smiled and extended her hand. Her nails had been chewed to the quick.

"Thank you, Ms. Reedy."

"It's Dale." Stale tobacco smoke clung to the beige carpets and drapes. She waved me over to a table in the corner where copies of today's *Wall Street Journal*, the *New York Times*, and both Chicago papers lay. I pulled out a wicker chair and stumbled over a pair of shoes. I bent down to pick them up.

"Sorry." She laughed. "My running shoes. Just pitch them in the corner, would you?"

Another fitness geek. "You're a jogger?"

"I am. No time for a health club. I run along the lakefront."

Okay. I could handle that. I sat on the chair and snuck a glance at the headlines. She settled in the opposite chair and pulled out a pack of Royals.

"Slow news day." She struck a match.

I looked up. She was smiling, but her brown eyes had a hard-bitten look, as if life had let her down somewhere along the way.

"Wait until summer." I stared at her cigarette.

"For the record, I still do an eight-minute mile. If I quit, I could probably do a bloody triathlon." She touched the flame to her cigarette, then exhaled a stream of smoke. "You're better looking in person than you are on the telly."

My stomach turned over. She knew about the trial. I'd never get the gig.

"Bloody hell." She jumped up, the wicker on the seat of her chair crackling. "I forgot my notes."

Her desk was cluttered with papers, books, a desk phone, and a cell. Underneath the mess was a sheet of brown blotting paper inside an old-fashioned leather blotter. Behind the desk was a credenza with two shelves. A framed photograph of two boys sat on the top shelf. With dark hair and dark eyes, both were in the universal soccer pose: one knee on the ground, a ball in their hands. Curious. She was fair; they were dark. Rachel and I, in reverse.

She moved back to the table.

"So you joined Great Lakes after the merger?"

She nodded. "They needed some shaking up. Especially here in T&D. Early retirement, attrition, deadweight." Which judging from her no-nonsense style, she must have promptly jettisoned.

"How long have you been Stateside?"

"About eighteen months."

I gestured toward the photo of the boys. "Long enough for them to join a soccer team, I see."

"They're back in England." Her face was impassive. "I didn't know how long I would be here. So they stayed." She stubbed her cigarette out in a large ceramic ashtray. No mention of a husband. "Now Ellie. What do you know about shale oil?"

I dug out a file from my bag. I'd done a little research last night. "It's a fossil fuel that's extracted from shale by heating it to very high temperatures. But the process isn't widespread, mostly because of the cost. There are also environmental issues. Greenpeace raised a fuss about greenhouse emissions in Australia—so much that the company developing the shale down there ultimately pulled out."

"Quite right."

"Here in the U.S., the federal government owns a lot of the shale reserves, but they're leasing or selling them off bit by bit. And because environmental controls are more restrictive here, there hasn't been the same outcry. At least not yet. The entire process was looked at during the first energy crisis. But because of the cost, nothing much was done." I closed the file.

"Impressive." She leaned back. "Tell me. Do you like to ski?"

I raised an eyebrow.

"Great Lakes has some shale reserves in Colorado that we're starting to develop, and we want to produce a training video about them. Well—" She tipped her head. "Part training. Part PR. We want to take a leadership role within the industry. Position ourselves on the leading edge of an emerging—or reemerging—technology, I should say. Twenty-first-century vision. That kind of thing."

"Why now?"

"The costs are more manageable." She laughed. "And who knows? It might even become profitable."

"I read that Great Lakes had an opportunity to bid on the Australian project but declined. Why?"

She extracted another cigarette. "We wanted to start fresh. Without any baggage." She stole a look at me. "You can understand that."

I leaned my elbows on the table. "Why me?" *Given my baggage,* I almost added.

She took her time lighting her cigarette. "You come highly recommended."

"By whom?"

"Midwest Mutual. The Mayor's Office. Brisco Chemicals." She blew out another stream of smoke. "And as for the others, well, bugger them, I say."

I sat up straighter. I liked Dale Reedy.

We spent a few more minutes discussing the audience, the timetable, the budget, and possible elements. I imagined myself on the slopes of Aspen, gracefully crisscrossing a hill. A nice fantasy, considering I've only skied twice.

"So when can you get me a proposal?"

I was about to answer when a knock interrupted, and an older man appeared at the door. Gray hair, stylishly cut. Nice suit. Cuff links. "Dale, I wanted to make sure you got those RFPs—oh, sorry. I didn't mean to interrupt."

Sure you didn't.

Reedy rose and introduced me to her boss, the vice-president of Training and Development. He clasped my hand.

"You look familiar." He tipped his head to the side, then aimed a finger at me. "Aren't you the woman who was on TV a few weeks ago? That trial business."

I felt myself color. "Guilty."

He studied me, then looked back at Reedy. Her face was curiously blank. "I see. Nice to meet you." His voice reeked with false politesse. "Dale, come see me when you're done." His lips tightened.

She nodded and watched him go. My spirits sank. Dale dabbed at her hair. Had she noticed? "Sorry. Where were we?"

"I—I brought a demo reel for you to screen. It's not my most current version, unfortunately, but I can supply references."

"I should think the reel would be sufficient." She fixed me with a serious look. "Ellie. May I ask you something?"

"Of course."

"It's about that trial."

I'd been wondering whether she was going to bring it up. I braced myself. "Go ahead."

"Do you still think he's innocent? I mean, now that it's over?"

I wasn't sure how to answer. If I went into any detail, I might scare her off. She'd think I was unreliable, too flaky to work with. But if I didn't say anything, she might think I was holding out on her, something you never do with a client.

"Yes," I said slowly. "I still think he's innocent. And if I'd been smarter, or more persuasive, maybe the jury would have agreed."

"But everyone else was so certain."

"I know."

"I thought they had quite a bit of evidence."

"I suppose so. But nothing's happened since to change my mind. In fact—" I stopped. "Never mind. It doesn't matter."

She cocked her head.

I shrugged. "His lawyer is dead, and I don't see anyone jumping into the ring to take his appeal. Although the court will have to appoint someone eventually."

She tapped her pen on a pad of paper, shutting me out. "Of course."

"To be honest, I've been trying to put it all behind me." I looked out the window. Most of the fog had burned off, leaving wispy clouds scuttling across a blue sky. She followed my gaze. I looked back at her.

"But you still think about it."

"A little," I admitted. "Especially when I'm driving down Lake Shore Drive. You know, the cribs are only a few miles from here. And Olive Park is even closer." I waved a hand. "You could probably see them from your window."

"I doubt it," she said crisply. "I have a southern exposure."

The room felt suddenly chillier.

"Oh. Um, by the way, is there someone—some resource person I could call while I'm working on the proposal?"

"Resource person?"

"I'm sure to have some questions that I don't need to bother you with. Background on Great Lakes Oil. And shale development."

"Let me give you our librarian's name. I'll tell her to expect a call."

Back at her desk, she pulled out a flat board that looked like a drawer and ran her hand down a page that was taped to it. Scribbling down a number on her pad, she tore off the sheet and handed it to me.

"So then, why don't we set up a meeting for next week?" She picked up her PDA and pushed a few buttons. "How is Monday, the fourteenth? I'd like to get moving."

"Sounds fine." I stood up.

"Ellie, it's been a pleasure. I look forward to working with you."

"Same here. I'll be in touch."

I felt her eyes on my back as I left.

A YOUNG STUD in the parking lot brought my car around, his head bobbing to the beat from my radio—some rap tune encouraging him to kill The Man. After shelling out twenty bucks for a measly two hours' parking, I could relate. I peeled out of the garage, my tires squealing impressively.

Traffic slowed on the expressway. Sandwiched between a truck and a van, I took out my cell and called Dad. A woman answered.

"Hello?" The voice was throaty but sweet.

"I'm sorry. I must have the wrong number."

"This is Sylvia Weiner."

"Oh, hello, Sylvia. This is Ellie Foreman. How are you?"

"I'm fine, dear. Just fine. And what can I do for you?"

"Uh—is my father there?"

"Your father? Who are you trying to reach, dear?"

I hesitated. "Jake. Jake Foreman."

"I'm sorry. I don't know anyone named Jake. You must have the wrong number."

I heard a slight commotion, followed by the swish of the phone being transferred.

"Ellie?"

"Dad? Is that you? Is everything okay?"

"Sure, sure," he said. "Everything's fine."

"So that's Sylvia?"

"That's Sylvia," he replied. "A hell of a girl." I heard giggles in the background. His voice dropped to a whisper. "She doesn't remember so good."

"Is it—"

"I think so," he answered. "Just starting."

I sighed. "I'm sorry."

"Hey. Nothing's forever. That's why you gotta enjoy every day."

"In that case, I'll let you go."

"No. I'm glad you called. *Nu?*"

"I just wanted to remind you about the Eskin Bar Mitzvah this weekend."

"What time?"

"Service at nine. Kiddush and lunch afterwards."

"Long day."

"Your friends."

The Eskins and my parents played bridge together for years. Their son, Danny, was the same age as I, and our parents had hoped we'd find each other. For a while, I thought it might happen. In Sunday school, he used to borrow *tzedakah* money from me. A high honor when you're five. But after he borrowed a twenty on our one date in high school, I decided he could bestow the honor elsewhere. He became an accountant and got married, but we kept in touch in that almost-family kind of way. I went to their wedding; they came to mine. They weren't invited to Rachel's Bat Mitzvah, but we'd kept it small.

"The Torah service starts at ten," I said. "I'll pick you up at nine-thirty."

"Sounds good."

"Say hi to Sylvia for me."

"Who?"

Such a joker.

TWENTY-SEVEN

I WAS GOING over my notes from my meeting with Dale Reedy the next day, thinking how much I admired her for blazing a trail in the corporate world at the expense of a family life when David called.

"Hi. How's the jet lag?" I tried for a cheerful tone, but it sounded artificial.

"I'm okay. I got back Sunday." Today was Tuesday.

We chatted about unimportant things, both of us tiptoeing around the edges, as if confronting what was really on our minds would bruise us, scrape our skin raw. He sounded pleased when I told him about the Great Lakes proposal. He said Abdul was still working on his deal. When we ran out of prattle, I took a breath.

"I called you in London. The night after we spoke. There was no answer in your room." He didn't say anything. "Were you with someone?"

"Are you accusing me of something?"

"I—I was upset."

He was silent a moment. Then, "Ellie. I wasn't with anyone. I knew it was you. I didn't feel like talking."

"But we've got to."

"Why? We're not going to resolve anything over the phone."

"Then how do we? Resolve things?"

"I don't know." His words reverberated over seven hundred miles of fiber optics. "Have you done any thinking?"

"Yes. But I don't know if you'll like it." I glanced down at my notes on shale oil. The words looked garbled and meaningless. "You told me—just after the trial—how I'm always trying to right what I see as injustices. Maybe I do. But I try to be careful. I don't look for danger. Occasionally, though, events do spiral out of control, like they did last summer."

"What about now?"

"I don't know that I can change the way I approach life. Or that I want to." I paused. "You know, sometimes I get the feeling you want to put me in a glass jar where I'll be safe. I know it's motivated by love, but that's not what I need. What I need is your support. It doesn't help when you tell me how I'm going out on a limb or making a fool of myself. I do enough of that for myself."

"So now I haven't given you enough support?"

"David, you're the best thing in my life. It's just I can't crawl into a cocoon with you and hide from the world."

"Is that your impression of me?"

"Well . . ." I paused again. "You are pretty quick to tell me when I'm venturing too far afield."

He didn't answer.

"I—I know it's because you care. And I know you don't want to cramp my style. It's just—" I stopped. "Sometimes I think I'm a bad influence on you. That I'm forcing you into situations and circumstances you'd never find yourself in were it not for me."

"You don't trust me very much, do you?"

I winced. He was veering far too close to the truth.

"What do you mean? Of course I—"

"No, you don't. Listen to me. Whether I steal a flower

at a hotel and put it in your hair isn't your responsibility. I'm an adult. I make those decisions myself. By the same token, if I choose to share your life, unpredictable as it may be, it's because I want to. But I can't just let you put yourself—and Rachel—in jeopardy, if it can be helped. And you can't expect me to."

"You're sorry I ever testified, aren't you?"

"That's not the issue."

A streak of anger shot up my spine. It was easier to react. "Yes, it is. And you should know that given the same circumstances, I'd probably do it again."

"I understand," he said tiredly. "That's where this conversation began. Look . . ." He paused. "I hope you understand what I'm about to say. I think we should take a breather."

My body went still. *This is how it starts,* I thought. *With stillness. No movement. Just words.* "A breather?"

"I think we both need to decide—before we get any deeper—whether this is something we want to work out." His voice was shadowed with pain. "That can't happen when we're seeing each other. We get—distracted."

I had an image of us in bed, his body against mine. I pushed it away. "How long of a breather?"

"I don't know."

More silence.

"What do I tell Rachel?" My voice was small.

"That I love her. You, too."

The stillness dissolved. My throat got thick. "Then why?"

His voice filled up. "You know why. Don't make me say it again."

It was useless to try to change his mind, and he cut the connection before I could. I stared at the phone, thinking about the flower I'd torn out of my hair at the Four Seasons. If I'd been trying to sabotage the relationship, I'd been more successful than I'd imagined.

* * *

I STAYED UP late burying myself in research so I wouldn't have to think about David. I found out more than I'd ever wanted to know about shale oil from Googling, but there wasn't much on Great Lakes Oil's web site. I'd have to call the librarian tomorrow. I rummaged around for the sheet of paper Dale had ripped off her pad.

The light must have hit at an odd angle, because as I held up the sheet, I noticed a residual imprint of numbers near the top of the page. She must have jotted them down on a sheet of paper she'd torn off before. *She writes with a heavy hand,* I thought, because the numbers weren't hard to discern. The first three were three-one-two, the area code for downtown Chicago. Then seven digits. And four more. A phone number and an extension. I squinted at them. Something about the extension was familiar: four, five, two, zero.

I stared at them for a while, then typed them into my notes. Maybe they were one of those numbers I call all the time and just don't realize—like tech support at my ISP. Or somebody's fax number, which somehow had burrowed into my memory. I couldn't quite grasp it. I balled up the paper and pitched it into the trash.

I rolled my shoulders, then shut down for the night. I checked on Rachel. She'd kicked the covers off and was curled on the edge of her bed, a stuffed tiger in her arms. I covered her with the sheet. But it was a cold night, and her window was cracked. I added a quilt.

I padded into my bathroom and peered into the mirror. Where would I be in twenty years? Was I destined to spend the rest of my life alone? Rachel would be living her own life. Would I become one of those bitter old women who wait all week for a call from their children and then complain about everything when the call came?

Enough. The best thing I could do now was end this day. I climbed into bed. It wasn't the Four Seasons, but it was soft and warm. I pulled the covers over my head, felt myself getting drowsy, falling free.

TWENTY-EIGHT

"**HOW COME DAVID'S** not here?" Rachel asked the morning of the Bar Mitzvah. Sipping a glass of orange juice, she alternately kicked her heels against the legs of the chair and pointed her toes. *People* magazine was open to a picture of Tom Cruise and some Hollywood babe. "Is he still in Europe?"

I looked up from the newspaper. "No, honey."

"Is he sick?"

"No." I folded the paper and propped it on the table.

"You're fighting again, aren't you?"

A tic of irritation passed through me. "We're not fighting." Rachel's frame of reference as far as relationships were concerned was rigid: people either fought, or everything was okay. There was no gray, no middle ground. But, then, with Barry and me as role models, what did I expect? "We both have some thinking to do."

"About what?"

I flicked the newspaper so I could read below the fold. "If it were any of your business, I'd tell you."

She wrinkled her nose.

I stood up and straightened the cropped silk jacket Susan and I had found in the Lord & Taylor outlet. Smoothing out my black silk pants, I said, "Let's get moving. We have to pick up *Opa.*"

As I drove down to Skokie, I wondered why Dale Reedy had Abdul's number. He had said he was working on a deal with Great Lakes Oil, but Training and Development is a long way from Acquisitions. Maybe he wanted to find out how to train his people to manufacture the additive he'd been talking about.

AFTER THE SERVICE, during which Sean Eskin, Danny's son, recited a dogged *haftarah* and an even more dogged *drush,* the audience decamped to a hotel for lunch. Dad, Rachel, and I piled into the car, speculating on how lavish it would be.

"Danny's an accountant. He knows the value of a dollar," I said. "I'll bet he chintzed on the food."

"I don't know," Dad said. "The kid's an only child."

"You think it's gonna be *Goodbye Columbus?*"

He shrugged.

"Care to put down a slight wager?" I grinned.

He grinned back. "You really want to gamble . . . with me?"

"Five bucks says it's a tightfisted affair."

"You're on."

OUR FIRST CLUE came outside the ballroom, where two hundred table assignments were alphabetically laid out on a table. Instead of a number, guests were assigned to a "team." Dad and I got the Bears, Rachel the Blackhawks. On each side of the table were life-sized blowups of Sean posing in different sports uniforms. In one he was wearing a Sox uniform with a bat slung across his shoulders. In the other, he was shooting a hoop in a Bulls uniform.

Dad clapped an arm around my shoulders and held out

his palm with the other. "Like taking candy from a baby."

Groaning, I pushed through the door to the ballroom, which had been transformed into a sports arena. Stadium lights blinded us with their glare; a set of real bleachers hugged the walls. A regulation hoop was set up at one end of the room; a ball-pitching machine occupied the other. Over a dozen kids were lined up waiting to take a swing.

Silver and blue balloons covered almost every surface, including the ceiling, and a quilted thermos bottle with Sean's name engraved on it sat on each plate. More blow-ups of Sean in a Bears, Cubs, Blackhawks, and Fire uniform were strategically placed around the room.

But the highlight of the decor—if you could call it that—was Cubs pitcher Rusty Steiger. Live. Dressed in his uniform, he was signing autographs over at the ball machine. Dad tapped me on the shoulder. I dug out a five from my wallet and handed it over. He palmed it cheerfully.

Once we were seated, the room went dark, and that twinkly, twangy music they use to introduce the Bulls spilled out. The DJ, in a creditable imitation of announcer Ray Clay, shouted. "And now, your host . . . the incomparable, the one, the only . . . Sean Eskin!"

A spotlight was thrown up. A moment later, Sean, one hand in his mother's and the other in his dad's, skipped into the room. At the DJ's exhortation, the crowd applauded wildly. All three Eskins looked slightly embarrassed but gamely raised their arms in a salute.

The lights snapped on again, and chatter filled the room. Before digging into my fruit cocktail, I waved my spoon. "Play ball!"

By the end of the main course, which consisted of baked chicken dressed up in some kind of sauce with wild rice and something that resembled green beans, I felt like asking Dad for my five bucks back. But before I could, Sean's parents rose to thank the rabbi; the *chazzan*, the tutor who'd worked with Sean on his Hebrew; and everyone else in the universe. Then Sean's grandmother, my parents' old friend, made her way onto the parquet dance floor. She was wearing a Chanel suit. Blue and silver. Not a hair out of place.

"Sean," she said in a quavering voice. "I only wish your *zaideh* Leon was here to see you today." Sean's grandfather had passed away six years earlier, around the same time as my mother.

"If he did, he'd have another heart attack," Dad whispered.

The grandmother went on to *kvell* about the wonderful job her grandson had done, then proceeded to name all her siblings and those of her late husband. I looked at my watch.

During dessert, the DJ led the kids, Rachel among them, around the room in a conga line. After snaking past all twenty tables, it ended up on the dance floor where a limbo pole suddenly appeared. When it was her turn, Rachel slid gracefully under the pole. The DJ threw one of those neon necklaces around her neck. Blushing, she straightened up and tried to pretend she wasn't having a good time.

Dad's eyes sparkled as he watched her. "She's beautiful, Ellie."

She was wearing a satiny white blouse that barely skimmed her waist, a short gray skirt, and heels.

"She's going to be fighting them off with sticks."

"Tell me about it," I said.

"You'll live through it." Chuckling, he squeezed my hand with both of his. "So, you're okay now, sweetheart?"

I nodded. I wasn't going to tell him about my visits with DePalma, Morelli, or the FBI, but I did tell him about Dale Reedy. "Looks like I might be getting some work after all. I met with a woman from Great Lakes Oil."

"You see? All that worry for nothing. You should listen to your daughter. What does she say? Take a chill pill."

I smiled. "Yeah. But something odd did happen. Do

you remember us talking about David's new client? The petrochemical sheik from Saudi Arabia?"

Dad released my hand and rubbed his nose.

"He's buying one of Great Lakes Oil's chemical plants in Indiana. But apparently, he called my client. Dale Reedy."

"So?"

"She's in Training and Development, not Acquisitions."

"Like I said, so?"

"So, when we had dinner together a few weeks ago, he said he didn't know her. In fact, at the time, we both thought she was a he."

Dad's eyes slid toward the dance floor where the Eskin family was gathering. "I'm still waiting for the punch line."

"Dad, why would he call her? I can understand him talking to the lawyers. Or the Acquisitions people. But Training and Development?"

"How do you know this happened?"

"I found *his* number on *her* pad of paper."

"Maybe some question came up about training people at the plant."

"But he specifically said he didn't know her. And he knew I was going to be meeting her. Don't you find that coincidental?"

My father fixed me with one of his stares; the one that says, *Back off and stop making trouble.* Then he got up from the table and walked over to Rachel, who was scooping up the last of her ice cream. He bowed and held out his hand. A minute later, they were dancing.

Dad still did an excellent fox-trot, and Rachel followed beautifully. As he waltzed her around the room, people at some of the tables pointed at the elderly gentleman with the young girl. When the music ended, he dipped Rachel with a flourish. She bent back almost prone and pointed her toes like a pro. I heard a smattering of applause.

It was after four when we got back into the car. The

afternoon light was fading, but I felt disoriented, like you do when you come out of a movie in the middle of the day. As I turned out of the lot, Dad fidgeted in the front seat.

"What's wrong?"

"Something's poking me in the back."

I pulled to the side of the road. He eased himself off the seat and shoved his hand into the space between the seat cushion and back.

"Something's stuck in here."

"Hold on." I started to open my door so I could walk around.

"No. I got it." He shook his head and pulled out a piece of silver jewelry. The bracelet from Calumet Park. "What is this?"

I looked over, surprised. "That's strange. How did that get there?"

"What is this, a bracelet?"

"I found it a few weeks ago. I thought it was in my bag."

Dad looked puzzled. "You should keep it in your jewelry box."

"I guess I should." I was about to shove it into my pocket when something made me check the rearview mirror. Rachel, her eyes down, kept winding a strand of hair around her fingers. She didn't look up.

Mystery solved.

I retrieved my canvas bag from the floor under Dad's feet and dropped the bracelet into it. She and I would have to have a chat about privacy. Subset two, paragraph six of the Boundaries discussion. But that was later.

Once we were on our way again, Dad looked over and grinned. "I have a confession to make."

I raised an eyebrow.

"I'll tell you the truth. I never wanted you to hook up with Danny. It was your mother's idea."

"It wasn't you? How come?" I expected him to launch

into his we-are-German-Jews-and-the-Eskins-aren't routine, but he surprised me.

"Danny wasn't what you'd call an Einstein. And it's obvious the kid's not much better."

I smiled.

"By the way, where's David?"

My smiled faded. "He's in Philadelphia."

My father cocked his head, as if to ask why.

I shook my head.

Rachel dangled her arms over the front seat. "Mom says they're—"

My father placed his hand on her arm. "Rachel. *Iz genug.*"

That's enough.

TWENTY-NINE

A CHILLY BREEZE swayed branches against the darkening sky but after the brittle noise of the party, the feel of the wind was soothing. As we pulled into the driveway, I noticed a silver sports car parked at the curb. I didn't think too much about it until Rachel squealed.

"Mother, look. I can't believe it. A Spyder. Right in front of our house."

"A Spyder?" I shivered.

"The car, Mother. It's only one of the tightest cars ever."

"Tight?"

"Cool, Mom. Tight is cool."

I looked, but I'm not much of a car person. Or a teenage linguist.

"Look, Mom, a guy's getting out." She craned her neck and let out a wolf whistle. I giggled, but the giggle died in my throat when Nick LeJeune slid out of the driver's seat. I threw the Volvo in park.

Rachel looked over. "You know this guy?"

"You do, too. He was here last week."

I climbed out of the car and adjusted my jacket. Le-
Jeune leaned against his car. He was wearing jeans and a
black leather jacket, and his Different Drummer hat was
pulled low on his forehead. I walked over, aware that
under the brim, his eyes were on me. "What brings you
back this way, Agent LeJeune?"

"Is this your daughter?" He looked past me.

I turned around. Rachel was eyeing him curiously. "Rachel, this is Nick LeJeune."

He flipped up his hat. "You're almost as pretty as your
mama." He held out his hand.

I could see her color, even in the dim light.

"You didn't answer my question," I said.

"I told you I'd get back to you."

"On a weekend?"

"The Bureau never sleeps, *chér*."

Chér? I paused. "You're lucky you caught us."

"I agree."

I made a show of looking him up and down. "So, what
can I do for you?'

"I was hoping you'd go for a ride with me."

Rachel sucked in a breath.

TWENTY MINUTES LATER, I squeezed into the Spyder
next to Rachel. I'd changed into jeans, work boots, and a
heavy jacket. LeJeune made a loop around the village,
cruising the main streets well over the speed limit. Rachel
pumped him with car-talk questions, and he seemed gen-
uinely pleased to reply. I kept my eyes peeled to the road,
only half listening to their chatter. Our village is known
up and down the North Shore for the cops who lurk on
side streets just waiting to snare speeders.

Thankfully, there were none today, and as we dropped
her off at Katie's, Rachel was full of smiles. She agreed
to be home by eleven and to call my cell if she needed a
ride. Then she raced inside to tell Katie and everybody
else she'd ever known about her adventure. LeJeune

turned onto the Edens and headed downtown.

"You made a friend," I said.

"She's a cute kid."

"The best."

"Knows her stuff about cars."

"Rachel?"

"She knew the model number, the horsepower, the torque. Even knew the manual transmission doesn't have a clutch."

I looked down. Sure enough, there was no third pedal on the floor.

"It's controlled by computer now."

I ran a hand through my hair. I should have listened more carefully. Where did she learn that stuff? Her father? Or someone else—like some kid who'd just gotten his license? Should I worry?

"You want to know who taught her, don't you?" He read my mind. "And what she had to fork over in return."

My hand dropped to my lap. The guy was pretty sure of himself. Probably thought he was God's gift to the world of crime fighting. Women, too.

He grew quiet as he threaded through traffic. The Spyder sat lower on the road than I liked, but it *was* well balanced, and LeJeune was a good driver.

"I got it this spring," he said. "A twenty-year reward to myself."

It occurred to me that a sports car was something a single man would buy. Unless the man had money to burn. Which FBI agents didn't. Or wouldn't flaunt if they did. "You've been an agent for twenty years?"

"That's right."

"But you said you were from Cajun country."

"I've been here since eighty-two."

He was quiet again. The Spyder slipped through traffic with ease, the air was crisp, and the lights on the highway sparkled. I felt lighter than I had in weeks. I didn't even care where we were going.

At Fullerton, he turned east and then south when he

reached Lincoln Avenue. The street hasn't changed much, despite the yuppie invasion that followed the urban pioneers. More fake gas lamps and wrought iron, maybe, but a lot of the same restaurants and clubs. The area used to be a mecca for blues joints; some are still there. But the front end of the Chevy that once jutted out of a brick wall twenty feet above the street was gone, and so was the Blues club underneath it. In its place was a Thai restaurant with an uninspiring façade.

"I miss it, too," he said, following my gaze.

We parked in a lot just off Lincoln. Summer is Chicago's best season, but people don't hibernate until January, and despite the cold, the sidewalks were crowded. As we rounded the corner, we heard the wail of a saxophone. The guy who stations himself on the Michigan Avenue bridge Monday through Friday was moonlighting here tonight. LeJeune threw a bill into his case.

"Where are we going?" I zipped up my jacket.

"I thought we'd have a drink . . . listen to some music."

"A drink. Music?"

"Unless you've got other plans . . ."

Before I could answer, he opened the door to Blues Alley, and we walked into a large room. Muddy Waters spilled out of the jukebox. Twenty tables surrounded a stage, half of them filled. The blades of a ceiling fan circled lethargically, not doing much to disperse a thick cloud of smoke.

I sat at a table while LeJeune went to the bar, returning with a draft and glass of wine. I wondered how he knew what I drank.

"Okay," I said. "What's going on? Why did we come all this way?"

"You like blues?"

"Yeah, but—"

"Well . . ."

A woman in jeans and a tight green sweater squeezed by us, her attention so focused on LeJeune that when she brushed the edge of the table, a few drops of beer spilled out of his glass. He pretended not to notice. He tapped a fist on the table to the music.

When the riff ended, he looked over. "You've got balls, cher. You know that?"

"Excuse me?"

"Going to DePalma's—that took guts. And the way you handled Morelli. You don't let people give you any shit."

An official commendation from the Bureau? Was this why I was here? "I told you. I was desperate."

He smiled. "Thoreau says, 'It is characteristic of wisdom not to do desperate things.' But I'd make an exception in your case." The jukebox went quiet. "So, Ellie Foreman. How did you get involved with video?"

The guy jumped around as unpredictably as a fly. He was either very cunning or totally incompetent.

Feeling off balance, I curled my fingers around my wineglass. "My mother took me to see *Old Yeller* when I was eight, and I cried my eyes out. Then I saw it again with my best friend and realized I was being jerked around. I decided to figure out how they did it."

He laughed. "I was right. You're a Valkyrie."

A literate FBI agent. Wasn't that an oxymoron? "Thoreau says it's better to be the jerkor than the jerkee," I said.

"Take no prisoners."

"War is hell."

"C'est vrai, ma petite."

"Speaking of being jerked around, what's with the *chér* and *petite* stuff?"

His grin deepened. "That's the way we talk to our women back home."

"Except you're not home, and I'm not your woman."

He looked away. Smoke from a nearby table drifted over. LeJeune rose and left the table. For an instant, I started to second-guess myself. Had I been too harsh? Too abrasive? Was he ticked off? Maybe I should make nice. Well, at least courteous. He came back a minute later with another round of drinks.

"So." I smiled. "How'd you get to be an agent?"

He leaned back. "I wanted to catch the bad guys."

"Which ones?"

"Oilmen, for starters." He sipped his beer. "My daddy tried a *vacherie*, but he lost his shirt."

"*Vacherie?*"

"Cattle ranch," he said. "He didn't make it, so he took a job with the oil company. Had over twenty years in when he lost his leg. They fired him. A year short of retirement. Never gave him another penny."

I winced.

"It's an old story—at least in my part of the world. Hell, even the Kingfish couldn't bring them to their knees."

"Kingfish," I said. "As in Huey Long, Kingfish?"

He nodded. "Before he became governor, he sued an oil company. Trying to get workmen's comp for men like my father. He lost, but he kept on fighting for the little guy. Problem was, the corporate interests didn't like that too much, so the same oil company tried to impeach him ten years later. They lost, too."

"Nice story." I shifted. "But the FBI wouldn't be at the top of my list of crusaders against corporate greed."

"You would know."

I once wrote for an underground newspaper. I read my three *M*s: Marcuse, Marx, and Mao. I tried hard to be a revolutionary. Unfortunately, it didn't take. I was told I was too bourgeois. That the most I could aspire to was running a safe house. "You've been checking up on me."

He didn't answer.

"Then you should know I don't do that kind of thing anymore."

"That's okay. Chasing down wise guys isn't what I do, either."

"What is it you do?"

"Take pretty ladies out for drinks."

Who was this guy? First he comes to my house and asks about mafiosos. Now he's flirting like I'm some Friday night special. I tilted my head, wondering whether I had enough cash for a cab home but hoping I wouldn't have to use it. Despite his pretense, if that's what it was, I was enjoying his company. I changed the subject. "Was your mother Acadian, too?"

"Italian. My daddy met her in New Orleans."

"Are they still down there?"

"My daddy is. My mother passed about five years ago. Cancer."

"Mine, too." And her death burned a hole in my heart that would never heal.

I finished my wine. "Sit and Cry" jangled out of the jukebox. Buddy Guy.

People jostled our table as they passed. Though it was barely seven, the place was filling up. LeJeune got the check.

"Let's get something to eat." He stood up and took the check to the bar, ignoring the interested look of the female bartender. I allowed myself just the tiniest gloat.

THIRTY

We drove north and east to Diversey Harbor. A veil of navy blue edged the western sky, pierced by an orange glow from Chicago streetlights. LeJeune drove around the inlet and stopped at the end of the Diversey boat launch, a ramp of concrete that slopes down to the water. Hundreds of boats anchor here during the summer, but now only a group of skinny pilings stood sentinel. He cut the engine and leaned an arm across the back of my seat. "There's a settling quality about water, you know?"

"Settling?" Traffic whined on Lake Shore Drive.

"It gives you what you need."

Black waves slapped against the pilings. "How do you figure that?"

"My daddy used to take me fishing on the bayou in our bateau. Sometimes it was so quiet you could hear the heartbeat of a hummingbird. Sometimes it was meaner than a wasp with two stingers. But every day, it gave me something to remember." He looked out. "You might not like what it's offering, but it's there for the taking."

A sudden gust of wind rocked the Spyder. I thought

back to the rapids of the New River in West Virginia. No metaphysical discussion could ever convince me water would meet my spiritual needs.

"Water doesn't give up its secrets. Even when it tears your heart out."

"Sounds like Cajun folklore. With a little voodoo thrown in."

He grinned, keyed the engine, and made a graceful one eighty. Soon we were heading down Clark Street. He parked on Arlington and guided me to Federico's, a restaurant with red-checked tablecloths, soft music, and garlic-scented air. As we walked in, the host gave me a once-over and led us to a table in the back. LeJeune took off his leather jacket and draped it over his chair. He was wearing a white button-down shirt that made him look like a young collegiate.

A waiter appeared. "They are fresh today, Signor Nick. And large."

Without asking me, LeJeune ordered a bucket of steamed mussels and more drinks. He settled back in his chair, looking very much at home.

"You like mussels?"

Enough already. I blew out a breath. "Look, it's nice of you to buy me drinks and dinner, but I think you ought to tell me why we're here. I got that it's not just social, but I don't take too well to . . . to subterfuge. If you want something, ask."

"You're right. It's time." He looked over and smiled. "But I want you to know I have been enjoying myself. I don't meet many women with looks and brains."

I started to say something, but he cut in. "We looked at the tape you gave us." His voice was low; I strained to hear him over the music.

The waiter came with our drinks. Wine for me, Molson's for him. LeJeune waited until he left.

"I need you to answer some questions."

I nodded.

"You went out to the crib the same night you took those shots of Santoro, right?"

"That's right."

"What did you shoot out there?"

"We shot a reenactment of what might have gone on during the twenties. We hired actors, dressed them up, staged a speakeasy kind of scene."

"That was last summer, right?"

"Mid-July."

He looked off into space for a moment. "Did you screen the tape after you recorded it?"

"Of course. We had to log in the time code."

"Time code?"

I explained that time code is a series of numbers that pop up on the bottom on the screen and allow you to select precise frames for editing.

"Does time code correlate to real time?"

I shook my head. "It's an arbitrary clock that's set at the beginning of the shoot."

He looked disappointed.

"Why?"

He took a sip of his Molson's. "Doesn't matter. So you looked at the tape, and it was fine."

"Right."

"But then, a year later, it turns out to be damaged."

"Right."

"Did the damage show up on more than one tape?"

"Not that I know of."

"You checked the others?"

"Mac, my director, did. It was only on the one tape. Why?"

He didn't answer. We were moving on his timetable, not mine. "So . . . going back to last summer, you screened the tape, and then you took it back out there a couple days later?"

"We needed it to set up the match dissolve."

"The what?"

I explained that a match dissolve was a special effect

in which you dissolved between two shots made from the same location and angle, but at different times.

"Kind of like time lapse?"

"Exactly. But just one shot."

He pulled out a sheet of paper and a pen. "I need you to walk me through everything you did with that tape the day you went back out there. Draw me a diagram. Show me exactly where you were."

"Are you crazy? I can't remember that. It was over a year ago."

"You have to."

I stuck out my chin, about to tell him what he could do with the crib, the tape, his paper, and his pen, but the look on his face stopped me. The intense, engaged man across from me was nothing like the smart aleck who'd been spouting Cajun shtick an hour ago. I took the pen.

"What's the first thing you did when you got down to the harbor?"

"Well, we boarded the *Versulis*—that's the tug that took us out to the crib from Navy Pier."

"How many people were on the tug?"

"Come on. You can't expect me to—"

"Try. Please."

I searched my memory. It had been a cool day, I recalled, shrouded in fog, but the chop on the lake whipsawed the tug, making a steady shot impossible. I remember asking Mac if he thought it would be stable enough to shoot. The cameraman was there. And the soundman. And the PR guy from the water district. And the crew on the tug. "I think there were five of us. And three of them." I ran it through my mind again. "Eight, all told."

"Good. See, you can remember."

"Maybe a little," I said grudgingly.

"What happened when you docked on the crib?"

"We unloaded the gear—"

"Where?" He motioned to the paper.

I sketched a rough diagram of the crib's surface, point-

ing out where we'd docked and unloaded the equipment.
"We shot some exteriors near the entrance. Then we went
inside to tape."

"Draw me a sketch."

I turned over the paper and sketched out the living
quarters, the kitchen, the eating area, the large half-filled
tank that sat to one side.

"Where was the tape from the reenactment at this
point?"

"It was in my bag."

"Your bag?"

I leaned over and felt for my bag before I realized I
didn't have it with me. "I usually carry a canvas bag on
location. I keep a stopwatch in it, a penknife, gaffer's tape,
sometimes a mike."

"You carry it over your shoulder?"

I nodded, wondering why that was important.

"Okay. Then what?"

"We set up in one of the bedrooms." I pointed it out
on the sketch. "The same room where we did the party
scene. Then we took the reenactment tape and played it
back through the camera so we could duplicate the same
shot."

"What was the shot?"

"Actually, there were two. We did a shot of the rolltop
desk, moving in and out—I'm sorry, zooming close and
then moving wider on it. Then we also did an establishing
shot of the bedroom. They were both on the reenactment
tape. We figured we'd decide later which worked better."

"Now, tell me something. Where on that reenactment
reel was the shot that you used for the match—whatever
you call it?"

"Dissolve. But I don't understand the question."

He repeated it.

"You mean where on the cassette did it physically lie?"
When he nodded, I answered. "Pretty much toward the
tail. The end. We'd already recorded a good deal before
we got to it."

"And what did you do with the reenactment tape afterwards?"

"After what?"

"After you used it for the dissolve."

"I put it back in my bag."

"Good." He took another pull on his Molson's. "Then what?"

"Then, nothing." I was growing impatient. "Come on, Nick. What's this all about?"

A determined look passed across his face. He shook his head.

"Yeah, well." I pushed my wineglass away, feeling cranky. "Maybe if I knew why I'm supposed to remember, I could be more helpful."

He studied me, as if weighing how much to say. "I'll tell you as much as I can when we're done. Okay?"

"This better be good." I studied the wall behind him, where a still life of a bowl of fruit and bottle of wine hung. "*Cher.*"

He gave me a little smile. "Then what?"

"I think we went outside to grab some exteriors. Yes, that's right." It was coming back now. The fog had burned off, but it was still cool and cloudy. The lighting would be flat but even. "That must have been when we went up to the suspension bridge."

"Show me."

I penciled in the bridge that connects the two structures on the crib. "A guy was up there painting, or coating it with rust remover or something. We thought it would be a cool angle, so we went up."

"Did you take your bag up with you?"

"I—I don't remember."

His jaw tightened. "Try."

I struggled with the memory. The bridge was narrow and not very long. About thirty feet. Because of that, Mac didn't come with us. It was just me and the cameraman. "I'm not sure—it was pretty cramped up there."

He shifted. "Okay. Let me ask this. Where on the bridge did you position the camera?"

That I did remember. "The cameraman was about half-way across so he could pan across from the lake to the guy on the bridge." I placed an *X* where he had set up.

"And where were you?"

I looked at the sketch, then at LeJeune. "I would have to have been behind him—out of camera range. Near the candy striper."

"The pink and white structure?"

I nodded.

"Show me."

I put another *X* at the end of the bridge.

He angled the drawing toward him. "How much tape did you shoot up there?"

"Not much. A total of maybe two or three minutes."

"Okay. What did you do after the scenes on the bridge?"

What did *we do?* I closed my eyes. I remember standing up, leaning over the railing of the bridge, looking down, waving to Mac.

My eyes flew open. I got it. "Before we came down, we shot down onto the surface of the crib. Four or five overhead shots." I paused. "And then we went back down to the surface of the crib and shot more workmen."

"That's good." His eyes glittered. "And then?"

"We came back down." I remembered the whistle of the wind, the sound of the gulls, the dense, gray light.

The light.

"I forgot! We lugged a light kit up with us, in case we needed some fill on the bridge. In the end, though, we managed to squeak by with available light. When we were done, the cameraman picked up the camera, and I picked up the light kit and my bag, and we—" I stopped. "My bag!" I concentrated on the memory, testing its veracity. Yes. "My bag *was* there, between the light kit and the wall. Wedged against the candy striper."

A grin broke across his face. "Show me."

We leaned over the diagram, and I drew it. Then he folded the sheet of paper and put it in his pocket.

Our mussels arrived in a black bucket with a cloud of steam.

"Dig in," he said.

I pried apart the shells, extricated the meat, and, after dipping them in butter sauce, let them slide down my throat. The waiter was right. They were fresh and large, and the smooth, hearty scent of garlic infused each bite.

We were quiet as we ate.

When there was nothing left but broth, LeJeune pushed the bucket to the side and tore open one of the wipes the waiter had brought to the table. "I like a lady who's not afraid to eat."

I wondered whether I could sop up the broth with a piece of bread. If I'd been with David, I wouldn't have hesitated. As LeJeune handed me the other wipe, an image of a restaurant in Philadelphia sprang into mind. David, Rachel, and me last summer. Newspapers on the table, wooden mallets, a pitcher of soda, a mountain of hot, spicy hard-shells. All of us sucking juice out of the tiny orange legs, laughing when it dribbled down our chins. A sharp pang stabbed me.

LeJeune didn't seem to notice. "Just one more thing." He tossed the wipe into the bucket. "When you were done with the reenactment tape, did your cameraman rewind it before he took it out of the camera?"

"Come on. How would I remember that?"

He kept his mouth shut and his eyes on me.

"Lemme think." I sighed. "If he's in the middle of a setup or scene, he usually dumps the cassette and loads a new one right away so he can pick up the shot."

"Is that what he did?"

"I'm sorry. I wasn't watching." I searched his face. "Your turn now. Why is that important?"

He didn't answer.

"Come on, bayou boy. Why is the location of the cassette or whether it was rewound important?"

He spoke in that hushed voice again. "We went out to the intake crib a few days ago. We took a look around. Listened with some equipment. We were out there for hours, but we didn't pick up any radio signals."

"Radio signals?"

"Your tape, Ellie. The RF."

An uneasy tingle ran through me.

"Our analysts say there's a possibility that the degradation on your tape was the result of a powerful blast," he said quietly. "Not a recurring signal. Just one. From a very close distance."

I thought about the grilling he'd just put me through. "Are you saying," I said slowly, "that the tape could have been damaged out on the crib?"

"It's possible."

"Where?"

He folded his hands on the table. "That's what I'm trying to find out."

"Why does it matter? What's so important about this signal?"

He shrugged and looked away. If he knew the answer, he wasn't about to tell me.

"Who are you, Nick LeJeune?"

He raised his eyebrows. "I told you."

"Bullshit. You show up at my house with an agent who tracks mobsters. But you're not on any mob squad. You tell me stories about RF signals from the intake crib. Why do you need to know about the tape? What made you seek me out? At least tell me that much."

"You're right." He cleared his throat. "Okay. Coates comes into the men's room down at the Bureau a while back. I'm there doing my business, and he's shaking his head, telling me he's gotta follow up on some ditsy broad who's riding around with mafiosi on the North Shore. So we're having a laugh about it, and then he says, 'It's the same broad who testified in that trial about the intake cribs.' " He steepled his hands. "I didn't have much else going on, so I came with him."

"Yeah? What do you do at the Bureau, monitor the Coast Guard?"

"Me?" He hesitated a fraction too long. "I do odd jobs."

"Odd jobs."

"That's right. Hey." He unfolded his hands and waved one in the air. "You want some pasta? The stuffed shells here put Maggiano's to shame."

BANDS OF RAIN streaked across the windshield on the ride home. The Spyder's headlights barely pierced the gloom. LeJeune switched on the defroster while I wiped the inside of the windshield. We were behind an SUV, a Ford Explorer. As LeJeune swerved around it, it occurred to me I hadn't seen any dark SUVs recently. Since the day I'd been driving around with Morelli, in fact.

I looked over. "You remember that Keystone Cop routine you and Morelli and that SUV went through the other day?"

"Yeah."

"Did you ever find out who was in it?"

He was quiet for a minute. "Someone muddied the plates up. We couldn't get a read."

"So you don't know who they were?"

He shook his head.

"Or if they were following Morelli?"

He shrugged.

"Rhonda Disapio thought she was being followed by an SUV. And she died."

"But you're alive. And how many SUVs have been following you recently?"

"None," I admitted. "But—"

"So maybe it was a coincidence."

"And maybe it wasn't."

"You said you were through ·with conspiracies."

"Then why are you pumping me about the cribs?"

He didn't answer, and we drove the rest of the way in

silence. As we pulled up to my house, he kept the engine running. I took that as a sign to get out.

"Thanks for dinner." I opened the door.

He leaned across and tipped up my chin with his finger. "You know, in this light, *cher,* you're a dead ringer for Vivian Leigh." He paused, as if waiting for my reaction.

"Does this usually work for you? I mean that Cajun shit just keeps oozing right out."

He grinned, not at all disconcerted. "Just like mud on the bayou."

THIRTY-ONE

I GOT INTO my PJs, trying to make sense of the evening.

The tape with the shots of Johnnie Santoro might have been damaged on the cribs. By a nonrecurring radio signal. Okay. Fine. But why was the FBI so interested?

There had to be a logical reason. I checked the clock. Almost eleven. Rachel would be home soon. She knew something about radio. I could ask her.

I turned on *Saturday Night Live*. A skit about homeopathic medicine was followed by a heavy metal band screaming their way through a song about war. I suffered through it with gritted teeth, then checked the clock again. Eleven-twenty.

Rachel was late.

I went to the window. Rain sluiced down over the glass, and the disk of the streetlight at our end of the block was rimmed in fog. Beyond it stretched a dark expanse of space. I went into the kitchen and poured a glass of wine. When I came back out, it was eleven twenty-two.

No Rachel.

I picked up the phone and dialed.

Katie's mother answered.

"Patsy, Hi. It's Ellie Foreman."

"Oh, hi, Ellie. How are you?"

"Should I come get Rachel now? She didn't call for a ride, but it's past her curfew."

I heard a slight hesitation. "Umm, Rachel's not here."

"Oh, did Frank give her a ride home?" Frank was Patsy's husband.

"Ellie, Rachel left a long time ago."

"What?"

"Her cousin picked her up around nine."

I gripped the phone. "Her cousin?"

"She said you knew all about it."

I kept my mouth shut.

"My God, Ellie—you didn't? Oh no. What can I do?"

"Did you see this 'cousin'?"

"No. I think they honked—the rain and all—and she went running out." She sounded more upset than me. "Tell you what. Let me wake up Katie and ask her. She'll probably know."

"I think that would be a good idea, if you don't—" A pair of headlights threw beams of opaque light through the window. A dark SUV was pulling into the driveway. I tensed. The side door opened, and Rachel emerged, jacket over her head. The SUV backed down the driveway.

"You know what?" I said into the phone. "She just pulled up. Thanks, Patsy."

I was at the door when Rachel jabbed it with her key. I planted my hands on my hips and waited. It seemed to take her a while to open it. I thought I heard her humming. When the door finally opened, she took her time withdrawing her key.

I cleared my throat.

She looked up. Her mouth split into a wide, lazy grin. "Hiya, Moommmm."

"Rachel, where have you been? And who was that?" I motioned toward the driveway.

She didn't answer but slowly walked into the kitchen, deliberately putting one foot in front of the other. Her shirt was bunched up above her waist, and her hair was tangled.

"Rachel?" I followed her in.

She stumbled over her feet, arms flailing. I caught her before she fell. She tried to push me away, but she missed. Her fingers clumsily flicked across my arm.

"Rachel?"

She looked at me with flat, glassy eyes.

"Rachel, sit down." She ignored me. I tightened my hold on her arm.

She flopped down at the table and propped up her head with her hand.

"You've been drinking."

"No, I haven't."

Stay calm, Ellie. You can handle this. "Who were you with?"

She shook her head in a slow, exaggerated way.

"I know you weren't at Katie's. I talked to Mrs. Shearson."

She didn't say anything.

"Where were you, Rachel?"

She slouched lower in the chair.

"Rachel, were you with Carla and Derek?"

She lifted a finger to her lips. "Shhh. Can't tell." Her shoulder dropped, and she slumped to one side. Bleary eyes slid from my face to the table, then rolled back in her head and closed. "Rachel, do you need to throw up?"

She opened her eyes and gave me a lopsided smile. "Nooope. I'm fine." Then she threw up on the table.

I CALLED EARLY the next morning. "Barry, it's me."

"How ya' doing, Ellie?" He sounded chipper.

"I've been better."

"What's wrong?"

"Your daughter came home drunk last night and puked on the kitchen table."

He went quiet. Then, "Is she all right?"

"She's still passed out." I stood up. "Barry, I've been meaning to talk to you about this. Did you know she's been hanging around with Carla and Derek?"

"Marlene's daughter?"

"Yes." I restrained myself from adding her "aerobics queen" handle. "Apparently, she was with them. I wondered if you'd ask Marlene if that's true. And then, maybe we can all sit down and—"

"Hold on, Ellie. What makes you think she was with Carla?"

"Well, for one, she admitted it."

"You asked her?"

"Of course." I started to pace around my office, the familiar irritation of dealing with Barry surfacing.

"Well, what did you expect her to say?"

"The truth."

"The truth." He snorted. "She'd say anything to get you off her back. What evidence do you have?"

"Evidence? What evidence? This isn't a court—"

"Where did she go? Who drove? Who slipped her an ID? Come on, Ellie. Instead of running off at the mouth, show me the evidence."

"Running off at the mouth?" I clenched my jaw. "Barry, lose the attack mode, will you? Rachel's in trouble. We have to deal with it responsibly."

"Attack? You accuse my girlfriend's daughter of corrupting Rachel, and you don't have a shred of evidence to back it up. You tell me who's attacking."

I squeezed my eyes shut and counted to five. No way would I make it to ten. "Barry, I insist that Rachel and Carla stay away from each other. If not, I'll have to take action. In the meantime, you might want to have a little talk with Marlene, just to make sure she knows where her daughter is when she's flexing her glutes or abs or whatever else she's doing all day."

A hostile silence followed. Then, "Ellie, you're the one who doesn't know where your daughter is or who she's with. If you can't handle Rachel, maybe we should re-consider her living arrangements."

A swell of fury shot through me. I slammed down the phone.

I didn't want to admit it, but Barry was right. I *didn't* know where Rachel had been. She'd lied to me. Katie's mother, too. But up until now, it never crossed my mind not to trust her. I always thought we had an honest relationship. But maybe an honest relationship with a teenager was an oxymoron. I'd been no angel myself, I recalled. If Rachel was dissembling at thirteen, what would she be doing in a few years?

I sank into a chair. When Rachel was young, I joked about raising children according to the school of bribes and threats. But that was when parenting consisted mostly of cuddling, potty training, and making sure they ate a tablespoon of vegetables a day. Now that she was becoming a person, I felt ill equipped and clumsy. What was the right tack? Cajole or insist? Negotiate or demand?

I gazed at the picture of her and David on my desk. I'd taken it at the Botanic Gardens last summer. Why wasn't he here with me? He might not know what to do either, but at least we could muddle through it together.

BY EVENING RACHEL was a palette of miserable colors: her eyes were yellow, her nose red, and there was a green-ish cast to her skin. I brought ginger ale and aspirin and tucked her back in bed. Her bedside lamp threw an arc of light on a clutter of stuffed animals in the corner.

"Now I know what a soccer ball feels like." She moaned.

"Sounds about right."

"I'll never do that again."

"You heard her," I said to a poster of four young men with black T-shirts and tattoos, who were glowering at me from the wall.

"Why do people get drunk?"

I didn't answer.

"It wasn't even fun."

"You want to tell me about it?"

She sighed. "Derek got this stuff. Sloe gin. We drove to the park and drank it."

Sloe gin fizzes. Tasted like punch but kicked like tequila. The kind of drink you give to underaged kids. I remember worshiping the porcelain goddess myself years ago, thanks to sloe gin. I also remember why my date kept pouring them down my throat.

"Rachel, did anything happen—I mean—after you were drinking?" I imagined Derek fondling my baby. Or worse.

"Carla and Derek started to make out, but then she threw up, and we came home."

"What about you? Did Derek try anything, well . . . inappropriate?" If she answered yes, I'd claw his eyes out.

"Mom, I was in the backseat. He was driving."

I relaxed.

"I'm sorry, Mommy."

"Shhh." I stroked her forehead. Maybe it had taught her a lesson. Maybe she wouldn't be so eager the next time. "Try to get some sleep."

"Will you read to me?"

We hadn't done that in years. "What did you have in mind?"

"Harry Potter? I never finished number four."

I grabbed *Goblet of Fire* from her bookcase and started in. Harry and Malfoy had set to each other using their wands as weapons, and Hermione's teeth were growing at an alarming rate. Snape cut off the scuffle in the nick of time, but no one seemed happy it was over. When I looked up at Rachel, she was asleep. I finished the chapter myself.

THIRTY-TWO

RACHEL AND I discussed the consequences of her behavior at breakfast. She was grounded until Thanksgiving: no play dates, mall trips, or evenings out. Especially on weekends. She would write a letter of apology to Mrs. Shearson for lying, and she'd volunteer at the soup kitchen twice a week.

"What about Science Club?" she asked. "We're starting chemistry. Can I still go?"

I thought about it. "Yes, that's permissible."

She beamed and polished off her cereal. I'd pictured her spending her teenage years in a dusty basement, fooling around with transistors, crystals, and diodes. But hey, if it meant she wouldn't be cruising around raves or getting drunk in the park, I'd throw in a chemistry set, too.

After I dropped her at school, I put on my black Garfield and Marx suit and headed downtown. Traffic clogged the expressway, the sky was bleak with hard-edged clouds, and a bitter wind tossed the last of the leaves around. November had arrived. We'd be lucky to see any sun before April.

Ninety minutes later, I was ushered into Dale Reedy's office. She was wearing a gray suit, almost a replica of her navy, but either the color was bad or she hadn't slept well. She looked more chalky than a British complexion would suggest.

"How are you, Ellie?" She came around the desk and shook my hand.

"Fine. And you?"

She led me over to the table. "I'm anxious to see the proposal."

No chitchat today. I dug out my copy, wondering if something was troubling her but knowing I couldn't ask.

"I think it turned out well," I said. "But I do have a couple of questions. I noted them with asterisks."

She took the papers. "I'll just start going through these, shall I?"

As she read, I looked around. She'd moved the pictures of her boys to a different shelf, and the daily newspapers were stacked in a chair. I didn't see her running shoes. Had she suspended her jogging for the season?

"This is good." She pointed to a paragraph on the second page. "Especially the bit about the leadership role we're taking."

You spoon-fed that to me, I wanted to reply. "Thanks."

She flipped through the document. "Yes. I think this will do. I'll have to show it to Tribble, of course, and take some time to—"

"Tribble?"

She yanked a finger toward the door. "My boss."

I remembered the older, gray-haired man who'd been so cool, even disapproving. My expression must have telegraphed my concern, because she added, "Oh, don't worry about him. He lets me do whatever I want. He's usually ripped by afternoon, anyway."

We exchanged knowing looks, and she turned to the last page. "Let's go over the budget, shall we?"

I cleared my throat. "I wasn't sure whether you wanted me to take a crew from Chicago or pick up one out there. Either way would work." I leaned forward. "And I wasn't sure how much you wanted to invest in postproduction."

"Postproduction?"

"Editing and special effects. And duplication. But the special effects are the prime consideration. If we—"

"Duplication?" She tapped a pencil. "What are we duplicating?"

"We'll need to know—at some point—how many copies you're going to want of the finished show. We use a duplication service, and the price breaks according to how many dubs you order. I listed them here." I pointed to a line item at the bottom of the page.

"Oh, I see." She gave me a rueful smile. "But tell me. How many copies do you make of the unfinished tapes?"

"Unfinished?"

"The tapes that you shoot in the field."

"You mean the originals we shoot on location?"

She nodded. "If that's what you call them."

I shrugged. "We normally don't make any. Most clients aren't interested in the elements. They just want the finished product."

She frowned. "But didn't I hear about a copy of a tape you made on the telly?"

I tried not to react. "That was the tape for the water district. That . . . that was a special situation."

"Did you make copies of everything for them?"

"No. In their case, we returned the originals. At least most of them." It was my turn to frown. Where was she going with this? "But the tapes are your property. If you think you're going to need copies, I'll be glad to make them."

"Well, now. I'm not sure."

"Most of our clients are happy to let us keep them in storage. That way they know they're safe, and they won't get damaged." I flinched as soon as I said it, but Dale already had arched her eyebrows.

I tried to backpedal. "Uh . . . the water district was an abnormality. An aberration."

"Indeed." Her eyebrows smoothed out. "But you returned all your originals to them?"

"Not all of them. They only wanted the ones that showed the operation of the filtration plant and the cribs. For security reasons."

"Of course. But then—" she paused "—how were you able to use that tape at the trial?"

A muffled trill cut through the air. "Blast. I thought I turned that off." She slid open her drawer, picked up a cell phone, and looked at the LED. Then she flipped off the switch. "Sorry. Where were we?"

"It's all right. As a matter of fact, the tape that we played at the trial, the one with the shots of Santoro was one of the ones I didn't have to return. It was a reenactment. We used actors and dressed them up in costumes. The only thing we shot were interiors. We probably could have done the shoot in a hotel room, and no one would have known the difference."

She smiled. "But you ended up making copies of it, anyway. For the trial."

"That's right." I was puzzled by her questions, but she was the client.

"So, how many—" Her office phone rang. "It never ends." She looked back at me. "I'll let my secretary get it. Give her something to do besides read the *Enquirer*."

But the phone kept ringing. She glanced impatiently at the phone, then held up the proposal and tapped the edges of the papers on the table. Finally, the ringing stopped. She laid the papers flat and clasped her hands together.

"Now . . ."

I was about to continue when there was a knock at the door.

"Yes?"

The door cracked, and a woman with dark hair and darker skin poked her head in. "I'm sorry, Ms. Reedy, but a Mr. Sam says he needs to talk to you now."

Dale's jaw tightened. "Tell him I'll call him back."

"He was very persistent."

"Lavinia." Dale's voice was icy. "I told you—I'll call him—"

The woman tensed, her face saying she didn't want to be held accountable if Dale refused the call.

Dale got it. "Oh never mind. I'll take the bloody call."

Lavinia withdrew, looking relieved. Dale stomped to her desk. "Twit. Doesn't even know how to screen calls."

I shifted in my seat.

She picked up the phone. "Yes?" A pause. "No." Another pause. "That's correct."

I stood up and wandered over to her window, trying to give her some privacy. The cloud cover had lifted to a high overcast, and her window, was larger than most office windows. If I pressed close to the glass, I could see both east and west. To the west was the heart of the Loop, a patchwork of irregularly shaped buildings. I could even see the Eisenhower Expressway, which runs west from the junction of the Kennedy and Dan Ryan. Millions of commuters use one of those three highways every day.

"Listen to me." Dale's voice grew more agitated. "I will handle it. Don't worry. I'll call you back."

I looked the other way. The traffic on Lake Shore Drive was a shifting pattern of dots, and the lake, gunmetal today, looked deserted and cold. Leaning my forehead against the glass, I could just make out the intake cribs in the distance. If I craned my neck farther left, maybe I could see Navy Pier.

As I looked, I noticed something running the length of the window at the edge of the glass. At first, I thought it was a crack. I reached up a finger to touch it, but it felt bumpy, not smooth, like you'd expect with an embedded break. I ran a finger down its length. A delicate wire, with a clear insulation, was taped to the window. It was barely more substantial than a thread, not something you'd see if you weren't looking for it.

I took a step back and followed its path with my eyes. Down to the floor, across the baseboards, around the corner, behind Dale's desk. I looked up. Dale was watching me, her phone in her hand, but when she caught me looking at her, she flicked her eyes away and returned the phone to its base.

She didn't say anything.

Neither did I.

RACHEL'S SCIENCE CLUB teacher had said antennas were flexible. You could put them anywhere. But why would Dale Reedy have an antenna in her window, I wondered on the way home. Did she have a radio setup there? Was there some connection between the oil company and the cribs?

There must be another explanation. Maybe Dale had a shortwave radio. Or a ham setup. Maybe she used it to keep in touch with her boys back in England. Families did things like that when they were separated by distance, didn't they?

But then, where was the rest of the equipment? And why didn't she say anything about it? Because it was clear from her expression when I found it that I wasn't supposed to. In fact, her behavior during our entire meeting was strange. Our discussion about the video was perfunctory. The enthusiasm she'd mustered during our first meeting was gone. The only thing she'd been interested in was the duplication of the tapes.

I thought back to our conversation. How she'd seemed to have trouble grasping the difference between originals and edited shows; how she kept coming back to the water district tape. Wanting to know how many copies we'd made. Whether I'd returned the original. My stomach tightened. She was pumping me about the tape we'd shot at the cribs! The tape with the RF on it.

The familiar landmarks on Ontario Street took on a sinister aura as I headed west. Buildings were darker, more hulking, cars and trucks more aggressive. Pedestrians wore menacing leers. What was so frigging important about that tape? First, LeJeune. Now Dale Reedy.

But Dale had a wire on her window. And a direct line of sight to the cribs.

WHEN I GOT home, I dug out LeJeune's card and punched in his number at the Bureau. His voice mail picked up. I left a message, telling him I needed to talk to him about my meeting at Great Lakes Oil.

I was still uneasy two hours later, and on the way home from school, I quizzed Rachel. "Sweetheart, remember those radios your Science Club teacher brought in for Parents' Day?"

"Sure."

"What are they used for?"

"Which ones?"

"Wasn't there something called a packet?"

She nodded. "Packet's awesome."

"Why?"

"Once you hook up a computer to it, you can do just about anything. Transmit voice, data, send signals to make things happen."

"Yeah?"

She twisted around. "We told you all that at Parents' Day. Weren't you listening?"

"I was, and you did a great job."

She nodded, as if the compliment was her due. We pulled into the garage.

"But tell me something, Rach. Can you send just one signal with the radio if you want? You know, just one blast at a time?"

"Of course." She pointed to the garage door opener. "That's what that thing does."

"Gotcha. But you'd still need an antenna with a line of sight between the two points, right? Even with only one signal?"

"Uh, duh."

I went upstairs to change. But as I hung up my suit, safe in the confines of my home, I started to second-guess myself. Could I have misinterpreted the situation? What if the wire wasn't Dale's? Perhaps it had been left by the former occupant of her office. She hadn't been in the country that long. Maybe her predecessor had an affinity for shortwave or ham radio, and when Dale inherited the office, she never got around to removing it.

For all I knew, moreover, Dale's behavior today could have been job related. God knows she was in a high-stress environment. Maybe she was in political trouble. It had been known to happen. Zealous female outstrips boss. But if said boss is a member of the old boys' network, guess who gets the shaft?

I put on jeans and a turtleneck and went outside to rake leaves. Fouad hadn't been around for a while, and a thick layer of them covered the grass. They were wet and heavy and speckled with black rot. It felt like moving rocks. I cleared a section of lawn, then bagged the debris and dragged the bag into the garage. I'd been working less than half an hour, but I'd worked up a sweat, and my hands tingled. I went back inside. I'd mulch the bulbs later.

Back in the kitchen, Rachel threw open the fridge. Grabbing a can of pop, she snapped off the top and swilled down half the can in one gulp. Then she let out a long, resonant burp.

"Lovely." A wave of cold air drifted over me. I closed the refrigerator door.

"Ummm." She took another swig. "By the way," she said on her way out, "he called while you were outside."

"Nick?"

She shot me a curious glance. "No. David."

"Oh."

She stomped up the stairs.

*   *   *

I CALLED DAVID back after dinner, but he didn't pick up. I left a message, then channel surfed for a while. The late news was full of the terrorist's trial. Acting as his own attorney, he was raging about the injustice of the American legal system. I turned off the TV.

After checking my E-mail, I started to clean up my desk. I'm fairly casual about housework; with a teenage daughter, you have to be. The only exception is when I feel life slipping out of control. Then, I charge through the house like an army of cleaning ladies, straightening, dusting, and scrubbing, as if the imposition of physical order would magically extend to my mind.

I pitched scraps of paper, rubber bands, and candy wrappers into the trash. Then I took everything off the desk and wiped the surface. As I was moving a couple of paperbacks, I noticed a corner of yellow paper inside one. I slid it out of the book. It was the sheet of paper from Dale Reedy's legal pad. With the imprint of the Four Seasons' phone number. And Abdul's suite.

Was there a connection between them? It was possible. Except that a few weeks ago he said he'd never heard of Dale Reedy. Didn't even know she was a woman. An uneasy sensation hummed my skin.

THIRTY-THREE

WHEN DAD HAS to walk any distance, he uses a cane that once belonged to his grandfather. Made of dark, polished oak, it has a knobbed silver handle that resembles a crown. It's a work of art, with delicate engraved motifs and carvings. He was rubbing it as we parked outside Irv's clothing store for men.

"We'll just run in, find a wool overcoat, and come out," he said impatiently.

"Okay." I got out and took his arm. "But you might want to consider a down jacket."

"Why would I want to do that?"

"Dad, it's a new century. They have different materials. They're really comfy. And warm."

"What's wrong with a nice, double-breasted camel's hair?"

"Not a thing. I'm just saying you could try something new."

He sniffed as we pushed through the door. Irv's is one of those no-nonsense places that sells menswear at a discount.

"So, how's Sylvia?"

He thumped his cane on the parquet floor. "Lovely lady, that Sylvia. Makes a mean batch of chicken soup."

"We've moved up to soup, have we?"

"She made Shabbos dinner last week. You know. Makes brisket just like Barney Teitelman's mother used to. Lots of onions and gravy."

I smiled. "Anything else going on you want to tell me?"

"If there is, you won't hear it from me."

We moved down aisles filled with men's clothing. To me, all those suits, jackets, and slacks are drab—too many pinstripes, grays, and browns—but I soldiered on. A salesman hovered at a discreet distance.

Coats were in the back. I thumbed through a rack and held out a dark green down coat with a zippered lining and hood. "How about something like this?"

He looked over from the rack he was browsing. "What am I, an explorer in the tundra?"

He turned around and pulled out a long brown wool with a reddish orange fleck weave. "How about this?"

"It looks like it was made in the forties."

"Exactly." He took out the hanger, slipped on the coat, and moved to a full-length mirror. "So what's going on with David?"

I cleared my throat. "Thank you for rescuing me the other day in the car."

He gazed at me in the glass and buttoned the coat. "You're having *tsuris?*"

"We—we have some things to work out."

"You should work them out quickly. You never know how much time you're gonna have."

"Dad, don't be maudlin."

"Just being realistic." He pirouetted in the mirror, then unbuttoned the coat and shrugged out of it. "Okay, let's see that Alaskan snowsuit."

I held out the down coat. He tried it on, checked himself out in the mirror, and arched his eyebrows. "Is that why you look like somebody shot your best friend?"

"That's part of it."

"What's the other part?"

I told him about Rachel's bout with sloe gin.

At first Dad looked concerned. Then his face smoothed out to a knowing look, and, by the time I finished, he was chuckling. "Sloe gin, huh? Reminds me of the time I was fifteen. Barney and I found a bottle of hooch behind the bar at Teitelman's. Figured it was left over from Prohibition. So we drank it. Boy, were we sorry."

"But Dad, she's only thirteen. Two years is a big difference."

"If she had anywhere near as bad a hangover as I did, she learned an important lesson."

"Are you're saying I shouldn't worry?"

"Tell me something. What were you doing at thirteen, Eleanor?"

I opened my mouth. Nothing came out.

"I rest my case." He waved a hand. "Don't worry. Rachel's a smart cookie. She'll be all right."

"Maybe." I sighed. "But the worst part is that Barry and I can't talk about it rationally. It was his girlfriend's daughter Rachel was with. I've been thinking I might call the woman. You know, discuss it mother to mother."

His answer came fast. "Don't do that."

"Why not?"

"If your husband thinks—"

"My ex-husband."

"Him, too," he shot back. "If he thinks you're sneaking around behind his back, he'll make your life miserable."

I didn't want to admit it, but he was right.

"Promise me, Ellie. . . ."

"All right. You win."

Nodding, he shrugged out of the down coat. "And now, just so we're even, so do you."

I cocked my head.

He patted the down coat, a twinkle in his eye. "Let's get out of here before I change my mind."

On the way home, Dad tapped his cane on the floor of

the car, humming tunelessly. I smiled. I should start thinking about Thanksgiving. I'd told Dad to invite Sylvia, as
well as his buddies Marv and Frank. Rachel would be
with us, too, and she was planning to invite a classmate
who'd just moved here from China. I needed to round up
a turkey. Buy sweet potatoes, green beans. I'd make up a
Jell-O mold, of course, and pecan pie. And the apple and
chestnut stuffing recipe Susan found in a gourmet magazine. We'd probably have way too much food, but we
could take the leftovers to the soup kitchen.

I was mentally preparing my grocery list when it occurred to me I didn't know whether to count on David.
A pang went through me. We'd only been together a few
months, and our relationship was already fraying. Was I
too reckless for him? Or was he too cautious, unable to
loosen up? Or was all of this just an excuse to ignore my
own demons? I chewed my lip. Analyzing the situation
wouldn't help if he stayed in Philadelphia while I was
here. Why couldn't things go back the way they were?
Why couldn't we rewind the past few weeks?

Rewinding my life made me think of the tape, Dale
Reedy, and the wire on her window. I looked over at Dad.
He might use a cane to get around, but his mind was still
sharp. I'd been reluctant to get him involved: last summer
he'd ended up in the hospital because of me. But David
and I were hardly talking, and LeJeune was who knows
where. Mac and Susan didn't want to get involved, and I
didn't want to burden Fouad. I didn't have many options.
I needed to talk it through with someone.

I edged out of my lane to pass a Mercedes. "Dad, I
need your advice."

He looked over, still rubbing the knob of the cane.

"I was wrong about something. You remember the lawyer who was killed? Brashares?"

"Santoro's lawyer?"

"Right. Remember how I thought the mob might be
involved?"

His sigh sounded like escaping steam. "Ellie, I thought that was over and done with."

"I thought it was, too. But a few things have come up. And I can't—well, I'm starting to worry." I paused. "It started again at Mac's studio. I was working late there one night when a fire broke out, and—"

"You were in a fire?"

"I wasn't hurt," I added hastily. "At the time, I thought it might be connected to my testimony at the trial."

"What are you talking about?"

"I guess I need to tell you the whole thing."

I explained what I learned about Santoro, how that led me to DePalma and Morelli, how the FBI suddenly took an interest in the tape. "They're trying to identify the source of the RF on the videotape. They think it's somewhere on the intake cribs."

He squinted. I had his full attention.

"But now I'm not sure who's doing what or why." I told him about Dale Reedy and the wire on her window.

Dad put a hand on his cane and the other on the handle. "You say the fire department hasn't solved this arson?"

"They don't have any suspects."

"But somebody set that fire."

I nodded.

"And you thought it was the Mafia coming after you—because of something you were supposed to know. That Brashares and the Disapio girl probably also knew."

I nodded again.

"But now not only the FBI but this oil executive is asking you questions about the same tape. The tape you showed at the Santoro trial."

I considered telling him about Abdul and his possible connection to Dale Reedy but decided not to. I wasn't sure how—or even if—they were connected, and the fact that Abdul was in touch with David would just give Dad another reason to worry. "That's about it."

I exited the Edens on Old Orchard Road and drove east.

Dad looked straight ahead, a frown on his face. The only sound in the car was his cane tapping.

He seemed to become aware of something slowly. "Maybe you've been looking at it the wrong way."

"What do you mean?"

"Maybe it wasn't you they were after. Maybe it was the tape."

"The tape?"

"It sounds like some people don't want that tape to exist."

"The woman at Great Lakes Oil?"

"Among others."

"Because of the RF."

"Which the FBI is trying to analyze." He looked over. "Tell me. How many copies of that tape did you make?"

"That's what Dale Reedy wanted to know."

"What did you tell her?"

"Actually, not much. We were interrupted by a phone call." I thought back. "And then I saw the wire on her window."

He rubbed his chin. "So, how many are there?"

"Let's see. I made two copies before I testified. One of which I took with me to Brashares's office the first time. Then there was the original Beta that we played at the trial. There was also the master dub that we made for the files—in case we never got the original back. That's the one that was destroyed in the fire." I stopped at a light. "Brashares may have copied the copy for the prosecution, but then again, he was so cheap he might have just lent them the original."

"If the prosecution wanted a copy, they would have paid for it."

"Okay. So, I'm not sure what Brashares did."

"Too bad you can't ask him." He cleared his throat. "So, as far as you know, we're talking about four tapes."

"Yes."

He laid the cane down and ticked them off on his fingers. "You gave Brashares the original and one copy."

I nodded.

"And there was another one in the studio that was burned."

"Right."

"What about the fourth?" He squeezed his pinkie.

I didn't answer. It had been in my bag until I gave it to the Feds. But nobody, except Dad now, knew I didn't have it.

THIRTY-FOUR

THERE WERE TWO calls on my machine when I got home. The first was a terse message from LeJeune. He'd be out of town for a few days but would be in touch when he got back. That was it. No mention about getting my call. Nothing about looking into Dale Reedy or Great Lakes Oil.

The second was from Abdul, who was back in Chicago. "I am sorry I did not reach you," he said on the tape. "Please call me back." He reeled off the number of the Four Seasons.

As if I didn't know.

I deleted the message.

A bone-chilling rain mixed with sleet pounded the area that night. The weather people congratulated themselves on accurately predicting the first snow of the season. Never mind that they'd predicted the same thing a few days ago, and nothing materialized. It's as if they can't wait to proclaim that winter has, in fact, arrived in Chicago. It must be written into their contracts. I turned up the heat and threw extra quilts on the beds.

Dad wanted me to let Dale Reedy know that I had given the fourth tape to the FBI. I wasn't so sure. Given her off behavior the other day, that seemed like the wrong kind of signal to send. If she thought I was onto something she didn't want known, telling her I had surrendered the tape wasn't going to convince her I was suddenly not a threat.

But that left me not knowing what to do—or whom to trust. I punched in LeJeune's number again. I knew he wouldn't be there, but maybe he'd call me back. "Hey, Nick. It's Ellie. I know you're out of town, but I really need to talk to you . . . Give a call, okay?"

As I hung up, I heard a grunt from the hall. Rachel stood in the doorway, hands on her hips. "You're dumping David, aren't you?"

"What?"

"You're dumping David for Nick."

"Are you crazy? Of course not."

"I don't believe you. You're lying."

"Rachel, what's gotten into you?"

"You know something? Daddy was right." Angry red patches flared on her cheeks.

"What are you talking about?"

"He said you're too dysfunctional for a normal relationship. He said you'd probably run through a lot of men."

I stared at her, slack jawed. "He said what?"

She didn't answer.

"Rachel, there's nothing between us. You'll have to trust me on that. And, as for your father—"

"I saw how he looked at you the night he came over. He asked me a lot of questions, too."

"Rachel, he's an FBI agent. That's his job."

"Questions about David and Daddy?"

"Young lady, I don't know what you're getting at, but I don't like it one bit. I think—"

Her face was turning purple. "You get after me for drinking, for breaking the rules. But you're the real hypocrite. You dump one guy, then go out with another. I wonder who it'll be tomorrow? You know something? I want to move in with Dad. At least he and Marlene are stable."

She stomped out of the room.

THIRTY-FIVE

ANGRY GRAY CLOUDS skudded across the sky as I pulled into the lot at the supermarket the next day. They matched my mood. I grabbed a cart, and headed inside. Rachel's outburst had been unnerving. Not just because of her emotional swings, which I knew were the result of hormones kicking in. Or even her anger, which was understandable—she'd seen me with David, and then, a short time later, with Nick. She could be legitimately confused.

What *was* making me crazy was Barry. I thought, after years of hostility, we'd reached a plateau where we could interact with civility if not warmth. But he had blindsided me again, spinning half-truths behind my back. In the past, I could usually work around him. Stop—or at least deflect—his blows before he did any damage. But this time I'd played into his hands. David was gone, LeJeune had appeared. I was his best accessory.

I snatched two bags of chocolate chips off the shelf. I tore one open and shoved a handful in my mouth. As the chocolate slid down my throat, I wasn't sure who to blame: Barry or me.

*   *   *

HANK CHENOWSKY LIVES in a three-flat in Wrigleyville, not far from the ballpark. It was an older building, and as I climbed to the second floor, a musty smell sifted through the walls. Hank opened the door, a surprised look on his face. I wondered why; I'd called him from the grocery store. He was taking the day off, the editing room wasn't quite ready. I got my answer when I sniffed the air.

I swore off grass years ago, choosing alcohol instead. It was a Hobson's choice. I was all for "better living through chemistry," but I knew weed could lead to lung cancer. Some studies linked it to brain damage. Alcohol could trigger heart attacks and brain damage. Since brain damage was a given, I went with liquor, figuring a heart attack would kill me quicker than cancer. Oh. And booze is legal.

Hank's eyes were bloodshot, his pupils dilated. "Oh, man. You did say you were coming down. Sorry."

I looked around. "Where's Sandy?"

"Giving a music lesson."

"Too bad. I was hoping I could meet her."

"Me, too." He smiled beatifically. "She's awesome."

At least somebody's love life was good. I followed him back to the kitchen, feeling envious. His apartment had hardwood floors, high ceilings, and a back porch off the kitchen. My first apartment in Old Town had a similar layout. A memory of winter weekends with Barry flashed through my mind. Both of us stripping off boots, Levi's, turtlenecks, and sweaters, desperate to get our hands on each other, even though we'd just gotten dressed. Passion and sex are easy when you're young.

Hank opened the fridge and scratched his head. "You want something? Juice? Tea?"

"I'll settle for diet soda."

He whirled around, a look of horror suffusing his face. "Ellie, do you know how bad that shit is for you?"

Considering his present state of consciousness, I bit my lip.

"You should purify your system, you know? Cleanse all the additives polluting your body. Your body is your temple, man." He sniffed with the zeal of a convert. "Sandy won't bring anything into the house that isn't organic." He rummaged in the fridge and pulled out a pitcher of something dark and murky. "Here. Try this oolong. It's organic. It flushes out toxins." He poured a glass.

I took a sip. Bitter and sharp. I had a sudden craving for a Big Mac. "I feel better already."

Brightening, he poured one for himself, and we went into the living room. A framed eight-by-ten photo rested on a table. Hank with a young woman. She was almost as tall as Hank, had long, frizzy red hair, and wore granny glasses. Her skin was so pale it was almost translucent. Their arms were wrapped around each other, and they both wore loopy smiles. I saw the lake in the background.

"Hey, this is the first time you've ever been here," he said, as if the thought had just occurred to him.

"That's right, Hank."

He nodded his head. "Cool, man."

I settled back on the couch. Hank has a big-screen TV with every conceivable accessory attached to it: DVD, video deck, satellite receiver. He even has a connection to his computer in case he needs to see something he's downloaded on a really big screen.

"So why are you here?"

"Well, like I said, I was hoping I could meet Sandy." I pointed to the picture.

He flashed me the same loopy smile. "She's working. Teaching."

"A music lesson."

"How'd you know?"

I set the glass down on the table. "So how have things been going since the fire?"

"We're getting there. Another few weeks, we'll be finished."

"Still no word on who might have done it?"

"No. Mac says the case is still open, but since the insurance came through, I don't think he cares too much."

I nodded. Next to the picture of Hank and Sandy was a frog in a red and white striped shirt, steering a gondola.

"Hank, do you remember the RF on that tape from the cribs?"

He rolled his eyes. "Oh, man. Not again."

"Well, a few questions came up recently, and you know so much more about that kind of thing than I do."

"I don't know. I kinda wanta forget about that."

"Just a couple of questions. Please."

He flipped up his palm. "Let's have it."

"Thanks." I set down my tea. "Okay. Let's say you have interference on a tape, and you find out that rather than being continuous, it might have been just one single, powerful burst. What does that tell you?"

He squinted and rubbed his chin with his fingers. "I give up. What?"

"Seriously, Hank. The tape is being analyzed"—I didn't say by whom—"and they're not sure the interference came through the camera."

"That's weird."

"Not if the tape was sitting next to a source that was transmitting radio waves."

"Is that what they're saying?"

"They're not saying anything. I'm asking."

He rubbed his chin again. "Man, I don't know. Anything I say would just be a guess."

"Guessing counts."

"Well, when you're talking about one burst, no matter where it's coming from, you might be looking at some kind of data transmission."

"Data?"

"Voice transmission is continuous. More or less steady. Depending on the conversation, of course. But when you transmit data, it comes in a binary burst. Kind of like . . ." He paused and then expelled a loud noise, part belch, part word. "BRAAAP."

I suppressed a giggle. "So the signal might have been one of those—er, BRAAAPs?"

"Yeah. BRAAAP." It sounded like an imitation of a sick frog. "BRAAAP. BRAAAP." He grinned like a kid who's discovered a new way to annoy his mother.

"That's pretty much what Rachel said, too. Well, not in as many words." I shifted. "So it could be a data transmission. Theoretically."

"Sure." He nodded. "You have enough power, you can put an RF signal on anything that's magnetic."

"Power? How much power are you talking about?"

"Man, I don't know. I'm a video guy, Ellie, not an engineer. Enough to trigger the signal." He tossed his long hair, then gathered it as if he was making a ponytail. "Where was it?"

"The transmitter?"

"Right."

"I don't know. But is there any way to tell whether a signal is transmitting voice or data from the pattern of RF on video?"

"What do you mean?"

"Well, hypothetically, could there be streaks on the tape if the signal were voice, but snow if it were data . . . something like that?"

"Sorry, Charlie."

"Why not?"

He squinted at me. "You ever take any science courses?"

"As few as possible."

"It shows. Listen. You're dealing with the electromagnetic spectrum. It's all the same shit. The only thing that changes is the frequency. The wavelength."

"Which means?"

"In your case, it means that just because you see it doesn't mean you can tell what's causing it."

I sighed. "Okay. I got it."

"Really?"

"Well, maybe."

He grinned. I stayed a few more minutes, thinking Sandy might show up, but when she didn't, Hank walked me to the door. As I took the steps down, I turned around.

"Hey, thanks for the tea."

"BRAAAP." He saluted.

ANGRY WHITECAPS ROILED the lake as I took the Drive north. Between the afternoon rush, which seems to start around three these days, and an early dusk, it would take over an hour to get home. I was heading west on Peterson when I noticed the SUV following me. At first, I tried to put it out of my mind. If I ignored it, it didn't exist. But three minutes later, when it was still there, I checked the rearview mirror for plates.

There weren't any.

At least in front. I pulled over to let it pass so I could spot the ones on its rear. But as I slowed, it did, too. A ripple of unease ran through me. Finally, it turned off onto a side street.

Susan showed up after school, looking chic in black wool pants and a royal blue sweater. I've never seen her with a hair out of place, a stain on her shirt, a snag in her panty hose. I don't know how she does it. She's just as busy as me—maybe busier. I brewed coffee, feeling grungy in my sweats.

We took our mugs into the family room. A rerun of *Nova* was on TV. It was a show about sharks and the divers who photographed them off an island near Costa Rica. There were lots of dreamy underwater sequences where hammerheads and manta rays peacefully coexist. I wondered what kind of video equipment the divers were using and how they could shoot film and breathe at the same time.

Susan settled into a chair. "I have a good one for you."
I flipped off the tube. "Shoot."

Susan has her fingers on the pulse of village life, a
situation for which I'm exceedingly grateful. Without her,
I'd be bereft of the giggles and snide comments a good
gossip supplies.

"You know Carol Bailey, right? Two small kids, really
involved in IAS?

I nodded. The Infant Aid Society luncheon is an annual
September tradition on the North Shore. Over five hundred women, in elegant fall finery, gather inside a huge
tent on a palatial Winnetka estate for lunch and a fashion
show. The proceeds help provide day care for disadvan-
taged mothers struggling to get their lives in order. Having
gone to the luncheon once or twice, I feel nothing but
admiration for the hostess who sacrifices her lawn to a
thousand shoes and metal stakes every year.

"Which one is Carol?"

"She's on the board. Always talking up the Society and
the vital services they're delivering."

A hazy image floated into my mind. "Tall, thin, blond,
I-hate-you-'cause-you're-gorgeous looks?"

"That's the one." Susan paused, a twinkle in her eye.
"Well, Carol was arrested last week."

"What?"

She dropped her voice to a whisper. "Child endanger-
ment."

"No."

"She left her kids in the car to go in for a manicure,
and when she came out, two police officers were waiting
for her. She had to beg them not to call DCFS."

"My God. What happened?"

"Her husband eventually showed up." Susan tore open
a packet of sweetener and dumped the whole thing in her
mug. "I guess they worked it out. But still. There's this
new state law, you know. Twelve thousand dollars if you
leave your kids alone in the car."

"You think she paid it?"

She sipped her coffee. "Probably not. Family connections, you know."

"I know." I sipped my coffee. "People like that make me mad."

"People with connections?"

"No. People who are hypocritical about themselves." I waved a hand. "Like people who drive to an Earth Day rally in their SUVs."

"Or give money to MADD and then drive drunk?"

"Or get ticked off when a dog poops in *their* yard, but won't use a pooper scooper on *others'*."

We both laughed. She raised her mug. "This is good."

"It's vanilla."

There was a clatter from the kitchen. I turned to see Rachel righting a cereal bowl she'd somehow upended on the counter. I watched as she got milk out of the fridge, poured it into the bowl, and grabbed a spoon from the drawer, all the while conspicuously avoiding my eyes.

I turned back to Susan, whose eyebrow was arched so high it could have been in Saint Louis. "All is not happy in paradise, I see."

I shrugged.

"What happened?"

I told her about Rachel's tantrum.

When I finished, Susan fixed me with a penetrating look.

I braced. "Okay. Let's hear it. You're not happy with me, either."

"The issue isn't whether I'm happy, Ellie. It's whether you are."

"Susan, you need to understand something. David was the one who said we needed to take a break. Not me."

"Why?"

"You know what's been happening since I testified. Things around here haven't been what you could call normal."

"Oh, I don't know. Maybe getting trapped in fires is part of your self-improvement program."

"David can't handle it."

"Can you blame him?"

I fumed. "I know he's concerned, but if it were up to him, I'd live in a perfect little room with perfect furnishings—you know, like that room Keir Dullea ended up in in *2001*."

Susan put her mug down. "Ellie, you're probably my closest friend. You could rob a bank, overthrow the government, and I would still love you. But sometimes I wonder if you know what you're doing."

"Susan—"

"No, let me finish. You have this wonderful man who adores you and your daughter. There's nothing he wants more than to be with you for the rest of your life. So, what do you do? Dredge up some lame philosophical excuse why it's not working out, push him away, and then go running around with an FBI agent, who—" she made imaginary quotation marks in the air "—you're suddenly 'helping' on an important case."

"Susan, I told Rachel, and I'm telling you. There's nothing there. It's a totally professional relationship."

"Okay."

"Anyway, that has nothing to do with David."

"Except for the fact that he's not around, and this guy is." She peered at me over her coffee cup. "Oh yes. And the fact that David loves you."

I frowned. I thought of the weekend at the Greenbrier. The surprise at the Four Seasons. The way he took care of me after the trial. The plans he was always making. "But he's always doing nice things."

"Always doing nice things, huh? As in 'I love you and want you to be happy' nice things?"

I didn't answer.

Susan flipped up her palm. "Hmm . . . Let's see. Here we have a generous man, who wants a loving, intimate relationship." She flipped up the other. "And here we have an FBI agent who gallops in like the Lone Ranger, and will probably gallop right out after whatever 'case' you're working on is over. But, of course, he'd be glad to give you a ride on Silver first." She alternated raising her hands, as if weighing the scales of justice. "Gee, I wonder which is the better deal?"

The way I was feeling, a ride on Silver might not be a bad idea. Fast. Fun. No strings attached. But I couldn't say that. "Susan, you can't really believe I'd break up with David for an FBI agent who thinks he's God's gift to the world at large. He's out of town anyway. I haven't talked to him in days."

She nodded toward the kitchen. "I'm not the one you have to convince."

I caught a glimpse of Rachel, pretending to do her homework. She had to be listening to every word. "But I will admit to one thing."

"What's that?"

"He's about the only one who's taking me seriously."

Susan picked up her coffee cup. "Ellie, do you think you might have a few issues with intimacy? Maybe you should consider seeing someone."

THIRTY-SIX

MAYBE SUSAN WAS right, I thought, as I pulled into the gas station the next morning. Maybe I was incapable of sustaining an intimate relationship. I'd never thought of myself as any more or less dysfunctional than the rest of society, but given my problems with Barry, David, and Rachel—even a near brush with Susan—perhaps I should reevaluate.

I wrestled the hose into the tank, imagining a *dybbuk* inside gleefully laughing at me, though whether it was because of my mood or the fact that gas prices were bleeding me dry, I wasn't sure. While I waited, I decided to clean out the back of the car. It beat watching dollars and cents zoom up at lightning speed. Or dwelling on my shortcomings.

I started with my canvas bag, which was wedged underneath the front seat on the floor. I took it over to a large metal trash container. I set it down on the concrete island and felt around the bag. Two objects seemed to be stuck together. I pulled them out. The silver bracelet from Calumet Park was tangled up around my stopwatch.

As I started picking at the bracelet to unravel it, I thought about the VHS copy of the tape I'd given to LeJeune. If Dad was right, and someone *was* after the tape, they'd been going to extraordinary lengths to get it. Break-ins, arson, and—assuming Brashares's death was part of it—even murder. But that didn't explain why Rhonda Disapio was dead. Or Mary Jo Bosanick. They had nothing to do with the tape. Mary Jo Bosanick never knew it existed.

I studied the bracelet. I was willing to concede that my theory about drug dealing and gangsters was far-fetched. Even harebrained. But how likely was it that the two women's deaths were random acts of violence? Two girls, best friends, party at Calumet Park on a summer night. Two men motor into the boat launch. One woman dies, the other makes a narrow escape. A year later, she dies, too. Meanwhile, the men disappear. No one knows or believes they exist. Except me. And the only thing I knew was that one called the other Sammy.

Someone at the next pump whistled. I jumped back, nearly losing my balance. I looked at the pump; it was still. I went inside to pay, the bracelet and stopwatch in my hand. I set them down on the counter and dug out a twenty.

The young man behind the counter looked at his digital readout. "It's twenty-two fifty, ma'am."

Damn. I try to keep gas at twenty bucks a pop, purely on principle. Never mind that I make more trips to the gas station; those are the little ways we fool ourselves. As I fished out a few more dollars, the guy behind the counter eyed the bracelet.

"Looks like the one I bought my girlfriend."

I looked up. "The bracelet?"

He was wearing a striped uniform shirt with his name, Sam, embroidered in red on the pocket. He pointed. "The heart thing. I got the same one for her."

I picked at some grime on the charm. "I hope your girlfriend's was in better shape than this."

"It was." He grinned as he handed me back my change, and I headed out to the car. I was two steps away when I froze.

I'd found the bracelet in Calumet Park, where one of the men called the other Sammy.

Someone named "Mr. Sam" had called Dale Reedy the day I was with her.

I climbed in the car, threw the bracelet on the seat, and started the engine. Sammy was one of the guys in the boat. Coming into the boat launch the night Mary Jo was killed. According to Rhonda, it was Sammy and his cohort who killed her.

As I swung out of the gas station, my mind started to race at warp speed. What—exactly—had Rhonda said? A hot, humid night. Mary Jo and Santoro had fought. Mary Jo took Rhonda to the park to drink it off. While they were there, two men came into the boat launch, their boat loaded with gear.

I'd assumed they were running drugs, partly because of Santoro's background but also because of the comment Mary Jo made: "What makes you think I don't know about dealing?"

I had been wrong. But if it wasn't drugs, what was it? Why would two strangers kill a woman they didn't know—and then her friend as well? I circled the village park, deserted and bleak in the November chill. Frigid water collected in troughs and depressions around the field.

People kill for many reasons, but one of the biggest is fear. Fear that they'll be killed first. But Mary Jo and Rhonda weren't threatening.

Fear of being caught is another. Rhonda thought the men were just fishing, but were they? Or were they doing something else? Something they didn't want revealed. Something with such high stakes—at least for them—that killing two young women was their only option.

A lone figure struck out across the park. His jacket was pulled close and shoulders hunched against the cold.

What was it? What were they hiding? Something on the boat? The boat was carrying some cargo. Rhonda had said something about it. But what? "A lot of shit" were her words, I recalled.

I turned the corner and headed back to Willow Road. As I passed the dry cleaners and hardware store, the sun made a brief appearance, glinting off the Volvo's hood.

Glinting. Something glinting in the moonlight. That was it.

Metal. Logs. Metal fireplace logs.

I frowned. Something that looked like metal fireplace logs. What was Rhonda trying to describe? I squinted through the windshield.

A metal container of some kind.

Sure.

One of those metal trash containers with a foot pedal to open it up. Maybe they held a stash of drugs.

Or maybe something else.

A fire extinguisher? No. Most fire extinguishers are red; they wouldn't necessarily glint in the moonlight. And someone would have to be pretty hard up to kill over a fire extinguisher.

Think, Ellie.

The men were coming in off the lake. Late at night. With metal containers. What if those containers had something to do with the water? Maybe they held water. Or you used them in water.

An image of divers filming hammerhead sharks sprang into my mind.

A tank. An oxygen tank.

Scuba diving equipment.

Is that what Rhonda saw? A boat filled with diving equipment?

Why would someone be diving in the middle of the night in Lake Michigan? And why wouldn't they want anyone to know about it?

I tried to piece it together. A man named Sammy was

at Cal Park a year ago. The night Mary Jo Bosanick died. Possibly ferrying scuba diving equipment.

Dale Reedy got a call from a man named Mr. Sam. She had a wire taped to her window. She'd been quizzing me about a tape I'd shot at the intake crib. And she had a line of sight to the crib.

The sun disappeared behind a cloud.

RACHEL'S DOOR WAS locked, and when I knocked, there was no answer. I went into my office and went online. The computer chimed I had mail. The return path read Greatlakesoil.com. I clicked on the message.

> I'm frightfully sorry, Ellie, but we're going to have to cancel the project. The economy has been bumpier than we anticipated, and we simply can not justify further discretionary expenses at this time. I know how much work you put into the proposal, and I would be happy to compensate you for your time to date. I hope there will be an opportunity for us to do business together in the future.

Short. Concise. Definitive. And obviously code. Something had happened.

It could have been her boss, Tribble. When he'd come into her office during our first meeting, I was sure he knew who I was. He would never have forbidden her to hire me; the corporate world doesn't work that way. But, drunk or not, he might have asked pointed questions about my credibility, reliability, perhaps even my talent. Dale might have started out defending me, but faced with his volley of questions, she would have realized something was off, and, over time, she might have concluded it wasn't a battle worth fighting.

Then again, maybe it was wasn't Tribble. Maybe it had

something to do with the wire, the tape, and a man named Sammy.

I stood up and started to pace. There was no way I could find out, and I could only think of one person who could. Where was LeJeune?

THIRTY-SEVEN

RACHEL SPENT SATURDAY camped in her room with the door locked. An occasional exclamation through the door was the only proof she was alive. I made her favorite pasta and tomato sauce for dinner as a peace offering. I wasn't convinced it was up to me to make peace, but Jewish American guilt goes a long way toward accepting responsibility for sins you haven't committed. But she waited until the sauce had turned cold and the noodles rubbery before sneaking down for a plate.

Around nine, I made a run to the video store. I'd get something we could watch together. Maybe we'd even start talking. I grabbed an Adam Sandler tape and a comedy with Cameron Diaz and was back on my block in less than thirty minutes. I was passing my neighbors' house when I slammed on the brakes.

A dark-colored SUV was pulling away from the house. Two figures were in the front. I tried to make out the license plates as it sped away, but it was too dark. I swerved into the driveway and raced into the house.

"Rachel?" I yelled. "Rach, where are you?"

Silence.

I ran upstairs and checked all the rooms. No Rachel. I checked the closets. No one. My pulse throbbed in my ears. I ran downstairs. The basement was empty. I raced back up and opened the front door. It was a frigid night, and an icy wind stung my skin.

Where was she? Maybe she'd left a note. If she did, it would be in the kitchen. I ran in. Nothing. I checked the clock. Almost nine-thirty. She knew her curfew was eleven. Had she gone out deliberately? Maybe I was wrong not to give her a cell phone or a pager. Lots of parents did these days, but I'd considered it excessive. A badge of conspicuous consumption.

I picked up the phone and called Barry. The phone rang four times, after which his machine kicked on. Another weekend in Door County with Marlene, no doubt. But no Rachel. I called Katie's house. No answer there, either. I thought about calling Susan, but I knew her machine would pick up; she and Doug are always out on Saturday night.

I huddled on the couch struggling to keep panic at bay. A plane flew low overhead, triggering an instant of fear. But it passed safely, its thunder shaking the walls. A nightmarish conspiracy unspooled in my mind. What if the men in the SUV knew the exact moment I'd be alone and vulnerable and deliberately chose that moment to strip me of the only thing in my life that held any meaning?

I flashed back to the New River in West Virginia, when I failed to rescue my daughter. Was it happening all over again? They had taken Rachel, and they were going to do something unspeakably horrible to her if I didn't—but what? What was I supposed to do? Give them the tape? Tell them what I knew? What did they want?

I gazed around the room. The walls, the bookshelves, the furniture all looked solid, almost comforting in their ordinariness. Still, an overwhelming sense of futility washed over me. I sank back on the couch. If she wasn't home by eleven-fifteen, I'd call the police.

At midnight I was about to pick up the phone when a sweep of light tore through the window. I raced to the hall, my heart pumping, and before I could really think about it, grabbed my father's Colt .45. Checking to see that it was loaded, I released the safety. I hoped I still knew how to chamber a round.

I flattened myself against the door. My mouth felt like it was filled with cotton. I waited—for a window to shatter, a knob to turn, a door to fly open. When the bell rang, I sidestepped to the glass panel inset on the door. Under the porch light, looking hollow-eyed and slightly green, was a cop.

I sagged against the wall. I should have realized anyone ringing the doorbell in the middle of the night wasn't out for a nefarious purpose. I slipped the Colt back in the cabinet.

"Good evening. Ms. Foreman." The officer was one of the cops who'd questioned me after the fire at Mac's studio. "I came by to tell you your daughter's okay."

My breath caught. "What do you mean, okay? Where is she?"

"She's—she's at the station."

"At the police station? Why?"

"Ma'am—er, we brought her in on an unlawful possession charge."

Over on the expressway, a truck rumbled by. Its echo reverberated through the trees. I stared at his badge, uncomprehending. He could have been speaking Chinese.

"What?"

"I was there when they brought her in. Detective O'Malley sent me over as a courtesy."

"Rachel's been arrested? What for?"

"For unlawful possession of a weapon, ma'am."

My jaw dropped. "A weapon?"

"A firearm."

I gasped for breath. "A gun?"

He nodded. "She's in custody now."

"In custody?" When he didn't answer, I added, "What's going to happen to her?"

"Well, ma'am, that kind of depends on her. And you. She's with the youth officer now."

"Oh my God." My hand flew to my mouth.

"Don't worry. She's fine—a little shaken up is all. But you need to get down there."

THE VILLAGE POLICE station, a modern brick building, sits in the middle of an upscale residential neighborhood. Set back from the road, it could pass for a school or a community center, except for the phalanx of cruisers in the parking lot. After parking the car, I ran past a flagpole to the front entrance. White boulders, bloodless in the weak moonlight, lined the walkway.

The lobby resembled a modest office complex with tiled floor, white walls, and fake plants. Doors led off both sides. Near one of the doors was a pass-through window, behind which lay several desks and an array of communications equipment. The combination of fluorescent lights and crackles from the radio was unworldly.

I announced myself to the dispatcher, an older, heavyset man with thin bands of white hair stretched across a pink scalp. Then I sat in a black molded plastic chair. I felt like I'd stepped through the looking glass.

"Ms. Foreman?"

I looked up. An attractive blond stood in front of me. Her name tag read Officer Georgia Davis, but she was dressed in a pair of tailored black slacks, black boots, and ivory sweater. Her shoulder-length blond hair was curled in a perfect flip, and her eyes were large pools of brown.

She flashed me a hesitant smile. "I'm the youth officer. I'm handling your daughter's case."

A wave of embarrassment washed over me.

"Why don't you come with me?" Again, a tentative smile.

She waited for me to gather my bag, and we pushed through one of the doors.

"Is she okay?"

We went down a long hall and rounded a corner. She pointed to a door. "She's been waiting for you."

As I opened the door, I clamped down on my tongue. I was in a small, windowless room, about eight by ten. The walls were cinderblock, and a built-in bench stretched along one wall. Two vertical steel bars, the kind you see in wheelchair-accessible bathrooms, were attached to the walls. A pair of handcuffs—*handcuffs*—dangled from one of them. Rachel was curled in a ball at one end of the bench.

At the sound of the door opening, she looked up. Her skin was waxy white, her expression one of abject fear. When she realized it was me, her eyes widened like they used to when I'd come home from an out-of-town trip. She propelled herself into my arms.

"I'm sorry, Mommy." Tears streamed down her face. "I'm so sorry."

I hugged her tight. "It's okay, baby. Mommy's here."

There was a knock on the door, and Officer Davis came in. Rachel pressed herself more tightly against me. Spying a box of tissues at the other end of the bench, I gently disengaged from Rachel and handed her the box. She cringed, but I brushed a hand across her hair, trying to telegraph that it was okay. Davis leaned against the back of the door and read from a clipboard with papers attached.

"At about eleven o'clock Officers Randall and Brewster stopped a black SUV Lexus speeding south on Waukegan Road near Dundee. At first the driver attempted to outrun the officers, but eventually he pulled over. They apprehended Derek Harrington, Carla Sager, and Rachel Goldman. When they began questioning the youths, they observed a thirty-eight caliber handgun on the floor of the passenger side of the vehicle. A revolver." Davis looked up. "It was loaded."

"A loaded revolver?"

Davis held up a hand. "Your daughter was in the back-seat at the time we apprehended them. We have no reason to believe she handled the gun at any time. Is that right, Rachel?"

Rachel sniffled into her tissue.

Davis went on. "The officers who took them into custody ran a check on the car and found it was registered to Robert and Alexa Harrington of Glencoe. No one in the vehicle had a Firearms Identification—"

"Where are the other kids?" I cut in.

"In our other interview rooms. The Harringtons are on their way down, but we haven't been able to reach Mrs. Sager or Mr. Goldman."

"That's because they're—"

"I understand. Rachel told me they're—away. We were able to contact an aunt. She's coming down."

I felt oddly relieved I wouldn't have to explain how Rachel's father happened to be with Carla's mother. "So, what happens now?"

Officer Davis looked at Rachel, then at me. "Well, Ms. Foreman, Rachel and I have talked. Why don't you tell your mother what happened?" Davis gave her a slight nod.

Rachel ran her tongue around her lips. "Well, Derek and Carla rented *Natural Born Killers*—you know with Woody Harrelson and Juliette—"

I nodded. Oliver Stone's New Age *Bonnie and Clyde*. Two young serial killers shooting their way across the country and loving it.

"They picked me up and we went back to Carla's to watch it. I thought it was creepy, but they thought it was awesome." She looked down. "Then we went back to Derek's, and he found the gun."

"Where?"

She shrugged. "It was his father's, I think."

"What the hell did you think you were doing?"

Rachel fell silent.

"Rachel?"

"I didn't know."

"Were you high?"

"No. No one was doing anything."

I cut my eyes to Davis. Had they been stoned, maybe I might have understood. But they were cold sober. Davis raised her eyebrows back at me as if to say, *This is the way it is these days.*

"Derek found some ammo in his garage, so we started to ride around. Derek started saying all these things, like first we'd shoot out some windows, and then—" She shuddered. "We'd get you, and—"

"Me?"

She wouldn't meet my eyes. I looked at Davis, who gave me a brief shake of her head. A fresh torrent of tears started down Rachel's face.

"I didn't mean it, Mom. I was just really mad. I would never have—" She hunched over again, bowing her head in her hands.

I put my arms around her. "It's okay, Rachel," I whispered. "I know."

Davis cleared her throat. "It's clear to me that Rachel feels very remorseful. We've been talking about choices, and she realizes she's made some unwise ones. Particularly in the area of friends. We've also talked about things she can do the next time she feels angry and upset. And she's promised me that we'll talk again after Thanksgiving—if that's okay with you."

"That's fine."

When Rachel looked up, I flashed her a smile. So did Davis. The anguish on her face started to recede.

"What happens now?" I asked.

"She can go home."

Rachel's face brightened. "I can?"

Davis nodded. "Get some rest. You've had a rough night."

Rachel stood up and moved to the door. Then she

turned around and came back to Davis. Standing on her toes, she kissed her on the cheek. Davis colored.

"Thank you," I said.

"She's a good kid." She put an arm around Rachel's shoulder. "I've explained this to Rachel, so I should tell you." She extracted some papers from her clipboard. "Your court date is in five weeks. She doesn't have to appear; her lawyer can be there for her. I'll be there, but I'll recommend that the charges be dropped."

Officer Davis and I shook hands.

As we left the station, I noticed a couple, about my age, in the black plastic chairs. The woman was sobbing into a handkerchief, and the man's arm was around her shoulders. Derek's parents, probably. I pushed through the door without stopping.

THIRTY-EIGHT

RACHEL AND I slept late the next morning. Then we did a huge Thanksgiving shopping at the supermarket. She was subdued; we chatted about inconsequential things. I wanted to fully process last night before we talked. For now, I was grateful that she wasn't hurt. And that the SUV turned out to be Derek's.

When we got back, Fouad was on the front lawn removing the last of my annuals. It was hard to believe the wiry twigs and stems he was pulling out were once petunias and impatiens. He helped us unload the groceries. Rachel put them away.

Back outside, he started in on the prairie grass flanking my driveway. The weak November sun made the dry stems seem luminous. Against an empty, lavender sky, the effect was pure Georgia O'Keefe.

Fouad's red and black lumber jacket was open at the neck. Wiry black chest hairs spilled out above his T-shirt as he slashed through the grass.

"They're saying it might snow tonight," he said.

I drew in a breath. Sometimes there's a tangy, metallic

scent that precedes snow, but I didn't smell it.

"Where have you been?" I asked. I haven't seen you in a while."

"My son had some problems. We went to Duke to work them out."

Ahmed was a stellar premed student. I couldn't imagine what kind of problems he'd have. I asked.

"Someone set fire to his dorm room."

I swallowed.

Fouad didn't look up. "Fortunately, the damage was minor."

"Fouad, I'm so sorry. What did you do?"

He shrugged. "We spoke to the dean, his advisor, and the dormitory monitor. They were full of apologies." He kept hacking through the grasses.

I waited for him to say more.

He didn't.

I shook my head. "I don't know how you do it, Fouad. You've been here thirty years. How do you deal with it—with such—equanimity?"

He was quiet. Then he got up, looked at me, and moved to the other side of the driveway. "I want to tell you a story. It was told to me by your friend David."

"My David?"

He nodded and started in on the grasses on that side. "Last summer, the night we went looking for you, we were here. . . ." He motioned to the house. "We were worried. We did not know where you were. So we agreed to wait for a few minutes."

I remembered the night.

"While we waited, we talked. He told me about a young girl in Germany. During the thirties. About the same age as your Rachel is now. Maybe a year or two older.

"She grew up in Freiburg. Her father was a tailor. Not a wealthy man, but he managed. She had a brother and a sister. She went to school, had friends. She had a happy childhood." He threw a glance over his shoulder. "But then, she was told she could not go to school anymore.

Her friends were no longer permitted to play with her. Her father was forbidden from working. The family was restricted as to where they could go. They were forced to wear a sign on their clothing. They endured cruel taunts from neighbors who a few months before had been their friends. One day she was forced to watch her father strip down to his underwear in the middle of the street while others—their former friends and neighbors—gathered around to jeer."

He put down the scythe and looked up. "Whenever I think it is bad here, I remember the story about David's mother. And I thank Allah I am where I am." He scooped up the ends of the prairie grass and stuffed them into a plastic bag. "You understand?"

I nodded.

"There are many Muslims who share my view. Despite what you hear on the television." He stood up, the bag in one hand, the scythe in the other. "I take care of the landscaping at the mosque over in Northbrook, you know. I hear the young men, the students, talking before and after prayers. Most of them love this country. They are grateful to be here." We walked back toward his truck. "They do everything they can to fit in. They dress American, they eat American, they even Americanize their names. Fariq becomes Frank, Samir becomes Sammy, Rayann becomes Ray—"

I stopped. "What did you say?"

He turned around. "I said they do everything they—"

"No. The name. Sammy. It's short for what?"

"*Samir.* S-A-M-I-R. It means entertaining companion." He tilted his head. "Why do you ask?"

I shook my head. "I—I—it's probably nothing. I mean, there are probably lots of Samirs in Chicago, right?"

"Yes. It's a very common name. Surname, too."

"A surname, too?"

"Sam is." He went on. "If the family name is Sam, a young man might call himself Sammy. There is also Sami, which means high, lofty, or elevated. Or Samman, which means grocer."

I followed him to his pickup. "Is there any way to determine which name someone who calls himself Sammy might be using?"

He shook his head. "It would be like someone who calls themselves Al. Are they Albert, Alfred, or Alphonse?" He lay the scythe in the bed of the truck. "By the way . . . speaking of names . . . I spoke to my friend the other day. The one from Riyadh."

It took me a few seconds to focus. "Riyadh?"

"Your friend from the royal family."

A jolt of uneasiness shot through me. "Abdul."

Fouad nodded. "My friend said there is a database on the Saudi royal family on the Internet."

Of course. Why hadn't I thought of that?

"It is not an official site, you understand. Just a private effort to keep track and organize some of them. Over two thousand names are listed. It is not complete by any means; there are over five thousand royals. I searched for the name you gave me."

"You didn't have to."

He held up his palm. "No, do not thank me. I found nothing."

I stiffened.

"But you see, most Muslim family records are based on the progeny of the mother, not the father."

"Like Jews."

He nodded. "If a mother is not listed, it could mean that no one, including the Sauds themselves, is sure who was doing what with whom. There also is the issue of polygamy. It is sometimes difficult to identify the children when there are four or more wives in the family. And there is also the desire for privacy, particularly where females are concerned. Sometimes information comes to light only when the mother's obituary is published."

"What are you saying, Fouad? Is Abdul a phony?"

He answered carefully. "I can only tell you that the

name does not come up on any of the branches of the family that are publicly known."

I COULDN'T SLEEP that night. I'd gone online and found—or didn't find—the same thing as Fouad. Did that mean Abdul was an imposter? Posing as a Saudi royal while David helped him purchase a chemical company? And if he wasn't, why would he lie about it? What was he trying to hide? Even if it turned out he was a member of the royal family, he was still spending a lot of time and money in Chicago. And harboring some kind of connection to Dale Reedy.

And now there was a man named Sam who called Dale Reedy. Plus a man named Sammy from Calumet Park, possibly ferrying diving equipment, who may have killed Mary Jo. And Sam and Sammy were common Arabic names.

I bunched up the pillow in front of me. I'd read how terrorist operations were sometimes financed by wealthy, seemingly legitimate Arabs, who, in reality, were covertly supporting a terrorist cell or two. Was Abdul one of them? He conducted business at the highest levels of society: the Greenbrier, international currency markets. He seemed to have money to burn. And I had reason to doubt his veracity.

Was Sammy part of his cell? He wasn't enrolled in flight school—he took diving lessons instead—but what difference did that make, if the goal was some terrorist action?

I rolled over and turned on the light. I couldn't accuse Abdul of terrorism; that would be the worst kind of racism. There was always the chance that Abdul *was* a member of the royal family. Maybe his mother, an exotic princess or daughter of an emir, had slipped through the family records.

Still, there seemed to be some connection between the RF damage on a videotape, a British woman at Great

Lakes Oil, the intake cribs, and possibly an Arab. Something just beyond my grasp.

I threw the covers off. I felt as if I were in the maw of some mysterious creature, unable to figure out what it was. My theories might make sense if I knew its genus, its habitat, its routine. But it was keeping itself out of reach. Hidden. Unapproachable.

I stared at the phone, feeling frustrated and helpless and alone.

THIRTY-NINE

DAVID ANSWERED ON the second ring. "Linden here."

"Hello, David."

"Ellie." His voice was unreadable. "How are you?"

I felt like skipping the ritualized dialogue that begins most conversations, but David probably needed the words—and the time. "Okay. You?"

"I'm good," he said. "It's pretty late."

I checked the clock. Almost midnight. "Sorry."

"So, what's up?"

Pass the ball. State your case.

"I—I need to ask you a couple of questions. About Abdul."

"Abdul?" Disappointment colored his voice.

I felt like I should apologize and irritated that I felt that way. "It's important."

He sighed. "What's the question?"

"How did he become your client?"

"What kind of a question is that? You know how it happened. You were there."

"He met you at the Greenbrier, was impressed by your credentials, and decided to hire you?"

"Well . . . basically, yes."

"Well then, why did you take him on?"

"What is this, the third degree?"

"I'm sorry. I guess what I'm asking is why you didn't delegate him to one of your staff."

"He needed someone with expertise in foreign exchange. I'm the head of the department. Ellie, what's this about? Have you been bothering him? Because if—"

My irritation grew. "Actually, it's the other way around. He called me a day or so ago. He was here."

"I told you before, he likes you."

"David." I hesitated. "I think he's a phony."

There was silence. Then, "What the hell are you talking about?"

"David, I don't think he's related to the Saudi royal family—Fouad checked. And now I'm starting to wonder if he's really a businessman."

"Ellie. Stop. Don't go any further. Abdul and I are working on a major purchase. I don't need any interference. Especially from you."

"Okay. Answer this. Where are you in the deal, David? Has Abdul put up any money yet?"

"That's none of your damn business."

"David. I would never insinuate myself into your business dealings without a good reason, just like I know you wouldn't insinuate yourself into my work."

Silence.

"He hasn't put up a dime, has he?"

"We're not at that stage yet. You heard him at dinner a few weeks ago. We need to rethink a few things."

"David, he's stalling you."

"Why would he do that?" His voice sounded less certain.

"Because he isn't who he says he is. Because he's using you as a cover for what he's really up to."

"And what would that be?"

"I'm not sure."

I heard a long exhalation. "Ellie—"

"David, listen to me. I can't explain it. But the timing is suspicious. You meet him, and barely a week or so later, he's your client."

"It happens."

"And he just happens to want to buy a plant near Chicago?"

"Ellie . . ."

"Which forces him to come out here on a regular basis."

"So what?"

"How do you know he doesn't have some ulterior motive? That he's playing you?"

"What possible reason would he have to do that?"

I should have told him my suspicions. Explained everything that was happening. But I was afraid he wouldn't believe me. And given our problems, he might even think I was sabotaging him. I couldn't risk it.

"Remember how he played host at the Four Seasons? He was smooth, wasn't he? It made me wonder if he was a pro."

"A pro? At what?"

"Pumping me about the trial and the tape and the RF."

It takes David a long time to trust someone, but once he does, he's enduringly loyal. It would never occur to him to question a friend's motives.

"Ellie, what are you accusing him of?"

"Didn't you ever wonder how he knew about the abandoned coal mines at the Greenbrier?"

"What are you talking about now?"

"David. Remember the rafting? When I hiked back through the woods with Rachel? Abdul knew we would be passing the old coal mines in the area. Tell me something. How does a Saudi sheik know that?"

"Maybe he took a walk. Maybe he has been there before. What's your point?"

"Something isn't right. It hasn't been since I met him. I get the feeling he already knows the answers to the questions he asks. And now, I've discovered a connection between him and a woman at Great Lakes Oil who—"

"I would hope so."

"David, this woman doesn't have anything to do with his acquisition. She's in Training and Development. I did a video proposal for her, and I found out they've been in touch with each other. Then she abruptly cancels my video. It's all getting very bizarre."

He cut me off. "Ellie, I know things are not going well for you right now. I know you've got some problems. But this is off the charts. You can't make my client out to be some kind of scam artist. I won't permit it."

A flicker of anger pulsed through me. "Fine. Just remember it was our trip to the Greenbrier that started everything."

"What do you mean by 'everything'?"

"Everything you can't seem to handle." Damn. It slipped out.

"I see. We're back to me now. Ellie, I don't have to justify myself to you. Who I do business with is not your concern. If you want to pick a fight with me, you're going to have to do it another way." He cleared his throat. "Look, it's late. I need to get some shut-eye. I think this conversation is just about over."

"No, wait," I cried miserably. "I'm sorry. I didn't mean it."

"Then what do you mean?"

As an instrument of communication, the telephone has its limitations. "I—I don't know. Things are just—very strange. And I miss you."

He was quiet. Then, "That's not what I hear."

The bitterness in his voice jarred me. "Who have you been talking to?"

"You're not my only friend in Chicago."

"Rachel. You've been talking to Rachel. I can't believe it. You and she—"

"Ellie—"

"It is her, isn't it?" He didn't answer. "Tell me."

"No." His voice was soft but emphatic.

"Damn you, David. Someone is spying on me, and you won't tell me who it is? How dare you? I have enough trouble with that right now."

"Ellie, what—"

I couldn't take any more. "You know something? You're right. This conversation is over."

The phone hit the base unit with a thud.

FORTY

AFTER DROPPING RACHEL off at school on Monday, I came home and went online. A quick thirty minutes on the net surfaced over a dozen places in Chicago that offered scuba diving lessons. An equal number were scattered around the suburbs.

I sighed and started down the list. Many had already closed for the season, and their machines told me to leave a message. I frowned. That wouldn't do me any good. On the ninth listing I reached a human, but he didn't want to reveal anything about his customers and seemed annoyed I had the chutzpah to ask. Another man accused me of engaging in industrial espionage.

I took a break and reassessed my methodology. Clearly, a different approach was required. I thought about it. Ten minutes later, I hung up the phone in triumph. It had worked; the person I called actually checked their customer database but didn't find any Sammys or Samirs. Still, I was buoyed by my progress. I refined my technique on the next call. Again, they checked their records, but no luck.

Finally, on the twentieth call, I reached a friendly female voice.

"Diving Unlimited."

"Hi," I said cheerfully, sliding right into character. "My name is Grace Barnett Wing. I work in the personnel department at Walgreen's."

"Yes?"

"I'm checking up on the application of a young man who says he took diving lessons from you." I heard the soft click of keys in the background. "We like to verify our applicant's extracurricular activities, as well as their professional ones. Would there be someone I could talk to about that?"

"Extracurricular activities? You're kidding."

"I wish I was. You can't be too careful these days, you know what I mean?"

"I guess."

"I know it's an imposition. But I really would appreciate the help."

"What's the name?"

"Well, you're not going to believe this, but I did a really stupid thing." I paused. "I spilled coffee all over his application, and it's kind of hard to read. And I know my boss'll kill me if I screw up. The guy's being considered for a management position."

She hesitated. "Well, what do you think the name is?"

"His first name could be Sammy. But then again, that could be his last name."

She was quiet for a moment. "Miss, what did you say your name was?"

"Grace Wing. Barnett Wing." Forgive me, Grace.

"Well, Miss Wing, if all you've got is one name, I don't know how I can help."

I lowered my voice to a stage whisper. "Well, I'm not supposed to say this—I'm sure you can understand—but he—um—he's definitely—well, we're pretty sure he's Arabic. You know, from the Middle East."

I heard an intake of breath.

"And, well, I was just wondering if you could check your customers for the *S*'s to see if, well, you know, you'd find any names like—"

"You say you're from Walgreen's?"

"Yes. The corporate office. I know I was careless, but—"

"Do you know when he signed up?"

"I'm sorry, but I don't."

"Sammy, you say?"

"Yes. But it could be Sam." I considered whether to tell her it was a common Arabic surname. No. Not good.

"Well, let me check last names first." More clicks. Silence. I held my breath. "No Sammy."

"What about Sam?"

"Nothing. We have a Samson, and a Samos, but nothing that looks Arabic."

I crossed my fingers. "Can you run down first names?"

"I don't know. That might be kind of tricky. I could try to pull up every Sammy or Sam we have on our database, but how would I know if it's the right person?"

"Maybe his last name will pop up, and, like I said— well, it might be obvious."

She sighed. "I suppose it's worth a try."

I heard the clicks of her fingers on a keyboard. Outside, the sound of a truck roared down the block.

"Well, now, this is interesting."

My pulse picked up.

"When did you say he was here?"

"I didn't."

"I have a Samir Hanjour. He enrolled a year ago last spring."

"Really?"

"Yes. It looks like he took some lessons but never completed the course."

"I'm surprised. He seems like the type who would follow through."

"People stop for all sorts of reasons, you know. Sometimes their ears can't take it, you know. The pressure.

Other times, they move, or their jobs change. It's not so unusual."

"No, I suppose not." I hesitated. "Tell me, is he the only diving student you had with the name of Samir, or Samman, or Sami?"

"Hold on." A few moments passed. "Yes. That's it."

"Then that's got to be the young man I'm looking for. The address I have looks like he lives in—well I can't tell." I cleared my throat. "The coffee."

"We have him living in Orland Park."

"That's it. Yes. Where in Orland Park?"

She reeled off an address. I copied it down. "Do you want the phone number?"

"Sure."

She gave me a number with a 773 area code. I wrote it down.

"Oh, hold on. You know what? There's a "w" by the number I just gave you. I think I might have given you his work number by mistake. Do you want the home number instead?"

"Sure."

She repeated another number with a 630 area code.

"You've been wonderful. You probably just saved my job. I can't thank you enough. What's your name?"

"Mary. Mary Rhodes."

"Thank you Mary. I'll be sure to note how helpful you were in our files."

"My pleasure."

As soon as I disconnected, I tried the home number, but it was out of service, and there was no forwarding number. Then I punched in the work number. After five rings, a man's voice picked up.

"Yeah?" Gruff. Breathing hard. I'd pulled him away from something.

"I'm trying to reach Samir Hanjour. Is he there?"

"Who?"

I repeated the name.

"There ain't no one by that name here."

"Oh, dear. Maybe I have the wrong information. I thought he worked there."

"Well, maybe he did, but he don't no more. I never heard of 'im."

"I'm sorry to have disturbed you. This—this is—Walgreen's, isn't it?"

"Walgreen's? Lady, you got the maintenance room at People's Edison."

People's Edison? The huge utility that provides most of Chicago's power?

"Oh. I'm terribly sorry. I must have the wrong number."

I carefully put the phone back on the base. I picked it up a second later and called People's Edison's corporate headquarters and asked to be connected to personnel. A moment later an officious voice told me there was no way she could release any information about PE employees unless I had clearance from her department head. I thanked her and hung up.

I stood up and started to pace. An Arabic man named Sammy took scuba diving lessons last year. Apparently, he also worked at People's Edison. Or did when he started the scuba lessons. I wondered if he drove an SUV.

I ATTACKED THE lump of dough with a rolling pin like a tiny steamroller. The dough bulged, cracked, and finally surrendered to a higher force. Once it was uniformly thin and even, I transferred it to a nine-inch pie plate, trimmed off the extra, and fluted the edges. I rotated the plate and smiled. Martha Stewart had nothing on me. I was starting in on the filling when the phone rang.

"Hello?"

Silence.

"Hello?"

A click. I hung up and wiped a floury hand across my brow. A wrong number. That's all it was.

I finished the filling and put it in the fridge. Then I

rummaged in the cupboard for onions. As long as I was feeling domestic, I should get a head start on the stuffing. Damn. I was all out. But it was barely one o'clock. I threw on a coat and grabbed my keys.

I noticed the SUV on the way home from the store. A hundred yards behind, keeping a steady distance away. It was still there when I turned onto Happ Road. Two figures were inside. Men.

Fear skittered around in me. I pressed down on the gas and sped past my block, praying that the cops who hide at the side of the road were there. But they must have been taking the day off. The SUV accelerated and kept pace.

My fear spread.

I got to the end of Happ, careened around Sunset Ridge and onto Voltz. I checked the rearview mirror. Nothing. But Voltz twists and turns and cuts off your sight line. At Lee, I turned right and raced toward Shermer.

I needed to find someplace safe. Someplace no one could get to me. The mall? No. Too big. Too isolated. Too many empty corridors. The library? It was close by, and it was my sanctuary as a child. But it had been remodeled recently; there were lots of small study rooms and cubicles. I needed a place where everything was out in the open. Where there were people.

I was still deciding when the SUV reappeared in the mirror. Closer now. Shortening their rope. My heart hammered in my chest. I flew across Shermer, then Dundee, and sped back to the grocery store. I tore into the parking lot, threw the car in park, and sprinted through the door.

My breath was ragged, and I was trembling. Positioning myself so I had a clear view of the front window, I walked up to one of the checkers, a woman I've known for years. I hugged my arms across my chest.

"What'd you forget this time?" She smiled, then took a closer look. "Hey. Are you all right?"

"Couldn't be better." I tried to take a long, cleansing breath. "How's the handicap?"

"My handicap?"

"Yes." I panted. She was a golfer.

"Good," she said uncertainly, as if she had no idea where I was coming from but was too polite to say so. "I shaved off another stroke this summer."

I looked out the window. The SUV had pulled into the lot and was inching down the lane where the Volvo was parked. I jumped back from the window and said a prayer. The SUV slowed, stopped, and then slowly pulled away.

"That's great, Debbie." I blew out a breath. "Just great. Golf sure is a great sport."

I WANDERED THROUGH the supermarket aisles, thinking I'd hide out there until it was time to pick up Rachel. I was stunned to find heart of palm was over three dollars a can; a tiny jar of caviar was only six. I wandered over to the candy aisle. More my style anyway, but even here, the prices were up to nearly a dollar a bar.

As I scanned the array of brightly colored packages, a familiar itchy feeling rose in my throat, and it dawned on me that a grocery store was not a good place for me to be right now. I felt alone. Defenseless. Out of control. It would be easy to find myself with a case of sticky fingers. I forced myself to walk to the coffee bar at the front of the store, where I bought a latte and made myself sit to drink it.

Once I had Rachel, I drove down to Skokie, taking Hibbard and Illinois instead of the expressway. Every few yards I checked the rearview mirror; no one was tailing us.

"Where are we going?" Rachel asked as we wound through the quiet streets.

"To Dad's."

"Is *Opa* okay?"

"He's fine. I—I just want to check up on him."

"Oh." Rachel seemed abnormally quiet, and I wondered whether I'd subconsciously projected my fear onto her. I needed to be more careful. As we turned onto Hunter, we passed a yard already crowded with Santas, candy canes, and a large sleigh filled with packages.

"Look." I waved. "It's not even Thanksgiving, and they'll probably leave them up until February."

Rachel didn't say anything.

"If we can live through this," I cracked, "we can live through anything."

Rachel recoiled as though I'd struck her.

"Christmas, honey. The decorations."

She burst into tears. "I don't want to go to *Opa*'s."

"Rachel, what are you talking about?"

She sobbed. "He's going to yell at me. And so will you."

"Oh." Now I knew. I pulled to the side of the road. "Honey, that's not it."

Her sobs grew louder. I drew her into my arms. She threw her arms around my neck and buried her face in my shoulder.

"I thought—I thought I was going to jail, Mommy." She wailed.

"Shh." I brushed my fingers across the curls framing her forehead. When she was little I always thought she looked like one of those angels with golden halos. "It's okay, honey. It's over now."

A few minutes passed. Her sobs began to hiccup. "They—were—so—mean."

"Officer Davis was mean?"

"Not—her." She sniffled. "She was—okay."

I thought she was okay, too. Better than okay.

"The others. The ones who arrested me." She took a shuddering breath. "They told me if I got into trouble again, I'd go to juvenile detention. They treated me like I was—like—I—was a—a—" She started to tear up again.

"A criminal?"

She nodded, her eyes glassy and wet. "When we got to the station—they took our fingerprints—and then they put me in that cell—and—they handcuffed me to the wall."

I winced. I remembered the time I was arrested for shoplifting. How frightened I was. How ashamed. How alone. I hugged her tighter.

"Then they asked me all these questions. But in a really mean way. They kept saying they knew someone at school was dealing, and I had to tell them who it was. And then—" She stopped short, a horrified look on her face. "Mother, are they going to tell the school what happened?"

I pushed an unruly curl behind her ear. "No. The school doesn't know anything about it."

"What about *Opa?*"

"I haven't told him."

"Mommy . . . please . . . don't."

I looked over. "I won't. Unless you say something first."

"Never." She shook her head and sniffed. "Never." She looked up. I saw the determined tilt of her chin. "I never want to see Carla again. Even if I have to make all new friends."

I forced a smile. "How about we talk about it over the weekend? I don't want you to forget, but I don't want it to ruin Thanksgiving. We'll figure out how to keep our noses clean after Thursday."

"Our noses?"

"Ours," I said, silently thanking God hers was on just fine and that she seemed to have survived her ordeal with only minor damage. "Yours and mine. I'd like to spend more time with you."

She nodded and wiped her eyes with her hands. For the first time in days, the hint of a smile cracked her face. "Mom?"

"Yeah?"

"Do you think I could set up a chemistry lab in the basement?"

FORTY-ONE

"**MY FAVORITE GIRLS!**" Dad swung open his door. "What a surprise."

"We just happened to be in the neighborhood . . ."

Dad squinted as we trooped inside. He knew I was lying. "Are you okay?"

"We're fine," I said hastily, exchanging a glance with Rachel. "We—er—wanted to have dinner with you."

He looked at me, then Rachel. "Chinese?"

Rachel nodded eagerly, and Dad went into the kitchen to hunt for the take-out menu. Rachel took off her coat and plopped down on the couch.

I prowled around the apartment. With only two rooms and a kitchen, it didn't take long to make a circuit.

"Sit down, Ellie," Dad said as I passed the kitchen. "You're making me nervous."

I sat at the dining room table. Dad brought in the menu, and after a group consultation, called in an order of egg rolls, sweet and sour chicken, and lo mein with Cantonese noodles. "Can't fill up too much." He winked at Rachel, "Not with turkey day coming up."

My cell phone trilled. I jumped up and dug it out of my purse. "Hello?"

There was no response. "Hello?" Silence. "Damn it." I looked around. "No one's there."

Rachel and Dad watched me with curious expressions. I looked back at the cell, hoping a "missed call" display might pop up along with the number. Nothing. I shoved the cell back in my pocket.

"How about a game of chess?" Dad asked.

"Cool." Rachel went to the cabinet, pulled out his chess set, and proceeded to set it up on the table.

"I'll skip this round," I said.

Dad nudged Rachel. "A comedian, your mother."

Rachel giggled.

I went to the window. It was close to five, but the skies, swollen with thick gray clouds, were more luminous than usual. A snowstorm was coming. For real, this time. I looked back at Rachel and Dad, engrossed in their opening moves. I ducked into the bedroom.

"Ellie, your *schpilkes* are driving me crazy."

I came back out. I was driving myself crazy. "Why don't I go pick up the food?"

"Awesome," Rachel said. "I'm starving."

Dad stared at me through his glasses. "We could have it delivered."

I felt around in my bag for my cell phone. "I need some air. It's okay."

"You sure?"

I nodded. I headed to my car, trying to be aware of everything in front and behind me. Five painted rocks bordering the lawn. Four cracks in the sidewalk. Two streetlights angling in on the lot. I started to count how many cars were there, but lost count when I dug out my keys.

As I fitted the key in the lock, I felt a sudden presence loom over me. Closing in fast. I didn't have time to get in the car. What should I do? My key! I'd rake the car key across his face. When I sensed he was almost on top of me, I threw my hand in the air and whipped around.

LeJeune caught my wrist.

I staggered back. "Jesus Christ!"

"I wouldn't go that far, *cher.*"

He was wearing a dark, bulky parka, and his Different Drummer hat was pulled low on his face. But his eyes smiled down at me.

"Damn you!" I waved my keys. "You almost lost your smooth Cajun skin."

He loosened his grip on my wrist. "You do have a way with words."

I shook off his hold. How dare he act as if he was just casually dropping by? As if nothing was wrong, the past week never happened?

"How did you find me?"

"The Bureau has its ways, *cher.*"

I didn't know whether to curse him or just walk away. I started to open the car door, but now that he was back, the fear, the not knowing, the sense that things were closing in on me—it all suddenly seemed to be too much. My composure snapped.

"Oh God, Nick." My voice trembled. "I've been so alone. And scared. I'm being followed. And I don't know who or—" Burying my face in his coat, I started to cry.

He waited patiently, his arms around me, until I calmed down. When there was only a sob or two left, he tilted my chin up with one hand and brushed away my tears with the other. He leaned over, and the next thing I knew, his mouth was on mine. Doing things I hadn't felt in a long time.

As we drove to the Chinese restaurant in the Volvo, I wondered what had just happened between us. But he didn't say anything, just looked through the windshield with a half-smile on his face. Maybe it wasn't that important to him. Just the cost of doing business. It was probably in the FBI handbook: kiss hysterical woman, calm her down, then get what you need.

Whatever it was, we'd have to sort it out later. There were more important issues at hand. I told him the SUV was following me again. I also told him how I'd shaken it—for the moment. He nodded but didn't ask any questions. I wondered why.

"What am I going to do?" My voice sounded shrill as we parked and headed inside. "I can't go back home tonight. It's too dangerous."

"I know."

"You know?" I looked over. "Damn you, again. If you know I'm in danger, where the hell have you been for the past week? Didn't you get my messages?"

"I got them."

"Then why you didn't call me back? I might have been—Rachel and I might have been—"

As we reached the door to the restaurant, he cut me off. "I was out of the country. I couldn't talk on an unsecured line."

We pushed through the door. Basically a carry-out, the restaurant was small, with a high counter that stretched across two thirds of the room. Three small tables sat in front. The sound of splattering oil drifted out from the kitchen, and the scent of Asian spices permeated the air.

"When did you get back?"

"This morning."

Now that we were in the light of the restaurant, I saw the stubble on his face and the dark pouches under his eyes. When he realized I was checking him out, he dipped his head. I checked the bag of food on the counter. The name Forman was scribbled on the receipt. They always forget the *e*.

I gestured to the bag. "You want something?"

"Just coffee."

I nodded at the proprietor, who filled a plastic cup and handed it to LeJeune. As he took it, his movements seemed jerkier, less fluid than usual. A subtle tension seemed to have come over him.

After paying, we headed back to Dad's.

"Nick, I need to tell you what's been going on."

He sipped his coffee. "This is good. They still don't brew coffee right in London."

"London? You were in London?" I stopped at a red light. Dale Reedy was from England. I thought about the length of time he'd been gone, what had happened before and since. When the light changed, I said, "You're on an antiterrorism squad, aren't you?"

He looked at me for a long moment. Then he nodded.

"Why didn't you tell me?"

"I couldn't." He leaned his arm across the back of the seat. "A few months ago we received credible information from Saudi intelligence about a planned terrorist attack in the Midwest. Something specifically involving water. It was confirmed by the Mossad. And British intelligence. They said it would go down after the verdict."

"What verdict?"

"The guy who's on trial now. If he's convicted—"

"Which, in all likelihood, he will be. . . ."

He shrugged. "Yeah. Well, if he is, there's supposed to be a nasty surprise afterwards."

"In Chicago?"

He nodded.

"Why here?"

"Why not? Chicago's been relatively unscathed so far. It is the Second City. And we have reason to suspect there's a sleeper cell here."

"This is all connected to the RF on my tape, isn't it?"

"Yes."

I parked behind Dad's apartment and switched off the engine. I sat very still. "How did you find out? That it was connected to me?"

"We didn't. Not at first. But you testified at the Santoro trial about RF interference. Out on the water. In the Midwest." He shrugged. "It just seemed like something we ought to check out. Especially after we got word you were taking rides with Outfit guys."

"What did you find out in London?"

He motioned to the bag of food. "Why don't you drop that off?"

I hesitated. Dad had never met LeJeune, and, aside from his car, Rachel wasn't too fond of him. But now that he was back, I didn't want to let him out of my sight. I wrestled with what to do. "Do you want to come up?"

Nick must have sensed my indecision. "Why don't I wait here."

Relieved, I opened the door and took the bag up to Dad's. I told him I wouldn't be staying.

"Why?"

"It's kind of hard to explain."

"Try."

I told him how LeJeune found me in the parking lot. "We—we have some things to work out."

Dad fixed doubtful eyes on me.

"Business," I added hastily.

Dad took the bag of food. "Be careful."

I gave him a hug. "I will. I'll be back."

LeJeune was on his cell by the time I got back to the car. I climbed in. When he was done, he stretched out his arm on the seat and nuzzled my neck.

"Come here, *chér*." His voice was hoarse.

I looked over. I saw in his eyes that he wanted me, and I realized, with a jolt, that I wanted him to. He moved close and traced a finger down the side of my face. My stomach fluttered.

"I've been meaning to do this for a while."

I tried to steady myself. "Before we get—distracted . . ." I pushed his hand away. ". . . there are things we need to discuss."

He curled his fingers around mine. "Like what?"

"Like Sammy. I think I know who he is."

"Sammy?"

A few droplets of sleet spattered the windshield, fat and heavy. I switched on the wipers. "The guy who was at

Calumet Park the night Mary Jo Bosanick was killed? The one who came in on the boat? I think there's a link between him and the intake crib."

LeJeune cocked his head.

"His name is Samir Hanjour. He lived in Orland Park. He was enrolled in a scuba diving course at Diving Unlimited. But he dropped out."

He sat straight, fully alert now. "How'd you find that out?"

I told him about the calls I'd made. "There's more. There's a woman involved. A British woman who works for Great Lakes Oil."

The lines on his forehead drew together. "What do you know about her?"

I told him about Dale Reedy and the wire on her window. I'd barely finished when he punched in a number on his cell and repeated what I said.

"Yes. Could be. Get a team out there ASAP and get back to me." He paused. "Have them meet at the police marina." He listened. "Call him." Another pause. "And we got a possible ID on the cousin. Samir Hanjour."

"Cousin?"

He held up a finger and repeated the address in Orland Park. Then he snapped off the phone. "You've been a busy woman."

I shot him a look. "Are you patronizing me?"

"No, I assure you, I'm not."

"Then, what is this about a cousin? And why do I get the idea you already know about Dale Reedy?"

"We didn't know about the antenna."

"But you do know about her."

"That was one of the reasons I was in London."

"But you couldn't tell me."

He didn't answer.

I crossed my arms. "Let me see if I get this. You've known about her—since when?"

"We got the first intelligence in May."

"You knew she might be part of some terrorist action, and you let me deal with her anyway?"

"We hadn't confirmed it, and by the time we did, she'd already made contact with you."

Snow started falling in earnest. I turned the wipers on high. "So you let me go ahead and risk my life doing business with her?"

His eyes flashed in the dim light. "Tell me something. Would you have broken off with her if we'd asked?"

He had a point.

"You tipped us off to her, anyway."

"Me? How?"

"When we first came to your house, you said something about a call from an executive from Great Lakes Oil. Look, Ellie. We didn't know anything concrete. It was only when she surfaced a second time—through you—that we started to piece it together."

"How did it surface the first time?"

He shook his head. He wasn't going to tell me.

I tried another tack. "So you went to London because of Dale Reedy?"

"That's right. Turns out the woman's got quite a track record. Fringe human rights movements. A real left-winger. Came to the attention of Scotland Yard when a bomb went off in Grosvenor Square fifteen years ago—she was indirectly involved. But then, she suddenly turns herself around. Changes her name. Gets married. Takes a straight job. Starts working her way up the corporate ladder."

"She wouldn't be the first. Look at Jerry Rubin."

"Jerry Rubin wasn't married to a Saudi Arabian expatriate."

"What?"

"Dale Reedy, aka Darlene Eaton, is married to a suspected terrorist by the name of Dani Aziz. British intelligence has been looking for him for years. But he's slippery; he stays underground. Always travels. Meanwhile, she's here. And their kids live with her folks."

I remembered the photo in Dale's office. Two boys in soccer uniforms. Cute. Dark hair. She'd never mentioned a husband. I'd assumed she was single.

I felt stupid. "Are you saying her husband, this Dani, is Samir?"

He shook his head. "Pakistani agents saw *Aziz* in Peshawar last month. But he has a cousin. And no one has seen him for over a year."

I paused, trying to assimilate the information, but I kept coming back to a question. "Why are you telling me all this now? What's changed?"

"You've been followed, right? By someone in an SUV?"

At my nod, he pulled out a piece of paper and unfolded it. "Turn on the dome light, *chér,* and take a look at this."

I stared at the scan of a photo. It was a lousy quality. Grainy. High contrast. Probably a copy of a copy of a passport picture. My stomach lurched anyway. The dark eyes. Mediterranean features. The cold expression. "I know him," I whispered.

LeJeune's eyes burned into me. "Is he the one in the SUV?"

I shook my head. "He was at Santoro's trial the day I testified."

"You're sure?"

I remembered how he looked at me as if I were some inanimate object. A piece of garbage to be disposed of. I shivered. "He was sitting in the row behind my father."

LeJeune reached for his cell phone.

I reached across to stop him. "Wait. I'm not finished. I think there's a link between Dale Reedy and the financier of the thing. Whatever the thing is."

LeJeune reached for his coffee instead. "Financier?"

"Abdul Al Hamarani. He tells people he's related to the Saudi royal family. Spreads money around as thick as butter. Stays in fancy hotels. His cover is that he's buying a chemical plant from Great Lakes Oil."

"Abdul, eh?"

"Abdul Al Hamarani. He's a client of my—of a man I know. He and Dale Reedy have been in contact." I explained how I found his number on her pad of paper.

Before he had a chance to reply, his cell phone trilled.

FORTY-TWO

LeJeune stared through the windshield, his answers short, deferential. A superior giving him orders. When he was done, he twisted around.

"Our men found an antenna on the crib. I have to go. You'll have to—"

I grabbed his arm. "I can't—you can't leave. Not again. Not with Samir—"

"But I can't—" He checked his watch. "Shit. There's no time. I need to borrow your car."

"Only if I'm in it."

"But I can't—"

"Nick . . ."

He looked through the window, then at me. "Okay. Let's go."

Relief and fear swept through me simultaneously. An odd duality of emotions. "What's going on?"

"I don't know." His face was grim.

I called Dad as we pulled away and told him where I was going. He didn't say much. Then, "Rachel can stay here. I'll wait up."

"I love you, Dad."

A mixture of snow and sleet fell as we slogged through traffic. The streets were slick, but rush hour was at its peak. I wiped the inside of the windshield with my sleeve. LeJeune kept up a fast tap on the floor.

Over an hour later, we parked downtown near the police marina. One of their boats took us out, but the ride out was nothing like I remembered. A bitter wind raked the lake's surface, turning my face numb in minutes. My stomach pitched with the waves, and for the first time I could understand how the *Edmund Fitzgerald* got into trouble. By the time we stepped onto the Carter-Harrison intake crib, almost two hours had passed.

The crib was swarming with men, most of them in FBI jackets. A complement of Chicago police officers was there, too, and a few others, I guessed, from the water department. Arc lights were strung up, and the snowflakes caught in their glare looked iridescent. A boat, which might have been Coast Guard or possibly military, was anchored a few yards away with tanks and scuba diving equipment on its deck. Funny. Rhonda Disapio was right. From this distance, they did look like logs. Metal fireplace logs.

I peered into the lake, watching snowflakes dissolve and disappear into murky black water. What was going on? Was something hidden in its depths?

LeJeune joined a group of men at the limestone and brick structure. Some of them glanced my way. Feeling self-conscious, I studied a bronze fish that sat like a gargoyle on top of the limestone wall. Flakes of snow blew into my face.

Two men up on the suspension bridge pointed at something. I squinted, trying to see. It was a set of double windows near the top of the pink and white structure.

LeJeune came over. "They turned off the pumps."

"Why?"

"So we could send divers down in the candy striper."

"What for?"

"So they can find whatever the antenna's attached to."

"Where was it—the antenna?"

He pointed up to the bridge. "It was attached to the wall. Just above those windows. Next to the suspension bridge."

The suspension bridge. "I left the damaged cassette on the bridge. Right next to the candy striper," I said slowly.

"Right," LeJeune said.

A swell of noise on the other side of the crib distracted us. A couple of men gestured. LeJeune went over to listen. Then he got on his cell. He came back over, his face unreadable. "The divers found something."

I tensed.

"We're gonna bring in some help. You're gonna have to clear out."

I started to object, but he cut me off. "Go home. I'll call you later."

I shook my head.

He looked over at the men, then at me. I sensed him come to a decision. "Okay. There's a white van parked over at DuSable Harbor. No one will be in it. Wait for me there."

I nodded. "Who does it belong to?"

"A friend."

"There's no way you can come?"

He shook his head. "Not yet."

"Are—are you going to be okay?"

He brushed a hand across my cheek "You can count on it, *chér.*"

Twenty minutes later a marine police boat docked at the crib, and half a dozen men in bulky dark haz mat suits and spacesuit helmets disembarked. Seven of us, including the cops and the men from the water department took their places, and we motored back to shore. Crowded into the semienclosed cabin behind the pilot's chair to keep warm. Nobody talked. As we approached shore, the Great

Lakes Oil building loomed over the cityscape, its pale walls a mosaic of reflected light.

We docked at the police marina, and a cop walked me over to DuSable Harbor. A white van was parked on the semicircular drive. Four stubby antennas protruded through a metal plate on its roof. The plate looked like a stop sign laid horizontally. Two more antennas stuck out from other spots on the roof.

"What is this?" I asked the cop who'd walked me over.

"Don't ask me. Some kind of radio gear, I think."

"You sure I can go inside?"

The cop motioned to the police boat that had ferried us ashore. It was just backing out of the marina. "The guy who it belongs to just hopped a ride out."

There was no answer when I tapped, so I slid the door open. A beam of light spilled out of a tiny desk lamp clamped above the driver's seat, but most of the van was in shadows. There were no seats in the back, and the space was crammed with equipment. I saw VU meters on a few pieces. Speakers hung on both sides of the wall.

The only other light was a greenish hue from a laptop on the floor of the van. I crawled over and saw a green bull's-eye, almost chartreuse, with brighter green circles inside it. A bright green splotch in the center looked like one of those TV radar maps of a storm, except here a dotted radius ran from the center of the splotch to the circle's circumference. Numbers and words, including Display Source, Sector, and Decay Rate, appeared around and on the circle. I had no clue what they meant.

The interior of the van gave off a slightly stale odor, but compared to the crib, it was warm and dry. I hunkered down behind the front seat. The window was streaked with sleet, but I thought I saw a large boat move slowly past, its dark shape massed against the darker black of the lake. A metal chain clanked in the distance. Despite the tension, or maybe because of it, my eyes felt heavy. I yawned.

The next thing I knew, the van door was opening, and

a blast of cold air rushed in. I startled awake to see Le-Jeune.

"Getting your beauty sleep, *chér?*"

"What—what's happening?"

He climbed in and brushed his lips across mine. His jacket smelled fishy, but his lips were soft. I closed my eyes and kissed him back.

When we broke apart, I was breathless.

He grinned. "For a welcome like that, I'd go back and do it all over again."

Before I could answer, the door slid open again, and someone else climbed in. A man crawled past me, settled himself in the front, and turned the tiny desk lamp to high. I blinked in the harsh light. The man was in his twenties, I thought. He was wearing a blue warm-up suit with a white stripe down the side, but a thickness around his middle implied the clothes were just for show. A headband around his forehead held back a mane of curly, dark hair.

"I'm Clarence." He dipped his head. "A friend of Drummer's."

"Drummer?"

He pointed to the words Different Drummer Fishing Charter on LeJeune's hat. Now that I was thinking about it, I'd never seen him without it.

"Are you with the FBI?"

"Sometimes."

I leaned up against the side of the van. "Why is it I can't ever get a straight answer from any of you guys?"

Clarence cleared his throat and looked at LeJeune. Then he crawled over to his laptop.

"You will this time," LeJeune said. "I want to tell you what we found." He took a breath. "It was a watertight, hermetically sealed box. The size of a suitcase—maybe thirty-six by twenty-four by eight. When we opened it up, we found two compartments. One contained radio equipment: a small transmitter, a receiver, and built-in power source. The other held—" His face was impassive. "An explosive device."

"A bomb?" I clamped a hand over my mouth.

He nodded. "Don't worry—it's been disabled by now." He flicked his eyes over to Clarence. "But—" He faltered. "—it was nuclear."

I bit down on my hand to keep from crying out. I'd heard about suitcase nukes. Small nuclear bombs. Both the Soviets and the U.S. made them, but some had gone missing when the Soviet Union collapsed. Experts feared they'd ended up in the hands of terrorists.

"Was it—was it—one of the Russians'?"

"We don't think so." He shifted. "Let me rephrase that. It's unclear if any Soviet nuclear tactical weapons would even work after twenty years. They need regular maintenance and upkeep, which, given what's going on in that part of the world, isn't happening. But someone may have gotten one to use as a prototype. Or maybe they built one from scratch."

"That's possible?"

"Given enough money, there are plenty of disaffected Pakistanis, former Soviet nuclear scientists, even Iraqis, who would do it in a heartbeat."

"I thought the technology was way beyond—well, too sophisticated."

"The hardest part is getting weapons-grade uranium. We've heard rumors it's been coming out of Turkey." He waved a hand. "Who knows? Assuming you can get your hands on some, you can cut corners, and—well—it can be done."

I felt sluggish and heavy, as if I was trying to tread water but was sinking into its depths. I wondered if I was in shock. "How small?"

"Excuse me?"

"You said it was a small device. How small?"

"It's just a guess at this point, but probably less than a kiloton. One fifteenth of what they used at Hiroshima."

"But powerful enough to take out a couple of city blocks," Clarence said.

"Or the water supply of Chicago," LeJeune said.

"That's what they were doing? Sabotaging the water supply?"

Clarence and LeJeune exchanged another glance.

"What? What is it? Why are you looking at each other like that?"

"Because that's the good news," LeJeune said. "If it had detonated, the radiation would have made parts of downtown Chicago uninhabitable." He paused. "For at least a century or two. And, if the wind was blowing the other way, the lake would be poisoned for about that long."

I opened and closed my mouth like a fish, half expecting him to break into a grin and tell me this was all a joke. A prank he and his Bureau buddies were playing. His expression was hard as granite.

"But that's just for starters," he went on. "A blast like that, if it had gone off in the Loop, would incinerate anyone within a one-block radius. A quarter mile away, over 250,000 people would die within a day from radiation sickness. A half mile away, you still have thousands dead. Within five to ten miles, the environment would be irreversibly poisoned."

"Did you know there's only one fucking hospital in the entire country that knows how to deal with radiation sickness?" Clarence said. "And that's in Tennessee, for Christ's sake."

"There's something you can take to ward it off, can't you?" I asked.

"Iodine tablets," Clarence said. "But they only work when you know it's coming in advance. And even if you knew, how are you gonna get enough to everyone in Chicago?"

"But they didn't target the Loop," I said. "They sank it on the crib."

"I guess we can be thankful for that," LeJeune

said. "Although obliterating the water system is plenty serious. Humans can't survive without water more than three days. Think what would have happened if all the bottled water was gone."

I pressed my lips together.

"Order would break down. You'd have looting. Panic. Chaos. Hospitals overwhelmed. Downtown Chicago's evacuated. Abandoned. No commerce. No transportation. Nothing. For decades to come." He shook his head. "*Chér,* you're looking at something that would make September eleventh look like a birthday party."

I covered my face with my hands. A tenuous silence settled over the van, broken only by the whine of the laptop.

LeJeune gently pried my hands away from my face. "But that's not going to happen, Ellie. None of it."

I looked up.

"You know why?" He tipped up my chin with his hand. "Because you came forward at that trial."

"The RF," I said softly. "On my tape."

"That was our break." He motioned to Clarence. "Tell her."

"It wasn't just a simple transmitter and receiver. It was a sophisticated packet radio setup. We found gauges that indicate they were monitoring the internal environment of the box and reporting all that data back. Temperature, humidity, pressure, battery strength. Other stuff, too."

"That was all transmitted back to the Great Lakes Oil building?"

"Yeah. But who knows where it went from there? That's the beauty of it, see. The scientists monitoring the box—or the guys with their finger on the button— could be anywhere. Chicago, the Middle East, Asia. All you need is a computer and a modem."

"But we shot out at the cribs over a year ago. Are you telling me the suitcase has been underwater since then?"

Clarence nodded. "Looks that way."

"So it was planted before September eleventh."

LeJeune nodded.

"How did they get it there?"

"Probably brought it in through a port. In a steel container. Then barged it up the Mississippi."

I felt my eyes grow round. What if Santoro had offloaded it? What kind of irony would that be?

"Where is Dale Reedy?"

"We're looking for her," he said. "She won't get far. And we have a team on their way over to Great Lakes."

I rocked forward and hugged my knees. "I don't get it. How could no one have found the antenna on the crib before now?"

"There weren't many people out there, even in summer. Plus, you can't find something you're not looking for. They used thin, flexible conduit. Against a surface, it's almost invisible." His hands sketched out the path in the air. "They ran it from the pit of the candy striper, up the wall, and out the set of windows above the suspension bridge. The antenna itself was less than six inches long."

"But you went out there to look around."

Clarence answered. "We used the van for a couple of hours, then took a field strength meter out on a boat, but we weren't out there long enough. Looks like the transponder woke itself up every six or eight hours to transmit or receive a signal. No way we would have caught it."

"But we did," I said, "because we were shooting out there over ten hours."

Clarence aimed a finger at me. "Exactly."

"How did they power it?" I asked, thinking back to my conversation with Hank. "What kind of battery lasts almost two years?"

"A fuel cell battery," Clarence replied. "They use 'em on the space shuttle. They're just starting to show up commercially. They convert small amounts of fuel into electrical energy. Make a power source that lasts for years. Somebody built one into the suitcase."

"How much you want to bet Samir studied electrical

and computer engineering at DePaul or IIT?" LeJeune said.

"In between his scuba diving lessons," I said.

"It was his job." LeJeune shrugged.

"But how were they able to sink it on the crib without anyone seeing?"

"Before September eleventh, security on the cribs was a joke. Kids used to swim out there, smoke weed, dive off the side at night. And in winter, there were weeks when no one was out there at all." He smiled thinly. "Hey. You bring everything out on a boat late at night, break into or dive down in the candy striper, hook up the cable and the antenna, then sink the box. No big deal."

I rocked back on my haunches. "They accounted for every contingency," I said bitterly.

"Except one. They never expected your videotape would end up near their antenna."

I shook my head slowly. "It was luck. Blind, stupid luck."

LeJeune smiled. "My daddy always says luck is 'Labor Under Correct Knowledge.'"

FORTY-THREE

I DIDN'T WANT to stay in the van. I wanted to go home to Rachel and Dad. I was just about to ask Clarence to drop me off at my car when LeJeune's cell buzzed.

"Yeah." He picked up. "Got it. Okay." He turned to us. "The bomb squad finished disabling the device. They replaced it with pipe, and they're taking it to the lab."

"Thank God." I slumped against the side of the van.

LeJeune pocketed his cell. Clarence started to fiddle with a plastic box about the size of a paperback book.

"What's that?" I asked.

"A display unit."

"What does it display?"

"If I tell you, I'll have to kill you." He glanced at me. "Just a joke," he said with an edgy laugh. "It's part of the Doppler direction finder. It helps detect the direction that a radio signal is coming from."

"Is that metal stop sign on top of the van part of it?"

"Drummer said you were smart." He nodded. "The Doppler is mostly used by amateur radio buffs—you wouldn't believe the games they play with it—but it does come in handy in situations like this."

"I thought you said it didn't work the last time."

"That's because we weren't listening long enough, and we didn't know the frequency. But now . . ."

"You have the frequency?"

"It was on the transmitter. They were using an out-of-the-way ham radio band. In the 220 megahertz band." He looked at me over his laptop. "Which was smart."

"Why?"

"Less chance of being picked up by people like me." He went back to his toy.

"So what are you doing now? Isn't it all over?"

He looked up. "It is."

"Then why are you setting up more equipment?"

"Uh—uh . . ." His voice trailed off, and he threw a glance to LeJeune.

LeJeune's jaw tightened.

It occurred to me that since his last call, LeJeune was preoccupied and distant. I was willing to chalk it up to his reluctance, maybe his inability to express emotion, but now I wasn't sure. The danger was over. Why wasn't he more relieved? Where was his cocky FBI shtick? I reviewed what he said, after the call. They took out the bomb, he'd said and replaced it with pipe.

"They replaced the explosive with pipe," I said slowly. "Why did they do that, Nick?"

Clarence moved to the front of the van and started the engine. We pulled away from the harbor.

"Why did they replace it with pipe?"

After a long pause, LeJeune answered. "So we could drop it back in the crib."

Why were they doing that? They should have removed the bomb and disconnected the radio. Stripped everything down. Shipped it to the NSA or CIA or whoever did the kind of analysis they needed. I felt a bite of anxiety.

"Why?"

Clarence made a wide turn and headed west.

LeJeune seemed to be choosing his words with care. "We have a line on Reedy. But we still want to flush out Samir."

"Samir? He's probably on his way back to Saudi Arabia or Yemen."

"Not necessarily. He might not know we've disabled the device. But even if he does, he might stick around."

"What do you mean?"

"Ego. It was his thing. He wants to see it through."

"So why not let Dale Reedy lead you to him after you pick her up?"

"There's no guarantee she'll cop to anything when we find her. Remember, the asshole from the World Trade Center—the one who's on trial now—still isn't talking." He went quiet.

I didn't like the feel of it.

"Ellie," he said slowly, "we need you to help us out."

I sat very still. Snow thudded against the windshield, splattering into tiny craters on the glass.

"Samir thinks you know what's going on. We want him to keep thinking that."

"You want him to think the bomb is still there?"

"We want to keep the signals going. So we can flush him out. And you're the best way to make that happen." He leaned forward, his voice perversely soft and sweet and full of Cajun lilt. "We want you to go back out there. Pretend you're doing another video for the water district. A sequel."

My jaw went slack. "That's crazy. No one goes out there this time of year. He'll know it's a setup."

"Not if the water district announces they've decided to finish the video they started last year. And that they've rehired you to produce it."

"Who's going to believe them?"

"We only need to convince one person."

I sat in stunned silence. He must have taken it as acquiescence, because he leaned in closer.

"But, even if he doesn't believe it, he can't afford to let it happen. He can't risk any more attention focused on the crib."

"You want to use me as bait."

He didn't answer.

I scuttled away from him. "You want to use me as bait," I repeated.

He acted as if he hadn't heard me. "We're pretty sure we didn't miss any cycles, and unless he's got a spotter out there, which is almost impossible, given that the crib is a few miles offshore, he's not gonna know we intercepted the bomb.

"On the other hand, since we exchanged one material for another, the data values that are transmitted back to them may change."

My body itched with anger.

"With lead pipe in there instead of a demolition charge, the internal environment—the pressure, the temperature—will be different. That's going to confuse them. They'll be anxious. They'll want to know what's going on. Obviously, they can't go out and check it themselves. So the fact that you are going out there will make them crazy."

"Great. Why don't I just paint a bull's-eye on my back?"

"Ellie." He faced me. "You won't be in danger. We'll be waiting for them. Agents. SWAT teams. Coast Guard. Chicago marine police. We'll be with you every step of the way. If Samir or his people get within fifty yards of you, we'll pick them off. I won't let anything happen to you."

I glared at him. "Is there some reason I should believe you?"

He pushed up the brim of his hat. "Is this the same woman with the finely tuned sense of justice? The one who wanted to clear her reputation?"

"That finely tuned sense of justice is tempered by an equally fine-tuned sense of survival."

An edge crept into his voice. "In that case, you might

want to think about your daughter. Or your father. You sure as hell won't be much use to them dead."

"You bastard." I hissed.

He grabbed my shoulders. "Listen to me. Who was on the bridge next to the antenna? Who had interference on their tape? Who saw Reedy's antenna? Hanjour's been trying to get those tapes for weeks. Now he's obviously coming after you. Damn it, Ellie. It's only a matter of time. He's panicking, and panic makes people dangerous."

He let that sink in.

My fingers prodded my forehead. He was right; I had no choice.

He leaned back. "Here's the deal. We want you to go back out there. Friday morning, day after Thanksgiving. Just before dawn. To scout the location or do whatever it is you do." He went on. "The thing is, we want you to make sure Dale Reedy knows what you're doing. E-mail her. Leave her a voice mail. Tell her it's okay the project got canned. That you got something else. And be sure to tell her what it is." He looked over. "You know how to do that."

"I thought she was gone."

"We're confident the message will get to the right ears."

I swallowed. "Then what?"

He explained that the *James J. Versulis* would be waiting for me at the pier. I was to board and proceed out to the crib.

"What if he tries something before that?"

"We'll have a sniper team in the parking lot. And a SWAT team on the docks. We'll have men on the tug, too, and a team on the crib."

"And if they try before Friday?"

"We're posting men at your house. Starting tonight. Twenty-four/seven."

"No. I have family coming on Thursday. And guests. What if they—"

"You'll be all right. So will your family. I guarantee

it." A muscle in his jaw pulsed. "In fact, *chér,* there's only one person you should be scared of."

"Who's that?"

"Me."

"Why is that?"

"Because I always finish what I start."

FORTY-FOUR

Sleet dribbled sideways, then up. Layers of clouds raced across the sky. Clarence inched through the snow and sleet, trying to maintain traction. I stared out the window, catching glimpses of our surroundings.

I shifted uncomfortably. It might be hours before I got back to Dad's. But maybe that was good. I could just see us on Thursday. The table groaning with food. Dad about to carve the bird. The guests coming up to the house, skirting a gray Plymouth with two sullen men inside.

"Don't worry, folks," I'd warble cheerfully. "I'm the target of an FBI sting. An Arab terrorist is after me; he could strike at any time. But the FBI says not to worry, they'll protect me. You, too. Happy Thanksgiving."

We'd been driving ten minutes before I realized we were headed in the opposite direction from the marina where my car was parked. When Clarence turned onto the Eisenhower Expressway, I twisted around.

"Where are we going?"

"To my place," LeJeune said after a beat.

"Excuse me?"

"I live in Oak Park—it's close. The roads are a mess, and all of us need some shut-eye. Clarence will run you back to your car in the morning."

"I want to go home." Back to Rachel and Dad. To the people I love.

"Ellie, it's after one in the morning. You can't drive in this mess. We'll get you home by seven."

"No. Turn the van around."

"*Chér,* it doesn't make—"

"BRRAAAP!" A loud noise blared out from the van's speakers. It sounded like a cross between a foghorn and a wounded goose.

I looked at LeJeune. "What was that?"

LeJeune scowled. "Clarence, what the fuck was that?"

A series of high-pitched tones beeped, like a microwave oven completing a cycle. Clarence slowed and pulled over. He threw the van into park and crawled back to his laptop.

The same green bull's-eye was on the screen, but there were more lines, and it looked like new numbers and words had appeared. Clarence studied the monitor, then pressed his lips together. His expression was grim.

"What is it?" Nick's voice was tight.

Clarence pressed a key, bringing up a screen with columns of three-digit numbers. He tapped another key, and a different column came up. He sucked in a breath.

"Well?"

"It's another signal."

LeJeune shook his head. "It can't be."

"It is. On the same frequency as the crib."

"But we're miles away from the crib."

"That may be, but I've got a signal registering three on my S-meter."

They exchanged looks.

"What does that mean?" I asked quietly.

Neither of them answered.

"What are you saying, Clarence?" I asked, my voice louder.

He turned around. "Another signal, tuned to the same frequency as the device on the crib, was just transmitted—from somewhere around here."

"But we're heading west on the Eisenhower? Away from the lake."

"I know."

Another signal. "Does that mean there's another . . ." I hugged my knees, trying not to panic. My throat suddenly felt full of dirt. We were on the Eisenhower. Going away from the crib.

The Eisenhower.

Something about that picked at my brain. Something I should know.

The snow swirled up, then down, then circled in a vortex of its own design. I couldn't see farther than a few feet. The Eisenhower. The complicated cloverleaf design connecting the Eisenhower to the Dan Ryan and the Kennedy. Could that be—

"Oh God!" I turned to look at LeJeune and Clarence. "Dale Reedy has a line of sight from her window to the Eisenhower! I saw it from her window."

There was dead silence. Then everything happened at once.

"Holy shit!" Horror spread across Clarence's face. "Fuck it, Drummer! You gotta stop the team at Great Lakes! Now!"

LeJeune dug out his cell phone and started punching in numbers.

"Why?" I asked shakily. "What's going on?"

"Because—because—" Clarence started rubbing his palms up and down his thighs, gazing wildly around. "Christ! Shit. We may have already set things in motion. Jesus, man. You gotta get through."

"Clarence, why? What's going on?" He kept rubbing his hand up and down his leg. My heart thundered in my chest. Anxiety was contagious.

I grabbed one of his hands. The rubbing stopped. "Tell me."

He stared at me. His eyes looked haunted. "We haven't had time to analyze the system. We don't know how it's programmed. There might be a code that needs to be entered when you disconnect the system." He let out a shuddering breath. "Which means if there is a second device, and if the right code wasn't entered . . ." His voice trailed off.

"Which means what, Clarence? What are you trying to say?"

He took another long breath. "If those guys mess with the head end at Great Lakes, and they don't have the right code, the device could blow. The other bomb will go off."

Blood shouted in my ears. I whirled around to Nick. His cell was in his ear, his face ashen.

Nobody said a word while we waited for his cell to connect. I held my breath. It felt like hours. We heard fast, repetitive beeps.

A false busy. LeJeune snapped it off and tried again. Snowflakes danced and spun past the car. Again, a false busy.

"Fuck." LeJeune threw the phone down. "We gotta head back to the Loop."

"In this shit?" Clarence motioned outside. "We'll never make it."

"We gotta. We can't let them fuck with the system."

"How much time do we have?" I asked.

LeJeune didn't answer.

"Nick?"

"I don't know. I don't know where they are. They could be in her office already."

Ice replaced blood in my veins.

LeJeune turned to Clarence. "What can you tell me about the source of the signal? Where's it coming from?"

"The range of the Doppler is about two miles. The signal could be anywhere within that radius."

"Can we track it?"

"Hold on." Clarence crawled to the front seat of the van where he picked up a small black box about the size of a cell phone. A stubby antenna extended through its top, and there was a digital panel on the front.

"What's that?" I asked.

"A frequency finder," he said.

"I thought you already knew the frequency."

"We do, but if we happened to be within 100 to 150 feet of the signal, the Scout'll give me a readout." He depressed a few buttons, muttering. "Come on. Come on. Gimme a break." He shook his head. "Nothing." He put it down. "We're gonna need at least one more transmission—probably two—to plot it on the Doppler."

"But that might not be for another six hours," I said. "What if—"

Clarence cut me off. "Keep tryin' that phone, Drummer."

Nick punched Redial. The cords on his neck were stretched taut. Another false busy.

We stared at each other. Panic started to seep through my body. I smelled fear in the van.

LeJeune unzipped his parka. I could see beads of sweat on his brow. He turned to the laptop. "I'm gonna pull up a map."

Clarence started rubbing his thighs again. "If you can't connect on your cell, how you gonna get online?"

LeJeune squeezed his hands into fists. "Shit. Where's the closest exit?"

"Paulina, I think. Near UIC."

"What else is around here? Clarence? Ellie? Come on. Think. What the fuck is around here?"

"Forget it, man." Clarence shot him a resigned look. "There's nothing we can do. Except pray."

"No." LeJeune's face turned hard. "It's not fucking over. We're gonna think our way through this. What's near here? UIC? The United Center? Sears Tower? Come on. Help me out."

Clarence took his time answering. As if he was just humoring LeJeune. Going through the motions. "I don't think it's Sears. The signal looks like it's slightly south of us. Sears is due east."

LeJeune frowned. "But you don't know for sure."

"Not without another plot point."

"But if this one was planted before Nine-Eleven like the other, all it would have taken is some guy in a gas or phone company uniform. He could have stowed it in the basement. Or the loading dock. Even a parking lot. Like the first Trade Center." LeJeune bit his lip. "We should send men over there."

He grabbed the phone, punched in more numbers, and · shut his eyes while he waited. I heard the fast beeps. "Goddammit."

I sat up and rolled my shoulders, trying to shake off some tension. "You know, the fact they planted it on the crib might be significant."

A small vein on LeJeune's forehead throbbed. "What do you mean?"

"They wanted to sabotage the water supply. To inflict maximum damage to the infrastructure—as well as people."

"Yeah?"

"Maybe they're doing the same thing with the other."

Nick's eyes widened. "That's good, *chér.*" He nodded. "Infrastructure. So what kind of infrastructure is out here?"

"Shit man. Everything," Clarence said. "Electric. Communications. Highways. Trains." He ticked them off on his fingers.

"You can see the Eisenhower from Dale Reedy's window," I said.

Clarence bolted upright. "Fucking A! The junction! Where the Eisenhower, Dan Ryan, and Kennedy come together!"

"What about it?" LeJeune asked.

"It's the most heavily used access in and out of the Loop. That blows, you got practically no access to downtown."

"And if it happened during rush hour . . ." LeJeune added, his head nodding, ". . . with thousands of commuters pouring into the city . . ."

"My God!" I covered my mouth with my hand.

"That's it." LeJeune's eyes caught fire. "Now it makes sense!"

"What?"

"I've been trying to figure out why they took a chance on the wind."

"The wind?"

He hunched forward. "The crib bomb. If the wind was blowing from west to east when they detonated it, most of the radiation would drift out over the lake, not the Loop. It would poison the water, but fewer people would die."

"So?"

"So . . . these bastards are vicious. And smart. They'd want to inflict maximum damage." He nodded again, more to himself than us. "I couldn't figure it out. I kept wondering whether they had something else up their sleeve. But they must have taken the wind into account—"

"Cross-contamination." Clarence breathed.

"Yes." LeJeune slammed a fist into his other palm. "With two, on both sides of the Loop, it doesn't matter which way the wind blows."

"The crib's east, the Eisenhower's west," Clarence finished. "They'd have the Loop covered."

LeJeune and he exchanged looks. Clarence moved to the driver's seat.

"Where are you going?" LeJeune asked.

"The signal seemed to be just south of us. We've got to do something. We've got to move."

As we pulled onto the highway, tires swished against snowy asphalt.

LeJeune picked up his cell and dialed one more time. His eyebrows shot up. "It's going through." He thrust it against his ear. "Shit man, it's LeJeune. Where are you?" He listened, then yelled. "No. Don't touch it. You gotta stop. Right now. We got another signal. There may be a second package!"

I heard the exclamations from his phone, but I was only half listening. Part of my brain was tripping over another connection. It was half there. Buried in my subconscious.

LeJeune was watching me. "What is it, *chér?*"

"I'm not sure. Something you said earlier."

"I said a lot of things." He grinned.

I was astonished he could kid around at a time like this. I tried to call back the conversation. Infrastructure. Power. Electricity. Uniforms.

LeJeune went back to his call. He was frowning when he got off. "We have a problem."

Clarence twisted around.

I sat up straighter.

"You were right, buddy," LeJeune said. "We disconnected the radio temporarily when we disabled the device on the crib. We reconnected it as soon as we could, but our guys are saying there's no way to tell whether that altered the sequence of codes. And there's no time to go into the program to find out."

"What does that mean?" I asked.

"Disconnecting the system—even for a second—may have alerted the computer that something was different. That the system has been penetrated. Tampered with. As a result, the blast we just heard . . ." He paused. ". . . may have tripped the code to detonate."

My stomach clutched.

"They said it can take about thirty minutes to run through the codes for detonation." He looked at his watch. "It's one-seventeen now. And we heard the signal about ten minutes ago."

"Are you saying we only have twenty minutes to find it?"

"If we're lucky."

FORTY-FIVE

DESPAIR, NOT NECESSITY, is the mother of invention. I know that now, because it was while I was staring out the van's window in stunned silence, trying to absorb the fact that life in this city might end, that thousands of people might perish, and that I might be one of them, that it came to me.

It was one of those moments when the future lies in your hands. And you know it. Not one of those times that, in hindsight, turns out to be significant. You know—right as it's happening—that your actions will have a huge impact. That they might even change the world.

Some people welcome those moments. They feel it's their destiny. Not me. I felt nothing but terror. I spoke anyway.

"When I was calling scuba diving schools," I said quietly, "a woman gave me a number for Samir at work. Or at least where he might have worked at one time. When I called it, a 773 area code by the way, the man who answered said it was the maintenance room at People's Edison."

No one said anything. Then Clarence drew in a long, slow breath. "There's a PE substation just south of the junction."

LeJeune's eyes widened. "Let's go."

WE VEERED OFF at the next exit, crossed over the highway, and reentered the Eisenhower going the other way. Clarence pushed, but in this weather, we couldn't go faster than thirty. I checked the dashboard clock. One twenty-one. Four minutes had passed. Sixteen left. I was desperate to hug Rachel, to brush her hair off her forehead one more time. I wondered if I'd have another chance.

LeJeune spent most of the time on his cell, and Clarence concentrated on the road. I found myself measuring my breaths, trying to space them out evenly. Was I subconsciously devising an internal clock? Or hoarding air while I had it?

After what seemed an eternity, I felt the van turn south. I got to my knees and looked out. The van's headlights caught a small People's Edison sign at the edge of the road, and we pulled into a field that stretched at least two or three acres. A stand of trees, cloaked in an eerie snow-induced twilight, were in front, their bare branches curled upward as if begging for mercy.

We parked and got out. Through the trees was a forest of steel towers, strung together with thickly coiled wires. There must have been nearly a hundred of them, snow falling softly around them. They seemed almost haphazardly placed. Different shapes, too. Some were traditional towers, each side with steel bracing, but others looked like giant monkey bars you find on a playground. Still others were T-shaped poles.

On the ground between some of the towers were boxy units the size of refrigerators, and perched on nearly everything were strings of what looked like super-sized light bulbs. Insulators, I discovered, that help attach power lines to their structures. Though the snow muffled much of the sound, the hum of a gazillion volts zipped through overhead lines.

A Chicago patrol car pulled up and parked horizontally across the entrance, its revolving Mars light turning the snow into a veil of pink and blue specks. Within minutes, two more sedans pulled up. Men piled out. LeJeune went over to huddle with them. Another van arrived, and half a dozen more men climbed out wearing haz mat suits and carrying masks. Two of them were carrying a boxy piece of equipment that was small enough to fit in a backpack. They looked vaguely familiar.

"NEST," Clarence said. "Nuclear Emergency Support Team. They were out on the crib."

"What?"

"They run around patrolling for dirty bombs. They've got their sniffing gear with them."

"Sniffing gear?"

"Gamma ray and neutron flux detectors. Kind of like fancy Geiger counters."

The men split up into teams of twos and threes and scattered through the trees toward the substation. I stamped snow off my feet. "What are they doing?"

"Making sweeps of the area. Looking for the device."

"What time is it?"

Clarence checked his watch. "One-twenty-six."

Eleven minutes left. "What—what happens when—if— they find it?"

"They disable it." He started rubbing his hands together. "Actually, that's the easy part," he said. "Or it would be if they had enough time."

"What do you mean?"

"There are a couple ways to go. You could bring in a robot—disable it by remote control. You could also bring in a huge tent and fill it with foam." He blew on his hands. "To contain the radiation in case the bomb blows."

I winced.

"I don't know what they'll do this time. The military's supposed to handle these things. Maybe they'll try to blow the bomb's wiring."

A man ran out, opened a van, grabbed something, and ran back in. I stiffened.

"What time is it?"

"One-twenty-eight."

Nine minutes.

Lights flashed. More vehicles converged on the scene. Several men and a woman got out. One of the men was leading a dog. Then another van, filled with Chicago Police Department Bomb Squad personnel, pulled in. They disappeared through the trees.

Suddenly a man's voice shouted through a megaphone. The wind snatched the sound and tossed it around the air. "All unauthorized personnel must vacate the premises immediately. All unauthorized personnel out. Now."

I grabbed Clarence's arm. "What does that mean?"

He grimaced. "It means they found something. I have to go in. The radio."

"No! Don't leave me!"

But he was already running to the van. I followed him over. He opened the door, grabbed a mask from under the front seat, and headed into the trees.

Alone, I tried to wiggle my fingers, but they were numb. I should never have bitten my nails. It was an annoying habit. Rachel had inherited it from me.

I leaned in to check the time. One-thirty-three. Four minutes left.

I started to shiver. The snow was up over my shoes. I wished I had boots that buckled all the way up. Like the shiny pink boots I had as a kid. I never buckled the top strap. Mother always chided me about it.

Suddenly a shout went up. My stomach twisted. I strained to look through the trees, but the falling snow and parked cars blocked my view. LeJeune ran out and started dragging me toward the van.

"They found it! Get out of here!" His face was haggard. "Now!"

Panic radiated out from my stomach. I threw myself into the van. The engine caught right away. I tried to tell myself it would be okay. The bomb squad was handling it. I checked the clock on the dashboard. One-thirty-five. Two minutes left. They'd do it. They had to.

I threw the van in reverse. If these were the last two minutes on earth allotted to me, I wanted to be with my family. I started to back up, then stopped, the engine still idling. Dad and Rachel were twenty miles north. I'd never make it. With less than two minutes, I probably wouldn't even make it to the highway. But now what? What should I do?

I was deliberating the absurdity of spending my last two minutes alive with nothing to do and nowhere to go when a dark-colored sedan pulled up. Turning into the yard, it slowed to a crawl, and a window rolled down. I looked to see who was driving, but between the snow and the darkness, I couldn't tell. The car rolled a few yards forward, then stopped a few feet from the van. As the driver opened the door and climbed out, I gasped.

It was Abdul.

I cut the engine, my heart banging in my chest. Where was Nick? I had to warn him. That's what I was supposed to do. Make sure he got Abdul. I jumped out of the van and sprinted away from it. I was veering right, angling toward the substation entrance when there was a blinding flash of blue light, and the silence was rent by a roar. A scream tore out of my mouth. I threw myself to the ground.

It took a few seconds to realize I was still alive. There had been no explosion. No fireball. A chopper, its blue lights flashing and its motor whining, had broken through the overcast and was descending. It banked over my head, narrowly missing the utility towers, and landed fifty yards away in the street.

More men poured out, some of them suited up, some in uniform. The military. They ran into the substation.

I got up and brushed off the snow. LeJeune. Abdul.

There had to be less than a minute left. I counted steps as I moved through the trees, twisting around and seeing my footprints in the snow. I was just at the entrance to the substation when the megaphone voice barked again.

"Make way . . . make way! Everybody back! Let's get this sucker out of here."

A knot of men emerged from the substation. In the middle of the group were several men in haz mat suits carrying a steel suitcase on what appeared to be a flat wooden board. They were moving very slowly toward one of the vans; other men surrounded them. I caught a glimpse of Clarence in the group, his mask on. He gave me a thumbs-up.

Once the suitcase was in the van and the van had taken off, the men in haz mat suits tore off their masks. Others high-fived each other and laughed. A few wiped tears from their eyes. I looked for LeJeune, but I didn't see him.

I whipped around. I'd confront Abdul myself, although what I would say or do when I found him, I had no idea. I raced back to the van, cold, bone-weary, but resolute.

But when I got there, Abdul had disappeared. His car was gone. The only hint it had been there at all a set of tire tracks in the snow that were fast filling in.

I checked the clock. One-forty-one. More men poured out from the substation.

It was over. With nary more than a whimper.

FORTY-SIX

I NEVER FOUND LeJeune, and Clarence followed the van with the bomb. Someone else gave me a ride to my car.

When I got home, I took a shower and brewed coffee, then called Dad. Rachel and he were fine; she was still sleeping. I told him I'd pick them up around noon; he should pack an overnight bag so he could spend the weekend with me.

The snow tapered off, and a weak slash of sunlight inched across the kitchen counter, coming to rest on the wall. I prowled around the house, restless and unfocused, too exhausted to sleep. On the surface my world seemed normal and stitched up, but underneath was a crack, a fissure so deep I wasn't sure it would ever mend. I knew I would never look at the world in quite the same way again.

The doorbell chimed around ten. LeJeune. He'd put on a clean shirt, but he needed a shave, and there were dark smudges under his eyes. He kissed me. "What smells so good?"

I'd tried to pretend everything was okay, heating up the

oven, putting in the pie, starting to sauté celery and onions. "Pecan pie. For tomorrow. I'll get you some coffee."

While I poured, he wandered around the kitchen. I wondered if he was feeling the same way as I. I got out sugar and milk.

He leaned against the counter. "We picked up Hanjour and Reedy."

I spun around. "Both of them?"

"Customs nabbed Reedy trying to hop a flight to Frankfurt. She told us where to find Hanjour. We found him and one of his pals inside a White Hen in Orland Park. Stocking up on donuts and soda."

"Donuts? He was buying donuts?"

"His pal went for a knife, but we disarmed him. Hanjour just threw up his hands." He stirred his coffee. "Guess we won't need that sequel after all."

"It's really over?"

He hesitated, as if he couldn't quite believe it himself, then nodded. "We've already cased their apartment, and we're going through their E-mail. They were trying to get as far away as possible before it blew."

"They didn't want to die for the cause?"

"When you've been living stateside for a while, I guess martyrdom loses its appeal."

"And yet they wanted to destroy it."

"Ellie, no one ever said these guys had a tight grip on reality."

I refilled my coffee, then tore open a package of sweetener and dumped it in. "You know, I can't help thinking if I'd found the antenna the first time I met Reedy, none of this would have happened."

"Don't be too hard on yourself, *chér*. In a way Reedy may have saved your life."

"How do you figure that?"

"When you first met her, you had no reason to link any of the events to Arab terrorists. You thought it was a Mafia scam."

"So?"

"As long as you were running around looking for wise guys, she was able to rein in Hanjour. Convince him to go after the tapes instead of you. Persuade him she'd handle you."

I thought about it. He was right. The last time I'd seen the SUV—until a few days ago—was the day LeJeune and Coates came to the house. I met Dale Reedy the next day.

"She never had any intention of producing a video, did she? She brought me in just to find out about the tape. To play me and see how much I knew."

He nodded.

"Why did things change?"

"There's no guarantee of unanimity when you're dealing with terrorists. There probably was a disagreement over how to deal with you from the beginning. At least that's what she's saying."

"Reedy's talking?"

"Louder and quicker than a scalded cat. She's not stupid." He took a sip of coffee. "She did lay down one condition, though."

"What?"

"That MI5 or Scotland Yard pick up her kids and make sure they're safe."

"Did they?"

"She talked to them on the phone a few hours ago."

I tapped my spoon on the table. "What did she tell you?"

"The bomb was originally supposed to be detonated around the time of September eleventh, but in all the confusion, the final order never came down. Then, afterwards—"

"It was supposed to be part of September eleventh?"

"Apparently. But you know how splintered and isolated these cells are." He stared into his coffee cup. "At any rate, with all the attention on security and Arab terrorists, Samir's plans fell into disarray, and he had to abort. Months later, when things calmed down, Reedy got the word to put it back together. That's when they planted the second one."

My stomach twisted. "Got the word? Oh my God—I never got the chance to tell you, Nick. Abdul was there. At the substation. The one I think is in charge."

"Ellie . . ." He paused. "Abdul's a Saudi intelligence agent. We've been working with him since May. He's been tracking Islamic terrorists for years. He's the one who tipped us to the threat in the first place. Something happening with water. This summer. In the Midwest."

"Abdul's an agent?" I stared. "But he never . . ."

"He couldn't blow his cover." He grinned. "Of course, you managed to do that for him."

I wrapped my hands around my mug. "But I met him at the Greenbrier. What was he doing there?"

"He was trying to run down a training camp in rural West Virginia. A place where Arab terrorists reportedly train next to white separatists."

"No."

He shrugged. "When you're overthrowing a government, the enemy of my enemy . . ."

"So that's how he knew the countryside so well."

LeJeune looked puzzled.

"You remember. When he told us about the coal mines—" I stopped. I was confusing LeJeune with David. I bit my lip. I remembered the sheet of paper with Abdul's number at the Four Seasons. "If he was tracking Dale Reedy, why was he calling her at Great Lakes Oil?"

"He was trying to confirm her identity. She'd changed her name, remember? He was sure he would know her voice."

"So the plant acquisition *was* a pretext."

"You got it."

I sat back in my chair. "So if Abdul wasn't in charge, who did give Reedy the order to put it back together?"

"Aziz. Her husband."

"Why did they need two bombs?"

"Insurance. In case the first one didn't work. Remember, it had been underwater for almost a year."

"But they were still getting a radio signal."

He looked grim. "Maybe after they saw the devastation in New York, they decided to up the ante."

"So Samir got a job at PE and cased it on the side."

LeJeune nodded. "Terrorist or not, he needed to make a living. And what better place to rip off supplies?"

I shivered. "Do you think they were planting the crib bomb the night Mary Jo and Rhonda were at Calumet Park?"

"Hard to say. They might have been doing a test run. Or a safety check afterwards. But whatever it was, Samir panicked when he saw the two women."

"And killed Mary Jo."

He nodded again.

"After which he thought everything was under control—until I testified."

"That's why he showed up at the trial. He had to find out how significant that RF damage was. And whether you knew where it came from."

"Which is where he saw Rhonda Disapio. And realized she'd been the one with Mary Jo at the park."

"You got it. She'd always been a loose end."

"How did he kill her—tamper with her brakes or something?"

"Yeah. Reedy wasn't happy after that. She realized he was a loose cannon. That's when she came down on him. Told him to go after the tapes, not people."

"The fire at the studio."

"Yes."

"And Brashares."

"Like the cops say, he was in the wrong place at the wrong time." LeJeune drained his coffee. "They thought they'd patched up all the leaks. Until you screwed things up again."

"Because I saw Reedy's antenna."

"You also had the last copy of the tape." He looked

over. "You were in their sights from the beginning, *cher.*"

We were quiet for a moment.

"There is one other thing. Do you think she was sending me a message when she canceled the video?"

"A message?" He laughed. "Not hardly, *cher*. She was busy saving her own skin."

"She didn't have to E-mail me. She could have just disappeared."

"You sound like you're defending her."

I shook my head. "Just trying to understand."

"Don't waste your time." He ran a hand over his face. "You want some more coffee?"

"Sure." I handed him my cup.

"Black, right?"

How many times had we drunk coffee together? I pointed to the blue packet of sweetener on the table. He looked embarrassed.

I waited until he sat down again. "What else did Reedy say?"

LeJeune leaned back in the chair. "Well, for one thing, she said it was payback for the Gulf War."

"Huh?"

"When we bombed Iraq, we took out their water treatment plants. With no running water, people hauled buckets in from the Tigris, but it was filled with sewage. Thousands of people died. Typhoid, dysentery, cholera. Even polio. And because of the sanctions, they couldn't import any chlorine."

"Do you believe that?"

He made a noise that was almost a snort. "It makes a convenient excuse. But enough." He raised my hands to his lips. "We'll talk more later. Right now, you and I have some unfinished business." He smiled.

I pulled my hand away.

His smile faded.

"You know," I said slowly, "it's strange what happens when you think you're going to die. A certain clarity emerges." I tucked my hand under my leg. "Tell me something, Nick. The speech about your father losing his leg. And the bit about Huey Long. Was that part of the script?"

He tipped his head to the side. "What are—"

"Don't." I got up and went to the stove. "Don't."

He stood up and straddled a chair. "It wasn't just the job, Ellie. It—it never was. I realized it when I got back from London. I want you. We could mean something to each other."

"But . . ." I hesitated. "I don't want you."

He just looked at me.

"As long as we were working toward the same goal, it was easy to act *as if.* To pretend. But that changed when you agreed to use me as bait."

"You made that decision."

"You gave me no choice."

"I never wanted that to happen. I fought it. I nearly lost my job over it."

I bent my head, unsure if it was the truth but not wanting to find out. "It wasn't that it didn't have to be done. It did. But you were the one who talked me into it." I laced my fingers together. "Did you ever read *All the King's Men*?"

He didn't answer.

"I'll bet you have. Remember how Willy Stark started out as a reformer? Burning with the desire to do good? Along the way, though, he learned how to manipulate people. String them along."

He wouldn't meet my eyes.

"Eventually, of course, it corrupted him." I paused. "The thing is, even so, even with his lust for power, Willy Stark accomplished great things."

He looked up.

"You did, too, Nick. Most people would have given up. But you didn't. And if I ever get in trouble again, there's no one I'd want on my side more than you." I stood up. "But now I think you'd better leave. And . . . please . . . don't come back."

He ducked as if I'd lobbed him a stinging criticism. I turned away and pretended to fuss with the stove. After a moment his steps clicked across the floor and retreated in the hall. The front door opened and closed.

FORTY-SEVEN

"I WAS WRONG."

Dad and I were in the family room, watching flames from the fireplace dance, pop, and float up the chimney. One or two sparks landed on the floor and winked out. Strains of rock music drifted down the stairs from Rachel's room.

"What do you mean?" I picked up my glass of wine, which lay next to a plate of chocolate chip cookies.

"I thought you were on another one of your crusades," he said, balancing a cup of tea in his hand. "You know, trying to fit round pegs into square holes. I was wrong."

"I don't blame you." I twirled my wine, watching the firelight flicker and glint through the glass. "Who would have believed it?"

"I should have trusted you. You're my daughter."

"You know something?" I leaned over and squeezed the hand not holding the teacup. "It takes a *mensch* to admit he was wrong—especially to his child."

He squeezed back. "So tell me. These—these . . ." He couldn't seem to bring himself to say the word *bombs*.

"They were planted before September eleventh?"

"One was. The other one was added afterwards."

My father's brow furrowed. "Are there any more, you think? That haven't been discovered?"

"God forbid."

"Yeah, well, I guess praying is about all we can do." He gazed at me with worried eyes. "So why haven't I seen anything about it on the news?"

"LeJeune said they're keeping a lid on until the government decides how to respond."

"Good luck."

"They could have a shot. The action out at the crib was miles away from anything, and the weather last night was terrible. There weren't a lot of people around."

He sniffed. "That woman—the British one they picked up—she's talking?"

"That's what I hear."

"How did they identify her?"

"Abdul told them about her."

He set down his teacup. "Abdul?"

"The man we met at the Greenbrier."

"The one who's working with David?"

"The same." In fact, he'd dropped by the house that afternoon to apologize and ask my forgiveness. We'd had a long talk. "He's a member of the Saudi intelligence force, Dad. He's been tracking terrorists for years. The oil sheik role was his cover."

"Does David know?"

"Abdul says he explained it to him the other day. He said David wasn't happy about it. But he understands."

Dad bit into a cookie. I flashed back to Abdul's table manners. The match on the silk tablecloth. The caviar on the toast point. Not very royal. It should have been a tip-off.

"Reedy did make a huge blunder, though."

Dad stopped chewing.

"The antenna. Granted, I didn't notice until it was almost too late, but if I hadn't been so unobservant, I might have figured it out sooner. I don't know why she didn't try to disguise it."

"Probably the Empire mentality. You know how arrogant they get."

I remembered the photo of her two boys. "I don't know. I wonder whether, maybe in some subconscious way, she wanted me to figure it out."

Dad cocked his head. "What?"

"She has two boys. The Bureau thinks her husband was holding them over her head. Maybe this was her only way to get them out of his clutches."

"Have they caught him?"

"Dani? Not yet."

Dad frowned. "I'm an old man. What do I know?"

That was his way of telling me I was making assumptions again. Maybe I was, but I couldn't help thinking that men just don't get it. The extent to which a mother will go to protect her young. It's hardwired into our psyches. I started to reach for a cookie but stopped. Did that mean there was some unanimity between Dale Reedy and me? A subtle but mutually understood accord? I shifted uneasily.

"How's Sylvia?"

"You'll see for yourself, tomorrow."

"Dad, are you sure you're ready to handle this?"

He wiped his mouth with a napkin. "Listen, Ellie. She's great company, she plays a mean hand of gin, and I like holding her hand almost as much as yours. What more do I need?"

"If you're happy . . ."

"I'm happy." He covered my hand with his. "What about you?"

"I'm tired. I could sleep for days. But I keep thinking how much I have to be thankful for."

He patted my hand. I curled a leg underneath myself. "There's just one thing. I think Rachel's been calling David with updates about me all fall. The little *dybbuk*'s been spying on me."

Dad withdrew his hand.

"She and I are going to have one of those boundary discussions after Thanksgiving."

He toyed with his spoon. "I wouldn't do that if I were you."

"What do you mean?"

"You're blaming the wrong person."

"You?"

"Ellie, we're his only family. You may not want to be in touch, but I do. It's the right thing to do."

I scowled, but I wasn't totally surprised. As a young man, my father had fallen in love with David's mother. It hadn't worked out, but it had forged a connection between our families. Indeed, when David and I got together, in part because of the discovery about our parents, my father was convinced it was *bashert*.

"Love is never perfect," he said. "You young people still have a hard time accepting that. You'd rather head for divorce court than work it out."

I started to cut in, but he overrode me. "I'm not saying it wasn't warranted in Barry's case. But if you're lucky enough to have it come your way again, to find someone who loves you more than he loves himself, well . . ." He threw up his hand. "But what am I telling you this for? You're the hero. You do what you want."

"Labor under correct knowledge," I muttered.

"What is?"

"Luck."

"Exactly what I'm saying."

"You know what I want? I want to get away from here for a while. Go to some hot, dry desert where there's not a drop of water."

"Got any travel companions in mind?"

"I was thinking of you."

"My dance card is all filled up." He motioned toward my bag. "But I bet if you pull out that phone of yours, you might find someone who'd be thrilled to come with you. Especially if you feed him a home-cooked Thanksgiving dinner."

"Dad, I'm sure he's made other plans. He probably won't even take my call. I've—I've been pretty awful to him."

"Why don't you let him decide that?"

"If I were him, I wouldn't take the call."

"Then it's good you're not."

"Even if he did talk to me, how could he get here in time? It's Wednesday night."

"They have these things called airplanes, Ellie," he said. "Last I heard, they still fly on Thursday morning."

I considered it. Then I stood up. I thought I saw a twinkle in Dad's eye when I pulled out my cell, but with him you can never be sure.

"Maybe you should try him at his office. Maybe he's working late."

I felt my eyes widen and punched in the number.

A female voice answered. "Good evening, Mr. Linden's office."

My eyebrows shot up. I took a breath. "Is—Is he there? It's Ellie Foreman calling."

About the Author

A transplant from Washington, D.C., Libby has lived in the Chicago area twenty-five years. When not writing fiction, she writes and produces corporate videos. She has also worked in television news and public relations, and can occasionally be spotted in those venues. She holds a B.A. from the University of Pennesylvania, and an M.F.A. in film production from New York University. She lives with her husband, two children, and a beagle, shamelessly named Shiloh.